D0040627

*T*here sat his bride, perched on a wide branch like some silk-clad nymph, with one arm loosely around the trunk for balance. At least she'd looped and tied her skirts to one side of her legs for decency's sake, but as he gazed up from the back of his horse March still had a provocative view of frothy lace around bright green stockings on delicate, perfectly shaped ankles. The gauzy linen kerchief around her shoulders had slipped to one side, and the plump curves of her breasts rose above the neckline of her gown, all the more obvious above the boned bodice. Her skin was creamy and fair, her cheeks prettily flushed, her dark hair tousled beneath a small lace cap.

His first coherent thought was that Carter had been absolutely right: Lady Charlotte was a beauty, the kind of beauty destined to turn heads in every ballroom in London.

His second was pure amazement that such a lady was intended for him.

But his third and most urgent thought was why in blazes the soon-to-be third Duchess of Marchbourne—*his* duchess—was stranded in the lofty branches of a tree.

BOOK EXCHANGE
480-949-9507

Books published by The Random House Publishing Group are available at quantity discounts on bulk purchases for premium, educational, fund-raising, and special sales use. For details, please call 1-800-733-3000.

When You Wish Upon a Duke

Isabella Bradford

BALLANTINE BOOKS • NEW YORK

Sale of this book without a front cover may be unauthorized. If this book is coverless, it may have been reported to the publisher as "unsold or destroyed" and neither the author nor the publisher may have received payment for it.

When You Wish Upon a Duke is a work of fiction. Names, characters, places, and incidents are the products of the author's imagination or are used fictitiously. Any resemblance to actual events, locales, or persons, living or dead, is entirely coincidental.

A Ballantine Books Mass Market Original

Copyright © 2012 by Susan Holloway Scott
Excerpt from *When the Duchess Said Yes* copyright © 2012 by Susan Holloway Scott

All rights reserved.

Published in the United States by Ballantine Books, an imprint of The Random House Publishing Group, a division of Random House, Inc., New York.

BALLANTINE and colophon are trademarks of Random House, Inc.

This book contains an excerpt from the forthcoming book *When the Duchess Said Yes* by Isabella Bradford. This excerpt has been set for this edition only and may not reflect the final content of the forthcoming edition.

ISBN 978-0-345-52729-5
eBook ISBN 978-0-345-52730-1

Cover design: Lynn Andreozzi
Cover illustration: Alan Ayers

Printed in the United States of America

www.ballantinebooks.com

9 8 7 6 5 4 3 2 1

Ballantine Books mass market edition: August 2012

Acknowledgments

Traveling back to the eighteenth century is no easy voyage, but fortunately I didn't have to do it alone. Warmest thanks are in order to:

Janea Whitacre, Mark Hutter, Sarah Woodyard, and Neal Hurst of the Margaret Hunter Shop, Colonial Williamsburg, for sharing your endless knowledge (and patience) in explaining everything from shirt buckles to pocket hoops

Meg Ruley and Annelise Robey of the Jane Rotrosen Agency, for their support, optimism, and laughter when I need it most

Kate Collins, my editor at Ballantine, for making things even better the second time around

And, of course, Loretta Chase, my fellow Gemini-writer, for being the other half of my nerdy-history-girl-self

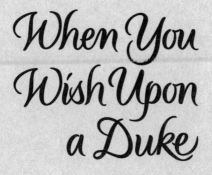

CHAPTER

1

It was only in the middle of the night that Lady Charlotte Wylder could remember the past.

She'd learned to wait until after the rest of the house was fast asleep before she slipped from her bed. With a shawl over her shoulders, she opened her bedchamber window and leaned outward, her dark hair tossing in the breeze. The moon was high in the blue-black sky, and beyond the garden wall, the waves in the sea made no more than the softest *shush* as the tide retreated over the sand. She breathed deeply, making herself think of nothing beyond the sea and the moon and stars. And then, only then, could Charlotte remember the distant days when Father still lived, and Mama still laughed, and her home and her world had been full of magic.

She closed her eyes, letting the memories come. She had been only four when Father had died, and she was eighteen now. They had lived in a grand house on Berkeley Square in the winter, and in an equally grand house in Somerset in the summer, as was fit for the family of the fourth Earl of Hervey. There had been servants in powdered wigs and livery trimmed with gold lace to cosset her, and elegantly painted carriages to ride in with

Mama and Father, and more silk gowns in Charlotte's own nursery wardrobe than most grown women possessed in a lifetime.

But the memories she sought were more humble. She wanted to remember her parents as they'd been then, the merriest and most beautiful young parents in London. They had been young, too, younger than Charlotte herself was now when they'd wed. They'd sung to her, and talked in funny voices to make her laugh, and used her dolls for impromptu puppet shows in the drawing room. Each evening while Mama dressed for the theater or a ball, Father would come to the nursery. He'd play hide-and-seek with Charlotte, and soon with her younger sister Lizzie, too. He would roar like a bear to make them shriek, and then they would pretend to capture him, and tie him up with hair ribbons.

Then later, much later, he and Mama would come kiss them goodnight when they'd returned home from whatever ball or frolic they'd attended. Mama's perfume always lingered, as sweet as a bouquet of flowers, while Father's kiss had been redolent of brandy and tobacco. But the best had come when her parents had paused in the doorway, Father's arms around Mama's waist as he'd drawn her close to kiss her, both of them chuckling softly as if they'd needed nothing more than their daughters and each other. What better definition of love could there be? For Charlotte, their love had been warm and comforting and secure, so secure that, with her child's certainty, Charlotte had been sure their life would always be so, and that—

"Charlotte?" whispered her youngest sister, opening the bedchamber door just wide enough to peek inside. "Charlotte, are you awake?"

Charlotte sighed and turned from the window. She could dream and fancy, but this was her world now, and had been for the last fourteen years: her two younger sisters and Mama and this ancient, windswept house overlooking the sea.

"You know I'm awake, Diana," she said, drawing her shawl more closely about her shoulders, "because from there you can see that I'm not in my bed."

Diana slipped inside the door, her eyes wide and her nightgown drifting ghostly pale in the moonlight. "You could be asleep somewhere else. In the chair, or on the carpet, or—"

"Or curled up like a dormouse, atop the tall clock." As much as Charlotte regretted the interruption of her reverie, she could never be truly cross with Diana. No one could. Though nearly fourteen, Diana would always be the baby, round-faced and guileless. "What is it you wish, noddy? Why aren't you abed yourself?"

"It's Fig," Diana said plaintively. "She went out the window and into the oak tree again, and now she's too scared to come back on her own, but keeps crying and crying. You must come fetch her, Charlotte. She'll come for you. You must come!"

"If only you'd keep the window latched, Diana, then Fig couldn't climb out." Fig was Diana's pet cat, a small, scrawny patchwork creature of much obstinacy and little sense, and naturally the recipient of Diana's slavish devotion. "If you love her as much as you claim, then you'd try your best to keep her safe."

"But I do love her, Charlotte." Diana's voice rose to a wail. "If I didn't, I wouldn't have come here for you, and I—"

"Hush, or you'll wake Mama." Charlotte tossed aside the shawl and from beneath her bed pulled out the oversized fisherman's jersey that she kept hidden there. The jersey was worn and not terribly clean, nor was it suitable dress for an earl's daughter, as their scandalized housekeeper, Mrs. Bain, had repeatedly told Charlotte. But Charlotte didn't care. She found the old jersey most useful and warm while on the beach or mucking about in boats, and especially for adventures such as rescuing Fig. She pulled the jersey over her nightgown and hurriedly braided her hair into a single untidy plait as she followed Diana to her bedchamber.

Diana's farthest window was open wide, with the twisting branches of the manor's oldest oak tree just beyond the sill. In those twisting branches was Fig, her mewling cries clear enough.

"Fig doesn't sound frightened to me, Diana," Charlotte said as she peered into the leaves from her sister's window. "I think she simply wishes you to know where she is, that is all."

"She *is* frightened, Charlotte," Diana insisted, "and she needs you to rescue her. Unless you want me to go to her instead."

"Don't consider it for so much as an instant," Charlotte said. "Mama'd have my head if I let you into the tree."

Mama would likewise have Charlotte's head for climbing trees again, which Mama declared was both dangerous and unladylike. But Charlotte would be punished only if Mama learned of it, which Charlotte would take care not to have happen. Being that Mama was inclined to be both forgetful and tenderhearted, avoiding her rare punishment wasn't really much of a challenge.

"Then you'll go?" Diana asked eagerly. "You'll save my poor little Fig?"

"You know I will," Charlotte said. She had rescued poor little Fig far more times than Fig truly wished to be rescued, and she'd earned the scratches on her forearms to prove it. "Hurry now, fetch me something to wrap her in."

Quickly Diana brought a cloth from the washstand, and Charlotte tied it loosely around her neck in readiness. She slung her bare legs over the stone sill, took a deep breath, and reached out for the nearest branch. It *was* dangerous, with the ground a good twenty feet below and the oak swaying gently in the breeze, but it was exhilarating as well, a challenge to be conquered. She'd always been the best tree climber in the family, pretending herself kin to the rope dancers at the mid-summer fair in the village, lithe men and women in gaudy silk costumes who skipped and pirouetted with breathtaking skill. That was how Charlotte imagined herself to be now, balancing deftly on the oak's branches with her nightgown fluttering around her.

"Do be careful, Charlotte," Diana called. "You can't fall. You must save Fig first!"

"I won't fall," Charlotte scoffed, her bare toes sliding over the smooth bark. "Rather, you should be telling Fig to be an agreeable pet, and come to me without a fuss."

Fig was within reach now. The little cat was sitting comfortably in the crook of a branch, her tail curled around her as she watched Charlotte's progress.

Charlotte inched closer, slowly pulling the kerchief from around her neck. "There's a good kitten," she coaxed. "Come, Fig, come to me, before Diana expires from worrying fits."

The cat stretched, her eyes gleaming in the moonlight, but made no move to come to Charlotte.

"Come to me, you base-born whiskered wretch," crooned Charlotte. "If you make me fall, mark that I shall be sure to take you with me."

A rumbling sound rose faintly in the distance, drawing the cat's attention. Quickly Charlotte grabbed her and wrapped her snugly in the cloth, only her head with its pointed ears poking free.

"Safe at last," she declared. "You see, Diana, that there was no reason whatsoever to worry."

But Diana's attention, like her cat's, had turned toward the unexpected sound.

"Look, Charlotte," she said. "It's a carriage. Why would a carriage be coming here in the middle of the night?"

"Why would a carriage be coming here at all?" Holding the swaddled cat tightly beneath her arm, Charlotte dared to learn forward over another branch for a better view. It was indeed a carriage, a rare sight when most of their neighbors consisted of fishing folk and farmers. Beyond the dutiful weekly call by the Reverend Mr. Ferris, there were precious few visitors of any kind to Ransom Manor. Fashionable London had long ago moved on to other tragedies and scandals and entirely forgotten the dowager countess and her daughters. Besides, the road to Ransom Manor was long, rough, and disheartening, and served as surely to keep the Wylders away from London as it kept Londoners away from them.

But this traveler had persevered. Beneath the tree, the carriage slowly came to a stop before the front door. The horses were weary, their heads drooping, and the driver moved stiffly as he climbed from the box to open the carriage door. The passenger who stepped forward was a gentleman, his traveling cloak swirling around him and a thick leather portfolio in his arms. As the driver thumped the butt of his whip against the manor's door to rouse the servants within, the gentleman looked upward, the cocked brim of his hat pointing like the beak of an inquisitive blackbird, and swiftly Charlotte slid deeper into the shadows to keep from being seen. The door opened, candlelight spilling out onto the steps, and Harbough, their butler, ushered the stranger within.

"Who could he be, Charlotte?" asked Diana with

growing excitement. "Why would he come here now, in the middle of the night? Maybe he's a pirate, or a French spy, or—"

"Oh, hush, Di," Charlotte said, scrambling back through the window. "Pirates and Frenchmen don't wait for Mr. Harbough to open the door. More likely he has word from one of Mama's London relations."

"I'd rather he were a pirate," Diana said, taking Fig from Charlotte and cradling her in the crook of her arm like a baby. "Or a Frenchman."

"You'd best hope he's not French, or you won't be able to speak a word to him," Charlotte said as she hurried through the room. "You'll wish you'd paid more heed in our lessons."

"You didn't either, Charlotte," Diana protested, trotting after her. "That's why Madame left. She said we were unteachable, like the cursed beasts of the forest."

"*Les maudites bêtes de la forêt.*" Charlotte might not recall much genteel French, but she did remember Madame's exasperated exclamations, which had been far more amusing than the verbs they'd had to memorize. "Come, don't dawdle. I don't wish to miss anything."

By the time they reached the front staircase, Harbough had just taken the stranger's cloak, the two men's shadows wavering in the light of the many-branched candlestick held by one of the maids. The three of them looked up to Charlotte and Diana on the landing. The stranger was definitely not a pirate or even a Frenchman, decided Charlotte with disappointment, but most likely a solicitor or other such dour fellow with papers or letters for Mama. Dressed in serviceable black, he was above middle age, his nose long beneath his snuff-brown wig and his lined features studiously composed. Yet even he couldn't entirely hide his weariness after his journey, and with no sign yet of Mama from her rooms, Charlotte realized it was her responsibility to welcome him.

Hastily she smoothed her palms over her hair and began down the stairs, her bare feet muted on the worn oak treads. Halfway down, she also realized that Mama would not be pleased to have her welcoming guests when she was dressed only in her night rail and a raggedy wool jersey, but at least the jersey was so stretched that it covered her to her knees, and besides, it *was* the middle of the night.

"Lady Charlotte Wylder," Harbough announced, as grandly as if she were entering a ballroom. "Lady Charlotte, Mr. Thomas Carter."

Charlotte smiled. Smiling generally eased any situation, however awkward.

"Good day, Mr. Carter," she said. "Or rather, good evening. Is Mama expecting you?"

"Good day, my lady," Mr. Carter said, bowing low. "Pray forgive the inconvenience of the hour, my lady, but it is you I have come to see, not Lady Hervey."

"I?" Charlotte's eyes widened with astonishment. "You must be mistaken, sir. No one calls on me."

"I assure you that there is no mistake, my lady," Mr. Carter said solemnly. "His Grace would never make such an error."

"His Grace?" Charlotte repeated warily. She folded her arms over her chest, the long sleeves flopping over her hands. From the landing behind her she heard a smothered giggle from Diana, and Charlotte's first astonishment now shifted to unabashed suspicion.

"His Grace, meaning a duke?" she continued. "A *duke*? Oh, what a pretty jest, sir, and I know you're party to it, too. Go on, then. Tell me why a duke—any duke!—would send you to call upon me."

"Forgive me, my lady, but His Grace would never jest

over such an important matter." Mr. Carter hesitated, choosing his words with care. "As the, ah, the fateful day of your nuptials draws closer, arrangements must be made."

"My *nuptials*?" Charlotte flushed. Now, this was dreadfully cruel, to tease her like this about marriage. She knew she was eighteen, already past the age when girls in the village wed, and also past the age when Mama and Father had been married. Yet because of who Charlotte was and where they lived, there were never any young men interested in her. Mama had always made vague promises to take them to London for suitable husbands when they were older, but always in some distant future, not now, and not to a *duke*. "A pox on you, sir, to show such unkindness toward me!"

But the gentleman only shook his head as he reached inside the leather portfolio. "Forgive me, my lady, but I assure that this is no jest, with no unkindness intended. Here is a gift His Grace sends to you, his portrait, as a token for the future you will share."

He stepped forward to hand Charlotte a flat velvet-covered box. For a long moment she could only stare at it there in her fingers. Then she slowly, cautiously unlatched the tiny golden clasp and opened it. Inside lay a small oval portrait of a handsome gentleman with dark hair, a blue sash across his chest. The portrait was painted on ivory and ringed with tiny winking brilliants. A painted stranger claiming to be a duke: how could this be her husband?

"Mr. Carter, good evening!" cried Mama, appearing on the landing beside Diana. Lizzie was there, too, yawning, evidently awakened by the commotion. "Pray forgive our makeshift welcome, but with the length of your journey, I was not given to expect you until tomorrow at the earliest."

"Good evening, Lady Hervey," Mr. Carter said, bowing gallantly. "The hour is unseemly, I know, but His Grace is a lord who expects promptness in all matters, and on this most important errand, I have traveled without stopping."

"Yes, I imagine dukes must be obeyed," murmured Mama, "no matter what the hour. Poor man, you must be weary beyond measure."

"Mama, please," Charlotte said, catching Mama by the arm. "About Mr. Carter, and this duke, and—"

"His Grace, Charlotte. You must call him His Grace," Mama corrected gently, looping her arm around Charlotte's waist and drawing her close. Her smile twisted, as if she was trying not to cry. "Mr. Carter, you have met my eldest daughter?"

"Yes, Mama, he has met me," Charlotte said quickly, her suspicions and uneasiness rising by the second. She pressed the miniature portrait into her mother's hand. "He brought me this as a gift."

Mama stared at the handsome painted face, her fingers pressed to her cheek.

"Heavens, heavens," she murmured. "Oh, how much His Grace favors his late father!"

"But who is he, Mama?" Charlotte begged. "How can you know him, while I do not?"

"Oh, my lamb, I am so sorry," Mama said, shaking her head with a sad regret that did little to calm Charlotte. "Everything was decided so long ago by your father, you see, when you were still in the cradle. I was going to tell you tomorrow, before Mr. Carter arrived, but now he is early, and I—I didn't."

"Then tell me now, Mama." Charlotte tugged the sleeves of her jersey over her hands, twisting them into the rough wool so that no one could see how her fingers shook. "What Mr. Carter says cannot possibly be true, can it?"

"Charlotte, Charlotte, my own dear." Again Mama tried to smile, a single tear sliding down her cheek. "It is true, every word. Within the week we shall all leave Ransom Manor for London, and as soon as it can be arranged, you will wed His Grace the Duke of Marchbourne."

CHAPTER

2

Greenwood Hall
Surrey

James Augustus FitzCharles, third Duke of March-bourne, stood in the center of the largest arched window in his bedchamber, his hands clasped behind his back. He was dressed for riding, and riding he would go, as soon as the tall French clock behind him struck eleven. That, he had calculated, would be the precise time to leave the stable, ride through the yard and the allée and across the north fields, and be near the London road when the coach passed by.

He could have waited until later next week, for the formal introductions that had been planned by his elders and their solicitors. To them his marriage was only a transaction of dynastic business, a calculated union of families and fortunes that had been blessed by His Majesty himself.

But for reasons that Marchbourne—or March, as he had been called by his friends since he'd inherited the dukedom—himself could not entirely explain, he'd no wish to wait for that chill formal introduction. Instead he'd decided that his first meeting with Lady Charlotte Wylder should appear to be by purest accident beneath the open sky, as if a whim of fate instead of their fathers had brought them together. He'd intercept her traveling party and graciously invite them to stop here at Greenwood for refreshment, as any host might. He'd already ordered tables arranged in the west garden, where his late mother's white roses were beginning to bloom, and his cooks were busily preparing a selection of temptations for ladies. But that would be all. A chance meeting, followed by civil hospitality, white roses and sweet biscuits and tea, an accident of love contrived by an ardent bridegroom.

More likely an accident of tomfoolery, March thought with disgust as well as despair. What was he thinking, anyway? He'd always believed himself by nature far too practical for this sort of ridiculous gallantry. His history with ladies was impeccably honorable, and as far as he could tell, he'd never once fallen in love. It simply hadn't been necessary. Lady Charlotte Wylder was already his, by right and by law, and had been betrothed to him since he'd been a boy of eight. There was no need for him to contrive a romantic folly with roses and biscuits to win her. He was twenty-six years old and a gentleman in his prime, master of all the land he could see from this window and much more besides, a peer of the realm and great-grandson of a king.

Yet here he was now, so beside himself with anticipation and dread and uncertainty that he didn't wonder the entire household couldn't hear his heart knocking away in his chest.

Eleven, and not before. He did not wish to appear too eager. Eleven, and—

The clock struck, the chimes as solemn as ever, and March nearly jumped from his boots. By the eleventh chime, he had composed himself once again and begun walking purposefully through the house, beneath the painted gazes of his long-gone ancestors in their stiff ruffs and gilded frames and before the occasional bowing servant. It took exactly nine minutes to walk from his rooms to the front door—he knew because he'd timed himself numerous times before calculating a useful average—so by a quarter past the hour, he had taken his hat and gloves from his servant and put them on, respectively, his head and his hands, had walked down the fifteen polished white stone steps, and had mounted the horse that the groom held for him. Two other grooms were also waiting, ready to ride behind as an escort. Waiting, too, was Carter, dressed in his usual gloomy black.

By trade Carter was the solicitor who oversaw all the niggling legal details that were part of every estate the size of Greenwood. But Carter had also been in the service of the Dukes of Marchbourne for so long that he'd earned March's trust as well in other, more personal matters. When his letters to the Dowager Countess of Hervey had gone unanswered, March had naturally sent Carter to call upon the lady and flush her out from the ancient, distant pile of a house where she'd hidden herself with her daughters. And, just as naturally, it made sense to have Carter at his side now—if for no other reason than that he could make proper introductions.

They rode down the drive, cutting off across the west fields, around the lake, and past the miniature Temple of Jupiter that his father had built on a whim. It was a splendid day, full of warmth and sunshine on the green fields and trees around them, but March's thoughts were turned so thoroughly inward that he saw none of the beauty around him. Fortunately, another of Mr. Carter's gifts was the ability to keep a companionable silence, and he rode patiently beside March until, at last, March could no longer keep his doubts bound within.

"You are certain the party of ladies left Tensmore this morn, Carter?" he asked without preamble. "You are sure of it?"

"As certain as I can be of anything, sir," said Carter, who was accustomed to this kind of abrupt conversation from the duke. "I had word that Lady Sanborn's coach left Tensmore shortly before dawn."

March shook his head. "How can you be so sure, Carter? If Lady Hervey is as—as *scattered* as you have portrayed her to me, then I find it difficult to believe that she would be capable of so prompt a departure."

"You are correct, sir," Carter said. "If arrangements had been left entirely in Lady Hervey's hands, then I doubt she and her daughters would have yet left Ransom Manor. But because they are now being guided by the countess, I expect that promptness is the order of the day, and that they left Her Ladyship's house exactly as planned."

March grunted, wordless discontent. The Countess of Danbury was Lady Hervey's fearsome aunt and Carter's secret weapon. Once she had heard (by means of an exquisitely worded inquiry from Carter) of Lady Hervey's procrastination, the countess had wasted no time appointing herself to bring her niece and grandnieces back into society—whether they wished it or not. It certainly wasn't the way that March had wanted matters to fall.

"You already know my thoughts on Lady Danbury, Carter," he said. "How you can consider letting those poor ladies be blasted by the flames of that old dragon as 'guidance' is beyond me."

"I would, sir," Carter said defensively, "so long as her flames will serve your purpose. Pray consider her ladyship as an ally in your purpose rather than a, ah, a dragon."

March sighed. Lady Danbury would always be a dragon to him, and now, unhappily, a dragon who would be bound to him by marriage. "I pray that Lady Charlotte will not prove to be a dragon in training."

"Oh, no, sir, not at all!" Carter exclaimed. "She is a young lady of the greatest beauty."

March didn't reply. He had steadfastly maintained that it was far more important that his duchess possess the character of an old and noble family than mere shallow beauty, and Lady Charlotte Wylder's bloodlines were impeccable. This had been the main reason that his father had long ago agreed to this match, to "improve" their own family's dubious heritage—that, and because his father and Lady Charlotte's had been boyhood friends.

But while March would never be so dishonorable as to say it aloud, deep down he did wonder if her face was fair or plain, if her form would be pleasingly curved and her skin soft to his touch. He wouldn't have been male if he hadn't. The fact that no one in London had seen Lady Charlotte since she'd been a young girl—apparently she hadn't even sat for a portrait—made her a complete mystery, and March was uneasy.

"Truly, sir, you need have no concerns," Carter said earnestly, correctly reading March's silence—though what else could he say of the future Duchess of Marchbourne? "Lady Charlotte is quite beautiful, as are the dowager countess and the younger ladies as well. To be sure, she has been raised in the country—"

"That is to the good, Carter," March said. "I admire the simplicity of the country."

"Oh, Lady Charlotte does have that," Carter agreed, with a little too much enthusiasm. "She is no lady of fashion. She is completely untainted by London's false airs, with no—"

"That's enough, Carter," March said sharply. "We will not speak of her ladyship further."

Carter looked away, and bowed his head with contrition. "Forgive me, sir."

"Damnation, man, I didn't intend a reprimand," March

said, more annoyed with himself than with Carter. The solicitor had only been answering the question, and besides, it was hardly Carter's fault that he'd met Lady Charlotte Wylder before March himself had. If he bumbled so badly with old Carter, how the devil could he be expected to do before Lady Charlotte?

With a muttered oath, March wrapped the reins more tightly around his gloved hand and dug his heels into his horse's sides. Beneath him the horse lunged forward, and March bent low, giving himself over to the animal's speed, carrying him to his fate. Lady Charlotte could be directly over that next hill, and they'd meet at last, and all the dreaming and dreading would finally be done. Dutifully Carter and the two grooms followed, but their horses were not equal to March's, and he was soon ahead of them. He raced up the last hill, knowing that on the other side lay the road to London, and upon it, if the saints did smile upon him, would be his bride.

He reached the crest and paused, drawing the horse's head to one side.

And swore again. Softly, under his breath, as befit a duke, but swearing nonetheless, for the scene that lay before him made less sense than a Covent Garden comedy.

An enormous, old-fashioned traveling coach had drawn to a halt near a copse of spreading trees, not far from the road. The coach was a distinctive shade of mulberry, like a giant glistening beetle, and even without being able to read the crest on the door, March knew it belonged to the countess. Though stopped, the coach did not seem to be in any distress; the driver had climbed down from the box, and the footmen who rode behind the coach were helping him loosen the team so they might graze. The baggage cart had also halted and the outriders had dismounted as well, standing in the shade of the trees. All this masculine activity seemed un-eventful enough, but the ladies—the ladies had all, it seemed, lost their wits entirely.

A beautiful gold-haired woman in a feathered hat stood beneath the broadest of the trees, staring upward into the branches. On either side of her were two younger girls that must be her daughters, both dressed in match-ing white gowns with pink sashes. The girls also stared up into the tree, wailing and sobbing as if their very hearts were breaking, and though their mother tried to comfort them by holding them close, they remained in-consolable, wringing and thrashing their hands about like bedlamites. Two small white fluffs of dogs on long leashes raced around and around these three, wrapping the leashes around their legs like a maypole ribbon, and barking, too, as if they hoped to outdo the girls' wailing.

The final touch of madness came from the countess herself. An angular woman laced too tightly, she tottered on high, unsteady heels through the waving grasses, leaning on the arm of a footman while she waved her ruffled parasol like a general's baton. She, too, stared upward, and because she shouted the loudest of all, March could hear her from the hill.

"Come down here at once!" she ordered. "No lowly mongrel beast is worth this sort of performance, and I will not have it. Come down, I say, come down directly! Directly!"

At once March urged his horse down the hill to join them. So long as they were on his land, they were his responsibility, and he would do what he must to calm them and bring order. It was only when he was twenty paces away that he realized Lady Charlotte—*his* Lady Charlotte—seemed not to be of the party.

"Good day, Lady Sanborn," he said, drawing up be-fore the countess. "Might I be of service to you? If there is some distress, some—"

"Distress, Duke!" She managed the slightest possible curtsey to him before she popped up again, her quivering cheeks pink with indignation. "That is, good day, good day. Pray forgive me, Duke, but my greatest distress must come from your very presence here. You must be gone directly. You cannot stay another moment in this place."

"But this is my place, Lady Sanborn," March said, thinking again of dragons. He wished she'd stop brandishing her parasol at him, too. All those shaking ruffles were upsetting his horse. "You are at present on my land and are therefore my guest. It's my pleasure and my duty to put you at your ease."

"This is not about my ease, Duke," she declared vehemently. "You know that as well as I. It is about you attempting to glimpse your bride before the time we agreed, and I will not permit it."

"It is your welfare that concerns me most at present, Lady Sanborn," he declared, sidestepping her accusation, which was, of course, exactly what he had been planning. "And how could I hope to glimpse Lady Charlotte Wylder when she is clearly not of your party today?"

"But Charlotte *is* here." The younger of the girls with the pink sashes darted toward March, her earlier tears forgotten. "She's the entire reason we must go to London."

At once Lady Sanborn swung her parasol down before the girl like a tollman's bar, blocking her path.

"You forget yourself, Lady Diana," she warned ominously as the gold-haired lady rushed forward, settling her hands on the girl's shoulders.

"Oh, Diana, this is a grievous mistake," the lady said hurriedly, mortified for her daughter's sake, "and I know I've explained this to you before, over and over. You are never to address anyone of His Grace's rank. You must wait until His Grace has first honored you with his notice."

"But he's noticed me now, Mama," the girl said, cheerfully undaunted as she gazed up at March on the horse. "He'll notice Charlotte, too. She's up there, sir, over your head."

The girl pointed upward. With a certain amount of reluctance—or was it dread?—March slowly looked up into the tree.

There sat his bride, perched like some silk-clad nymph on a wide branch, with one arm loosely around the trunk for balance. At least she'd looped and tied her skirts to one side of her legs for decency's sake, but as he gazed up from the back of his horse March still had a provocative view of frothy lace around bright green stockings on delicate, perfectly shaped ankles. The gauzy linen kerchief around her shoulders had slipped to one side, and the plump curves of her breasts rose above the neckline of her gown, all the more obvious above the boned bodice. Her skin was creamy and fair, her cheeks prettily flushed, her dark hair tousled beneath a small lace cap.

His first coherent thought was that Carter had been absolutely right: Lady Charlotte was a beauty, the kind of beauty destined to turn heads in every ballroom in London.

His second was pure amazement that such a lady was intended for him.

But his third and most urgent thought was why in blazes the soon-to-be third Duchess of Marchbourne—*his* duchess—was stranded in the lofty branches of a tree.

"Good day, Lady Charlotte," he said briskly, already determining a plan for rescuing her. "We shall make our formal acquaintance soon enough, I am sure, but more pressing now is that I save you."

"*Save* me?" she repeated, her eyes widening with charming astonishment. "But I do not require saving, Your Grace, not at all."

As if to prove it, she swung toward him with only the single arm around the tree's trunk for security, then swayed back again, almost as if she were dancing. It was gracefully done, to be sure, but it worried him to see her be so cavalier with her safety.

"No more of that," he ordered, swiftly guiding his horse to stand beside the base of the tree. "If you fall, I'll never forgive myself."

To his amazement, she laughed, a merry, rippling laugh. "But I won't fall, sir. Ask my sisters if you doubt me. I've been climbing in and out of trees for as long as I can remember, and this one is no challenge at all."

She balanced on one foot, raising and pointing the other elegantly before her.

The baser, male part of March's brain marveled at how fine her ankles appeared in those bright green stockings and how pretty her feet were in pink flower-patterned shoes with silver buckles, and wondered if she tied her garters below her knees or above them.

Fortunately, the more responsible part of that same brain stepped forward and reminded March of his duty.

"Take care, Lady Charlotte, take care," he cautioned, striving to concentrate on her safety rather than her knees. "Nothing will be gained, and everything may be lost."

He handed his reins to one of the waiting grooms, swiftly unbuttoned his coat, and tossed it along with his hat to another of the servants. He couldn't recall the last time he'd climbed a tree, but then he'd never had such a good reason for doing so. He swung his leg over the saddle and pulled himself up into the deep crook of the tree.

Behind him, he heard Lady Sanborn gasp again, though likely more with outrage than indignation.

"Please, Duke, do not put yourself at risk like this,"

she called. "Send a servant up after her if you must, but pray do not exert yourself like this. While Lady Charlotte is fool enough to believe herself a wild squirrel, there is no need for you to do so as well."

"Yes, sir, you must take care," Carter said, his voice adding another note of horrified concern.

March did not reply. Instead he looked across to Lady Charlotte, who still stood on her branch about ten paces beyond him, and another twelve feet or so above the ground.

"Be easy, Lady Charlotte," he said, wishing to reassure her. "Don't fear. I am coming to your aid."

But Lady Charlotte appeared neither uneasy nor fearful. She looked bemused.

"You don't have to do this, sir," she said wryly. "Truly. Not for me. I vow it's vastly heroic of you to make the attempt, but your riding boots will be too slippery on the bark."

"No, they won't." To demonstrate, he climbed up from one branch to the next, closer to her. She was right, of course: because his servants kept the soles of his boots as brightly polished as the shafts, he might as well have been navigating the smooth bark with sheets of glass beneath feet. But he'd never confess it to Lady Charlotte, not after she'd called him heroic.

She frowned, watching his well-polished feet sliding over the branch. "Take care, sir. Mind you keep one hand for yourself and one for the ship."

He climbed closer. "Are you a sailor, then, Lady Charlotte?"

"One need not be a sailor to see the wisdom in nautical maxims," she said. "I expect clambering through the rigging and mastheads is much the same as elms and oaks. Truly, sir, I can climb down perfectly well myself."

"She can, Your Grace," piped up her younger sister

Lady Diana, standing below them. "First Charlotte must save Fig, and then she'll come down on her own. She's done it hundreds of times."

March sighed with exasperation. He was accustomed to seeing a task to be done and doing it, and having his betrothed refuse his assistance like this was perplexing. Who would have guessed that life in the country would produce such independence in a young lady?

With fresh determination, he climbed up another branch. "Tell me," he said, "is Fig another sister?"

"My sister?" Lady Charlotte tipped back her head and laughed again, displaying a small freckle directly on the underside of her jaw that was unexpectedly enchanting.

If only she'd call him heroic once more.

"Fig is Diana's cat, sir," she explained, "and a wicked, ill-behaved little cat at that. She's watching us right now, you know, right up there, deciding when she'll let me catch her."

Dutifully March glanced upward, and for the first time he noticed the small piebald cat nestled in the leaves overhead. The cat looked content, her tail curled around her feet, and disinclined toward being caught.

"Can you reach up and seize the beast, Lady Charlotte?" he asked. "Then I'll guide you both down the tree."

She opened her mouth, likely to protest again, then thought better of it: a good sign, decided March, an excellent sign for their future together. It was one of the advantages of her being so young and impressionable. The sooner she learned to recognize him as her master and leader, as any proper husband should be, the better.

"Very well, sir," she said, bracing herself against the thick branch again. "I'll try to catch her. Here, Fig, here, come to me."

She reached upward, stretching her hands toward the cat. The cat did not move, nor did Lady Charlotte's stylishly close-fitting gown. With a tearing sound, the under-arm seams of both sleeves gave way under the stress and split. The pink silk gapped open, giving March an intimate glimpse of Charlotte's scarlet linen stays, the narrow boned channels holding her tightly. She grabbed at her sides, feeling the rent silk.

"Oh, goodness," she said, blushing. "Who'd have guessed that would happen?"

She laughed, and March laughed with her. He couldn't help it, nor did he wish to. With her, it seemed the most natural thing in the world, and one of the most pleasurable as well.

"Perhaps I should capture the cat, Lady Charlotte," he suggested, struggling to regain his focus on the rescue and forget the red stays and the laughter. Below them he heard a fresh torrent of dismay from Lady Sanborn, dismay he'd no intention of heeding as he climbed closer to Lady Charlotte. "I'll be able to reach the animal soon enough."

"Thank you, sir, but I have her." With her arms now freed from the confining sleeves, she gracefully stretched up and caught the cat in her hands. Fig didn't fight, turning happily limp as Lady Charlotte tucked her into one arm. Leaning back against the branch, she deftly pulled her white neckerchief from around her shoulders and wrapped it around the cat. Intent upon Fig, she showed no concern for the amount of pale skin she now bared to March's view, shoulders and throat and breasts. The little cat closed her eyes and rubbed her whiskered face against Lady Charlotte's arm.

March watched, wondering if it was possible for a duke to be envious of a cat.

"There," Lady Charlotte said. She turned back to face him with the bundled cat nestled in the crook of her arm, directly below the ripped seam. "I do this for safety's sake, sir. Most times Fig is perfectly content to let me carry her, but it is easier to climb down with her like this."

"Then let me help you, Lady Charlotte." He held his hand out to her.

She smiled over the top of the little cat's head and bent to kiss it between the ears. "You are persistent, sir."

"When I've reason to be, yes," he admitted.

"How fine to know I'm worthy of your persistence, sir." Her smile widened. "I feared that you would be old and wizened, like dukes are supposed to be."

"Is that what Carter told you?" he asked, surprised. It hadn't occurred to him that she might have had misgivings about him, just as he had had about her. "Didn't he give you the miniature of me?"

"The one circled with brilliants?" she said. "He did. But pictures can lie, sir, as can solicitors. I'm glad neither did."

"How fortunate for us both, Lady Charlotte." Only a few more feet separated them, and he easily reached his hand out to take hers. He was surprised by how small and delicate her fingers felt, how different from his own. Her expression was guarded, as if she could not make up her mind whether to pull her hand free or not.

He smiled, meaning to put her at ease, but also because he was, to his own amazement, thoroughly happy to be here, holding her hand in a tree as the breeze whispered through the leaves around them. The others below were forgotten, hidden by the leaves and branches.

"Take care now, and come closer," he coaxed, and after the merest hesitation she did, sliding along the wide branch toward him. "Take care, and trust me."

Her eyes were very blue here in the shadows of the tree. Her pale skin had a faint sheen to it, perhaps from the warmth of the day, perhaps from the excitement of it. A few stray wisps of dark hair tossed across her forehead, and impatiently she shook her head to move them aside. Then she smiled shyly and came to him.

He reminded himself this was for the sake of her safety and for no other reason, and that the wanton blood and impulses of his rakish ancestors were not the same as his. He reminded himself of this even as he slid his arm around the back of her waist: the sleekness of her silk gown, the rigid bones of her stays—those brilliant scarlet stays—and the vulnerability of her body within.

"There, sir," she said, her voice low and meant for only his ears to hear. She lifted her chin, clearly determined to meet his gaze as evenly as she could. "This is what you wished all along, isn't it?"

"No," he said, and that *was* true. He'd come here wishing to invite her to stop at Greenwood, and he'd wished for a word or two with her over a light repast under the watchful eyes of her dragon-aunt and her mother. He hadn't wished for more because, quite simply, he hadn't imagined any more was likely to happen. How could he ever have conceived of standing on the branch of a tree, hatless and in his waistcoat and shirtsleeves, with his arm at Lady Charlotte's waist, safely from the sight of those below? "Not at all."

"No, sir?" Disappointment filled her blue eyes. "Not at *all*?"

"I said I hadn't wished for this, Lady Charlotte, because I hadn't," he said quickly. "But now that we find ourselves together here, I wouldn't wish it any other way."

What he also wished for was to kiss her, here among the leaves, and with that as his only thought he slipped his other arm around her waist to pull her closer.

Yet as he bent his face over hers he felt, rather than heard, a low, rumbling growl between them. Ignoring it, he leaned in to Lady Charlotte, and the growl instantly rose to a banshee's screech. In the same instant, a score of tiny needles pierced the fine linen of his sleeve and dug deep into his arm.

"What the devil?" March exclaimed, attempting to free his arm.

"Let Fig go, sir, please." Lady Charlotte tried to work the cat free from March's arm. "Hush, hush, little one, he doesn't mean any of it."

"She most certainly does, and now she's—*aughh*!" Like the talons of an eagle, Fig's claws curved more deeply into his arm, and blood—*his* blood, blast the animal— blossomed through the white linen. He jerked his arm back, finally freeing his arm (and more blood) from the cat's grasp, only to realize that the rest of himself was tipping backward, too. One hand for the ship, Lady Charlotte had told him, and one hand for himself, but why hadn't she said a word about the hand that had been possessed by a bedlamite cat?

In compensation he lurched forward, barely recovering his balance as his boots scuffled on the bark. Lady Charlotte gasped, grabbing his shoulder to pull him back as she juggled the writhing cat in her other arm.

"Don't fall, sir!" she cried as they wobbled unsteadily together, the branch bobbing beneath them. "You *can't* fall!"

"Trust me, Lady Charlotte," he managed to gasp. "I'll keep you safe."

With a little yelp she flung her free arm around him and held tight, and he circled his arms protectively around her. It was an excellent moment, one of the very best he could recall in his life.

Followed, promptly, by one of the very worst.

With Lady Charlotte in his arms, March's tenuous balance vanished entirely. His feet shot out from beneath him and he toppled backward, falling, falling, falling. Someone screamed, but not Lady Charlotte. She trusted him to keep her safe.

And as they landed with a thump on the ground, he knew that he had. Because he was on the bottom, he'd absorbed most of the impact. He knew she was unhurt because she'd immediately scrambled up onto her hands and knees over him. Her blue eyes were wide with remorse and her hair was falling loose around her face, the most charming face he'd ever seen, even if it was spinning around in queasy circles.

"Oh, sir, are you hurt?" she said with a catch in her voice. "Merciful heaven, if I've injured you like this, before we've properly met—oh, it would not be fair at all!"

He smiled, or meant to. He wasn't sure if the order actually reached his lips. So much was spinning before him now: the tree, and the sky, and Carter's face, and Lady Sanborn's beside it, but mostly Lady Charlotte's. There was much he wanted to tell her, beginning with the white roses waiting for her admiration in the garden at Greenwood. Yes, that would be a good beginning, and a considerable improvement over plummeting from a tree like some damned rotten acorn.

"White rotheth," he said, shocked by his own slurred incoherence. He frowned as he concentrated, which hurt his head more, but for Lady Charlotte's sake, he would not give up. "Fo' you. White rotheth, an'—"

"There now, sir, do not tax yourself," Carter said, his earnest face replacing Lady Charlotte's. "Dr. Stapleton has been summoned, and a carriage from Greenwood to convey you home. Be easy, sir, and all will be well."

But he didn't care about Dr. Stapleton, or the carriage, either, and if Carter really wanted him to be easy, then he should let him see Lady Charlotte again.

"Lady Cha'lotte—"

"Lady Sanborn and the other ladies are continuing their journey to London, sir, as was for the best," Carter said, coddling him like some wretched nursemaid. "You will see the ladies in town next week, sir, and—"

"No' yet," March protested weakly. How could she leave him without saying farewell? He tried to push himself upright, meaning to go after her, but his arm gave way. Pain sliced through his shoulder as sharp as a sword, and then, mercifully, he felt nothing more.

CHAPTER

3

Charlotte woke the next morning when the maid-servant pulled open the curtains on her bed and let the bright morning sun fall full on her face. With a groan she turned away from the windows and buried her face back into the pillows. It was not so much the sun that affected her as the burden of her own conscience, and after yesterday's events, that burden was heavy indeed. The memory of the poor Duke of Marchbourne lying pale and still in the wispy grass because of her should have been sufficiently leaden on its own, but the icy silence of disappointment from both her aunt and her mother during the long drive to London had served to add even more.

With a clatter that Charlotte was sure was intentional, the maid set a silver tray with tea on the small table beside the bed.

"I am Polly, my lady," the maid said. "Lady Sanborn has bid me tend to you. She asks that you dress and come to her room as soon as possible."

Swiftly Charlotte rolled over to face the maid. "Is there any word from His Grace this morning?"

"His Grace, my lady?" Polly asked, her hands clasped tightly at her waist. She was a slight girl, not much older than Charlotte, with sandy hair and freckles over her cheeks. "Forgive me, my lady, but many dukes do attend Lady Sanborn."

"His Grace the Duke of Marchbourne," Charlotte said proudly, though still awed that so imposing a title could have any relationship to her. "The duke I'm supposed to wed."

Polly's expression did not change. "Then no, my lady. There has been no word come to the house from His Grace. At least none that I have been told."

"Then could you go and ask Aunt Sophronia for me, Polly?" Charlotte pleaded, pushing her hair back from her face. "Please?"

"I, my lady?" Polly drew back, clearly scandalized. "Forgive me, my lady, but it is not my place to ask such questions of Lady Sanborn."

"I suppose not." Charlotte sighed. "Though if His Grace had worsened over the night, then surely someone from his house would have sent us news of it. Surely we'd hear, wouldn't we?"

Charlotte was certain Polly raised her head an infinitesimal fraction, the better to look down her narrow little nose at her. The few servants at Ransom Manor—Mama hadn't kept a large household, nor had they needed one—had been more like friends, content to oblige and indulge her and her sisters. From Polly's obvious disapproval, that would clearly not be the case here at her aunt's grand house.

"Forgive me, my lady," she said, "but Lady Sanborn gives us strict rules about gossiping over our betters. Shall I pour your tea, my lady?"

In anticipation, Polly's hand already hovered over the curved handle of the pot.

Charlotte shook her head. "Thank you, no, I'll pour for myself."

The truth was that she much preferred chocolate to tea in the morning, but she'd already begun so badly with Polly that she didn't dare confess it.

But for Polly the question of tea was finished, and she'd moved to the next matter—or rather, she'd moved to the wardrobe, throwing open the tall double doors.

"Lady Sanborn said you were to dress for visiting the mantua-maker's, my lady," she said, surveying Charlotte's meager assortment of clothing, forlornly underoccupying the massive wardrobe. What had been adequate and appropriate for Surrey was evidently neither in London, and the longer Polly stared at the gowns hanging from the pegs, the more clear that became—which was the reason her aunt had determined a trip to the mantua-maker for the first round of new clothes must be today's agenda. "Will this riding habit do, my lady?"

"Yes, yes," agreed Charlotte hurriedly. The habit had seen much hard riding along the beach in harder weather, and in Polly's hands it now looked rumpled and worn, the once dark blue faded at the seams and cuffs and stained with salt from the sea air. "The hat must be still in one of the trunks."

"I will find it, my lady." With brisk authority, Polly dressed Charlotte, brushing and patting and pinning and tweaking and generally making the habit look more presentable. Next she dressed Charlotte's hair, deftly brushing it back into an artful, sleek knot at the back of her head. Finally came the hat, a plain black beaver cocked hat, which Polly pinned into place at exactly the right angle to give the masculine hat a coquettish air. When at last she held the looking glass for Charlotte's approval, Charlotte gasped.

"Faith, look at me!" she exclaimed. "I've never been so fine to go out on a pony."

"But you are not going out on a pony, my lady," Polly said firmly. "You are going in Her Ladyship's carriage, where you will be noticed and remarked on by all the world. I'd not be doing my duty if I did not make you look as handsome as I could, my lady."

"You've made me look much handsomer than I am." She smiled, and in their shared reflection she saw that Polly was now smiling as well. "How can I thank you, Polly?"

"You can go directly to Lady Sanborn, my lady, for she doesn't like dawdling," Polly said, giving Charlotte's shoulder one final pat. "Lord knows Her Ladyship's not so easy to please. And I hope His Grace is well, my lady. It's worrisome when the one you love is ailing."

Charlotte nodded and smiled, but her thoughts were far from easy as she followed Polly through the house to Lady Sanborn's rooms. She knew that Polly had intended only good wishes, but still it troubled her to hear the duke described as "the one you love." She didn't love him. She was betrothed to him. Truly, how could she love a gentleman that she scarcely knew?

Remembering yesterday only made it worse. She had fallen not in love with the duke but onto him, which wasn't the same thing at all. If she'd heard of this accident having happened to another lady, Charlotte knew, she would have laughed and laughed at the ridiculousness of it. But because she had been the one falling, and the poor Duke of Marchbourne had been the one fallen upon, it wasn't amusing at all. It was . . . tragic.

A footman showed her to her aunt's bedchamber. The room was enormous, running across the entire front of the house, with windows that opened out onto St. James's Square. There was much gilding on the walls, much crystal hanging from the chandeliers, and large looking glasses framed in gold to reflect it all a dozen times over. A thick

French carpet covered the floor, and the furniture, too, was trimmed with more gold, with plump silk-covered cushions.

Her aunt was sitting at a table in a distant corner before one of the fireplaces, breaking her fast. Several small white dogs lay near her on the carpet. She, too, was already dressed for the day, in a gown and jacket of mustard yellow silk edged with black lace. As soon as she saw Charlotte, she waved vigorously, like a passenger on a ship spotting an acquaintance on the shore.

"Here, Charlotte, here!" she called. "Don't hang back, child. You're a Wylder, not some impossible little milkmaid come to market. Though given how shamefully your mother has hidden you away in the country, I suppose the assumption could be forgiven. Sit, Charlotte, sit. Fah! Must I tell you to do everything?"

"No, Aunt Sophronia," Charlotte said, sitting on the edge of the nearest chair. She had only come to know her great-aunt in the last week, and in that time she'd also come to realize why Mama had retreated as far away from Father's family as she had.

Aunt Sophronia was *daunting*. There was no other way to describe her. She spoke how she pleased, yet in turn did not listen, and she expected all others to hop to instant obedience. Even her appearance was sharp, all bony angles and pointed lace and sharp-edged jewels that poked when she offered a perfunctory hug.

Yet Mama had assured Charlotte that Aunt Sophronia intended to be kind to her, and that her sharpness was only her way of showing favor toward Charlotte. More importantly, Mama had said that Aunt Sophronia was a special friend of the duke's, and that she could in time be an excellent ally in smoothing Charlotte's way both in London society and in her future marriage. Secretly Charlotte had her doubts about such an alliance.

But after yesterday's disaster, she knew she would need every advantage she could muster—even if it came in the prickly form of Aunt Sophronia.

"You have eaten, Charlotte?" she asked, tearing apart a piece of toast to toss to one of the dogs. "You must eat, now. No missish notions of not eating. We have a long morning before us, and I won't have you turning faint in a public street."

"No, Aunt," Charlotte said. "But I thought I'd wait for Mama and the others."

"You'll wait until supper, then, for we won't be seeing them sooner. Aren't you the best, best doggie!" She smiled at the dog who'd caught the toast, not Charlotte. "You will be in my company alone for the entire day, Charlotte, while your mother and your sisters will be doing whatever it is that they do."

"Yes, Aunt." Quickly Charlotte reached for the last piece of toast from the tines of the silver rack before it, too, could go to the dogs.

"More toast can be brought, my dear," said Aunt Sophronia. "I believe we do have at least another crumb or two in the kitchen."

Charlotte flushed. This was going to be a long, long day, perhaps the longest in her entire life. "Thank you, Aunt. This—this will suffice. Aunt Sophronia, if you please, has there been any word of importance? That is, have there been any words in reference to yesterday? Words from the duke?"

The older woman raised her painted brows. "By which I must infer you mean His Grace the Duke of March-bourne? I say, Charlotte, you do have difficulty expressing yourself with clarity. Do you mean have I had any message from the duke who you unceremoniously crushed yesterday?"

"Yes." Charlotte's cheeks grew warmer still. "His Grace

the Duke of Marchbourne. Has there been any word from Greenwood?"

"Nary a syllable." Magically a footman appeared with more toast, which the countess at once began preparing for the dogs. "But I believe His Grace must not have expired in the night, else the bailiff would have come to carry you off to the Tower. Murdering a peer is a most serious offense, Charlotte."

"Please, Aunt Sophronia, I didn't mean to fall from the tree, on him or otherwise!"

"You didn't mean to, no, but you did." She stirred more sugar into her tea, then pointed the spoon at Charlotte like a schoolmaster's rod. "What you did yesterday could have ruined your future and your prospects. No gentleman wishes to discover his future wife in a tree, clambering about like some half-mad hoyden."

"He didn't mind," Charlotte protested. "He climbed the tree to join me."

"He climbed to rescue you, as any gentleman might when a lady is in peril. He had no choice, really." She shook the teaspoon again, flicking drops of tea on the cloth. "By your impulsiveness, you put his very life in jeopardy—and him still without an heir, too. It was shamefully selfish of you, Charlotte."

"But you said he wasn't grievously hurt!" Again the horrible memory returned to her, with him sprawled on the grass and surrounded by his servants while she was being hauled back to the coach.

"Oh, I don't believe he was," Aunt Sophronia said. "Likely he has a fuddled head this morn, and there seemed to be some complaint about his shoulder, but I'm certain he'll survive. He is young and hearty. But what I fear is that as he lies there, moaning over his aching head, he'll have time to question what manner of lady you may be."

"He should know exactly what manner of lady I am,"

Charlotte said defensively. "I'm a Wylder, and the eldest daughter of an earl."

"I meant your character, Charlotte, not your blood-lines." Aunt Sophronia sighed and tapped the spoon against the cup for emphasis, the porcelain softly ringing with each tap. "The Duke of Marchbourne famously holds himself to an exceedingly high moral standard. Unlike most young gentlemen who come into their titles at an early age, his name has never been linked to any unsavory women, nor has he ever appeared as a scandal in the papers, peeking from behind a mask of asterisks."

"But that can't be true, Aunt," Charlotte said. "He tried to kiss me while we were in the tree."

"He did?" asked Aunt Sophronia, appalled. "Fah! It cannot be so!"

Charlotte was remembering every last pleasurable second before they'd lost their balance. When she had first seen him on his horse, she couldn't tell if he was as handsome as the painted miniature. The portrait wasn't really a fair likeness: in person, the duke had been younger-looking, and much more pleasing to her eye and tastes. His complexion was darker, as if he spent his days out of doors, and his features were stronger and less refined. His hair wasn't brown, either, but almost black, and once he'd climbed the tree it had begun to pull free from the black ribbon queue into unruly waves that Charlotte had longed to touch. Though, of course, if she had, she would have fallen much sooner, and missed the lovely feeling of his arm around her waist. Oh, if only he'd been content to hold her with one arm instead of two!

"He did kiss me, Aunt," she said wistfully, "or rather, he tried to. If we hadn't fallen, he would have, and I would have let him."

"Well, then, there you are." The dowager countess sat back in her chair with grim satisfaction, as if Charlotte had just explained every mystery of the world. "You must have enticed him."

"No!" Charlotte cried indignantly. "I wouldn't even know how to *begin* to entice him, or any other man!"

"Hrmph." Aunt Sophronia did not look convinced. "I suppose that's likely true. From what I've heard, Ransom Manor was as safe from men as any Dutch nunnery. But that is much in your favor where the duke is concerned. You see, although he is a duke, his blood is not quite as virtuous as it might be. His great-grandfather was king, as everyone knows, but his great-grandmother was only the king's mistress, some wicked little baggage of an actress. Of course, a dukedom is a dukedom, however it is got, or begotten, in this case. A dukedom eases everything, which is why your father was so proud of making this alliance for you. But they say this duke feels the shame of his family's beginnings, and tries his utmost to be a better man than that randy old goat of a grandfather."

This was intriguing. Mama hadn't told her a word about the wicked baggage of an actress, and she found the notion of a touch of roguery much more interesting than the saintly version of the duke that had been presented to her. Charlotte remembered how he'd looked at her when he'd leaned close to her, how his expression hadn't been saintly in the least.

"Perhaps that was it, Aunt," she said. "Perhaps it was being the great-grandson of the goatish old king that made him try to kiss me."

"Perhaps it was," Aunt Sophronia admitted. "Though you must never, never say so to him. In all other ways he is a paragon. He neither drinks nor plays to excess, he devotes much of his time to tending his estates, and he always takes his seat in the House when it is in session. He will expect that his duchess will be equally unsullied by tattle or ill behavior, and if he hears any of you, I've no doubt—no doubt at all!—that he will reconsider the match, and break it."

Charlotte caught her breath. When she had first learned she was to be married, the news had shocked her, and she'd wept alone at the unfairness of having to wed a stranger. Ever since they'd left Ransom Manor a fortnight ago, she'd felt like a leaf tossed into a running stream, carried this way and that and helpless to fight against the course that had been chosen for her. She had assumed— quite logically, she'd thought—that the duke must feel the same inevitability of the situation. She hadn't imagined him reconsidering, not even for a moment.

"But he can't change his mind, can he?" she asked. "Mama and Mr. Carter said the betrothal was a legal agreement between our fathers that could not be broken."

"Oh, child, child, matches have been broken over much less cause than this." With a dramatic clatter, Aunt Sophronia dropped the spoon into her now empty cup and pushed them both away from her. "There are no guarantees until the proper words are said over your head. That is the reason I wished to keep you and the duke apart until the wedding, you see, to make certain there were no accidents. Now we must simply pray to the heavens for a swift wedding date—the end of September, or early October, perhaps—and that yesterday's foolishness will not cause the duke to have a change of heart."

Abruptly Charlotte rose and went to stand before the nearest window, her back to Aunt Sophronia. The last thing she wished was for her aunt to see the disappointment that she was certain must be on her face— disappointment that she seemed to have inadvertently brought on to herself.

A week ago, if she had been told she might escape this wedding, she would have rejoiced. A week, hah: even a day, and her response would have been the same. But now that she had met the duke, everything had changed. Yes, he was handsome, titled, rich, and all those other things that gentlemen were supposed to be for ladies like her.

But what she remembered most of yesterday was how he'd smiled, and how they'd laughed together. She didn't love him, no. But laughing together like that seemed as good a start to love as she could imagine.

And now, if Aunt Sophronia was to be believed, it could all be done before it had fair begun.

She stared forlornly out at St. James's Square, thinking how its dreary emptiness suited her tattered prospects. To be sure, it was an excellent address—Aunt Sophronia would not reside here if it weren't—but the centerpiece of the square was a desultory pool of water, surrounded by a stone walkway and an iron fence, without a scrap of flower, lawn, or hedge to soften it. At least as long as she stayed at this house, she wouldn't be climbing any more trees. There wasn't a one to climb.

"What have you brought, John?" asked Aunt Sophronia suspiciously. "That's nothing I've ordered."

"Forgive me, my lady, but it's come for Lady Charlotte," the footman said. "The man who brought it said it must be given to her directly, my lady, and since he wore Marchbourne livery—"

"Charlotte!" Aunt Sophronia called. "Stop drooping by that window and come here."

But Charlotte was already hurrying across the room. The footman held an oversized willow hamper, which he gingerly set on the carpet before her. She unfastened the top and peered inside.

"A basket of straw?" asked Aunt Sophronia, mystified. "The duke has sent you *straw*? Whatever could be the meaning of that?"

"I'll wager there's something buried within," Charlotte said, plunging her hand deep into the straw. Immediately she touched something cool and round, something glass. She thrust her other hand into the straw and carefully drew the object out.

And sighed with awe.

In her hands was a glass globe, fastened to a squat vase of Chinese porcelain. Rising from the vase was a rounded arrangement of the most exquisite white roses she'd ever seen, the buds just begun to open.

Carefully she set the vase on the table and lifted away the globe. The heady scent of the roses filled the air, sweeter than any perfume, and Charlotte leaned over it, breathing deeply. She saw the card then, tucked among the blossoms, and drew it free. The pasteboard was heavy and cream-colored, and marked with a ducal coronet. But all she saw was his writing, an elegant dash across the card:

> *For my fair forest nymph,*
> *Until I might show you these roses as they bloom in*
> *our garden at Greenwood.*
> *Your servant,*
> *M.*

Charlotte read it, read it again, and then pressed the card to her breast with delight. She was his fair forest nymph, and the roses had come from *their* garden: oh, had any gentleman ever sent a more pleasing gift, or written a more perfect missive?

"I could ask you to read that aloud, Charlotte," Aunt Sophronia said dryly. "It is not proper for you to receive correspondence from a gentleman without my permission."

"Oh, please, no, Aunt!" Charlotte cried, dancing backward with the note clutched tight in her hands. To share it would be to lessen its magic; the words were from him, for her, and no one else. "But I promise you that His Grace has no wish to end our betrothal, none at all."

"That is agreeable news, I suppose." Aunt Sophronia bent over the flowers, giving them a perfunctory sniff. "But I still maintain that the sooner the wedding, the better."

CHAPTER

4

Three days later, March sat in his carriage and cursed the snarl of wagons, coaches, and other conveyances that blocked his path to Bond Street. Ordinarily he would not be in such haste to reach a mantua-maker's shop, and in general he avoided similar nests of swarming females as if they harbored the plague itself. Yet because he'd been told that one particular female was inside this particular shop, he could think of little else, to the point that he almost—*almost*—threw aside propriety and expectations and jumped from his carriage to walk the remainder of his journey.

But then, patience had never been one of his virtues, and these last three days had tested him greatly. The wrench to his shoulder when he'd fallen from the tree with Lady Charlotte had been nothing: an uncomfortable sprain, no worse than others he'd suffered before falling from a horse. The blow to his head, however, had been deemed sufficiently dangerous that he'd been confined to his bed with the curtains drawn and doctors hovering like vultures in his bedchamber.

So much idle time for reflection had been dangerous, too. Lying there in the dark, he'd played his first disastrous meeting with Lady Charlotte over and over in his mind, wincing at every inane word he'd uttered and every false step he'd literally taken. He'd even worried

that the roses he'd sent from the Greenwood garden—
and the trial of writing the card with his aching head—
was another blunder, an old-fashioned gesture that a
girl such as Lady Charlotte would dismiss. He hadn't
been able to tell her true feelings from the note of thanks
she'd sent the next day, the formal words so clearly dic-
tated by her aunt.

In fact, his greatest fear had been that she'd dismiss
him. Ever since his father had announced his betrothal,
Lady Charlotte Wylder had been a comforting, conve-
nient nonentity. When he was a boy, a distant mother
and a lack of siblings had limited his opportunities to
learn of female mysteries, and he hadn't really trusted
the women whose company, however pleasurable, had
been purchased. It had all made him uncomfortably shy
among ladies, and Lady Charlotte had become his protection.

Because of her, he didn't have to hear how, even as a
duke, he was an unsuitable match for young ladies from
older, more noble families because his great-grandmother
had been Nan Lilly, an actress and a whore. Lady Charlotte's impeccable name had protected him against the
less discerning women, too. It had spared him from
dancing with his friends' sisters on school holidays, and
delivered him from having to make the dreary bachelor
rounds of balls and routs in London and Bath. Ambi-
tious mothers with daughters to marry off avoided him,
and the daughters themselves ignored him. He owed a
sizable debt of gratitude to Lady Charlotte for this, and
had always considered himself fortunate to have such a
useful phantom in his life.

But now that phantom had a face, and a deliciously
tempting body, too, that had haunted his headachy
dreams. She *was* beautiful in a fresh and unstudied way,
and when she'd laughed, it had been the merriest en-
chantment he'd ever heard. He'd also realized that other

gentlemen would likely feel this way about her, too. Betrothal or not, her aunt the dowager dragon would make certain she was launched into society with a grand splash. Because he was himself wealthy, he'd never paid much attention to Lady Charlotte's portion, but her worth was sufficient to make her a prize heiress. If a more attractive suitor appeared, he'd no doubt that Lady Sanborn would contrive a way to break the engagement.

He could not let that happen. Because when Lady Charlotte Wylder had smiled at him, her cheeks rosy and her face dappled with sunlight, he'd realized with a jolt that he didn't wish simply to fulfill his obligation and marry her. He wanted to win her heart.

Which was why, when March had finally risen this morning with a clear head, he had escaped the hovering doctors and come straight to London, and now, at last, was stepping down from his carriage and through the green-painted door of Mrs. Damaris Cartwright, mantua-maker to ladies.

He hadn't been inside a mantua-maker's shop since he was a boy, attending his mother. It wasn't much different from the tailor shops he visited: neat counters with cushioned stools before them; rows of shelves with goods in boxes, bolts of costly cloth, and coils of ribbon; and several artful displays of finished gowns to tempt the customers.

What was different from his tailor's, however, was that the shop was occupied entirely by women, both behind the counters and before them and fluttering in the open spaces as well. As soon as he entered, all conversation stopped as every last one of them turned to look at him. No, they *stared* at him, as if he were some curious beast in the Tower menagerie. He wasn't imagining it, either. Almost in unison, they curtseyed to him, the soft *shush* of silk the only sound in the shop. Across from where he stood hung a large looking glass, and in it he saw his reflection: his tall, serious, male self, dressed in dark blue superfine with engraved silver buttons, his still-tender arm cradled in a sling contrived from a maroon silk scarf, standing like some righteous old Turk over a dozen obsequious women.

And yet, in the way of luck, there was not a hint of the woman he wished most to see. Blast, what he'd give now to be able to make a swift and honorable retreat back to the pavement!

"Good day, Your Grace, good day!" An older woman bustled forward from the back hall to greet him, elegant in dove-gray silk with a silver chatelaine and a worked pinball hanging from her waist. He wasn't surprised she already knew who he was; most likely one of her stitching-spies had seen the crest on his carriage and reported back to her. "I am Mistress Cartwright, sir, your humble servant in all concerns of correct fashion. How might we serve you this day, sir? What may we offer to please a special lady? We've silk lutestring fresh from Paris, as well as a shipment of castor fur for trimming, direct from Quebec and the most lustrous ever I've seen."

"Ah, thank you, Mrs. Cartwright, no," March said, clearing his throat. He wished all these women would return to their chatter and stop gawking at him as if he were some actor on the stage. "I've come to your shop to meet a special lady, not to, ah, please one with castor fur."

Mrs. Cartwright smiled and made a graceful sweeping motion with her head, offering everything to him. "Many gentlemen attend us with that express purpose, sir. Though perhaps in time you will wish to please the one you meet with a remembrance from our shelves."

Damnation, that sounded more like he'd come to survey the goods in a bagnio, not a mantua-maker's shop.

"I had hoped to converse with Lady Charlotte Wylder while you were attending her," he said hurriedly; he was not the sort of gentleman who preyed upon humble seamstresses or milliners for diversion. "But since Lady Charlotte is not here at present, I will—"

"But her ladyship is indeed here, sir," Mrs. Cartwright said. "She is in one of our parlors, having the final fittings for several new gowns. Lady Sanborn is with her as well. Shall I send word to them that you are here, sir, and wish to join them?"

"During the, ah, fitting?" he asked, startled by the prospect. Most specifically, he thought of Lady Charlotte's scarlet stays.

Mrs. Cartwright nodded, far too polite and too experienced a tradeswoman to show that she noticed his discomfiture.

"It is often done, sir," she murmured, "particularly during the final fittings. There is no immodesty in a gentleman witnessing the last adjustments. If you'll excuse me, sir, I'll speak with Lady Sanborn. I am certain she'll be delighted to have you join them."

March was just as certain that nothing would delight Lady Sanborn less than to have him pursue Lady Charlotte all the way to a fitting with her mantua-maker, but now that he'd come this far, he wouldn't back away. Besides, as Mrs. Cartwright had said, Lady Sanborn could hardly refuse to see him. It wasn't as if she could pretend she wasn't at home.

He watched Mrs. Cartwright glide quickly into the back of the shop, leaving him among the shimmering little pool of women. But once again Lady Charlotte had worked her magic. As soon as he had mentioned her name, the others had lost interest in him and his doings and had returned to their own purchases and conversations. At least the fashionable world seemed to regard the lady as still belonging to him.

"The ladies would be honored to have you join them, sir," Mrs. Cartwright said, ushering him back through the shop. "This way, sir, if you please."

March followed her down the narrow hall, decorated with prints of great ladies in even greater gowns and smelling faintly of flowery powder and sweet perfumes. It all gave him the distinct and unfamiliar sensation of entering some female sanctum sanctorum; as privileges went, he realized he rather liked it, too.

"Here, sir," Mrs. Cartwright said, opening a door to him. "My lady, His Grace the Duke of Marchbourne."

"Good day, Duke." The countess rose from her armchair and curtseyed, her smile chilly. "What an honor to discover you here, of all places."

"I'm the one who is honored, Lady Sanborn," he said, his gaze already turned from her to Lady Charlotte.

She was standing in the center of the small room, swallowed up by a gown so large it covered most of the floor. The gown was one of those outlandish silk extravaganzas worn at court and nowhere else, with yards of pale rose satin supported by the hoops that gave ladies the look of campaign tents. Two startled seamstresses had been crouched at Lady Charlotte's feet, pinning some sort of serpentine silver frippery along the hem, while another held the ruffled sleeve that she'd been ready to attach to the gown.

Yet all the costly display still couldn't take away from Lady Charlotte's own beauty. She was even more lovely than he remembered. Her cheeks had pinked and her eyes had lit as soon as he entered, and her smile was filled with such warmth and eagerness that he could scarce believe it was for him. All the doubts and misgivings that had plagued him these last days and nights vanished in an instant—or at least they would if he could speak to her alone.

"Good day, Your Grace," she said, her voice betraying a hint of charming shyness. "Did you come here just to see me?"

"What a bold question to ask of a gentleman, Charlotte!" scolded the countess, rolling her eyes with a dramatic show of dismay.

Any moment March expected the smoke and flames to spew from her dragon's nose. What would it take to make her leave them alone? He knew it wasn't considered proper, especially since in theory they'd not even been introduced, but damnation, he was already bound to marry the lady. He supposed he could try ordering the dragon away, but even given the differences in their rank, he wasn't sure she'd leave Lady Charlotte unattended.

No, it would likely take a silver sword to vanquish her, much like the one St. George had possessed. He could only imagine what the gathered ladies in the front of the store would say to that, too.

"Your Grace," the dragon said, "please be assured that you need not reply to my niece's impertinence."

"But I will," March said. "I did come here to see you, Lady Charlotte. What other reason could bring me to such a place?"

She laughed with unabashed delight. "Perhaps you desired a lace gown? Or a new pelisse?"

"Charlotte, please," the countess said. "Remember yourself, and what we have discussed between us. Do not give offense."

But March wasn't offended. He was enchanted. He'd liked how she'd spoken plainly to him in the tree, and he liked it even more here.

"A pelisse," he said, pretending to consider such a garment with the hope that she'd laugh again. "No, I do believe I'd rather see that pelisse on you."

But Lady Charlotte wasn't laughing. "Oh, sir, look at your poor arm in a sling," she said softly. "Does it grieve you much? Are you in great pain? Oh, and it's all because of my clumsiness, too."

"It's not my arm but my shoulder, and it's mending well enough," he said with what he hoped with was gallant nonchalance. "You're hardly to blame for it, Lady Charlotte, and I'd never think of you as clumsy. Not at all."

"Yes, yes, sir, and the less said of that little event, the better," the countess said, putting an unarguable end to the subject. "So how would you judge this gown, sir? Doesn't Lady Charlotte look the very picture of a peeress in it?"

Lady Charlotte grinned, holding her arm out for the seamstress to slip the sleeve onto it and slide it up to her shoulder. Most of her arm was bare below the sleeve of her shift, a slender, creamy expanse of seldom glimpsed skin, and March thought how ridiculously more seductive such glimpses could be than a score of oversized court gowns. To make things worse—or better—the seamstress was having some manner of difficulty attaching the sleeve, and pushed Lady Charlotte's white linen neckerchief aside, baring even more of her.

"Is the neckerchief in your way?" Lady Charlotte asked. "There's no trouble removing it."

Without waiting for the seamstress's answer, Lady Charlotte pulled the neckerchief from her shoulders, reminding March of how she'd likewise pulled off her neckerchief to wrap around the errant cat in the tree. Now, to oblige the seamstress, she tossed the kerchief on the bench to one side, leaving the deep, wide neck of her gown uncovered. Even March knew that this was how a court gown was meant to be worn, just as he'd observed such gowns on countless other ladies in his life. Observed, and approved; he wouldn't have been male if he hadn't.

But those other ladies had not been Lady Charlotte, and those countless other half-bared breasts paraded before him had not been hers. Raised up like an offering by her stays, her breasts were round and plump, more satiny than the silk below them, and so impossibly tempting that it took all his ducal willpower to drag his gaze back to her face, where it belonged.

If only the dragon could be driven away . . .

"You do like the gown, sir, don't you?" Lady Charlotte asked disingenuously. "I've never had any half as fine and I know nothing, *nothing,* of the fashions, but Mrs. Cartwright said this was exactly what every lady wished to wear to the palace."

"With the proper additions, Charlotte," Lady Sanborn said promptly. "The correct plumes in your hair, and of course jewels when you have them."

Jewels. Of course. And of course the mercenary dragon meant his mother's and grandmother's jewels, a not very subtle reminder that his wife would be entitled to wear them. March knew all this well enough, and he had in fact already asked Carter to retrieve the family's jewel boxes from safekeeping so he might decide which pieces to have cleaned and refurbished as wedding gifts for Lady Charlotte. He wanted to slip the rings on her fingers himself, and he wanted to fasten the necklaces around her throat and watch the pearls and other gems slip into that shadowy valley between her breasts.

But it should all be his choice, not Lady Sanborn's, and it irritated him that the dragon would dare think otherwise.

"There was a pair of pearl drops, sir, droplets crowned with diamonds," the countess was saying, "that I especially recall the late duchess wearing. I believe the tale was that the pearls were Italian."

"They were Italian, Lady Sanborn," he said, his voice dropping low. As all his friends knew, he seldom spoke of his mother in conversation, and he didn't want to discuss her, her jewels, or how or why or where she'd come by them—especially not with Lady Sanborn. "I believe they still are, too."

"Of course, sir, of course," she continued, ignoring the unmistakable warning in his voice. "Yet as handsomely as your mother wore those earrings, I can't but imagine them now on Charlotte, and how—"

"Leave us, please, Lady Sanborn," he said curtly. "Leave me with Lady Charlotte. Leave us alone."

The countess rose swiftly. "Sir, I cannot—"

"Now," March said. "All of you go."

The countess sputtered with wordless indignation, standing so righteously straight that she nearly bent backward. Biting back her anger, she waited until the three seamstresses had scurried from the room. She then made a stiff, self-righteous curtsey to March, and at the door paused to look back to Lady Charlotte.

"Recall who you are, niece, and what is at stake," she intoned, so loudly March was sure everyone in the shop must have heard her, and likely in the next shop as well. "Recall all that I have taught you, I beg you, and do not forget. I shall be directly outside if you desire me."

Head high, she stalked from the room, and the latch of the door clicked shut behind her.

And finally, inevitably, March was alone with Lady Charlotte.

CHAPTER

5

Charlotte stood in the center of the mantua-maker's small dressing room, exactly where the seamstresses had left her, and tried desperately to remember whatever it was that Aunt Sophronia had implored her to recall. Doubtless it was something to do with ruined opportunities and blighted futures, for both were favorite cautionary topics of her aunt. Or it might have been simply ruin, as it pertained to men. Ruin and men were always linked together. Mama had also warned her and her sisters about ruin during lengthy talks about how babies were created, especially after one of their kitchen maids at Ransom Manor had met her ruin with a sailor on leave from his ship in Portsmouth. Ruin, it seemed, lurked everywhere.

But when Charlotte looked across the narrow room at the duke, she thought not of ruin but only of him.

The first time she'd seen him, he'd appeared like magic to climb from his horse up the tree, determined to rescue her. It didn't matter that she hadn't needed rescuing. He'd still seemed like some fanciful prince from a ballad, with his hair tousled and his white linen shirt billowing in the breeze. When he'd asked her to trust him, she'd instantly agreed, mostly because she'd wanted to, but also because none of it had seemed quite real—at least until they'd fallen from the tree.

But here in this room, the duke seemed very, very real. He was taller than she'd realized in the tree, his shoulders broad and all of him powerfully male. He was dressed as elegantly as a man could possibly be, in a dark blue suit of clothes with a waistcoat covered in cream-colored Marseilles work. His dark hair was clubbed sleekly back beneath his black cocked hat, and there was no unseemly balladlike billowing to his immaculate Holland linen beyond lace ruffles at his cuffs. He wore a dress sword in a silver scabbard beneath his coat, and from his manner she'd no doubt that he could use it, too. He'd just bravely banished Aunt Sophronia, hadn't he?

In fact, he appeared entirely invincible except for two important exceptions, two chinks in his manly armor that Charlotte had noticed at once. First, of course, was his arm in the sling: a silk sling, artfully contrived, but an undeniable sign of a graver injury than he'd wished to admit, one that caused him to wince when he moved.

The second sign of vulnerability was not nearly as obvious. When the duke had ordered the countess to leave, his expression had been hard with anger that she'd dared to speak so to him, his dark eyes flashing and his jaw squared. But as soon as the door closed, the anger had drained his face, replaced by something so different that it shocked Charlotte. She wasn't sure if what she saw was sadness, melancholy, or simply pain from the effort of latching the door, and in her youth and inexperience, she accepted what was easiest to understand.

"Your shoulder, sir," she said softly. "I know my aunt wishes me not to speak of that day again, but I would have you know how sorry I am that you were hurt. Because of me. I know it was because of me, so please don't say otherwise."

He looked at her, and whatever she'd seen before in his face was gone. Now his eyes seemed only to focus on her, just as they had earlier.

"And I told you that my shoulder will mend and be well enough, Lady Charlotte, and so it shall." He smiled to prove it, but the smile seemed weary, a little worn.

"Oh, sir," she said. She felt silly standing here in this plain room in the lavish yet unfinished court gown, and woefully unsure of herself with him. How could she not, when he was so much older and more worldly than she?

"I know in time your shoulder will be well, sir," she said, "but I will be sorry until it does. Does that suffice?"

"It will," he said gruffly. "If you wish it so, then how could I want otherwise?"

"You're very kind, sir," she said, willing herself to stand still, hands clasped loosely at her waist as a lady should, and not fuss with her skirts or hair. "Most kind."

She could hear the others in the hall outside, bustling and rustling and whispering back and forth, and she could imagine her aunt there, too, just beyond the door, listening. She wasn't sure how long she'd have here alone with him before Aunt Safronia conceived of some reason for returning, and she desperately wished to make the most of that time. In the duke's presence, she felt uncharacteristically shy, and all the more awkward because of the importance of this moment. What was proper to say to him, this imposing lord she was contracted to marry, and yet right for the man whose bed she would share?

She smiled, albeit a little tremulously. "I suspect your doctors cautioned you against coming to town, sir."

He raised his head a fraction, all brave defiance. "They could not stop me," he declared. "They couldn't at all."

"Ah," she said, flattered, though startled by his vehemence. "I'm glad you felt sufficiently improved to make the journey, sir."

"That wasn't my reason, Lady Charlotte," he said. "I came because I didn't want you to become so distracted by—by the amusements of the town, and forget me."

"Forget you, sir?" she asked, stunned. "After only three days? Oh, sir, I'm not half so faithless as that!"

"I pray that you aren't," he said gravely.

"You needn't pray, because it's the truth," she said, surprised and a bit wounded that he'd believe such a thing of her. "Once you come to know me better, sir, you'll understand."

He nodded, agreeing to . . . something. If he didn't yet know her, then she didn't know him, either.

"I wish you wouldn't call me 'sir,' " he said, surprising her again. "That is, I know that 'sir' is considered proper, but my friends call me March, and I dare to hope that my wife will likewise be my friend."

My friends call me March. Surely such an informal freedom would not garner Aunt Sophronia's approval. Her aunt had told her that, from respect, many duchesses never called their husbands anything other than "sir" for their entire wedded lives. To Charlotte's delight, however, it seemed clear that the Duke of Marchbourne intended things to be different between them. He intended them to be friends: a daring notion indeed. She smiled, seeing her face reflected in his dark eyes.

"Yes, March," she whispered, feeling vastly bold. "I like to say it. March."

"I like to hear it on your lips, Lady Charlotte." He smiled, too, his whole face relaxing. He looked younger when he smiled, and much less daunting. She wished he'd do it more often.

"Now you must call me Charlotte, plain and unadorned," she said. "It's only fair."

"Charlotte, then," he said. "Unadorned, according to your aunt's wishes. But never plain."

She chuckled happily. "That's idle flattery, the words of some low, perfidious beau."

"No, it's not, Charlotte," he said, pretending to be indignant. "It's the truth."

Impulsively she stepped closer to him, her wide satin skirts rustling around her. Once more she was struck with how tall he was, and she'd a brief, foolish thought of how, again, she'd be scaling a tree.

"In that tree, you asked me to trust you," she said softly, "and I did, and I do. Now I must beg you to do the same. What sorry manner of wife should I make if you cannot trust me?"

He sighed, a deep, rumbling sigh that seemed pulled from his very heart, and one that in turn touched hers.

"How could I not trust you, Charlotte?" he asked, his voice rough. "As my wife, my duchess."

"My husband, and my duke." As gently as she could, she rested her hand on his upper arm, taking great care to avoid his injured shoulder. "What a sorry pair we must make! Your arm's in a sling, while mine has no sleeve."

"No sleeve at all," he repeated. Lightly he ran his fingers up along the inside of her bare arm. It was the most featherweight of caresses, but enough to make her shiver with unexpected pleasure.

"None," she whispered, her heart racing. "That is, not now."

His caress wandered further, lingering over her shoulder for a moment before finding the line of her collarbone. His hand was warm on her bare skin, or perhaps it was her skin that warmed beneath his touch. He traced higher, over the nape of her neck, until his fingers threaded into her hair.

She closed her eyes, relishing the feel of his hand against the back of her head. If she were Fig, she would have purred aloud, so pleasurable was his touch. Because she wasn't a cat, the best she could do was to relax even more, letting her lips part with a breathy small sigh of contentment.

She hadn't meant it as an invitation, not at all, and when she felt his lips touch hers, she gasped and fluttered from the strangeness of it. He drew her closer so she couldn't escape, nor did she wish to, not really, not when she realized that this was kissing, and that he was kissing her.

Could he tell that she'd never done this before, that he was the first man to kiss her? She didn't believe that kissing fell beneath the black cloud of ruin—she'd often seen men and women kissing publicly without shame—but she'd no idea how enjoyable it could be. She liked how soft his lips were against hers, how the slight stubble of his shaven jaw offered a rough contrast against her cheek.

She sighed her happiness, and he took that, too, as more invitation. He slanted his mouth to part her lips farther, deepening the kiss and the intimacy with it. She wasn't prepared for his taste, a male mix of black coffee and tobacco, or for the plunder of his tongue against hers. She may have been unprepared, but she was not unwilling, and soon all she felt was the dizzying raw impatience of it, and a fervent hope that he wouldn't stop, not yet.

Clearly, kissing her had made him forget any of the lingering pain from his shoulder as well, since he pulled his arm free from the sling to slip around her waist. Once she bumped his shoulder by accident, and she heard a slight grunt of surprise, but that was all, and hardly reason for him to push her away. Far from it, for from the way he held her, molding her body to fit his, it was as if he wished to blur the boundaries between them, and become one being, as man and wife should.

And—heaven forgive her!—that was a most thrilling thought. Instinctively she slipped her arms around the back of his neck to steady herself, the row of tiny hard buttons on his waistcoat pressing against her chest. She twisted to meet him, and knocked his hat from his head; he didn't notice when it thumped to the floor, nor did she. His other hand left the back of her head and somehow found itself on the front of her bodice, his fingers spreading over the flat, embroidered front of her stomacher.

Only a second more, and his hand had discovered the top of her breast where it rose from the gown's neckline. With a groan he twisted her around and pushed her back against the wall with a small thump, his legs tangling briefly in the silk-covered cane hoops.

The touch of his hand on her bare skin shocked her, for such a freedom would lead inevitably to ruin. Even she knew that. Yet what shocked her far more was how much her own traitorous body enjoyed his caress, and worse, how readily it seemed to know what to do next, arching against him to offer even more of herself. Her breath had quickened and her blood felt aflame, while the tatters of her conscience were unheeded and forgotten. All she could think of was kissing him more, holding him more tightly, and letting him do whatever he wished to her deliciously heated self.

Until, that is, the sharp rap on the door interrupted everything.

"If you please, Your Grace," Aunt Sophronia said, sharp and clear despite the latched door that was keeping her out. "You are keeping these good women from conducting their trade. Surely your conversation with Lady Charlotte must be at an end by now."

March sighed heavily, and though he took his hand from her breast, he kept his other arm still around her waist.

"I don't want to let you go," he murmured, his voice rough with urgency. "To leave this place and watch you go away, apart from me, will be unbearable."

"I have no choice, March, nor freedom to do otherwise, no matter how much I wish to stay with you." She spoke in a swift whisper, each word tumbling over the next. Her breath was still shallow and quick, and she wasn't sure her legs would support her when he finally set her free. "But Aunt Sophronia—"

"The devil take your aunt," he muttered, and kissed Charlotte once again, so fervently that she felt dizzy all over again.

"Charlotte?" her aunt called. "Is everything well, Charlotte?"

She twisted free of him, whimpering with frustration. "If we don't open the door, I vow she'll break it down herself."

"I wouldn't doubt it." He grabbed his hat from where it had fallen and jammed it onto his head. "Nor will I test her. She's a dragon, your aunt."

Hastily she pulled the neckline of her gown back in place over her breasts and shoved the pins back into her hair. She glanced at her reflection in the seamstress's looking glass. Oh, my, she did look the wanton, her lips red and full from kissing, her hair tousled, and her eyes—she knew not how to describe it, but her eyes were *different*. No matter what she did to tidy herself, her aunt would not be pleased, and unhappily she turned back to Marchbourne.

His clothes were once again perfectly composed. His handsome dark face was not. She'd never seen a man simultaneously look so angry, yet so disappointed.

"Charlotte?" her aunt called again. "Charlotte, the door, if you please."

"One moment, Aunt Sophronia."

She darted over to Marchbourne. "Trust me in this, too, I beg of you," she said softly. "Don't fear that I'll forget you, Marchbourne. I never could, and I never will."

She touched her fingers to her lips and then to his as a pledge. He seized her wrist and kissed her open palm, his gaze not leaving hers.

Her head spun. Could there be anything more perfect than this gentleman?

"Charlotte!"

She pulled her hand free and hurried to unlatch the door. Her aunt swept inside, furiously studying Charlotte, then the duke, then Charlotte again.

The duke nodded to the countess as if nothing were amiss. Perhaps to him there wasn't.

"I'll leave you ladies to conclude your business," he said. "It has been my pleasure to share your company. Good day, Lady Sanborn, Lady Charlotte."

Charlotte curtseyed beside her aunt, watching sadly as the duke left. She considered what might happen if she ran after him in the hall. She'd seen plenty of girls in their old village running after sailor-sweethearts who were bound for their boats and ships, and begging (and receiving) one last kiss had always struck her as tragically romantic. But she wasn't a village girl and he was a duke, not a sailor, and besides, he was only bound for his carriage, not for sea, and her aunt—ah, Charlotte was quite sure her aunt would not approve.

Certainly her aunt was close to expiring now as she shut the door to the room against the seamstresses who still hovered waiting outside.

"You shame me, Charlotte," she said in a furious whisper so that the others would not overhear her. "You shame our entire family, and your dear father's memory as well. But most of all, you shame His Grace and yourself."

"But he came to me, Aunt Sophronia," Charlotte said, clinging to whatever scraps of a defense she could muster in the circumstances. "He wished to see me, that was all, and to ascertain for himself that I'd not been hurt when we fell from the tree."

"No tales, Charlotte, no lies." Her aunt's face was so flushed with anger that the red showed through her face powder in ruddy blotches. "Not when the guilt's written so plainly over your face."

Her cheeks hot, Charlotte self-consciously smoothed her palms again and again across her untidy hair. "Forgive me, Aunt Sophronia, but where is the harm in conversation with the gentleman I am to wed?"

"A *conversation*," repeated her aunt with disgust. "I'd vow far more than words alone were exchanged between you two. Look at you!"

She reached out to pull Charlotte's bodice square across her chest, tucking the frill of her shift back inside.

"How long do you think it will take before word of your *conversation* with the duke flies from this shop?" she demanded. "Before the sun sets, you two will be the talk of every supper table, high and low, in London, and by midnight your name will be common in every rum shop and alehouse as well. Surely the duke must have been aware of that when he shut this door. Surely he must have been aware of the consequences, even if you are so woefully, foolishly ignorant."

She groaned and shook her head, and then took Charlotte's chin in her fingers so that she could not look away.

"Oh, my dear Charlotte," she began, her face softening as her first anger turned to dismay. "Why must you insist you know what is best? Why won't you heed what I say? Yes, yes, you are to wed His Grace. But he is expecting an honorable wife, not a sluttish mistress who is discussed by all his friends. No gentleman will refuse what's freely offered, but they will turn away with disgust from such a freedom in a wife."

Troubled, Charlotte remembered every pleasing freedom she'd just granted to her duke. She wished to be contrite, for she did not doubt that Aunt Sophronia's intentions were only the best, despite her sharpness. Nor did Charlotte doubt the wisdom of her words. When she'd considered the cost of ruin, she hadn't thought of a scandal of a London-sized magnitude, and she still couldn't comprehend the interest that the rest of the world took in the actions of the Duke of Marchbourne, and by connection to him, hers as well.

Yet the harder she tried to repent of March's kisses, the more she recalled their delight instead. Instead of the danger of a possible scandal, she recalled his caresses, his fingers in her hair and his palm on her breast. She remembered them so vividly that she felt herself begin to grow warm all over again, and she had to lower her lashes to shield her eyes from her aunt and keep those recollections to herself.

But to Charlotte's good fortune, Aunt Sophronia misread her downcast gaze.

"I suppose a modest demeanor is better now than never, Charlotte," she said with a smidgeon of approval. "But I have already resolved that you won't be coming with your mother and sisters to the playhouse tonight. Far better for you to spend the evening in solitary reflection, considering how to change your behavior in the future."

"Yes, Aunt Sophronia," Charlotte said as obediently as she could. She was sorry she wouldn't go with the others to the play, but if that was the worst punishment that her aunt could muster, then she knew she'd escaped. There'd be other plays to see; even better, there'd be plays to see with the duke.

No, with March. *Her* March. How vastly fine that sounded!

CHAPTER

6

"I've brought the rings as you requested, Your Grace," said Mr. Boyce, the jeweler. "An exquisite selection indeed."

Boyce stood on one side of the small table, while Carter, ever vigilant, stood on the other. For the best light for viewing the jewels, the table had been set before the tall window overlooking the park and its surface covered with the same dark green velvet cloth that was found in Boyce's shop. A dozen small dome-shaped boxes, some covered in silk and others in leather, were lined up awaiting individual presentation, their lids still hooked shut. It was as if Boyce had set up shop here in the front parlor of Marchbourne House, thought March wryly, except that it was a shop where everything already belonged to him.

"Well, then, let's see what there is," he said, sitting in the tall-backed armchair placed for him before the table. "I'm sure we'll find something to suit."

Yet March wasn't sure what to expect. Although the contents of these little boxes (and a good deal more, according to Carter) were technically his property, he'd never been much interested in jewels. The jewels had always reminded him a little too much of the baser origins of his family's nobility, and it was uncomfortably easy for him to imagine his round-faced great-grandmother,

Nan Lilly, the king's mistress, covered with the glittering stones that her royal lover had given her. It wasn't that he was ashamed of Nan. Her portraits were hung proudly in all his houses—even the one reputed to be the king's favorite, with her as a barefoot shepherdess with one shamelessly naked breast slipping free of her gauzy classical chiton.

No, it was more that March didn't wish to think too closely of how his great-grandmother had pleased the king to be rewarded with this ring or that bracelet in those bawdy old days. He didn't want to imagine his grandmother, either, who had been as famous for the quality of her diamonds as for her liaison with a French ambassador, nor his own mother, who, even in the country, had always worn so many jewels that she'd sparkled from afar like some distant heathen idol.

No. Much better instead to imagine Lady Charlotte wearing the jewels and bringing much-needed respectability to them. Her family was so venerable that they'd likely been the ones to offer a hospitable welcome to the Conqueror himself. There were no royal mistresses or French ambassadors lurking among the Wylders' skeletons. Just as March had done his best to make people forget his father's profligate drinking, gaming, and whoring, so he was sure Charlotte would make them think only of her as the new Duchess of Marchbourne.

He smiled with pleasure, remembering Charlotte's fresh, eager face and the innocence of her kiss, and how earnestly she'd asked for his trust. How could he not trust a lady like her? How could he not—

"Sir?" asked Carter. "Is there, ah, a problem I might address for you?"

Carter's face bore such perplexed anxiety that March realized he must have been thinking of kissing Charlotte longer than he'd realized.

"Thank you, no," he said quickly as he pulled his chair

closer to the table. "Pray show me what you've discovered for me, Mr. Boyce."

"Of course, sir, of course," the jeweler said. With practiced grace, he took the nearest box, unlatched and opened it, and displayed the ring inside. "This first is a whimsy that might please a younger lady. It is in the shape of a pomegranate, sir, with rubies, emeralds, and diamonds in gold."

March took the ring from the box, carefully, as if it might melt in his fingers. He studied it with what he hoped would seem a critical eye, wondering what the devil he should be seeing.

"Constancy, marriage, fertility, birth, sir, all are qualities ascribed to the pomegranate," the jeweler explained, watching March over the tops of his wire-framed spectacles. "A most suitable choice for a betrothal ring, sir."

March frowned. Constancy, marriage, fertility, and birth seemed like a great burden for any ring. It came too close to tempting the fates, too, invoking so much with a single jewel.

"A pretty ring, yes, but I do not think it would suit Lady Charlotte," he said, returning it the box. "What is next?"

Boyce hurried to oblige. "This is a lovely table-cut diamond, sir, placed within a pyramid setting, and surrounded by other stones," he said, handing March the next. "The very finest quality, sir. I believe the diamonds were purchased in Florence."

March recognized this ring immediately, and he'd no pleasant memories of it, either. His mother had worn the ring so frequently that it had become associated with her, as was often the way with grand ladies of fashion.

But what March remembered was how, when he'd been very young, he'd broken a favorite Chinese vase of his mother's. At once she'd struck him for his clumsiness, and the ring's sharp setting had cut into his cheek, so deep that he'd the scar still. His mother had then burst into tears over what she'd done, but the raging quarrel that had resulted between his parents later that night had been far, far worse than the cut.

"Not that one," he said, snapping the box's lid shut himself.

"Then what of this, sir?" Quickly the jeweler handed him another. "An old-fashioned style, perhaps, with the silver foil behind the diamonds for brightness, but the stones are of a quality that they could be reset to her ladyship's taste."

March did not know himself if the ring was old-fashioned or not. It was large and weighty, with a cluster of rose-cut diamonds set together like a bouquet of white flowers, much like the white roses he'd sent her from the Greenwood gardens. The band of the ring was a warm, rich gold, worked with a curving vine that curled completely around the finger. The back of the setting was gold as well, and engraved with two hearts, intertwined. Surely it must have been meant as a token between lovers, and yet the ring clearly had never been worn, the band still a perfect circle and the curving lines of the engraved hearts crisp and new.

"Do you know the history of this?" he asked. "Who in my family wore it last?"

Boyce's face fell. "Alas, sir, I do not know," he said sorrowfully. "Most of the pieces have a connection to certain noble ladies in Your Grace's family, but I could find nothing concerning this ring."

Chagrined at having no better answer, the jeweler held his hand out for the ring, expecting March to discard this one, too, as he had the others, but instead March kept it.

"Then we shall leave it to Lady Charlotte to create her own history with it, Mr. Boyce." March smiled with satisfaction, pleased that the task had been so easily accomplished. "This is the ring."

The jeweler bowed. "A most excellent choice, sir. Though I would be remiss not to show you the others—"

"Another time, perhaps," March said. "I'm sure in time Lady Charlotte would like to see them all for her own choosing."

He looked again at the ring, turning it this way and that in the bright sunlight. It was easy to imagine the clustered diamonds on Charlotte's slender hand, even if that hand was endearingly marked with scratches from tree climbing and her infernal cat. She'd like this ring. He was sure of that, though he couldn't quite say why. It would suit her.

And, of course, he hoped it would come to mean the world to her because he'd been the one to put it on her hand.

He tipped it toward the jeweler to show the back of the setting. "Is it possible to engrave our initials there, inside the hearts?"

"Of course, sir, of course." Mr. Boyce smiled indulgently. "A pretty notion, sir, and easily done."

Behind him the door opened, and a footman announced a visitor. "His Grace the Duke of Breconridge."

"Breck!" March rose, turning eagerly to greet his cousin. "Come, see the ring I've just chosen for Lady Charlotte. I mean to give it to her next week, when we're formally betrothed."

Brecon entered with his usual reserve, every movement and expression thoughtful and considered. Though he and March were cousins, there was fourteen years between them, and in many ways Brecon had acted as both an elder brother and a father to March, particularly once March's parents had died. They shared the same dark good looks and strong-cast features, an undeniable family resemblance.

But Brecon also understood the challenges of a dukedom founded on illegitimacy, for they shared the same portion of royal blood, with the same profligate king for a great-grandfather. Brecon's great-grandmother had been an elegant French lady who'd shrewdly traded her virtue and honor for the considerable rewards of a royal mistress, and there was probably still a good deal of Gallic perspicacity in the third Duke of Breconridge.

There was also undoubtedly a sizable appreciation of Gallic fashion. While most English gentlemen dressed for a June afternoon in the dark breeches and simple coat that they'd wear for riding, Brecon wore a fawn-gray suit with silver flowers embroidered down the front and cuffs of the coat and across the waistcoat beneath, extravagant silver filigree buckles on his breeches and on his shoes, and silver lacing on his dark gray beaver hat.

If any man could pass judgment on a lady's betrothal ring, it would be Brecon, and eagerly March held it out for his cousin to see.

"A sweet bauble," Brecon said, squinting as he appraised the ring. "Sizable, too, with all those stones. I wonder that it won't be too large for the lady, however. Most young creatures seem to prefer a more dainty offering on their finger."

"I don't believe it's too large," March said confidently. "Not for Lady Charlotte. She's not one of those over-nice, missish ladies who'd require a dainty ring."

Brecon smiled, cocking a single black brow. "You're very certain of the lady's tastes. Or are there diamonds to be found in the trees?"

March flushed. Brecon was the only one of his London acquaintances to whom he'd told the truth of his injured shoulder. Everyone else believed he'd fallen from his horse, not from a tree, and certainly not with Lady Charlotte on top. For her sake, he wished that belief to remain, and quickly he turned away from his cousin and back to the jeweler.

"Have it engraved and back to me tomorrow, Mr. Boyce," he said. "I'll summon you again for sizing if the lady requires it."

"Very good, sir," Boyce said, carefully tucking the ring back into its plush-lined box. "I thank you for your custom, sir, and the honor of your patronage."

March nodded, determined to keep silent until Boyce and Carter and all the ring boxes left. Boyce's family had served his for at least the last century, but March doubted that even such a degree of loyalty would be able to resist spreading a delicious tale of the Duke of Marchbourne up a tree with Lady Charlotte Wylder.

"I'll thank you, Brecon, not to mention my first meeting with Lady Charlotte before others," March said as soon as the door was shut and they were alone. "My own people can be trusted not to speak of it, but tradesmen are altogether different."

"What, you worry now of what people will say of you chasing the lady up the tree?" Brecon grinned, unable to resist teasing. "First intercepting her coach on the road, then climbing to reach her among the lofty limbs! Upon my soul, you've been a veritable highwayman of love where this lady is concerned."

March groaned, dropping heavily into a nearby armchair. "It was not the wisest action of my life, no. I see that now. I was impulsive. I was foolhardy. I was—"

"Cease flogging yourself," Brecon said mildly. "No one enjoys a martyr, particularly when your martyrdom is of your own doing. You acted the ardent bridegroom, that is all. With her entire household clustered beneath you, there's hardly any question of your compromising your fair lady on a branch."

"The ardent bridegroom," March repeated with despair. "More like the ardent ass. I had my doubts even as I rode to meet the carriage, yet still I persevered. I never seem to know the right step with ladies, Brecon. You know that."

"What I know is that most of your missteps have been well intended and without any lasting damage," Brecon said, smoothing away the sting of his first teasing jests. "You cannot learn to dance without making a few stumbles along the way."

"I know, I know." Glumly March rested his head on his hand. "I cannot become a gallant overnight, no matter how much I might wish it."

Talking to Brecon like this usually made him feel better. It wasn't only that his cousin was older and wiser at forty-two. It was that Brecon had already managed to sail smoothly through most of the greater challenges of life, while March still felt mired upon the shore. Brecon had married happily. He had his heir, and more, for he'd fathered four excellent sons, handsome, cheerful, and accomplished. He spoke regularly in the House of Lords and was as much a favorite at the palace as he was among his tenants. His single sorrow, and it had been severe, was the loss of his wife to smallpox several years before. But after his grief had subsided, even being widowed had turned to his favor, and he'd become the darling of every hostess who wished an extra gentleman at their table as well as the matrimonial target of every spinster and widow in town.

March doubted very much he'd ever be in that singular position of rivaling his witty cousin's popularity, nor truly did he wish it. But he did hope he could find a measure of Breck's happiness before his whole life had passed him by, and he hoped even more to find love to go with it.

Now he ran his hand restlessly back through his hair, deciding how best to explain all this to Brecon.

"I want matters to progress agreeably with Lady Charlotte," he said at last. "She is a most excellent young woman, and exceptionally beautiful. I want to earn her favor and regard."

Brecon nodded, encouraging. "That is good. Most gentlemen in your position do not bother to win wives that are as much as given to them."

"Well, then, I am different," March said. "I feel certain she is my one hope for happiness in life."

"That's a sizable burden for the lady to bear alone." Brecon shifted in his chair, the sunlight dancing over the silver embroidery on his waistcoat. "I trust you'll be willing to do some of the carrying of this match as well?"

"I mean to do whatever is necessary for us both to be happy," March said. He didn't need to add the rest— that he was determined not to be miserable in his marriage the way his parents had been—because Brecon, more than anyone else, understood that. "I'll do whatever I must."

"Then you will be happy," Brecon said easily. "Deciding to be so is much of the battle, or so the philosophers tell us. But enough of your love life. Tell me instead how fares the shoulder. If you're here in town, then your injury must be improving."

March smiled resolutely, running his hand lightly over the silk sling. His shoulder did ache, enough that he had yet to visit his clubs or friends, but yesterday with Charlotte had been worth it.

"My shoulder's well enough," he said. "Stapleton and the other doctors would have me still malingering in my bed, but I saw no use to that, and came to town."

"Because Lady Charlotte is here?"

March nodded. He couldn't lie to Brecon, especially not about this. "Our betrothal is next week, and there are preparations that need to be made."

Brecon cocked his brow, more question than surprise. "There's not much to prepare, is there? A ring is all that's required from you, and you've done that. The solicitors will be the busy ones, negotiating and copying every last farthing of settlements and portions. All you and the lady must do is sign your name to the papers, and then wait until the appointed day."

March grimaced. "Precious little romance to that."

"There isn't supposed to be," Brecon said. "We're not the pretty folk in sentimental ballads. Marriage for gentlemen like us is more a union of property, a complicated transaction, than anything else. Your only responsibility is to pay sufficient visits to your wife's bed to produce an heir to carry on your title. Beyond not behaving too outrageously, your obligations to each other are done."

March knew this was the truth—he'd already signed enough letters and papers in connection with the match— but he hated the heartlessness of it all.

"I hope for more than that," he said. "You'd make it sound more like purchasing a cottage than marrying a wife."

Now both of Breck's brows rose. "Is it so very different? It would seem that you've already visited the lady and surveyed her qualities just as you would a cottage. Tested her foundations, as it were."

"What do you mean?" March asked defensively, though of course he knew exactly what his cousin meant. Breconridge being Breconridge, he surely would have heard by now of what had happened in Mrs. Cartwright's shop. Brecon heard everything.

And, apparently, he read everything as well.

"Haven't you seen this?" he asked, drawing a folded news sheet from inside his coat and handing it March. The page had been folded to highlight one particular article:

We have learned that Cupid's DART *hath struck the lofty Duke of* M****b****e *most keenly. With a huntsman's fierceness he yesterday did pursue the beauteous Lady C. W. from his estate in Surrey to her*

mantua-maker in Oxford Street, & in a private LAIR
*to the back of that establishment did keep alone with
her in close &* INTIMATE *company for considerable time.
Driven by his* PASSION, *did His Grace forswear the sweet
promise of the* HYMENEAL BOWER *& instead press home
his immediate advantage to seize the final* PRIZE?

Too furious to speak, March read the item again before he realized he'd become too furious to breathe, too,
and he let out all his breath in a single heated oath.

"You do not deny it, then?" Brecon asked.

"How can I deny what is so near to the truth?" With
the paper crumpled in his hand, March rose and stalked
to the window, staring unseeing at the park before him.
He should have guessed this would happen, considering
how many others had been in the shop with them. Yet
to read the result and see his encounter with Charlotte
reduced to a lurid tattle made his stomach churn. "The
lady has not been in London a week, and yet in one afternoon I have destroyed her honor and her name."

"You say this wretched scribbler has told the truth,"
Brecon said. "I trust that this is some exaggeration, and
that you did not in fact ravish the lady on the back coun-
ter of a mantua-maker's shop?"

"There was no, ah, consummation, if that is what you
ask," March said, still turned to the window. "But in the
warmth of our conversation, I did kiss her, and embrace
her, and in her innocence she—she did not rebuff me."

The disapproval in his cousin's voice was clear enough.
"March, she is to be your wife and your duchess. You
can't treat her like some common little strumpet. Thank
the heavens that her father's dead, else it could be swords
at dawn on the misty heath after this."

"Don't count me fortunate yet," March said with gloomy
resignation. What if this were enough to sour Charlotte

on marrying him altogether? What if she decided she'd had enough of London and of him, and returned today to her quiet old house by the sea? "I wouldn't put it past Lady Sanborn to send her second with a challenge."

"No jesting, now, no jesting," Brecon said, more concerned than disapproving. "Consider this business from your side as well. You say the lady is an innocent."

"She is," March said firmly, recalling the sweet breathiness of her inexperienced kiss and the wonder that had shown in her eyes. "I do not doubt her at all."

"I'm glad of it," Brecon said. "But what if your impatience had carried you further, and she were to be with child by the time you wed? The world counts months with great glee, and what if your son and heir should arrive as a six-month babe? There'd be plenty of whispers as to whether the child was even yours, whispers that, however false, would haunt you and your son the rest of his life. Given our peculiar shared heritage—"

"There must be no more bastards," March said curtly. It wasn't enough that he had publicly dishonored Charlotte. How had he not thought of this, of the inadvertent curse he could have placed on their unborn child?

"Exactly, cousin, exactly," Brecon said. "You're fortunate that the lady's beauty and form inspire such desire in you. If in time you can make yourself fall in love with her and she with you, all the better. But I can assure you that a little decorum, a little restraint, before your wedding will go far toward establishing an honorable marriage."

But for March there was another solution, and to him it was the most honorable one as well. Lady Charlotte needed the protection of his name and title, not the slander of it. He no longer saw the need for this prolonged betrothal until a Michaelmas wedding. In fact, he saw no need of a betrothal at all.

"There must be no more of this tattle about Lady Charlotte in the papers," he said firmly. "She doesn't deserve another word of it."

"That's the spirit," said Brecon with hearty approval. "Lead with your head, not your cock."

"Yes," said March. "There will no betrothal, nor a period of waiting. Instead I intend to marry Lady Charlotte at once."

CHAPTER

 7

Charlotte stood in the center of the stone-paved path in the garden behind her aunt's house. After the wild gardens and fields of the old manor in Dorset, this city garden seemed oppressively small and restrained, with tall brick walls on three sides and the house on the other. Everything was bound by geometric precision, with the neat stone paths crossing one another at perfect right angles, and every raised bed of flowers was so neatly trimmed that no leaves or tendril vines dared curl beyond their boundaries. Even the small lady apple trees that were her aunt's special pride were forced to grow to please her, their branches pinned to low fences in strict espalier and their miniature fruit at a level for Aunt Sophronia to pluck for herself.

Most of all, there were no tall trees for shade, nor trees fit for climbing, either, which was likely why Charlotte was permitted to be here by herself, unattended and unwatched. She'd come here now in this early hour purposely to be alone, the shadows of the walls long across the paths as she stood with her arms out at her sides and her knees slightly bent. With the paths as her ballroom, she began to count the rhythm of the minuet, striving to recall the steps that the Parisian dancing master had taught her yesterday.

One-two, one-two-three, one-two, one. She'd never

danced a minuet before, and the steps were wickedly complex, without any comforting pattern or reason. Monsieur La Farge had patiently explained that she must try her best because minuets were always danced by one couple at a time, while the rest of the company stood by to watch with respect. More shocking still was learning that the lady of highest rank in a room traditionally opened a ball by dancing the first minuet, and in many cases that would mean her as Duchess of Marchbourne.

As difficult as the dance might be, she was determined that March would be proud of her, not shamed by a clumsy, awkward wife before his friends. The one saving grace was that their wedding was still months away, and for that time she'd only be an earl's lowly daughter, safe from minuets. But still, here she was, practicing alone in the garden and trying to recall all the niceties of Monsieur La Farge's lesson.

She turned to her right and smiled, imagining March beside her. She remembered how he'd looked at her when they'd been together at the mantua-maker's, and how his expression had appeared almost bewitched, as if she'd cast some sort of magical spell over his wits: a thoroughly lovely moment.

"What in blazes are you doing, Charlotte?" Diana called as she and Lizzie came bounding through the garden from the house. With them was Fig, miserably tugging and nipping at her new leash of pink braided leather.

The leash wasn't the only alteration. Just as Charlotte herself had changed, her two sisters were now dressed neatly to follow London fashion (and Aunt Sophronia's expectations), Lizzie in a yellow-striped gown with a wide green sash at the waist and Diana in nearly the same gown except with blue stripes and a yellow sash. Instead of the haphazard plaits that they'd usually worn in Dorset, they now had their dark hair brushed and pinned neatly beneath ruffled linen caps.

But while their appearance might have changed for town, their manners clearly reflected what they'd left behind on the Dorset beach.

"Is this what Aunt Sophronia's French fop has taught you?" Lizzie said. She began taking tiny mincing steps with her back at an exaggerated arch to mimic Monsieur La Farge, while Diana waved her handkerchief like a flag and giggled. "Are you practicing how to shake your hands about and talk to yourself like a madwoman from Bedlam?"

"You hush, Lizzie," Charlotte said, crossing her arms over her chest. "You too, Di. Before long, Aunt Sophronia will find husbands for you, or at least she'll try to. If you'd any sense, you'd be joining me in Monsieur La Farge's lessons, so you'll be prepared when it's your turn."

"Why in blazes would I wish to do that?" Lizzie flapped her arms at her sides in a mockery of Charlotte's minuet. "We're only staying in London until you're married."

"That will likely be weeks and weeks," Charlotte said. "Aunt Sophronia thinks it won't be until autumn at the earliest. Plenty of time."

But Lizzie was too occupied in flapping her arms to care. "Look, Charlotte, I'm a flying Frog!"

"In London ladies don't say 'Frog' for French people," Charlotte said with exasperation, "and they don't say 'in blazes,' either. That's close to swearing, and gentlemen don't like ladies who swear like fishermen."

"You used to swear the worst of any of us." Diana gathered Fig up into her arms, trying to untangle the unwanted leash from the little cat's leg. "You used to hate lessons, too, and you were the one who behaved the worst with governesses, so they'd leave."

"Perhaps I've found a reason to pay heed," Charlotte said. She sat on one of the white-painted benches, taking care to keep her back straight and to arrange her skirts so they'd fall becomingly over her legs. At the last she remembered to cross her ankles, too, so the tips of her shoes peeped from her petticoats at a pleasing angle. These were more suggestions from Monsieur Le Farge, and every bit as frustrating to remember as the minuet. "Perhaps I've now an inclination, one that I didn't have before, to behave as becomes our rank."

"Because of your *duke*," Lizzie said, not bothering to hide her disgust. "You think because you're going to marry him and have people curtseying to you because you're a duchess that you're better than Diana and me, and Mama, too."

"I don't think of myself as any better at all," Charlotte said defensively. What she did think was how much older she suddenly felt than her sisters. "But becoming His Grace's wife is like any other task that I must learn. You wouldn't go off to sea without first learning to follow the currents and steer a course and trim the sails to match the wind, would you?"

"I suppose not," Lizzie said grudgingly. "Unless I were in a rowboat, and then all you'd need to do was fit the oars to the locks and row, which I can already do perfectly well."

Charlotte sighed, wishing this new life before her could be that uncomplicated. "His Grace isn't a dinghy, Lizzie, and learning to be an acceptable duchess is going to be much more difficult than keeping the oarlocks straight. If I am to be of any use to His Grace and not an embarrassment, I have a great deal of things to learn before our wedding."

Diana's expression remained stubbornly skeptical as she petted the cat in her lap. "I wish you didn't have to marry anyone, Charlotte. I wish you were coming back to Ransom with us, where you belong."

"Oh, Di." Charlotte sat on the bench beside Diana and hugged her close, striving to keep back the tears that suddenly stung her eyes. As exciting as these last days had been, part of her couldn't help but agree with Diana, and long to be returning to her familiar old life with her mother and sisters. "You know how much I'll miss you once you leave with Mama, but my place now will be with the duke. It will be the same for you one day, too, once you're married."

Lizzie wriggled in beside her on the bench, and Charlotte pulled her close, too.

"My two little geese," she whispered, overwhelmed. "You must promise to visit me at Marchbourne House, or Greenwood."

"Mama says we'll visit you as soon as you have a baby," Diana said. "Then we'll be aunts."

"You can be godmothers, too," Charlotte said. She knew that an heir was the main reason the duke was marrying her, and that everyone else knew it, too, but it somehow was disconcerting to hear her younger sister speaking so blithely of her producing a baby, as if it were not more involved than baking a cake. "You can come for the christening."

"Babies," said Lizzie with unrepentant disgust. "I'd rather come see the duke's stables and his horses than any *baby*."

Charlotte smiled. Not everything was changing, at least not where her sisters were concerned. "I expect His Grace has many, many horses, Lizzie, and likely a few ponies as well. He seems to have a great deal of everything."

Diana frowned. "You're having to learn so many new things to please the duke, Charlotte. But what is *he* learning that will make him any use to you?"

"I don't know," Charlotte confessed, surprised by the question. She'd been so busy worrying about her own preparations that she really hadn't considered what he might be doing for their wedding. "I expect because His Grace is older and has been a duke since he was a boy, he doesn't have much to learn. I doubt he's half so worried about blundering and shaming me."

"Then likely he won't care to see this." Lizzie pulled a crumpled scrap of newspaper from her pocket, smoothing it over her knee. "I saw it right away in one of the news sheets on the sideboard this morning. I tore it out so Aunt Sophronia wouldn't see it, leastways before you did."

Charlotte frowned as she took the raggedy paper. She gasped as she began to read it, and gasped again at its conclusion. Aunt Sophronia had warned her of the consequences of her encounter with March at Mrs. Cartwright's shop, but Charlotte hadn't expected the gossip to be printed in the papers like this, for all of England to read.

What would Aunt Sophronia say?

More important, what would March say?

"I'd say it's vastly impressive, Charlotte," Diana said with admiration, leaning over her shoulder to read it again. "To think that you're so *notorious* that the papers would make a puzzle out of your name, with initials!"

"Has Aunt Sophronia left her bedchamber?" Charlotte asked, rising from the bench. "Have you seen her yet this day?"

"Mama said they were going to take their tea together in the front parlor." Diana slipped from the bench, too, the cat cradled in her arms and her eyes bright with excitement, and Lizzie instantly followed.

"What are you going to do, Charlotte?" she demanded. "You're not going to show that to Aunt Sophronia, are you? Ooh, you'll be in so much trouble once she reads it!"

"I may be in trouble enough already," Charlotte said, her heels clicking on the paving stones as she hurried toward the house.

"We'll come with you," Diana said, trotting along beside her. "You'll need supporters. Besides, I want to see Aunt Sophronia's face turn red like a turnip when she reads the part about the sweet promise of your hymeneal bower."

"No, you won't," Charlotte said. "I don't want either of you there. This is something I must face by myself."

She ran up the stairs, her skirts bunched in one hand and the damning column in the other. She didn't wait for a footman to announce her to her aunt, but charged into the parlor on her own. Her aunt and her mother were sitting together at the table near the window, with tea, jam, and sweet buns before them and the fluffy white dogs sprawled on the carpet at their feet.

Yet the two women did not look happy as they sat there. They looked concerned and more than a little upset, and Charlotte's spirits sank even lower. One of the footmen stood beside the table with his flat silver salver in his hands, obviously waiting for some reply or order. Surely whatever Charlotte said next couldn't make matters worse, and without preamble she held the wrinkled scrap of newspaper out to her aunt.

"Diana discovered this in one of the papers," she said, her voice trembling. "They've pretended to disguise my name and His Grace's, but any fool could decipher it. Oh, Aunt, you were so right!"

But Aunt Sophronia only glanced at the article, not bothering to take it from Charlotte.

"That must be from the *Daily Courant*," she said. "I wondered where it had gone. Never to be outdone, the *Inquisitor* has its own version, too, and of an equally panting tone. It is, sorrowfully, to be expected, considering the lack of regard and respect in the modern world today."

Confused, Charlotte gave her head a small anxious shake. "Then—then you are not concerned by this?"

"Of course I am concerned," the countess said indignantly. "How could I not be? Isn't this exactly as I'd predicted?"

"Yes, Aunt," Charlotte said, tears stinging her eyes. "I can only guess what His Grace must be thinking, to see his name dragged into the papers like this."

"I would wager a guinea that His Grace isn't giving these tawdry words a single thought, or at least not the same thoughts that you are," Aunt Sophronia said. "Gentlemen perceive these things differently than we ladies do. In fact, I would wager a thousand guineas, if I could find a taker."

Only then did Charlotte notice the letter in her mother's hands, heavy white stock with a gold imprint at the top. Slowly Mama refolded the letter and placed it on the table, giving a small pat with her open palm.

"You aunt is so sure, Charlotte," she said softly, "because His Grace has already written to us."

Mama was trying to smile, but her mouth crumpled, and instead she pressed her handkerchief to her eyes and bowed her head.

Charlotte stared at the folded letter, the bright green wax wafer marked with the Marchbourne arms stuck unbroken to the edge. She recognized the bold, masculine penmanship from the note that had come last week with the roses, the strongly drawn letters without any frills or flourishes, much like March himself.

She probably could have read the letter for herself, especially since the contents seemed to be in regard to her. But to touch the letter, to read it, would make whatever awful message it bore undeniably real.

"Has he broken with me?" she asked, so washed with disappointment that she could scarce stand. "Is that it? Has he called off our betrothal because of the scandal I have caused?"

"Broken with you, my dear?" Aunt Sophronia tipped back her head and laughed, a throaty laugh that Charlotte did not want to hear. "That is what you believe he has done? Broken the match?"

"Yes, I do," Charlotte said, her hands clutched tight at her sides. "And if you were not so—so cruel, Aunt, you would tell me now, and spare me more misery."

"Silly girl," her aunt said. "The duke doesn't want to break with you. Far from it. He wishes there to be no betrothal, because he cannot wait. He wishes to marry you at once, Charlotte. At once."

Charlotte stared at her aunt, focusing on how the countess's amber and diamond earring swung gently against her powdered cheek, a tiny detail that she could concentrate upon and keep the room from spinning away. "You are not jesting? The duke still wishes to marry me?"

"He most certainly does," her aunt said, laughing again. "I do believe he'd marry you this day before dinner if it could be arranged. You've won His Grace so completely, Charlotte, that I do believe nothing would drive him off."

Still Charlotte could not make sense of it. "But you are not serious about me marrying at once, are you, Aunt Sophronia?"

Her aunt smiled and tapped the table with a teaspoon for emphasis. "I am quite serious, niece, and so is His Grace. We had already agreed to the plans for a small ceremony to mark your betrothal later this week. His Grace suggests that this be transformed into your wedding instead. A simple affair, to be sure, before a handful of witnesses, but it will accomplish the same business, and you'll be man and wife as definitely as if you were wed at Westminster."

In three days—and forever after—who she was would no longer matter compared to who she'd become. Oh, preserve her, it was all happening so very fast!

Charlotte groped for the nearest chair, sinking into it. "How can it be possible? What of the banns?"

"Charlotte, he is a duke with royal blood," Aunt Sophronia said, "and the archbishop himself will do whatever needs to be done in order to oblige him."

"And me?" Charlotte asked. "What of obliging me?"

"What obligation could there be?" Aunt Sophronia asked, genuinely surprised. "This suggestion of his could not be a greater triumph for you. A betrothal is well enough in its way, but the sooner you and the duke are joined before God, the better for everyone."

Until now, Mama had said almost nothing, letting Aunt Sophronia speak, but now she could keep silent no longer.

"If you please, Sophronia," she said. "I should like to speak to my daughter alone."

"To plan, no doubt." The countess smiled, gathering up a dog beneath each arm. She paused before Charlotte and bent to kiss her lightly on the forehead. "Congratulations, Charlotte. I'm thoroughly proud of you."

But as soon as she left, Charlotte dropped to her knees and rested her head on her mother's lap. "Oh, Mama, forgive me, but this is all happening so fast!"

"My own baby," Mama murmured, smoothing Charlotte's hair back from her face. "Don't be sad, sweet. Be brave, and try to think with a clear head. Your father planned this for you to make you happy, and in time I pray it will."

"But three days, Mama," Charlotte protested, her words choked with emotion. "Only three days, and then everything in my life will change!"

"It will, yes," Mama said, her voice gentle, but firm, too. "But it will change whether you marry His Grace or not. Nothing stays the same, Charlotte, no matter how much we might wish otherwise. At first I felt bad for not having given you more warning, but now I believe it was for the best, not to have had this wedding looming in your thoughts."

"You and Di and Lizzie will leave," Charlotte said, her words muffled by Mama's skirts, "and I'll be left behind and alone."

"You won't be alone, Charlotte," Mama said firmly. "You'll be with your husband, as is proper for a wife. You must learn to rely upon him, and he on you. If you have a real need or emergency, you'll also have your aunt here in town with you."

"But I don't know the duke, not at all!"

"He doesn't know you, either, Charlotte," Mama said. "That is how all marriages begin, with the two of you discovering each other."

"But Mama, I—"

Suddenly Mama's face clouded with concern. "Unless there is something about His Grace that has made you wary of him? Is there, Charlotte? Because if you fear him, or believe he might harm you—"

Charlotte raised her head, her hands still resting on Mama's lap. "Oh, no, not at all. It's not that."

Mama nodded, clearly relieved. "I've scarcely seen His Grace to form any impression of him, but he is a handsome gentleman, with a pleasing manner. A bit solemn, perhaps, but then he is a duke."

"He *is* handsome, Mama," Charlotte agreed quickly. "He has lovely dark eyes that speak his kindness, and his smile, though rare, is as pleasing as can be, and he is very gallant, that is, he can be gallant when—"

"Shhh, Charlotte, please," Mama said. "Speak more slowly, and with more care for the words you choose." Charlotte nodded and took a deep breath. "When the duke and I are alone, he hasn't been solemn at all."

"That he isn't solemn with you is in his favor," Mama said. "But that he has contrived to be alone with you is not. You are an earl's daughter, Charlotte, and both my family and your father's are a good deal older and more noble than his. You must take care that he always treats you with the respect you are due as a lady, even when you are alone together. *Especially* when you are alone."

Charlotte nodded quickly. "He was most kind to me when were alone together at Mrs. Cartwright's, and when he kissed me—"

"He did kiss you, then?" Mama asked tentatively. "It wasn't an invention of the papers?"

Charlotte blushed, and she looked down. "He did, and it was—it was very nice. *He* is very nice. But Mama, what I wish for, what I hope for, is to be happy and in love as you and Father were, and—and I do not know how to make that happen."

"Because you can't force love to happen, Charlotte," Mama said gently. "Love grows on its own, like the prettiest of weeds. You cannot predict where it will sprout, or even if it will. But if you nurture it with trust and respect, it will grow, and prosper. So it was between your darling father and me. Our match was arranged, too, and I was even younger than you when I wed, and oh, I was frightened of being a countess!"

"You were?" Charlotte asked. She remembered her parents as being so inseparable that it was hard to realize they hadn't always known each other.

"Oh, yes," Mama said. "I nearly fainted clear away at our wedding. But before long your father and I realized we suited each other quite well. We fell in love and stayed in love, and so I pray it will be for you and His Grace."

Though Mama's eyes were bright with unshed tears, she smiled, and her face seemed to soften and grow younger as she spoke of Father. To Charlotte's wonder, she glimpsed her mother not as she was now, but as she must have been long ago as a bride herself. She'd thought her parents had always loved each other, because that was how she remembered them. But now it seemed that they'd had to fall in love like anyone else. It was a wondrous, encouraging realization.

"I do believe His Grace likes me already, Mama," Charlotte said shyly. "Why else would he have come clear to town and followed me to Mrs. Cartwright's shop?"

Mama's smile widened. "More important, why else would he have braved your aunt to do so?"

"He called her a dragon, Mama," Charlotte whispered, lowering her voice even though her aunt was far from hearing. "I wanted to laugh when he did."

"You should have," Mama said, laughing now. "Because he is completely right. She *is* a dragon."

Her laughter faded, her expression growing more serious again. She took Charlotte's face in her hands, so tenderly that tears welled in Charlotte's eyes. Mama was right: once Charlotte wed March, her loyalty must shift from her family to him. Her family would return to Ransom Manor, and future moments like this with her mother would be rare indeed.

"My own darling daughter," Mama said. "How I will miss you! Yet I believe in my heart that His Grace will be the right gentleman for you. Be your own dear, sweet self, and how can he not love you?"

"And I *will* love him, Mama," Charlotte said, promising herself as well as her mother. When she and March took their wedding vows, she knew she'd have to swear to that, as well as a great many other serious things, but she was certain that loving him would be the easiest vow to keep.

"In time, sweet, in time," Mama cautioned. "You can't force love, no matter how much you wish to."

Tears welled up again in Charlotte's eyes. "What if it doesn't grow as you say?"

"It will," her mother said softly. "I don't doubt it. And once you love him, and he loves you, then you will be happy. You will. And that, Charlotte, is the very best I can wish for you both."

CHAPTER
8

"Rain," March said with disgust. "Can you believe this, Breck? I cannot recall the last day that it rained, and now see how it pours down for us today."

Brecon stood with him at the small arched windows, watching the rain stream from St. Paul's porches and splatter and puddle on the paving stones. They were waiting in a small vestryman's room beside the Morning Chapel, where the wedding would take place as soon as the bride's party arrived. They were not late; it was March who was early, as was often his habit. Usually he preferred arriving first, but today, standing here dressed in a blue silk suit in the late afternoon, waiting for the others only made his restlessness grow, ratcheting higher with every passing second.

"Be easy, March," Brecon said, handing him a glass of the Madeira that had been thoughtfully left on the sideboard for calming the groom. "There are plenty of folk who believe that rain on a wedding day only augurs the best. Love, happiness, fertility, and all the rest come dripping from the clouds upon you."

"Pox on your augurs." March emptied the glass, wishing at once that the Madeira weren't so cloyingly sweet. He'd had no appetite for dinner, and the wine on his empty stomach was not pleasing. That was all he needed, to be violently ill as he took his vows. "You would say something inane like that."

"I would," Brecon said mildly. "That is my role here today. To keep your spirits up by pouring more down your throat. Consider this, cousin. If you must play Noah, then at least you'll leave St. Paul's with Mrs. Noah."

"The woman must have a name." March smoothed the sleeves of his jacket, tugging the ruffled cuffs of his shirt free, then decided they hung too low over his hands and stuffed the cuffs back in. At least his shoulder had improved, so he'd been able to abandon the sling. "You cannot call her Mrs. Noah. Could there be a worse omen than that for the day?"

Brecon tipped his head to one side, thinking.

"I do not believe I know the lady's name. How curious." He leaned around the corner to call to the bishop and the two other clerics who were likewise waiting respectfully for the bride. "Tell us, gentlemen. What is the given name of old Noah's wife?"

The minister bowed. "I regret to disappoint you, Your Grace, but the Bible never gives the name of Noah's wife. It remains a mystery."

"Ah, well, cousin, there you have it," Brecon announced grandly, as if March weren't standing only a half dozen paces away. "Noah's wife remains Mrs. Noah, with nothing beyond that. Pity. Can't see your lady standing for that, though she'll have nothing to complain of now. 'Charlotte Wylder FitzCharles, Duchess of Marchbourne' is name enough for any woman."

March ignored him and turned back to the window. He wasn't particularly given to superstitions, but all this empty talk of what was lucky and what wasn't was making him think too much of good fortune and ill, and when he caught himself wondering if there'd been rain on his parents' wedding day, he knew it was time to steer his thoughts in a more practical direction.

"At least the rain has discouraged most of the gawkers," he said to no one in particular as he stared from the window. "I trust the men we've hired will keep the ones who have come at a distance."

Groups of soggy onlookers huddled beneath the porches, but the crushing crowds he'd feared had stayed away. Even with such short notice, the papers had seized upon the wedding, and had reported every morsel of news they could learn and had invented many more with a panting eagerness that had appalled March.

Still, though he didn't like the attention, he understood it. The English adored any kind of wedding, especially the wedding of a duke descended from a much-loved king. There'd also been all manner of claptrap invented about Charlotte, practically turning her into a fairy-tale heroine raised in a tower by the sea. It was nonsense, and it was . . . distasteful. The sooner he and Charlotte were decently made man and wife without the rest of the world peering at their every move, the better.

Restlessly he once again pulled his watch from his pocket, stunned that only five more minutes had crept past since he'd last checked the time.

"She's here, cousin," Brecon said quietly beside him. "Are you ready?"

March jerked to attention. "How can that be? I've not seen their carriage."

Brecon smiled. "Do you truly think we'd let you see your lady before the ceremony? Her party's come by the other door."

March felt an odd little lurch in his chest. "Have you seen her, then?"

Breck's smile widened. "I have, briefly. She's absolutely beautiful. Terrified, too."

"Terrified?" March repeated. "Why should she be terrified of me?"

"Not you," Brecon said, critically straightening the front of March's coat. "Rather, I suspect she's afraid of the same thing that's frightening you as well: the knowledge that you're soon to be joined for life to another you scarcely know."

March groaned. "If that's your notion of comforting support—"

"I'm merely reminding you, March, that you and Lady Charlotte are in exactly the same situation." He gave March's shoulder a final, fond pat. "Be kind to her, cousin, especially tonight. Never forget that she's a lady. She's very young, true, and gently bred, but if you're kind, she'll make you happy. That's the best advice I can offer you. Now come. You don't wish to make Lady Charlotte wait, do you?"

March nodded briskly, tamping down a curious mix of excitement, anticipation, eagerness, and, yes, a bit of fear. He had never been an officer, but surely this must be what military men felt before they went into battle. And if all this was roiling through him now, what could Charlotte be feeling? She *was* so young, not far from the schoolroom, really. Brecon was right. She would need him to support her through this day, and he squared his shoulders in preparation.

There was no denying it now. He was ready to become a married man.

With Brecon beside him, he entered the chapel behind the three clergymen, their black and white vestments billowing around them. The wedding was not a grand, princely affair. No flowers, singers, orchestra, or scores of guests, but instead a small ceremony with only family for witnesses. March had Brecon beside him and no others because, quite simply, he'd no one else left in his family.

He had chosen the Morning Chapel for both its privacy and its size, tucked away as it was from the main nave of St. Paul's. The dark polished wood of the pews and wainscoting were an elegant backdrop to the red and purple silk hangings and cushions, a most sumptuous setting by the light of the candles.

As he took his place at the rail, he couldn't help but glance up. If it had been a fair day, the afternoon sun would have been streaming down upon him and Charlotte through the tall arched window, something he'd anticipated as a sort of natural blessing. But the dark clouds overhead had put an end to that hope, the rain drumming against the glass, and steadfastly he tried to think of it more as an inconvenience than as one more inauspicious omen.

No, he'd make luck enough for him and Charlotte together. He heard a door close, and he turned eagerly.

And there, at last, she was.

She stood at the entry, surrounded by a flurry of women—her mother, her aunt, her sisters—who, like ghosts, left only the vaguest of impressions. There'd be no grand procession, and once she was ready, she was to join him here at the rail with her little flock of family.

She was still fussing with her gown, smoothing her skirts after they'd taken away her cloak, and perhaps shaking away a few drops of rain. Her hooped gown of silver silk shimmered as she moved, the skirts dabbled with some manner of sparkling stones and loops of silver ribbon and drifts of lace falling from the sleeves. Her waist seemed impossibly small by contrast, and as she bent forward he'd a heady glimpse of her breasts, pushed up above the gown's low neckline. She wore a fine lace kerchief pinned to the back of her hair, and through it glinted more sparkles in her hair, or maybe it was only more raindrops. He was glad they hadn't powdered her hair to follow fashion; he remembered how soft those thick dark waves had been to touch.

She straightened, visibly trying to compose herself with her eyes downcast and her hands clasped at her waist, the way every lady stands. But even that well-practiced gesture couldn't calm her: her fingers failed to link smoothly, missing first, then tangling and fumbling before she finally pressed them together.

March's sympathy went out to her at once. Brecon was right. She *was* frightened. She hadn't yet dared look his way, though surely she must know he was there. Finally she took a deep breath—how base he felt that he noticed how her breasts rose and fell!—and raised her gaze to meet his.

Her eyes were enormous in her pale face, as blue and fathomless as the sea. In them he saw her fear and uncertainty, but he also saw courage and determination. Most startling of all to him, however, was the hope that he saw there, too, and that was what won him completely.

Ignoring the instructions that had been given to him, he went striding down the short aisle to her. He didn't care at all about what was proper for a marriage in St. Paul's, but he cared very much about her, and he did not want to see her alone any longer. They'd do this together, just as they'd go through the rest of their lives together.

Startled, she barely remembered to sink low in a curtsey before he reached her, the sparkling silk of her gown making the softest *shush* around her. It would, he realized, be the last time she'd need curtsey to him, for as soon as they were wed, she'd be a duchess, and his equal.

He couldn't wait. He grasped her hand and lifted her up. She was dazzling, and it had nothing to do with her silver gown or the glinting stones in her hair.

He smiled, unable to help himself. "Does it still rain, Lady Charlotte?"

"Yes, Your Grace," she answered, a charming tremor in her voice. "Though the shower did seem to be lessening as we left the carriage."

He nodded. "I'm glad. We've had enough rain this day, haven't we?"

"Oh, yes." She smiled, and he forgot everything else.

"March," Brecon said behind him. "Please."

That was reminder enough. As if he'd planned it all along, he led Charlotte to stand before the bishop. Brecon stood at his side, and Charlotte's family gathered at hers, as witnesses should. He had a slight awareness of Lady Sanborn looking serious and faintly disapproving, Lady Wylder weeping into her handkerchief, and the two younger ladies—he'd have to learn their names—staring at him as curiously as if he'd grown an extra head.

For all he knew, he had. He could concentrate on nothing but Charlotte beside him: the little wisps of curls along her nape that the rain had coaxed free, the length of her lashes over her cheek, the sweet pout of her lower lip, the way her fingers were holding tightly to his as if she never wished to let go. He barely heard the bishop as he began reading the ceremony, and only judicious prodding from Brecon produced his responses at the proper time. Since there had been no betrothal ceremony, he had decided to use the diamond cluster ring as her wedding ring, and when he drew it from his pocket and slipped it on her finger, he'd been rewarded with a definite gasp. It also fit as if it had been made for her, which, at last on this day, he saw as a favorable omen.

But as March knelt beside her on the purple velvet cushions and listened to the bishop's final beneficent blessings, the significance of those blessings struck him with all their awful force. Charlotte was not only his wife but also his responsibility. He knew he was supposed to love her, which he'd every intention of doing, and to give her children, which he expected to be enjoyable, too.

But for the sake of their marriage, he was also bound to guide her, keep her from harm, and generally make sure she did her best to be a good wife as well as a good duchess. He thought once again of his parents, and how seldom they had been in each other's company. Would they have been happier if his father had heeded the words of their marriage vows and taken more care watching over his mother? Was it his father's fault that their marriage had been so thoroughly miserable?

There was no way of knowing now, of course, not with both of them long dead. But March wasn't going to take that risk with Charlotte. He would do whatever he must to preserve their happiness—for her sake, and for his.

"You may now kiss your bride, Your Grace," the bishop said, his smile jovial.

Charlotte blushed, as every bride is supposed to do, and chuckled as she offered her lips to his. Gently he pulled her close and she curled her arms around his shoulders. He kissed her, long and well, and perhaps with more passion than was proper for St. Paul's, but not for his new wife.

"Oh, March," she whispered, her blue eyes shining. "I'm so vastly happy!"

So vastly happy: that was right, he thought, that was how it should be, and with equal happiness he tucked her little hand into the crook of his arm.

At once her family seemed to swarm around them, a mass of females and their rustling, perfumed finery. Lady Hervey managed to weep and smile at the same time; Lady Sanborn smiled, too, in her usual disapproving, dragonlike fashion; and the two sisters bounced about in there as well. They congratulated him, and marveled over Charlotte's ring. They all kissed him, and he kissed each offered cheek. Brecon was laughing merrily, and kissing the women as well, because he could. One of the sisters stepped forward and bobbed a quick curtsey as she handed Charlotte a posy of white flowers. He hadn't considered that while Charlotte need no longer curtsey to him, her family must now curtsey to her.

"Congratulations, Your Grace," Lady Sanborn said with a tartness that struck him as wildly inappropriate. "You've become a member of our family now."

"That's true," he said mildly. For Charlotte's sake, he wouldn't let the dragon annoy him. "Just as the duchess is now part of mine."

He smiled, thinking of how fine that sounded, and drew Charlotte a little closer to him.

"Yes, yes," Lady Sanborn continued, as if he hadn't spoken. "You and the duchess will return to St. James's Square with us to dine, of course. Nothing elaborate, a small collation for the family."

His smile vanished. He wished she would cease reminding him that they were now related. And the last thing he wished was to return Charlotte to her aunt's house, bringing her back like some sort of faulty goods. This was their wedding day, and besides, he wished nothing more than to be finally alone with her.

"Forgive me, Lady Sanborn, but we must decline," he said. "The duchess and I will be returning to Marchbourne House."

The words came out perhaps more curtly than he'd intended, so curt that they managed to crush every bit of the goodwill around him as surely as a boot heel on a violet. The cheerful, chattering conversation stopped. Her weeping mother seemed stricken, and the sisters stared. The bishop and the other clergy looked down at the floor. Even Brecon seemed discomfited.

"But you cannot mean to take her away so soon, sir," Lady Sanborn protested, the only one who dared to speak what everyone else was evidently thinking. "Surely you cannot object to a small celebration to honor the nuptials. Her mother and sisters are set to leave town tomorrow at dawn, and this will be the last they will see of one another for a good while."

"The duchess and I already have plans for the evening, Lady Sanborn." Damnation, had he always sounded like such a fatuous ass, or was it only because *he* was now a *we*? He didn't dare look at Charlotte, not with the grim possibility that she might prefer her family's company over his. "We could, however, consider another celebration in the future."

"Thank you, Aunt Sophronia, but my place is with my husband," Charlotte said softly. There wasn't a breath of doubt or hesitation in her voice, and to make it even better, she gave a small, private squeeze to March's hand as well. "If the duke intends us to go home now to Marchbourne House, then we shall go."

"Yes," he said, returning the pressure on her fingers. He didn't know which pleased him more: that she'd taken his side as if it were the most natural, rightful thing in the world, or that she'd called Marchbourne House her home. "Good-bye, then."

It was, he thought, the most supremely awkward moment of his life. Perhaps if he'd family of his own, it wouldn't have seemed so, but he didn't, and their obvious disapproval of his decision was not pleasant to bear. There was more kissing from her aunt and her mother and more tears from the sisters, who now sobbed and wailed like professional mourners, and so much resentment from all of them that it hung in the air of the chapel like a heavy, wet fog. Yet through it all, Charlotte remained steadfast at his side, and if she, too, longed to weep, she bravely kept her tears unshed.

Hours passed, or so it felt to March. More likely it was five minutes, and their cloaks were retrieved and his hat was brought and then they were finally on the porch, her silvery skirts billowing around them both as she clung to his arm.

Suddenly Charlotte stopped and turned her face up toward the sky.

"Look, March," she said. "The rain has stopped, and the sun is out. What a pretty sign for us!"

He didn't look up because he couldn't look away from her face. She was smiling and she was squinting, and her cheeks were pink and the little curls around her forehead were tangling in the blowing lace, and he'd never seen anything as beautiful.

"A pretty sign, yes," he said. "A very pretty sign indeed."

CHAPTER

9

Charlotte grinned up at her tall new husband. It had been terribly hard to part with Mama and her sisters, but now that she'd said her farewells, she could look ahead to her future. She was happy, as happy as any bride should be, at least a bride who barely knew her groom.

"You say that as if you meant me, March, rather than the omen," she said, daring to be flirtatious now that they were safely wed. "I wasn't fishing for praise for myself, you know. I meant that our future would be as bright as the sun, and you turned my words around."

"But you *are* pretty, Charlotte, as is the omen," he said. "I didn't have to twist your words around."

He brushed the tangle of blowing lace from her face, leaning forward just enough that he blocked the sun. She didn't have to squint now. She could see his face clearly, and marveled again at how fortunate she was to be given such a handsome gentleman for a husband. But those handsome features were still solemnly composed, as if he hadn't realized she'd been teasing him, and she felt a small pang of disappointment.

But perhaps dukes didn't tease and flirt in public, she thought, swiftly excusing him, or perhaps this was his way of being nervous. Heaven knows she'd felt that way in the chapel, with the bishop intoning such serious prayers for them. Yes, that must be it. March likely was still feeling the solemnity of the occasion. Once they were alone, he was sure to relax.

Relieved, she took a small dancing step to one side, into the sun again and out of March's shadow. She looked back up the steps of St. Paul's to where Mama stood with her arms around Lizzie and Diana to comfort them, and a lump of longing and regret rose in her throat. She'd never been apart from her mother and sisters, not once, and now she was to be separated from them for weeks, even months.

"Come, Charlotte," March said. "It's unwise to keep the horses waiting."

She nodded, and gave one final wave of her posy to her sisters, blowing them a kiss for good measure. She *would* be brave. She hadn't cried yet, and she was determined not to do so now. As Mama had said, life was always changing, whether she wished it to or not. She swallowed the lump in her throat and forced herself to smile at March as he led her the rest of the way to his carriage, a huge, splendid affair with red-spoked wheels picked out in gold and his crest painted in more gold on the door.

"Goodness, look at the horses," she exclaimed. The team of matched dappled grays had elaborate rosettes of white silk ribbon on their bridles and harnesses, and the footmen, too, had white ribbons and sprigs of white sweet pea pinned to the breasts of their livery coats. "Oh, and the men, too!"

"I ordered everything in your honor," March said. "I'm glad it pleases you."

"It does, March. How can it not?" She considered kissing him, there at the carriage door, just to show how pleased she was. But in the instant she hesitated, he'd already begun to hand her into the carriage, and the moment for impulsive kisses was lost. She sat on one red-cushioned seat, her skirts spilling around her, and he sat on the other side, facing her and trying to place his feet without stepping on her petticoats. The footman folded up the carriage steps and latched the door, and the driver started the horses. Ragged cheering rose from the street, and curious, Charlotte leaned forward to the window.

"Who are they?" she asked. On the far side of the street stood throngs of people, waving and cheering, as a group of strong-armed men kept them from rushing forward. She waved her posy in acknowledgment, and they cheered all the harder. "Did you arrange for them to be there, too?"

"Hardly," March said, sitting back from view and clearly embarrassed by the cheering crowd. "They're here on their own, to gawk and sigh and use our marriage as an excuse for drinking in the street. I apologize for the nuisance."

"But it's not a nuisance," she said. "Whoever they are, I think it's vastly nice of them to wish us well."

He sighed. "You think that now, but in time it will indeed seem a nuisance. There's a great deal of curiosity about you, you see. My great-grandfather was a popular fellow with his people, and the Dukes of Marchbourne receive a bit of that old popularity whether we wish it or not. A new duchess is a rare occurrence. There hasn't been one since my mother. People feared I'd never marry, and that our line would end."

Charlotte nodded, equally solemn now. She well understood the importance of marriages and male heirs. Her own family had been tested by entail and inheritance, and nearly broken because of it. "You didn't know me. You could have wed another."

"You were chosen for me," he said. "By my father, and by fate. I never wished to marry anyone else. I waited for you."

"Oh, March." It was a simple explanation, honest and

direct, but to her it seemed like the most romantic declaration imaginable. Forgetting her finery, she crossed from her seat to his to sit beside him, squeezing her hoops against the side of the carriage. From the street came another burst of cheers; though most likely the cheers were in honor of their ribbon-decorated coach, she preferred to think they were cheering her onward.

"I know I promised before God to be your wife," she said breathlessly, "but I want you to know that I wish above all things to make you happy, and make you glad that you waited to wed me, and—and give you an heir so your line doesn't end."

For the first time since they'd left St. Paul's, he smiled. "As much as we both might wish that, Charlotte, it's not something we can control."

"I know," she said, blushing furiously. "But I understand how important it is to us. My mother bore three daughters and no sons, and when my father was killed, his title and our houses and everything in them all went to some distant cousin that we'd never met who wasn't even named Wylder. That's why Mama—my mother, I mean—took us to Ransom, which came to her through her family, not Father's. She could have lived in the Earl of Hervey's dower house, but she wished to be as far from that disappointment as she could be. She was brokenhearted, you see. In some ways, she still is."

"So that is why you were hidden away in Dorset?"

She nodded. "Because my parents had no sons," she said. "I understand why my father needed one, and why you must have them, and why I will do my duty to you to provide one as well as I can, but I am so vastly glad that your parents did have a son, because now you're here, and you're my husband."

"Charlotte," he said, and that was all. Though he was still smiling, he was also studying her closely, his dark eyes betraying either concentration, or confusion.

"I did not say that very well, did I?" Frustrated, she looked down at her lap and the brilliant new ring on her finger, and sighed deeply. "I know what I wished to say, but sometimes when a matter is important, I speak too fast, and babble like a fool."

"You made perfect and complete sense to me." He eased his arm around her shoulders, and she slipped against his chest as readily as if she'd always found comfort there.

Yet despite that proffered arm, she wasn't sure if he was teasing her or not. She hoped he meant to kiss her instead, which would be infinitely more agreeable than teasing. She looked up at him through her lashes, without lifting her chin.

"If that is true, March," she said, "then you are the first person on this earth that has admitted to the ability to understand me in trying circumstances."

"Then that, Charlotte," he said, leaning closer, "must be why I was chosen for you."

"Yes," she murmured, reaching up to run her fingers along his cheek. "A good thing you were, too."

He turned his head just far enough to kiss her fingertips. She realized he was going to kiss her next upon the mouth, and she smiled. He'd kissed her twice before, in the mantua-maker's shop and just after they'd been married. While she knew that two kisses hardly qualified her as knowledgeable, she thought she knew what to expect as she settled back into his arm and closed her eyes in readiness.

She was wrong.

This time when he kissed her, there was none of the impulsiveness of the first time, or the genteel pledge of the second. Oh, it began the same way, his lips on hers, but it quickly changed to something more. This kiss was about capture and possession and fire, dark, masculine things that she'd no name for. He was voracious, his hunger raw and demanding and unexpected. Yet the harder he kissed her, the more she felt a similar fire grow within herself. She clung to his shoulders as she answered his kiss, striving to match the warmth and urgency of what he was giving her.

She didn't care that they'd slipped to the seat of the carriage, or that he was as much as lying across her, or that it was possible that they were being glimpsed by others through the carriage windows. She ignored how her beautiful silver gown was being crushed, and how the twinkling brilliants were catching and snagging against his clothes, and even the ominous crack as his weight bowed and broke the caning in one side of her hoops.

All that mattered was kissing March, and being kissed by him. She understood that this was a kiss with a purpose, and that there was but one way that it was meant to end.

Unfortunately, that one way was not the carriage stopping, nor the telltale creaking of the springs as the footman jumped from the box to prepare to open the door.

March heard it first and broke away with a growl of frustration, pulling Charlotte upright on the seat beside him.

"We're home," he said gruffly, turning his body to shield her from the footman. The servant was wise enough to knock on the door before unlatching it, and to wait, too, for a response from within. As quickly as she could, Charlotte began putting her clothes to rights. Already she'd learned that March seemed to be very good at disarranging her clothing while he was kissing her, and that a certain amount of restoration was always going to be necessary afterward.

"That was fast," she said breathlessly, pushing pins back into place and smoothing her bodice.

"Too fast," he agreed, watching her dress with the same hunger he'd just demonstrated while kissing her. She liked it, too. It wasn't the way that he looked at her when he admired her gown or was happy to see her. Instead it was rather a wolfish look, as if he longed to devour her, and in turn it made her feel wantonly warm and wolfish, too. She leaned forward and kissed him quickly, just to let him know how sorry she also was that they'd had to stop.

"*Much* too fast," she whispered ruefully, picking up her posy. "I suppose I'm ready."

For another long moment, he did nothing but study her, then sighed.

"Oh, yes, we're ready," he said. With obvious reluctance, he called to the footman to open the door, climbed out, and turned to offer his hand to Charlotte.

In the full splash of late afternoon sun, her skirts were even more mussed and crushed than she'd guessed, the rumpled silk loudly proclaiming what she'd been doing with the Duke of Marchbourne.

No, with her *husband*. Surely that would make a difference. They were wed now, and after all, they'd only been doing what married people were supposed to do. There couldn't be anything shameful or scandalous about that.

Yet when she stepped down before the footman, she couldn't miss the startled surprise that showed in his eyes for the instant before he recomposed his features. She glanced up at March to find his face every bit as impassive as the footman's.

Well, then, if that was how he wished this to be, then she would oblige, and pretend along with him that nothing untoward had happened during the short journey from St. Paul's. In her head, she could hear Aunt Sophronia's scolding reminder that a gentleman like March expected his wife to behave with honorable decorum, not act like a sluttish mistress. She raised her chin and, with one hand in March's and the other holding her posy at her waist, she stepped forward exactly as a duchess should.

Or she would have if she could. As soon as she began to walk, she felt oddly unbalanced. Suddenly she remembered that moment when March had crushed and broken the canes in her left hoop. She glanced down, and saw that while the skirts over her right hip floated gracefully outward, the ones on her left did not, but hung limply, like a sparrow's broken wing. Without the hoop's support, the silk drooped and trailed forlornly, and the scattered brilliants stitched to her skirt seemed more to wink slyly than to sparkle.

But she *would* be a duchess. She would ignore it, and as best she could she sailed bravely at March's side.

She needed to be brave, too. In the short time she'd been in London, she'd never seen Marchbourne House. It rose before them now, dauntingly impressive, an enormous long building of red brick enclosed from the street by tall black and gold fences and gates. Here at the portico, she'd only a hasty impression of more chimneys than she could see and more windows than she could count. Ransom Manor could have been dropped here whole into the courtyard and not be missed, and Aunt Sophronia's house in St. James's would have been no more than one of the wings. She could just remember the splendor of her parents' old London house, but even that paled beside this.

"Goodness," she murmured, holding on more tightly to March's hand. "This is all very grand."

"Grand?" He looked up at the house as if seeing it for the first time himself. "Why, I suppose it is. I never give it much thought."

"But it's your house."

"One of them, yes," he said evenly. "I've four others besides. You'll see them all in time. As duchess, you'll oversee them now as the new mistress."

Charlotte stared upward, her lace kerchief drifting back from her head as she leaned back to try to see the roof. Aunt Sophronia had explained to her that her new responsibilities would include running the duke's vast household, and that in addition to making sure things were arranged to the duke's tastes, she'd also have dozens of servants who would look to her for supervision and guidance, and that wasn't including all the tenants and their families who lived and worked the duke's properties. Charlotte had believed herself eager for the challenge. She'd often helped Mama with the housekeeping books at Ransom, and their few servants had always seemed more like family than staff to be managed. To be sure, that was because of Mama's tender heart, and a ducal household would be much larger, but the basics surely must be the same. Yet how could she ever have imagined anything on this scale?

"You lived here alone?" she asked incredulously, staring up at the vast house. "All this just for you?"

"I'm never alone," March said. "There are the servants, and I often have friends visiting. But if one considers this as my home, then yes, I suppose I do live alone. Or did. Now it will be your home as well."

She didn't answer, not aloud. How could such an enormous, chilly place ever be her home? It wasn't even a house. It was a palace, and wistfully she remembered the comfortably rambling and slightly shabby scale of Ransom Manor.

"Come inside," March said, unaware of her misgivings as he led her up the white stone steps. "The staff will be waiting to meet you."

The tall double doors were held open for them by tall footmen in powdered wigs and plum-colored livery laced with silver. The lanterns in the entry hall had been lit, though they barely began to light the cavernous space. The floor was a checkerboard of black and white marble, with richly carved woodwork and polished brass everywhere she looked. Huge gloomy portraits stared down from the walls, men on horseback with long flowing hair and women with old-fashioned ruffs around their necks.

But most daunting to Charlotte was the long line of servants waiting to meet her, from the butler and housekeeper at one end to the lowest scullery maid in the distance. They stood as straight as any regiment of soldiers, and though they all wore the white ribbons with sprigs of sweet pea pinned to their breasts in her honor, she still felt not welcomed but thoroughly intimidated.

One by one, March presented each servant to her, and each in turn either bowed or curtseyed with a deferential "Your Grace." March had no difficulty reciting their names and duties, but he hadn't presented more than a half dozen before Charlotte, overwhelmed, had already forgotten the names and faces of those who'd come before.

Only one was familiar: Polly, from St. James's Square. Since she hadn't had a lady's maid of her own, Aunt Sophronia had "given" Polly to Charlotte to take with her to Marchbourne House. When Charlotte came to Polly in line, she very nearly hugged her from pure relief. Very nearly, but not, for she'd already determined that March wouldn't have approved of such a display, and besides, it could have gone ill for Polly below stairs.

Instead she simply waited until Polly had finished her curtsey. "Good day, Polly," she said. "I'm glad to find you here."

Polly's pale cheeks pinked, but she did not smile. "Thank you, Your Grace. I'm most grateful and honored to serve you."

And that was all that March expected her to say, too. "Now the parlor maids," he said, guiding Charlotte away from Polly to stand before the next well-scrubbed young woman.

At the end of the line, Charlotte nodded and smiled at March as confidently as she could.

"It appears to be a most excellent staff," she said. "I suspect it will take me a bit of time to learn everyone, but in a week or two, I promise to have the house running to your satisfaction."

March's brows rose with surprise. "A week or two?"

"Three at the most," Charlotte said. "You might not credit it, March, but I am a good household manager, and wise with money."

His brows rose higher. "That's not necessary, Charlotte," he said. "Nor is frugality, not for us."

She flushed. Of course he'd think that way; he was one of the wealthiest peers in the realm. "Frugality is always necessary, March," she insisted.

"It's a kind of virtue, and part of running a house well, no matter how large or small. I'm certain that once I've had a chance to look over the accounts, I'll find all kinds of small economies for us, as well as instances of tradesmen not being as honest as they should be in their reckonings with us."

"My own wife." He smiled, all fond indulgence. "I'm glad that you wish to help me in this way, but just as you are no ordinary wife, this is no ordinary household. Perhaps in time, when you are older and more experienced, you may wish to occupy yourself with domestic affairs, but it's unnecessary at present."

"But I wish to prove myself useful to you, March, as a wife should."

"All I ask is that you be happy," he said, and though he smiled still, it was clear he considered the question settled.

She sighed, for it wasn't settled at all as far as she was

concerned. She'd simply have to wait until she could prove to March that she wasn't too young to be useful to him and not simply ornamental.

"Now doubtless you would like to refresh yourself before we dine together," he continued. "Polly will show you to your rooms, and I'll join you again in half an hour's time."

He raised her hand to his lips and kissed it, his gaze never leaving hers. Perhaps bookkeeping and household accounts could wait. There were other, more interesting ways she could please her new husband, weren't there? As his lips lingered on her hand, a fresh little ripple of desire shivered through her, and she grinned.

"Only half an hour, March," she whispered. "Until then."

CHAPTER

❧ 10 ❧

Charlotte followed Polly up the staircase and down a long, echoing hallway. She'd never been in a place like Marchbourne House. Through the open doors, she saw beautiful rooms filled with valuable paintings and furnishings, yet not a soul within, like a haunted palace. She couldn't imagine how March could bear to live in such silence, and she resolved that they must fill these empty rooms with friends and acquaintances to give them life.

And children. She hoped she and March would have many children, and not just the required sons, either. She had always loved having sisters, and she knew her mother believed that only her children had kept her from losing her wits entirely when their father died. Now Charlotte in turn wanted to fill this huge, echoing house with the sounds of laughing children at play, and as soon as possible, too.

"These are your rooms, ma'am," Polly said, showing her into the last door on the hall. "I was told that these have always been the duchess's quarters. Her Grace the late dowager duchess—His Grace's mother—fancied things brought clear round from China, and that's how everything's still done now. Of course His Grace expects you to change it to suit yourself. This is your receiving room."

Charlotte caught her breath. She wouldn't dare change

anything, for surely this must be one of the most beautiful rooms she'd ever seen. The room filled one corner of the house, with tall windows on two sides and a view of the sun setting on Green Park. The curtains had yet to be drawn for the night, but because the daylight was nearly done, there was a cheerful fire in the grate and the candles had been lit, both in the silver candle stands and in the chandelier overhead. Green silk patterned with swooping gold and pink cranes was hung on the walls, and a pair of large red and gold lacquer cabinets, open to display a collection of porcelain figures, flanked the chimney.

There was a lady's desk before the window and several well-cushioned armchairs, and bouquets of fresh flowers perfumed the air. The flowers again were all bridal white, and Charlotte's heart swelled when she thought how March must have ordered those for her sake, too.

"In here is your dressing room, ma'am," Polly continued, showing Charlotte into a smaller chamber lined with chests of drawers and cabinets and a large, gold-framed looking glass. Swiftly Polly opened and shut the drawers to show that Charlotte's new clothes had already been unpacked and put away. A washstand stood to one side behind a tall, black-lacquered screen, and a lace-draped mahogany dressing table and bench were arranged before the window for the best light.

"And this last room, ma'am, is your bedchamber," Polly said. The walls were hung with more of the same pale green silk, with an enormous, opulent bed, crowned by a deep tester suspended from the ceiling and hung with embroidered curtains.

"The housekeeper called that bed by its French name, ma'am," Polly said proudly, as if by being Charlotte's maid these rooms and their contents now belonged to her as well. "It's a *lit à la duchesse,* and she said it's the only one like it in all London."

But Charlotte wasn't listening. Instead she was standing before the fireplace, drawn to the life-sized portrait that hung over it. It was clearly March as a boy, perhaps of eleven or twelve, and a beautiful boy at that. His cheeks were still childishly round, his dark hair long and falling over his shoulders. He was dressed in an informal version of a gentleman's suit, with his waistcoat exotically patterned to mimic a leopard's skin. His pose was studied, and he stood with one elbow leaning on a broken marble column, with more classical ruins behind him.

But what Charlotte noticed most was the openness in his face, how as a boy he hadn't had the guarded reserve that he stood behind now. What had happened between the boy and the man to put that guard into place? What had changed him so dramatically?

"That's His Grace's Roman picture, ma'am," Polly said. "He went all the way to Italy when he was a boy like that, with his father, the late duke."

Charlotte turned to face her. "What else have you heard in the servants' hall, Polly? Does this seem like a happy house?"

"Happy enough, ma'am," Polly said, choosing her words carefully. "It's a proud house, that's for certain, but then it would be the same with any duke. His Grace likes things done most particular, they do say that, yet they're fierce loyal to him. And they're very happy he's wed you, ma'am, very happy."

Charlotte smiled. At least that was good news. Her role as the new duchess was going to be difficult enough without having to face a mutinous household. She glanced back at March's portrait.

"Have you seen any pictures of His Grace's parents?" she asked. "His mother who had these rooms, or his father?"

"No, ma'am, I haven't," Polly said quickly, so quickly that Charlotte suspected there was more that she wasn't telling. "But oh, ma'am, mark the time! If I am to have you dressed to sup with His Grace, then we have not a moment to spare."

Charlotte let herself be shepherded into the dressing room, and stood in the center while Polly efficiently unpinned and removed her wedding gown.

"Is the duke coming here to join me?" she asked shyly. "That is, to dine?"

Through the open door, she could see her enormous new bed. Aunt Sophronia had told her that few titled couples shared a bedchamber, but that the husband would visit the wife's. She knew, too, what happened once he arrived. Growing up in the country among animals had put an end to that mystery. Mama had long ago explained the details where men and women were concerned, with Aunt Sophronia contributing a few more blunt instructions during the last few days.

But it was a considerable leap from knowledge in theory to knowledge in practice. Charlotte tried to imagine kissing March and then imagined the rest, all happening upon that very bed: having him undress her and touch and caress her as he pleased, and then finally take her maidenhead, and perhaps make their first child, too.

It wasn't that she was exactly frightened about tonight. March was a gentleman, and she trusted him too much for that. But she *was* uneasy, and worried that she would somehow not do things as a lady should to please her husband.

Wistfully she looked from the bed to the table beneath the window. She seldom thought of how her life could be otherwise than what it was, but oh, how much less complicated her wedding night would be if she and March were ordinary newlyweds!

"Perhaps His Grace and I could dine here," she suggested. "Things could be brought upstairs, and we could dine in our dressing gowns."

"His Grace sup here, ma'am? In your bedchamber?" asked Polly with surprise. "Forgive me, ma'am, but His Grace always takes his meals in the dining room, dressed properly as a duke should dress, as befits his station."

Now Charlotte was surprised. "He dines by himself in full dress for evening?"

"Yes, ma'am, he does, and he will expect you to join him there," Polly said, briskly pulling out one of Charlotte's new gowns. "I'm told the duke is a very particular gentleman about time, and he won't like to be kept waiting. Will this yellow silk polonaise please you, ma'am?"

Bewildered, Charlotte nodded. "That will do, yes."

"Very well, ma'am," Polly said, swiftly beginning to dress her. "I will be waiting for you here to help you undress, ma'am, whenever you and His Grace are done with your supper and return upstairs, and I'll take care that the maids turn down your bed."

Again Charlotte nodded, and wondered glumly if she was to be permitted ever to do anything for herself again.

Fifteen minutes later, the tall case clock in the hall was chiming the hour as she hurried through the long hallways and down the staircase to the dining room. She was flustered and flushed, but at least she was dressed as March expected and she was on time.

Or she had been until the footman at the door of the dining room informed her that His Grace was already within, and then insisted on announcing her as if there were a hundred guests waiting.

Blast, blast, blast, so now she *was* late! She raised her chin and struggled to compose herself, the way everyone else in Marchbourne House seemed perfectly able to do. She thought of Mama and reminded herself that she had always been a lady, the eldest daughter of the Earl of Hervey. Becoming a duchess would never change that. She was still who she'd always been, and with one final deep breath, she entered the dining room.

Another large, beautiful room—she was becoming numb to them now—with white walls covered with swirls of plaster garlands and more paintings. The endless mahogany dining table, covered in a damask cloth, could have seated sixty, with fifty-eight chairs pushed in close to the table. Branched silver candelabra marched the length of the table, their candles fluttering. At the distant end of the table, in an armchair that looked almost like a throne, sat March.

As soon as he saw her, he rose, and his face lit with such open pleasure that she was instantly relieved.

"My dear Charlotte," he said, coming forward to take her hand. "As foolish as it sounds, I cannot tell you how much I've missed you."

It was the first endearment he'd spoken to her as his wife, and small though it might seem, she treasured it.

"I've missed you, too." She smiled, feeling suddenly shy, exactly as she had earlier in St. Paul's. He was so *magnificent*. He, too, had changed his clothes for evening, and now wore a dark blue suit embroidered with gold vines, the linen of his shirt flawlessly white. But no matter how richly March was dressed, he still always outshone his clothes. He had a physical presence that she couldn't quite explain, and a male power that she couldn't resist—especially now, when he was regarding her with that same intense, hungry interest that he'd shown in the coach. It made her feel desired and oddly, pleasantly warm all over, with her heartbeat quickening just as it did when he kissed her.

"Sit here by me, as close as can be," he said, and she slipped into the other armchair across the corner of the table from his. "It's pathetically romantic, I know, but I pray that's forgivable on our wedding night."

"Oh, yes," she breathed. "It's entirely forgivable, and you are entirely forgiven."

At once a footman appeared to push her chair forward,

then remained standing slightly behind it. Another stood behind March's chair, and three more stood ready at the sideboard. Her goblet was instantly filled with wine, and a plate with the Marchbourne arms was placed before her. Charlotte remembered how March had said he was never alone, and now with dismay she realized how accurate he'd been.

"I hope you'll also forgive me depriving you of your rightful place at the end of this table," he said, covering her hand with his own. "But I wanted to be able to do this."

She turned her hand over so their fingers intertwined. Without looking away from her face, he began tracing small circles with his thumb on the inside of her wrist, in exactly the perfect place to make her catch her breath.

"That—that would be the least of it," she said, reaching for her wine with her other hand. "If I were clear down there, then you would have had to shout to converse with me."

"I would have done it," he said. "Mind you, I've climbed a tree for you already. But this is much easier. A toast, Charlotte."

She nodded, pausing with the heavy goblet in her hand. There had never been wine or strong waters at Ransom, and only in this last week had she first tasted wine. But Aunt Sophronia had advised that wine would help ease the wedding night, and for that reason Charlotte was determined to drink it.

"To you, my dearest bride and duchess," he said softly as he held the glass toward her. "To my Charlotte."

"To you, too, March," she said, "my dearest, dearest bridegroom and duke and—and everything else."

He raised a single dark brow, teasing. Perhaps he was following Aunt Sophronia's advice, too. "You would outdo me?"

She blushed but did not back down. "I won't outdo you, no. But I will match you."

"To you, then, Charlotte." He laughed and drank, and she did the same, emptying the glass.

"Goodness." She blinked, startled by the taste of so much wine in such an abrupt volume, and set the goblet down on the table with a thump. Instantly it was re-filled, and she steeled herself for the next toast.

"To your beauty and grace," he declared, grinning at her reaction. "Never was there a more lovely bride."

"Nor was there a more handsome bridegroom," she said promptly. "To your handsomenessnessness."

He set his glass down. "That's too many 'nesses,' madam. I cannot drink to an invented compliment."

"Very well, then," she said. "You are comely, sir. Can you drink to that?"

He winced. "I'm not sure 'comely' is an appropriate word for a bridegroom."

She frowned and tapped her finger on the stem of the goblet. The wine was making her feel exceptionally witty and daring, too. "Then what of 'virile'? Will that do? To my virile bridegroom?"

"*Virile?*" He widened his eyes with surprise and laughed. "You'd call me that?"

She laughed with him, though she wasn't sure of the source of his amusement. "Am I wrong to do so? Isn't that the proper word?"

He laughed even harder. "I should hope it's the proper word."

"Well, then." She raised her glass. "To my very virile bridegroom. Very, *very* virile."

She drank it down, before he could protest again, and he drank his as well.

But even after their glasses had been refilled, he still didn't offer a reply.

Charlotte scowled. "What, can you not think of an equal compliment for me?"

"I can think of a great many," he said, "but not one I'd wished spoken aloud of my wife."

"Hah," Charlotte said with a magnanimous flourish. "Then look elsewhere about my person for inspiration."

He nearly choked, he laughed so hard, and again she laughed with him. If marriage to him was always to be so entertaining, then they were destined to be happy indeed.

"I'll look to your other qualities," he said. "To my wife, a most excellent climber of trees."

She grinned. "To my husband," she said. "A most excellent gentleman to land atop."

"I trust I'll be the only one," he said, laughing still, and they drank again. "Here now, sweet, it would be a good notion for you to eat something along with all this wine."

Charlotte hadn't noticed when the footman had brought several dishes of food to the table. She leaned forward to consider them, and at once the footman behind her chair appeared to serve her, using a large silver spoon to ladle a grayish, creamy something onto her plate.

She stared down at it, unconvinced. The footman had carefully added a bit of the garnish to her plate, a purple flower that matched the Marchbourne livery.

"That's a fricassee of goose livers and mushrooms, with a sauce of red currants to the side," March explained proudly as he began to eat. "I'm certain you'll enjoy it. I keep both a French cook and an English one. You met them earlier. This is most likely from Monsieur Brière's kitchen, though they are both eager to please you."

She remained skeptical, both of the flowers and the livers. "Is he the one who has put the blossoms on the plate?"

"I expect it is," March said. "A pretty conceit, isn't it?"

But Charlotte's thoughts had already left her untouched plate. "Answer me true, March, if you please. Are you hungry?"

He set his fork back down on the plate with gratifying haste.

"You see, I'm not, not really." She plucked the purple flower from her plate and twirled it idly in her fingertips. "While you worry about your two cooks, I'm thinking of my poor lady's maid, waiting in my bedchamber to undress me."

"Is she now?"

Charlotte nodded, looking up at him through her lashes. That had gotten his attention earlier in the carriage, and clearly it had done the trick here again.

"I'm thinking it's barbarously ill-mannered of me to keep her waiting much longer," she said. "And I'm thinking that my virile husband would not ever wish me to—"

But before she could finish, March had pushed back his chair and dragged Charlotte into his arms. Her chair toppled backward with a crash, but neither noticed as it fell, or as a footman hesitantly replaced it. March kissed her furiously, his mouth slashing across hers with a dizzying urgency. Charlotte answered, as bold and eager now as he. Aunt Sophronia had been right. The wine had helped, and any last vestige of restraint or uncertainty had vanished—or had been vanquished—then and there. The heat that he'd stirred in her earlier in the carriage had returned as they'd made their way here, and now she felt it glowing again, a feverish fire low in her belly.

Desire, she thought, the very word titillating and forbidden. That was what it was. She *desired* her husband.

And March—March desired her, too. The way he was kissing her told her that.

"Upstairs." His voice was low and rumbling, the edge to it making her shiver with anticipation. "Now."

CHAPTER

11

This was not how March had planned this evening.

He'd envisioned his wedding night as a memorable occasion, one that he and his bride could reminisce fondly about for the rest of their lives. They'd begin with a quiet private supper in the dining room for the two of them, with wines and dishes that he'd chosen specially to please her. Afterward they'd shift to the drawing room for cordials and a special bride's cake baked in her honor. They would sit by the windows and look out at the park by moonlight (he had checked to make sure there was a nearly full moon), a favorite view that he'd anticipated sharing with her. Then they would retire upstairs, where he'd give her a decent interval to undress before he'd join her in her bedchamber and finally, joyfully yet solemnly, consummate their marriage.

That was what he had planned. But in all that careful planning, he had neglected a few important elements. He'd overlooked how lushly, lavishly beautiful Charlotte would be as a bride, and how, even in her innocence, she'd so tempted him that he'd practically tumbled her in the carriage coming home from St. Paul's.

He hadn't counted on drinking so much while he'd dressed for dinner, foolishly hoping to settle himself after the near debacle in the carriage. Nor that he'd drink even more when his genteel toast to their future had somehow lapsed into a riotous low drinking game that would rob them both of all their aristocratic decorum, nor that his bride would end up drinking to his virility in such an enchanting, enticing way that he'd wanted to demonstrate it right there. He certainly hadn't dreamed that the perfect supper would go untasted and the bride's cake in the drawing room forgotten, or that he and his duchess would act with such shameless abandon in the dining room.

And their half-drunken progress up the staircase—how could he have dreamed of that? Past more of his curtseying and bowing servants, and down the long hall to her rooms, holding so tightly to each other that they stumbled, so clumsy with desire that they laughed, then kissed, then laughed again. They reeled deliriously against walls and knocked into unnoticed chairs, and nearly tumbled back down the stairs. He had not been able to keep his hands from her, nor she hers from him, and it seemed that every dozen feet or so they'd had to stop to kiss again.

He had, in short, in all his careful planning, completely overlooked the fact that he hadn't married an icy, idealized duchess. Instead he had wed Charlotte, his Charlotte, the one lady in the world who had the charming power to both beguile and befuddle him to an astonishing degree.

And now it had come to this, with him pressing her flat against her bedchamber door while she laughed and kissed him and tried vainly to open the latch without looking. His cock was as hard as stone in his breeches, and every delicious chuckle and wriggle that she made only aroused him more. He had never wanted a woman more, and he couldn't believe that the woman was actually his wife.

Could she have any notion of how perilously close to his limit he was?

He reached around her to unfasten the latch, and when the door swung open, they stumbled forward together into her bedchamber. Charlotte's startled maid was sitting near the fire, and jumped to her feet to curtsey, some scrap of needlework in her hand. There were going to be plenty of tales told in the servants' hall tonight, and now she'd have one to contribute, too.

"Leave us," he ordered brusquely. "The duchess will call when she requires you."

The woman scuttled away into the next room, closing the door behind her. March glanced swiftly around the room. At least here everything was as he'd ordered, with flowers in the vases, the fire high, and the coverlets on the bed turned back. Unbidden, he thought of how this room had once belonged to his mother, then shoved the thought away. It wasn't his mother's bedchamber; it was the duchess's, and since Charlotte was the duchess, it belonged only to her.

With her maid gone, Charlotte looped her arms around his shoulders and smiled up at him.

"You'll have to undress me now, you know," she said, her voice a husky, confidential whisper. "I don't think I can do it myself without Polly."

"If that's a dare, Charlotte," he said, "then you are bound to lose."

He'd already made a fair start on removing her clothes somewhere on the stairs, and he'd magically shed his own coat and neck cloth as well. Her gown was pushed down over her bare shoulders, nearly uncovering her breasts, and her thick, dark hair was mussed and tumbled in charming disarray. He frowned down at her gown, trying not to be distracted by her breasts. For all the frippery, a lady's dress was not that difficult to remove. Quickly he began pulling the straight pins that held the front of her gown together over her stomacher, letting them scatter wherever they fell.

"It's not a dare," she said, and with a little harrumph she slipped her hands from his shoulders and began to unfasten the long row of buttons on his waistcoat. "Nor is it a race. Faith, why are there so many buttons to a gentleman?"

"To torment you," he said, but the sad truth was that he was the one who was being tormented. To feel her fingers moving down his chest, lower with every button, was torture indeed.

He yanked the last pin from her gown, slipped his hands inside the open bodice and pushed it back from her shoulders and down her arms, letting it fall to the floor in a soft rush of silk. She grinned and blushed, making him wonder how much of that grin came from the wine and how much simply from Charlotte herself.

"You're not afraid, are you?" he asked, wrestling the last buttons free on his waistcoat and tossing it aside.

She shook her head, heartbreakingly vulnerable for all her bravado. "Should I be?"

"I pray not," he said, more truthfully than perhaps she realized.

"You've not given me reason to be otherwise," she said, and laughed softly, a throaty little chuckle that almost undid him.

As if to prove it she untied the tapes at the waist of her petticoat and let it, too, drop to the floor. She stepped free of the pile of crumpled yellow silk, a step closer to him, and wriggled her stockinged feet from her slippers. Now she wore only her shift to her knees, and over that her stays—the same scarlet stays that he'd glimpsed in the tree, and which had haunted him for days.

Except now it wasn't a tiny triangle of imagining, but the entire tight-laced reality of Charlotte wearing them, her waist small and her breasts scarcely contained and offered upward, rising and falling with her quick breath. Her shift was such fine linen that it only seemed to accentuate what it pretended to hide. Her skin glowed through the sheer white, and through it, too, he could make out the shadowy dark mystery at the juncture of her thighs.

"I don't want you to be afraid of me," he said, reluctantly dragging his gaze back to her face. "Ever."

"I am glad of that, March." She smiled again, temptation incarnate. "But I'll have you know, too, that I am monstrously brave for a lady. Even for a duchess."

"Especially for a duchess," he said, his voice rough with the desire for possession. "*My* duchess."

He jerked his shirt free from his breeches and pulled it over his head, tossing it aside. Her eyes widened at the sight of so much uncovered male, but instead of shrinking away as he'd feared she might, she came closer, resting her palms on his chest. Slowly she spread her hands, exploring and tangling her fingers through the dark curls on his chest.

"Oh, my," she whispered with a certain pleased awe.

"You *are* brave," he growled, his hands settling on the narrowest part of her waist.

She smiled, lowering her gaze. Lower still, and her eyes widened abruptly as she saw the sizable proof of his interest in her, pushing forward through his breeches.

That was enough for him. He slid his hands down from her waist to cup her bottom, pulling her hard against his arousal. She gasped, and he kissed her hungrily, taking that little gasp into his own mouth. She slid her arms around his back, holding tightly, and slanted her mouth to let him kiss her more deeply.

Even as they kissed, it was easy enough for him to free her breasts from the rigid top of her stays, easier still to shove aside the thin linen shift to bare her nipples. He rubbed his hand across them, making them stand hard, then with his fingertips tugged and squeezed until they were even harder.

She broke away from the kiss, pressing her cheek against his with a startled little moan and arching her back to press her breast more fully into his hand. He kissed the side of her throat, where he could feel the pulse of her desire, and she shivered.

"Oh, March, what you do," she whispered. "What you do!"

But what he did next was bend down and slip his arms beneath her knees to scoop her into his arms. She gasped with surprise, a gasp that changed at once to another sweet small chuckle as he carried her the short distance to the bed. She sank into the featherbed, her dark hair fanning around her face. Her eyes were heavy-lidded with longing, and her lips were full and red from his kisses.

"What of my stays?" she asked breathlessly. "Shouldn't we try to—"

"Later," he said, climbing onto the bed beside her. He hadn't the patience for unknotting the clever lacing of a lady's maid now. Neither of them did. "I want you too much."

"I'll trust you," she said, and smiled.

Trust. She was trusting him not to hurt her and trusting him to lead the way in their lovemaking, as a husband should. He wished to be kind and patient. Respect, he knew, was key, and gentleness as well. Breathing hard, he struggled to recall the wise advice that Brecon had given him about pleasing a wife and the helpful suggestions about taking her maidenhead.

But as soon as she held her arms open to welcome him, he forgot it all.

He kissed her, and moved to lie over her, stroking her breasts and relishing the warmth of her skin. He shoved aside the skirt of her shift to discover more heated skin, and the long sweep of her thigh above her garters. She moved restlessly beneath him as she kissed him. Her hands roamed across his back, learning him, too, which only inflamed him more. His hand moved higher, unable to resist any longer.

To his shock he discovered she was already swollen and wet with desire, as feverish as he was himself. He stroked her as gently as he could, trying not to think of how tight she was around his finger, and how much tighter still she'd be around his cock. She made small shuddering moans of pleasure as he did, the most delicious sounds he'd ever heard, and she rocked against his hand as if striving to draw him inward.

He needed no more invitation. The last shreds of his self-control were gone. He tore open the buttons on the fall of his breeches to release his cock, and swiftly settled himself between her thighs. With only one thought in his mind, he plunged forward. She cried out with anxious surprise, trying to wriggle backward across the sheets and away from him, but he held her fast by the hips and pushed again. Once more, and he was buried deep.

If it was possible to find earthly paradise in a woman, then he had in Charlotte. To his remorse, he couldn't tell if Charlotte felt the same. She fluttered beneath him, with a small sound of unease that seemed infinitely worse after she'd proclaimed her bravery earlier. His conscience told him to say something, anything, to comfort and reassure her, but words of every kind seemed to have vanished from his grasp.

Damnation, what was he *supposed* to say? Her eyes were squeezed shut, closing him out, and he couldn't begin to tell what she felt. Finally he kissed her, the best he could offer in the circumstances. To his relief, she kissed him in return, her hands creeping back to clutch his shoulders, though her eyes stayed shut.

Unable to help himself, he began to move again. It didn't take long before he'd found his rhythm, his pleasure building at a thundering rate that matched his heartbeat.

But what was even better was how she'd found it, too. At first she'd moved only tentatively, but as he moved faster, so did she, rocking to meet his thrusts. He slipped his arms beneath her knees and raised them to be able to enter her more deeply, and instinctively she curled her legs around his waist, holding him in another kind of embrace. With each thrust, she began making breathy little cries that spurred him onward. Her beautiful eyes were wide open now and filled with pleasurable bewilderment over what was happening to her.

No, to them both. He'd never felt anything like this, not with any other woman. But as rare as it was, he knew he'd not last much longer. Suddenly she arched her back and stiffened, her release wresting a low, keening cry from her. He felt it, too, convulsing around him, drawing him deeper like a pond he couldn't resist. Nor did he. At once he joined her, throwing back his head to roar as he plunged one final time into her.

Exhausted, he fell forward, half on her and half to the side, his eyes closed. He didn't ever wish to move, not when he could hear her heart beneath his ear. He wasn't sure he could, anyway.

She sighed, and he felt that, too. "You told me to trust you, March," she whispered. "I did, and I—I'm so glad."

Trust. That was a word he didn't want to consider, not now, and it thumped like a thrown brick against his conscience. She had trusted him, and what had he done? Rolling away from her, he reached down to pull up his breeches and button them over his nakedness.

He felt her hand on his back, lightly tracing his spine with the tips of her fingers. He didn't deserve such gentleness from her, not after what he'd done.

"I'd no notion it would be that glorious," she said.

"Rather, it's *you* who are glorious. Ah, my own dear, dear husband!"

He was her husband, and she was his wife. There wasn't any denying it now. Reluctantly he turned and faced his new duchess.

She was curled against the pillows, her eyes heavy-lidded and wanton. Her mouth was so red it almost looked bruised from his kisses. Her hair was a bedraggled tangle around her face, with long strands pasted to her sweaty shoulders. What was left of her clothing was in crumpled disarray. Her breasts were still shamelessly displayed above the red stays and her shift shoved high over her bare thighs and stained with his leavings.

He had done this to her. She had given him her innocence, a gift a woman can offer only once, and he had ravaged it like a worthless mongrel. He had not been kind, nor had he been gentle. There had been no respect, no poetry, no wooing. He'd ignored every word of Breck's advice. He had sworn before God to honor her and promised to himself that he would only treat her with the highest regard, as a gentleman should. She had *trusted* him, and how had he responded?

He'd debased himself and dishonored her, and dragged her down to the gutter with him. He'd heeded only his lust, and forgotten everything else beyond satisfying himself. He'd torn away her clothes, thrown her to the bed, and used her like the lowest drunken sailor with a two-shilling whore.

He'd acted exactly like his father.

Her tremulous smile was enough to break his heart.

"I'm sorry, madam," he said, pushing himself from the bed and away from her. He grabbed his shirt from the floor and pulled it over his head. "I'm sorry."

"Sorry?" she asked, stunned. "Whatever do you have to be sorry for?"

He smiled bitterly. "You don't even know, do you?"

"No, I do not," she said, clearly perplexed. She crawled to the edge of the bed to watch him gather the rest of his clothes in a bundle. "You make no sense at all, March."

"I'm sorry," he said again, unwilling to say more. He'd already made enough of a shambles of this night without burdening her further, and all he could think of now was escape.

"Is it something I've done?" she asked, her voice breaking. "Did I disappoint you?"

He was appalled that she'd think such a thing.

"You will never disappoint me," he said at the door. "I only wish you could say the same of me."

Then he turned and fled.

For a long moment, Charlotte stared at the closed door. What had happened? Where had things gone so terribly wrong?

She grabbed one of the pillows, bunching it tightly into a ball in her arms to keep from crying. When Mama had explained the details of lovemaking to her, she'd thought it had sounded foolish and uncomfortable, and inelegant at best. Yet with March to guide her, she'd found joy and pleasure beyond description. He'd put aside his formal ducal self and revealed a wickedly ardent lover. She'd loved it, and she was sure now she was falling in love with him, too. Five minutes ago, she thought she'd been having the most perfect wedding night possible, with the most perfect of husbands.

And now it seemed she hadn't. She felt lost and hurt and abandoned and angry, and she couldn't begin to figure out what had made him leave as he had. With only pops from the dying fire for comfort, she was chilled and sticky and sore and stretched, with all the glorious pleasure gone with him.

She bowed her head and saw again the heavy new wedding ring on her finger. What did it signify now if her husband had no use for her? She wished she were once again with Mama and her sisters, and she wished she'd never heard of the Duke of Marchbourne, let alone married him. Finally she sobbed, unable to keep it back any longer, and punched the wadded pillow in her arms as hard as she could.

"Forgive me, Your Grace," Polly said, joining her from the dressing room. "But His Grace said you wished to undress for bed."

Charlotte's head jerked up. Polly's hands were clasped over the front of her apron and her expression was impassive, the way a good servant's was supposed to be. But if Polly had been waiting all this time in Charlotte's dressing room, as she'd been bidden to do, then she must have overheard everything that had transpired between her and March, from their first teasing encounter before the fire to the final humiliation of his departure.

Charlotte blushed, mortified, and swiftly pulled her shift up over her breasts and down across her knees. What had seemed exciting before March was shameful before anyone else.

Yet as her lady's maid stood before her, waiting for her orders, Charlotte realized that she, too, stood at a crossroads. She could throw herself weeping into Polly's arms and confess all of what had happened for the sake of the undeniable solace and commiseration one woman could give to another. Charlotte knew that, given her own age and inexperience, she was almost expected to make a confidante of her lady's maid. She'd already begun to do so while Polly had tended her at Aunt Sophronia's house, and she was sure Polly would be perfectly agreeable to continuing in that role now.

But Charlotte wasn't the same lady that she'd been even yesterday. Now she was Lady Charlotte FitzCharles, Duchess of Marchbourne, and her loyalty—as well as the rest of her—belonged to her husband. Confiding in Polly would be a betrayal of March, and no matter how much he tested her, she would not do that. Not to him, and not to herself, either.

She tossed aside the pillow and slipped from the bed. "Thank you, Polly," she said softly. "His Grace was correct. I am ready to undress for the night."

"Very well, ma'am." Polly nodded and moved behind Charlotte to begin untying her stays. "I have taken the liberty of requesting water to be heated for a bath, ma'am. The footmen should be bringing it up from the kitchen shortly."

"Thank you, Polly," Charlotte said gratefully. A hot bath was an unthinkable luxury—though not, it seemed, for a duchess. But a bath would help her to think and prepare for tomorrow. Tomorrow she would go to March and sort things out between them. Tomorrow she would make everything right.

She *would*. For what other choice, really, did she have?

CHAPTER
12

"There you are, Your Grace." Giroux, March's French valet, wiped the last flecks of soap from March's jaw and with a flourish held a small looking glass before him. "Ready for the new day."

"True enough, Giroux." Critically March studied his reflection, running his hand across his smooth-shaven jaw. There were gloomy circles beneath his eyes, and he looked like he hadn't slept. Which was to be expected, considering he hadn't. "What better way to begin a day than with a sharp razor?"

"*Tout à fait vrai,* sir," the Frenchman said, busily packing away his razor. "Shaving is what separates man from the beasts."

"Indeed," March said, turning to the coffee that the footman had just poured for him.

If all it took was having his jaw scraped free of whiskers by his valet to transform a beast into a man, then he would take it. After his disastrous wedding night, anything that would make him feel civilized was more than welcome. During those long hours alone in his bed, he'd thought far too often of his father and his poor mother, too, dark memories he'd rather not have come creeping back to plague him.

He wasn't his father, and wouldn't be. He was determined on that.

God knows he was trying his best this morning. He'd purposely followed his customary routine of replying to letters and reading the newspapers over breakfast, followed by a visit from Giroux. Next he would change his banyan for his morning clothes, and his day would begin in earnest, as it usually did.

Except that now his day must include his wife, a wife that he had treated most shamefully the night before. Inwardly he winced, remembering again how barbarously he had behaved toward her. He did not know whether she would forgive him or not, especially since he hadn't begun to forgive himself.

But they now were bound together as man and wife, and he and Charlotte would be expected to begin appearing as such today for the approval of the world, or at least their portion of London society. There were a great many people eager to make the acquaintance of his new duchess, especially since they'd wed in such haste. Fortunately, the king and the court were not at present in town, so Charlotte would be spared the ardors of a royal court presentation for another month or so.

Small grace, that. March set down his coffee cup and glanced up from the newspaper at the footman.

"Convey my morning regards to Her Grace," he said, "and inform her that the carriage will be ready at eleven to begin our calls."

He'd already decided that the carriage would be an excellent place to apologize for all his shameful actions and to vow to begin their marriage afresh. It would also be his first opportunity to prove what he promised. He would sit across from her as a gentleman should, engaging in pleasant conversation for the duration of the trip. He would make no attempts to touch her or kiss her, and he would definitely not maul her as he had yesterday.

Yet even before he'd completed that noble resolution, his lustful memory had overruled his conscience. What memories they were, too, of Charlotte sprawled wantonly before him, of her lovely, ripe breasts bared for him above those infernal scarlet stays, of how soft her skin had been beneath his hands and how warm her flesh had—

"Thank you, no," Charlotte said, suddenly not only in his thoughts but in his bedchamber, too. "I don't believe I need to be announced to my own husband."

He turned abruptly and there she was, striding cheerfully through the door. Colorfully, too: she was wearing a dark pink dressing gown of rustling silk taffeta that billowed and fluttered out behind her. The gown was tied neatly at the waist with a green sash, but it didn't begin to close the gown. Instead he had a tantalizing glimpse of her nightgown beneath, sheer white embroidered linen scarcely covering her breasts, the same round, full breasts that had filled his hands so perfectly.

Struggling to compose himself, he looked down, only to see the shape of her splendidly long legs through the fluttering silk and linen. She wore green silk backless slippers with high curving heels that clicked across the floor and, worse (or better), gave her a gait that made her breasts and hips and everything else sway and tremble. It was damnably enticing, and he would have been content to watch her walking up and down this room the whole day long.

Except he wouldn't be content at all, not until he'd been able to wrap those long legs again around his waist and—

"Good day, March," she said. "Polly asked if I wished a tray with my breakfast, but I told her I preferred to take mine with you."

Belatedly he rose to his feet to greet her, his coffee cup in his hand.

"Good day, madam," he said. "I was not expecting you."

She stopped still. Her smile remained, but he didn't miss the hurt flash quickly in her eyes, then disappear just as fast. "If you do not wish my company, why, then—"

"No, no," he said. "I did not expect you to be awake yet, that is all. I would be honored to have you join me. Please."

He looked sharply to the footmen, who hurried to bring a chair and another setting for her at his table.

"You are certain?" she asked.

"Of course," he said. "Please join me."

He sensed her relief, and hated himself all the more for having made her doubt at all. With a flurry of silk, she sat across from him. Morning sun spilled around her, turning her skin to golden ivory. If she hadn't slept, either, then it didn't show on her. Her hair looked as if she'd done it herself, a charmingly haphazard knot pinned at the top of her head. He liked it, until he realized that he liked it because it reminded him of how her hair had come down last night.

"I fear you will always see me at this hour," she said, smoothing her skirts. "I'm not a layabout kind of London lady. I'll still keep country hours, and rise with the sun."

"That is an admirable trait." He wished she hadn't called herself a layabout. He really wished she hadn't. "I generally prefer country hours myself."

"Ah, then you are a farmer at heart," she said lightly, pouring herself tea from the pot that a footman had brought. "Retiring to your own bed when the sun sets must agree with you. Do you read the newspapers like this every morning?"

"I do." So she was unhappy with him for leaving her bedchamber last night. Her reference to farmers was oblique, but he'd understood her meaning well enough.

At least she'd the sense not to make a fuss before the servants.

He refolded the paper and set it aside, determined to show that she would have his attention now.

"I have many interests and responsibilities," he explained, "with many people in my employ depending upon me for their sustenance. I regard it as my duty to be informed in the events of the day."

"Goodness." Delicately she sipped her tea, looking up at him over the edge of the cup in exactly the way she'd looked at him over her wineglass last night. "With your many responsibilities, I vow I must be grateful for whatever morsel of your attention I receive."

He grunted and frowned. It would seem that his apology to her needed to take place now, rather than later in the carriage. So be it; he'd rehearsed the words often enough as he'd lain sleepless in his own bed last night.

He motioned for the servants to leave them. As soon as they were alone, he stood and clasped his hands firmly behind his back. It was not so much that he wanted to loom over her—which, as a tall man, he couldn't help but do—but he always found it easier to speak of serious matters while standing.

Not that Charlotte understood.

"You don't have to stand in my presence, Marchbourne," she said warily, looking up at him. "I'm your wife, not a judge."

He took a deep breath. This was not going to be easy.

"Charlotte," he began. "Charlotte, there are certain things that I must say to you."

For the first time she said nothing, waiting in silence for him to continue.

"Charlotte, my dear," he started again. "My wife. I must apologize to you for last night."

She ducked her chin low. "For leaving me as you did?"

"For what I did before that," he said quickly, not wishing her to misconstrue. "I failed to treat you with the respect that you deserve, and for that I can never forgive myself."

She blushed, bewildered. "But there is nothing to forgive, is there? What you did—what we did—that is what husbands and wives are meant to do, isn't it?"

The devil take him, he was blushing now, too. "The act, yes, of course. But the manner in which I, ah, engaged, was not as befits you as my wife."

"No?" She seemed to be shrinking into herself. "I did not please you, March?"

"That is not the issue, Charlotte," he said. "The transgression was mine, not yours. You were entirely innocent, and I was in the wrong. But I give you my word of honor that it will never happen in that way again. When I come to you again in your bed, I vow to be the husband you and our children deserve, and address you only with the greatest respect."

There, he thought with relief, that was it, every word of the speech he'd so carefully planned. He smiled warmly. He expected she would thank him for his apology, or at least be grateful that there would be no recurrence of their barbaric wedding night fiasco.

She did neither. "Is that truly what you wish, March?" she asked, her voice pitifully small. "Because if it is, why, then I will agree."

"It is, Charlotte," he said firmly. "As your husband, you must trust me to know what will be best for us both."

She stared down into her cup, tracing her fingertip around and around the porcelain edge.

"I will trust you," she said finally. "Because you ask it, I will trust you. But it always returns to that, doesn't it? It's always a matter of trust."

She pushed back her empty cup and rose, drawing her dressing gown more tightly about her as if she were chilled. "Is that all, March? I should begin to dress if you wish to leave at eleven."

"That is all, that is all," he said heartily. "And I'll be proud of you whatever you wear."

"You are . . . *kind*," she said softly, then slipped around him to leave.

As she passed, her skirts brushed against his foot, and he nearly caught her arm to stop her long enough for a kiss. He wouldn't deny that he wanted to, nor did he doubt that she'd kiss him in return. But at the last moment he stopped himself, and wisely, too. How much would his word of honor as a gentleman mean if she couldn't walk through a room without him kissing her?

Instead he watched her go, the soles of her high-heeled slippers slapping gently at her bare feet as her dressing gown flicked through the doorway.

He told himself he should feel virtuous and noble. In truth he felt neither.

It was always a matter of trust.

Although the rules for new brides of a certain rank were not written down or published, they were as clear as any other law of the land to those forced to obey them. Both Aunt Sophronia and Mama had explained these rules to Charlotte, and even a male like March seemed completely familiar with their intricacies.

As the newly minted Duchess of Marchbourne, Charlotte was expected to call upon every other important lady in London society, over two hundred in all. The calls themselves were not of importance. A quarter hour in each drawing room and a swallow of tea accompanied by the most general conversation would do. What mattered was that Charlotte present herself in her new role, and with her presence grace those drawing rooms. If the Dowager Duchess of Marchbourne still lived, then she would have accompanied Charlotte, easing her

way and making the proper introductions. A FitzCharles
sister or sister-in-law could have performed the same
role. But since March had no female relations, he offered himself as Charlotte's companion for the first few
days, until she learned how the calls should be done.
While this was an unusual gesture for a husband, one
sure to be much remarked and whispered about, no one
dared say anything to his face. He was, after all, the
Duke of Marchbourne, and entitled to do as he pleased.

On that first day, Charlotte was grateful to have him
with her, too. She did not enjoy the calls. The other ladies were all at least as old as her mother, and most
were of an age to match Aunt Sophronia, and equally
intimidating. The conversations were almost exactly the
same. The state of the weather was followed by polite
queries about the wedding and congratulations on the
good fortune of the match. They recalled her parents
and his in the most general way. They admired her ring
and clothes, and purred and praised her to March as if
she were some costly, precious new acquisition.

Finally there was the inevitable, excruciating subject
of an heir. The appraisals of Charlotte's form for child-
bearing ("Forgive me for remarking it, Your Grace, but
you do appear a slender lady for producing sons."), the
comments about her breeding pedigree ("Your mother
had only daughters, did she not? Pity."), and the pre-
dictions of pregnancies ("I vow, Your Grace, that you
will be brought to bed nine months from this day.") pretended to be good-humored. But to Charlotte the comments were all not-so-subtle reminders of why she and
March had married in the first place. She found them
mortifying, and she was sure that March must feel the
same.

That is, she guessed he must, but she did not know
for certain. How could she? Though they had spent the
entire day in each other's company, he had behaved like

a well-mannered stranger. He had smiled with obvious admiration, and complimented her, and held her hand when they walked together, and listened to what she said with polite attention, but there had been no intimacy to any of it. He had steadfastly kept to the carriage seat opposite hers, and the extent of their kissing had been his mouth hovering over the back of her hand.

He could speak as much as he wished about how she had not displeased him last night, but how could she think otherwise, when the proof was right before her?

By the end of the afternoon, she was exhausted and perilously close to weeping before him. The last call had been to an elderly marchioness in St. James's Square, and as they left, she looked longingly across the square to Aunt Sophronia's house. Knowing how disorganized Mama always was, she wondered if their coach had already left for Ransom Manor, or if Mama and her sisters might still be within.

"I know we haven't planned it, Charlotte," March said, taking note, "but I have a bit of business to look after at my club, and if you'd like to visit your aunt while I—"

"Oh, yes, please!" she cried, then realized too late how that must have sounded. "That is, March, I would enjoy such a visit very much, if it is agreeable to you."

She wished he hadn't been quite so quick to agree, nor that he had looked so relieved to be rid of her, either. They'd only been married a day, she thought sadly. How could they already be tired of each other's company?

As she climbed the familiar steps to Aunt Sophronia's house, a footman in Marchbourne livery with her, she resolved to keep her sorrow to herself. She didn't want to worry her aunt or her mother, nor did she wish to seem like a selfish, spoiled bride by complaining that her husband was too thoughtful and kind. March didn't deserve that. All she longed for was a few comforting minutes in a familiar place, with family who accepted her as she was and wouldn't ask her if, after one night, she was already with child.

But she soon learned from the butler that Mama and her sisters had in fact left at dawn, as they'd planned. Her disappointment was so overwhelming that, combined with everything else about this miserable day, she promptly burst into tears as soon as she saw Aunt Sophronia in her parlor.

"Why, Charlotte, what is this?" her aunt said, rising with surprise. "What reason have you to weep so?"

"I—I haven't any," Charlotte said, her voice squeaking upward with tears, and when her aunt held out her arms to her, she fell into them, sobbing against her shoulder.

Aunt Sophronia let her cry, patting her gently on the back while her small white dogs barked and raced about from excitement.

"There now, there," she said when at last Charlotte was too exhausted to weep more. "Now tell me the reason for this. Don't say that there isn't one, because you wouldn't be spilling such torrents if there weren't. What's amiss? Where is the duke?"

"He—he's at his club," Charlotte said, fumbling for her handkerchief. "I can only stay for a little while."

"Every gentleman retreats to his club when he tires of women's company." Her aunt pressed her own handkerchief into Charlotte's hand. "Is that all this is? You are disappointed that he has not made you the entire sphere of his life?"

Charlotte shook her head, scattering her tears. "Last—last night, he came to my bed and—and loved me, and it was perfect and wonderful and I—I believed myself to be blessed to have such a husband."

Her aunt smiled. "Well, then. Most ladies would beg to have such troubles."

"But that *is* my trouble, Aunt!" Charlotte cried forlornly, pressing the handkerchief to her eyes. "Because

I thought what we did was wonderful and fine and perfect, and he did not. Last night, he—he left me as soon as we were done, and then this morning, when I went to him at breakfast in—in my new pink dressing gown, he only told me that he—he had behaved disrespectfully toward me in my bed, and that he was very sorry, and promised that he would never be that—that way again, when that is what *I* would wish!"

"The duke did not enjoy making love to you?" Aunt Sophronia asked, her mouth tight with dismay.

Charlotte shook her head forlornly, pressing the handkerchief into a tight, soggy ball.

"At first I thought that he did, but now I know he didn't," she confessed. "All this day he has kept to his word, and been very honorable, and not touched me or kissed me once. And—and I would rather it were the other way. Oh, Aunt, I must be such a harlot, to feel so!"

"Hush, don't say such a thing, even in jest," Aunt Charlotte said quickly, "because it cannot be true. You're a Wylder. You're not a harlot."

"Then why doesn't he desire me?"

"He hasn't said that, my dear," Aunt Charlotte said. "At least not how you've told it to me. What is more likely is that the duke, being a young man in the deepest throes of passion, fears that he treated you not as a lady but as a harlot."

Charlotte blotted her eyes with the wadded handkerchief, yet still the tears came. "That's exactly what he said."

Her aunt nodded sagely. "All his carnal experience will have been with courtesans, concubines, actresses, and other harlots, you see, as it would be with most bachelor gentlemen. Even a gentleman free of scandal such as the duke will have resorted on occasion to low congress with unfortunate creatures in brothels and bagnios. It gives gentlemen satisfaction and bodily relief, but no notion of how to treat their lady wives."

Charlotte nodded. She did not want to think of March with low creatures in brothels, but she couldn't deny that it was possible. While she had liked the way that, in their urgency, they hadn't bothered to undress all the way, even she could understand how that had not been entirely genteel.

"But what can I do now?" she asked, mystified. "How can I make him desire me again?"

"Oh, he already desires you," Aunt Sophronia said gravely. "I should think after last night's performance you should have little doubt of that. He was wrong to arouse you in the way he apparently did. But he is aware of this, gentleman that he is, and clearly he is trying to correct his errors."

"He is," Charlotte said slowly. What her aunt was telling her made perfect sense, and the more she considered it, the more relieved she felt.

"You must do your part, Charlotte," her aunt continued. "You cannot act like a slattern. You must turn that desire into a more honorable regard. A single glass of wine at supper and no more, so you do not lose hold of your own passions. Receive him to your bed as a lady would, and remember to remain so. Don't wail or thrash about, or use profanity or other lurid expressions only fit for Covent Garden. The duke is your husband and will be the father of your children. There is no need to entice him with brothel tricks."

Charlotte nodded eagerly. "So I should wear my new nightshift tonight?"

"I can think of nothing better." Her aunt smiled warmly, and patted her cheek. "The finest white linen, decorously embroidered, is exactly right for a duchess. Arrange your hair simply, and have your face scrubbed clean, without any paint. Give him nothing that will stir memories of those wretched women from his past. He will respect you the more, and in time love you for it as well."

"That is all I really wish for," Charlotte said wistfully. "For him to love me."

Aunt Sophronia smiled. "How can he not, when you are so eminently lovable? In time he will love you. I am sure of it. A bit of patience, a fine show of wifely virtue, and his love will be yours."

CHAPTER

 13

The business that March had claimed to take him to his club was not exactly business. He had gone there hoping to find his cousin Brecon, and his hope had bordered on desperation. His marriage was barely a day old, and already it was making him uneasy. He'd blundered badly on his wedding night, and though he thought he'd mended things this morning, he clearly hadn't. His first day as a married gentleman had only gone rattling downhill after breakfast, and he had a distinct suspicion that it hadn't reached the bottom yet. He'd only to recall how Charlotte had practically leaped from the carriage to get away from him and back to her family to understand that.

No, the sooner he could speak to Brecon, the better.

Fortunately, his cousin was a creature of habit, and March found Brecon where he always was at this time of day, sitting in the same leather armchair in the same corner of the upstairs parlor. He'd a glass, his pipe, and an open book, the perfect picture of a contented man, without any taxing strife in his house to disturb him. March envied him.

"Ah, the happy bridegroom," Brecon said, closing his book as March joined him. "I'm surprised your lady parted with you so soon."

With a groan, March dropped heavily into the next

chair. He was glad they were off in this corner, away from anyone who might overhear them. It was one thing to speak of Charlotte to Brecon, but quite another to bandy her name about the club, and he wouldn't do it.

"The lady is back in the dragon's lair," he said, "where she would much prefer to be than with me."

Breck's brows rose with surprise. "Not to stay?"

March shook his head. "I'll gather her back within the hour. She hasn't abandoned me. Not yet, anyway. Though I wouldn't wonder if she refused to come out to me when I call for her again."

"But what has happened? When I waved you two away in your carriage yesterday, I could not imagine a happier pair."

A waiter appeared to offer March wine or other refreshment, but he quickly shook his head. After last night, he wasn't sure he'd ever wish to drink again.

"We were happy as we left St. Paul's, and happier still as we dined. Brecon, I've never known another lady who was more agreeable, more amusing, more charming in conversation, more—"

"Until you landed in her bed," Brecon said shrewdly, pointing the stem of his pipe for emphasis. "That's it, isn't it? Were you too forcefully ardent for the lady? Did she weep and beg you to cease?"

March dropped his head back against the chair and looked up at the ceiling, unable to meet his cousin's gaze.

"I'll admit it freely," he said. "You don't have to say it. I didn't follow your advice. I didn't woo her, and I forgot the pretty compliments."

"Was it really so bad as that, cousin?" Brecon asked. "Compliments aren't everything, however pretty. Perhaps you are remembering it worse than it was."

"I was halfway to being drunk before we even sat at the table," March admitted. "We both drank more—a good deal more—without eating. Then we stumbled to her bedchamber, where I tore away half her clothes, shoved her on the bed, and took her."

"And for this performance, you were likely rewarded with tears and wailing," Brecon said. "Not that I could blame the lady."

March paused, still staring at the ceiling and wondering exactly how much to say, even to his cousin. After his own deplorable behavior, Charlotte should have been expected to cry and wail, as Brecon said. But she hadn't. Instead he would have sworn that she'd found her pleasure, too, which had only added to his own shame. Innocent that she was, she'd trusted him so completely that she hadn't even realized that what he'd done to her was wrong.

"We were both in our cups," he said finally. "I don't believe she was entirely, ah, aware."

He dared to glance at Brecon. He wished he hadn't. His cousin was glaring at him with a mixture of contempt and disgust.

"You poured wine down the poor lady's throat until she was too drunk to notice that you'd ravished her?" he said, incredulous. "*That* was your wedding night? No wonder she's retreated to her aunt's house. I wouldn't be surprised to learn that she'd run clear back to Ransom. Who could fault her?"

"I apologized this morning," March said quickly, leaving out how Charlotte had been the braver one, making the first step by coming to his rooms. "I promised last night's, ah, excesses would never be repeated, and that we would begin anew, as if they hadn't happened."

Now it was Brecon who groaned. "Cousin, cousin! Women are constitutionally incapable of pretending an event didn't happen. Their very beings cannot permit it. On the contrary, they will never forget anything, particularly any injustice perpetrated by a man."

At once March recalled the grim time with Charlotte

earlier today in the carriage. No matter how cheerful and respectful he'd attempted to be, Charlotte had only looked at him with the saddest possible eyes.

"Perhaps that explains it," he said slowly. "I'd thought she'd accepted my apology, but today she's made me feel as if I've kicked a puppy."

"Elaborate apologies don't work," Brecon declared. "The grander they are, the less women are inclined to accept them. Worse, they'll suspect you for them, too. And there is also the likelihood that despite the participation of Bacchus, she recalls a good deal more of last night than she has admitted to you. She may be as queasy with guilt and remorse as you are, and heartily wishes you'd stop reminding her of her part."

March frowned and leaned forward, lowering his voice even further. "She was a virgin, Brecon. I'd proof of that, and I won't have you say otherwise."

Brecon rolled his eyes. "I never did say that. I said she might have felt guilty after your, ah, initiation, which implies a nicely developed conscience."

March sat back in his chair, not entirely convinced, but Brecon was already circling back to his first topic, like a country preacher turned dogged with his sermon.

"No, no, cousin," he said. "There must be no histrionics, no breast-beating or gnashing of teeth. 'Tis much better to make your apologies heartfelt but brief, and then move along. Distract the lady from her wounds with a pretty bauble and then take her to some public place so she can display her trophy."

March nodded. Dogged or not, his cousin did make sense. He'd kept out a few more of the family's jewels—necklaces, bracelets, and earbobs—that Carter and Boyce had brought for his inspection. He could give Charlotte one of those tonight, as she dressed. A sizable pair of pearls for her ears would surely count as a peace-making bauble, and they'd be most handsome swinging against her neck, too.

"Here now, March, I've a notion," Brecon said, leaning forward. "Why don't you come as my guest to the old Theatre Royal tonight? Introduce your lady to the delights of the playhouse. I've seats in my box that will go begging if you don't, and you know how women love a good play."

Actually, March didn't. Once he'd passed the age of ogling actresses and dancers with his friends when they'd come down to town from university, he'd lost interest in the gaudy foolishness of the theater, and he never had attended a play with a lady.

But attending a play with Charlotte would be different. If his cousin recommended a diversion, then there couldn't possibly be anything more diverting than this. To enter the Duke of Breconridge's private box on the arm of her new husband, to have the whole playhouse turn to gaze at her as the new Duchess of Marchbourne and admire her clothes, her beauty, her general good fortune—what lady could wish for more?

"That is a fine idea," he admitted, imagining Charlotte's excitement. He was almost certain she'd never seen a play, and he liked being the one to take her to her first. "I'll accept your offer."

"It *is* a fine idea, and I cannot tell you how proud I shall be to have you as my guests." Brecon grinned and tapped the stem of his pipe against his cheek. "You'll see. After she makes merry with us and receives the admiration of the world, she'll go home in as delightful a humor as any woman ever can."

At last March smiled, his first honest smile of the afternoon. He'd much prefer to have Charlotte in a delightful humor than gloomy as a sad-eyed puppy.

"And then, cousin," continued Brecon, "when you return to your house and your lady invites you to join her in her bedchamber—why, you, sir, will be the beneficiary, as well as the most contented bridegroom in London."

Although tonight's play wasn't new—a revival of Otway's old *Venice Preserv'd*—the famed Mr. Garrick himself was again playing Pierre, one of his best roles. Every ticket was sold, and the crush inside the playhouse was rivaled only by the crowds on foot and in carriages outside in Drury Lane.

"Hurry, March, hurry," Charlotte said as they slowly made their way up the stairs to Breck's box. "I don't want to miss a moment of the play."

"We're going as fast as we can, Charlotte," he said, and in fact they were going faster than most others trying to get to their seats. Not only did they have footmen and ushers before them to clear their way through the crowd—for, as Charlotte was still learning, such was the power of a duke's rank and wealth—but they'd an added advantage in specifically being the Duke and Duchess of Marchbourne.

March would stand out in any crowd by merit of his height and presence, but tonight, dressed as he was in a magnificent suit of dark red silk, Charlotte was sure he must be the most gloriously handsome gentleman in all London. She liked how he refused to powder his dark hair or wear a fashionable wig, and she liked even more how he smiled only at her, no matter how many others greeted him.

But as she let him lead her through the crowd, she realized that just as many of the people were staring at her. She wore a gown so new that it had been delivered from Mrs. Cartwright's shop that afternoon. It was her first in the French style, a true *robe à la française* with a deep square neckline and graceful pleats that flowed down the back, drifting behind her as she walked. The silk was a pale gold stripe with puffs of lace and ribbon zigzagging along the two sides of the overskirt, and there were more ruffles and ribbons on her petticoat. Her stomacher was embroidered with pink silk carnations framed by gold lace, and she'd more lace at the deep cuffs on her sleeves.

Yet as grand as her gown was, it paled beside the earrings that March had presented to her while she'd been dressing. Teardrop pearls swung from clusters of diamonds, the pearls so large that if she'd seen them anywhere else she would have been sure they were glass. Of course they weren't, not from March. As she'd hooked them into her ears, he'd solemnly explained how the ladies in his family had always been famous for their pearls, and now she would be, too.

Best of all, as she'd sat before her glass after Polly had finished dressing her hair, he'd come behind her. She'd been sure he meant to admire the pearls, but instead he'd bent to kiss her on the nape of her neck, a place so sensitive that she'd gasped from surprise, and spread her fingers with pleasure against the edge of her dressing table.

He'd said nothing, nor had she, but the glances that they'd exchanged in her looking glass had been so intense that she'd blushed. She didn't believe that such a kiss qualified as unfit for a wife by Aunt Sophronia's rules, not after March had given her the astonishing pearls. At least she prayed it didn't, and as she followed his broad shoulders through the crowd, she dared to hope that that single kiss might lead to much more later that night.

"Here we are at last," March said as the usher bowed ostentatiously before the last little door in the hall. "Like fighting our way through Bedlam, that was."

Charlotte turned sideways to squeeze her hoops and skirts through the doorway, then caught her breath as she saw the scene before her. To Charlotte the curving rows of boxes seemed like some shopkeeper's fanciful display, with ladies and gentlemen dressed in so much finery that the crowd glittered and sparkled by the scores of candles. The stage was still empty, but below them the orchestra was already playing some spirited, exotic music that set the mood for the play to come.

"Ah, Duchess, I am honored," said March's cousin, the Duke of Breconridge, stepping forward to greet her. "Surely my box has never been graced by such a loveliness as yours."

He took her hand, kissing the air over the back of it, and gave her fingers a small fond squeeze for good measure. Charlotte had already determined that Breconridge was March's favorite cousin and his closest friend as well, and for that reason she'd resolved to like him, too. But then it was easy to like Breconridge: he was charming and droll, his eyes always full of merriment, and where March could be solemn and perhaps a bit too ducal, Breconridge's good nature could put a stone statue at ease.

Also unlike March, Breconridge cheerfully embraced the full extravagance of the French court's fashion, his suit embellished with winking brilliants and silver embroidery. On a lesser gentleman, the glittering effect might have dimmed the wearer, but not on Breconridge. He'd so much masculine confidence and presence that he could have been wearing the crown jewels, and all anyone would recall afterward was his intelligence, his wit, and his easy laugh. With so much grandeur about his own person, it didn't surprise Charlotte that Breconridge noticed her new earrings at once.

"If you please, Duchess, closer to the lights, so that I might admire your jewels," he said, peering at the earrings as he led her to one of the chairs at the front of the box. "March, are those the Medici pearls?"

"They are," March said. "She wears them well, doesn't she?"

Charlotte smiled and shook her head to make the heavy pearls swing. As pleased as she was by March's gift, she was happier still to hear the pride in his voice and to see it, too, as he looked at her.

"She does indeed," Brecon said. "Yet as extravagant as those pearls are, Duchess, they only enhance your own beauty."

Charlotte blushed. "You are most generous, Duke."

"Please, call me Brecon," he said with a bow. "After all, we are cousins now, too. Come, you must show your earrings to Mrs. Shaw, while I pray she won't crave a pair for herself."

Belatedly Charlotte realized there was another lady in the box. She was small and round, with green eyes and red hair that gleamed, unrepentant, through the heavy white powder. She was richly though quietly dressed, a subdued dove in dark gray silk beside Breck's gaudy male peacock. She'd also a prodigious bosom that threatened to spill forward as she curtseyed deeply to Charlotte. March had mentioned that Brecon was a widower of many years, and it made perfect sense that he'd have a lady with him for companionship.

"Duchess, this is Mrs. Harriet Shaw, a dear friend of mine," Brecon said. "Harriet, Her Grace the Duchess of Marchbourne."

"Your Grace," murmured Mrs. Shaw, smiling as she rose. "May I offer my best wishes upon your recent marriage."

"Thank you," Charlotte said, her cheeks pinking. No matter how many times she'd heard that today, she still hadn't wearied of being reminded that she'd married March, and she curled her fingers more tightly into his, hoping he felt the same.

But clearly what he was feeling at that moment had nothing to do with Charlotte.

"Mrs. Shaw," he said curtly, then devoted himself

to settling Charlotte in her chair. He moved his closer to hers, possessively claiming her hand again. Though Charlotte smiled happily up at him and he smiled back, she couldn't help but sense that something was amiss.

"I hope my box pleases you, Duchess," Brecon said, taking the chair on her other side. "They say the best boxes are to the center of the ring, as close as can be arranged to the royal box. But I much prefer to be here at the farthest end."

"I can see why you do, Duke," Charlotte said, leaning over the edge of the box for a better view. "You can see the stage perfectly."

He laughed. "Oh, what occurs on the stage is of little interest to me, Duchess. The real drama takes place in the audience. From this seat, I can watch all around me without the trouble of craning my neck. But more important, they can watch me."

He smiled winningly, but on her other side, March grumbled in disagreement.

"You're mistaken, Brecon," he said. "It's not you they're ogling. It is my divine duchess, born of the star-filled firmament, that draws their eye and holds it."

Swiftly Charlotte looked up at him. In the short time they'd known each other, he'd never made her that kind of pretty compliment. She liked it, liked it very much, and liked it all the more because she suspected he'd likely written it out and practiced it carefully beforehand. She knew because his smile was lopsided and more than a little self-conscious. She knew, too, that he'd done it solely to please her, and that pleased her most of all.

Impulsively she reached up and kissed him, her lips brushing lightly over his. To her surprise—and delight—he slipped his fingers around her jaw and held her there, kissing her in warm return.

"There you are, cousin," Brecon said dryly. "You see

how much wifely goodwill you've earned for yourself by giving her those pearls."

"Forgive me, but I am not so shallow as that," Charlotte declared warmly. "My regard for my husband has nothing to do with the pearls, and *everything* to do with the duke himself."

"Then you are wise beyond your years, Duchess, and your husband is fortunate among men." Brecon smiled in concession and swept his hand through the air to include the rest of the theater. "But there, didn't I tell you? The best show is to be found not on the stage but in my box, and the rest of these folk agree."

She looked back at the rest of the audience and realized that he hadn't exaggerated. Nearly every pale face was turned toward her, eagerly watching and waiting for her to kiss March again.

"Enough, Brecon," March said, defending her just as she had him. "My duchess doesn't know you as I do, and she's far too generous in her nature to understand that what you say is teasing and nothing more."

"Very well, cousin, very well," Brecon said with an affected sigh. "But I meant what I said about your good fortune."

Before March could answer, the curtain rose, and the play began with a thundering of drums. Charlotte sat back in her chair, prepared to enjoy herself. The only plays she had seen before were the ones presented on a makeshift stage by traveling companies at the midsummer fairs, and she couldn't wait to see one performed properly.

But while she was sure the acting was most excellent and the actors and actresses all knew their lines properly (which could not have been said of those plays at the fair), Charlotte found the play difficult to follow. The language of the play was old-fashioned, the lady who was supposed to be some sort of beautiful queen wasn't beautiful at all, and the story, as much as she could make sense of it, was all politics and murder and betrayals that weren't very interesting.

Before long her attention began to wander. Brecon was right. The dramas in the audience were much more interesting than the one on the stage. In the boxes across the theater and in the pit below people were quarreling, flirting, eating, drinking, playing with pet dogs, falling asleep, and making love, and the clothes they were wearing were better than the costumes on the stage, too.

Their own box was no exception. Not long after the play began, March had rested his arm across the back of her chair. When Charlotte didn't rebuff him—which of course she wouldn't—he let his arm gradually slip forward until it rested against her back. She smiled and forgot the resolutions she'd made to her aunt about being the perfect, reserved lady. Instead she leaned against March's side, pretending as he had that it had happened by accident, and he finished things by curling his arm around her entirely to hold her close. With a happy sigh, she rested her head against his shoulder, and thought it the most pleasant place in the world to be.

But as distracted as she was by March, she didn't miss what was happening on her other side. Brecon and Mrs. Shaw appeared engrossed in the play, their gazes never leaving the stage. Below the edge of the box, however, Mrs. Shaw's plump little hand made speedy progress from his knee to the inside of his thigh and finally vanished beneath his coat and into the fall of his breeches. Nor was Brecon idle, either, his own hand finding the pocket-opening on the side of Mrs. Shaw's petticoats.

Curious, Charlotte leaned forward, wondering how far matters would progress.

"For God's sake, Charlotte, don't watch them," March whispered. "At least act as if you don't notice."

She looked up at him and flashed a conspirator's grin.

He frowned, trying to look stern, but his mouth kept twitching as he tried not to smile in return.

Charlotte hadn't that much self-control. Instead she snapped open her fan and used it to hide the lower half of her face. But still her quaking shoulders betrayed her as she struggled to swallow a wave of inappropriate giggles, even as Mrs. Shaw's ministrations were making Brecon shift restlessly in his chair.

"Charlotte, stop," March whispered again. "Please. Pay them no heed."

But beneath her shoulder she felt the telltale tremors of his own suppressed laughter, which made it all the harder to keep her own back. It didn't help that the scene on the stage was a quiet one, with much whispered plotting and conniving, and if she and March laughed aloud, the whole theater would have known it, too. She rather wished he would. To her mind, he didn't laugh nearly enough.

But the playhouse perhaps wasn't the best place for that. Purposefully she sat upright, apart from March, and it was only by thinking the saddest thoughts—and not looking once at March—that she was able to recover.

But later, when the play was done and she and March were finally alone in their carriage with the footman latching the door, it was another story altogether.

"Oh, *goodness*!" she exclaimed gleefully, bubbling with laughter. "Your cousin and Mrs. Shaw! What *were* they doing during the play?"

"You know perfectly well what they were doing, Charlotte," March said as he tossed his hat on the seat beside him.

"No, I don't," she protested. "That is, not exactly. That was why I was so interested."

March groaned. "I suppose you don't, which is much

to your credit as a lady. Which is considerably more than can be said of Mrs. Shaw."

"Why?" Intrigued, Charlotte's eyes widened. "I thought she was some manner of respectable widow, a friend of your cousin's."

"Widow?" March said with a disgusted snort. "If there ever was a Mr. Shaw, then I pity the wretch. Mrs. Shaw is my cousin's mistress, Charlotte, and has been for over a year."

"She *is*?" Charlotte's mouth dropped open. "Oh, March! I've never been in the company of a true ruined woman!"

"You shouldn't have been in the company of one tonight," he said. "I would never have accepted Breck's invitation if I'd known she'd be there, too. Nor would I have brought you to that play if I'd known it would feature a Venetian courtesan for the heroine."

"She *was*?" Charlotte laughed uproariously. "March, I am such a noddy! I thought she was some sort of noble lady. A duchess like me."

"That was Belvidera," he said. "Aquillina was the courtesan, and she is in no ways like you. I love and respect my cousin as I would a brother, but there are times when he entirely forgets himself. I do not know what devil possessed him to suggest I bring you here this night."

Still grinning, Charlotte looked slyly at him.

"Perhaps, March, Brecon judged the evening to be a good way to make you laugh, and be a little less stern."

He stared at her, genuinely shocked. "I am not stern," he said. "I am responsible, but not stern. You don't truly believe I'm stern, do you?"

Too late she realized she'd wandered into dangerous territory, but now that she'd dared this far, she couldn't exactly turn back.

"You are not stern to me, no," she said carefully. "But

there are other times when I fear the world must see you that way."

"That is because the world expects me to be a worthless, drunken, whoring rake," he said, his voice suddenly both bitter and weary. "The world will say that it's in my blood, that I cannot help it. The world has the lowest of expectations for me, Charlotte, and would like nothing better than to see me fulfill them."

"Oh, March." She came to sit beside him, taking his hand in hers. She remembered that lascivious old king who was his great-grandfather, but she'd never dreamed it would weigh so heavily on March after a century. "The world is quite an ass if it believes that of you."

He didn't smile as she'd hoped, but stared down at their linked hands.

"The world will believe what it pleases, Charlotte," he said in the same weary voice. "I can only do and say what I believe to be honorable and right, as a gentleman, a peer, a husband, and, God willing, as a father as well."

"You are all those things to me, March," she said fervently. "And we will be blessed with children. I know we will."

He did not answer, leaving the sounds of their horses' hooves on the cobbles and the creaking of the carriage's springs to fill the silence. She leaned her head on his shoulder, the same way she had in the theater.

"I should like it above all things if you came to me tonight," she said softly. "So we might, ah, begin again. If it pleases you, that is."

And at last he smiled. "My own Charlotte," he said. "Nothing could ever please me more."

CHAPTER

14

"You look most lovely, ma'am," Polly said, folding the coverlet neatly over Charlotte's lap. "Forgive me for speaking plain, ma'am, but I'm sure His Grace will be enchanted."

"Thank you," Charlotte murmured, too anxious to say more. She wanted March to be enchanted. She wanted him to forget last night and remember only this. She wanted everything to be perfect. Most of all, she wanted to be loved.

Because, heaven help her, she was already more than a little in love with him.

As soon as they'd returned home from the theater, he had gone to his rooms, and she had come here to hers. Polly had undressed her, replacing the elaborate gown with the embroidered white nightshift that she'd planned to wear last night. Charlotte herself unhooked the pearl earrings from her ears and put them back in their shagreen case for safekeeping. She'd been tempted to wear the pearls to bed, but somehow she doubted that Aunt Sophronia would approve.

Polly had unpinned her hair and brushed it out over her shoulders and down her back, and then had helped her into the bed. Charlotte sat in the exact center, propped against the mounded pillows that Polly had carefully arranged, just as now she was arranging the sheets and coverlets and smoothing everything over Charlotte's legs so there wasn't so much as a wrinkle in all that sea of cloth. Finally she twisted a few locks of Charlotte's hair over her shoulders, coaxing them into curls. With a satisfied nod, she stepped back.

"Will there be anything else, ma'am?" she asked.

Charlotte shook her head, but carefully, so as not to disturb any of Polly's careful arranging. She glanced down at her hands, flat on the edge of the coverlet because she hadn't known what else to do with them, the heavy diamond wedding ring winking on her finger. She'd done everything that Aunt Sophronia had advised to be the model duchess to receive her duke, and she prayed March would find it all agreeable.

She felt like a precious doll, placed on a high shelf so she'd not be mussed.

At least she didn't have to wait long. Soon after Polly left, March tapped at her door and entered.

"Good evening, Charlotte," he said solemnly, pausing at the door. He, too, was properly ready for bed, and over his white nightshirt wore a long black silk banyan embroidered with fierce red dragons. He looked very tall and very imposing, like some sort of mysterious ancient lord. He also looked very handsome and manly, and as he crossed the room toward her, she felt a warm flutter of excited anticipation gathering low in her belly.

"You're beautiful," he said, sitting on the edge of the bed beside her. "That is, you are always beautiful, but like this—it's for me."

"It is." She smiled shyly, and touched her fingers to the edge of the banyan. "I like the dragons."

He smiled crookedly. "I'd rather hoped you'd like the man inside them."

"I do." She reached up to lay her hand across his jaw. He'd shaved again: a small favor for her that she appreciated. "Will you join me?"

"Thank you, madam," he said solemnly. He shrugged the banyan from his shoulders and lifted the coverlet.

She moved across, making room for him. She tried to recall her aunt's directions about how she must leave everything to him and not be forward or slatternly. The advice about being a perfect duchess had made perfect sense in her aunt's drawing room, but here, in bed with March, it would be much more difficult to follow. She was more anxious now than she'd been last night.

He settled beside her on the bed and leaned forward to kiss her. His unbound hair slipped forward beside his face, and abruptly, horribly, she began to giggle.

"What is it?" he said, drawing back with a frown. "What have I done?"

"Nothing, March, nothing," she said, mortified. "It's only that I've never seen you before with your hair untied and not clubbed back in a queue, and—and I do not know why, but it made me laugh."

But to Charlotte's dismay, he saw no humor in it. "If my hair disturbs you," he said, "I can go have it tied back, and return."

"No, please don't go," she said, daring to touch the front of his nightshirt. The opening at the throat was unbuttoned and deep, and she'd a tantalizing glimpse of the dark hair that curled on his chest. She remembered how that hair had teased her nipples last night when he'd moved over her, how much she'd enjoyed it even though, in retrospect, it had been another of those slatternish things she'd done wrong. "Please stay. Please."

"You are certain?"

"I am," she said. To prove it, she reached up and ran her fingers through his hair. "I like your hair, anyway. It's thick, like a lion's mane."

At last he smiled. "I promise not to bite."

"How kind of you," she said, reassured by that smile. "A lion, then. I like lions."

"I thought you liked dragons."

"I do," she said. "I like lions and I like dragons. And you, Duke. I like you best of all."

He kissed her then, and she slipped her arms over his shoulders. Surely that wasn't slatternly, but oh, how difficult this was going to be to remain a well-bred duchess!

While his kiss began as gentle and reverent, exactly as he promised, the longer her kissed her, the more demanding it became. Without removing her nightshift, he began caressing her breast, and though his touch was as delicious as she remembered, it was muted by the linen between them. She longed to remove it, to shrug it over her head and toss it aside, but she didn't dare. Aunt Sophronia had been most specific about the nightshift, and she didn't want to disappoint March again.

At least he didn't seem to be disappointed so far. Breathing hard, he moved across her, pulling her nightshift to her hips and no farther. He eased her legs apart and settled between them. His cock was already hard, the way it had been last night, and she held her breath in expectation.

Last night she'd been stunned by how easily her body had accommodated him and how rapidly her first discomfort had blossomed into such exquisite pleasure. She had shamelessly wrapped her legs about his waist to take him deeper, and she had writhed and rocked and cried out with him. Brothel tricks: that's what Aunt Sophronia had called that, and if resisting them would make March love and respect her, then she would, no matter how pleasurable it had been.

But when he entered her now, she couldn't help but gasp, it felt so right. She hadn't the words to explain it better than that. Could it mean that she truly was a low woman at heart? Was that why she was having such a difficult time not acting like a slattern? This time he had managed to be more respectful of her, and focusing all his attention on stroking her from within instead of fondling or caressing her in an inappropriate manner.

For her part, she struggled to lie still as she'd been told, her eyes squeezed shut as she tried to keep back the cries that keep rising up in her throat. She made herself think sad, somber thoughts, the same way she did to keep from laughing at the wrong times. Yet still the heat built as her body coiled more and more tightly, and the more swiftly he plunged into her, the more she ached for the joy of release. She was almost there in spite of herself, almost there with her whole body reaching for it, when with a grunt he drove into her one final time and fell forward upon her, breathing as hard as if he'd run a race.

"Charlotte, my own," he said, kissing her again. "My own dear wife."

He withdrew and sprawled beside her, his head on the pillow next to hers. His eyes were closed and his smile content.

But Charlotte's eyes were wide open, and as she stared up at the pleated canopy overhead, she was anything but content. She had done what she'd been told to do and she knew she'd pleased him, yet her own body remained unfulfilled, as if she were dangling from a cliff with no hope of rescue. Slowly she felt the tension ebb away from her limbs, but it wasn't the staggering burst of joy she'd discovered last night. All she was left with now was his seed, wet between her thighs, and the hope that perhaps they'd made a child, a son, between them.

That was what she was here to do, and the reason he'd married her. So what right did she have to feel so ridiculously disappointed? She shoved her nightshift down over her legs, and moved away from the damp place on the sheet. A single tear slid down her cheek and onto the pillow, and with a muffled sob she dashed it away with the heel of her hand.

"What's wrong?" he asked with concern, turning to face her. "If I have hurt you—"

"You didn't," she said quickly. "Not at all. But you are pleased?"

"I am," he said, and smiled. "How could I not be with you?"

"I'm glad," she said, and tried to smile back. He was happy with her, the way Aunt Sophronia had predicted he'd be, and his happiness would lead to love, and love was what she wanted.

He wiped his thumb along the curve of her cheek, following the path of the single tear. If he wished her not to cry, then he shouldn't be looking at her like this with such kindness.

"You must be tired," he said. "I've made you traipse all over London with me today. I should let you sleep now."

He sat up and swung his legs over the side of the bed to leave, and she caught his arm to stop him.

"Please don't go, March," she said. "Please."

He looked surprised. "Don't you wish to sleep?"

"Not alone," she confessed wistfully. "Please don't leave. I know that we've our own bedchambers and that's where we're supposed to sleep, but I'd much rather you stayed with me here."

"To sleep?" he asked, as if this were some unfathomable mystery. Perhaps to him it was.

"Yes, to sleep," she said. Though her parents had kept separate bedchambers and dressing rooms, too, she'd always remembered them sleeping together, or at least she remembered going to them early in the morning and finding them in the same bed. "Neither of us slept well last night, so perhaps we will do better this way. As man and wife, rather than duke and duchess."

He smiled. "I suppose we are both."

"Yes," she said softly. "We are. Will you stay?"

By way of an answer, he slipped back under the covers. He put his arm around her waist and drew her closer. At once she snuggled into him.

He made a low grunt of contentment and shifted closer still. He swept her hair to one side and kissed the back of her neck, and she smiled to herself. Her body fit so neatly against his, as if it were always intended to be there, and his arm around her waist made her feel safe and protected.

No, better than that. He made her feel wanted, and surely being wanted was one step away from being loved.

"Happy now?" he whispered, his voice already drowsy and thick.

"I am," she said, drifting to sleep herself. "I . . . am . . . happy."

March climbed down from his horse and tossed the reins to the waiting groom. He'd spent the last hour riding in the park, riding hard, too, through the mists and trees of early dawn. He'd thought the exercise would bring him some peace. To his grumbling discontent, it had not, and as he climbed the steps to the house, his grumbling continued at a furious pace.

Charlotte's request had seemed innocent enough. The majority of English husbands and wives shared the same bed every night. Although he himself had never slept in another's bed, he'd been willing to try it, for her sake. Her bed was nearly as large and comfortable as his own, and besides, at the time, the long walk back to his own bedchamber hadn't seemed nearly as charming as remaining where he was.

And charming it had remained. Too charming. Though he'd fallen asleep quite agreeably with his lovely wife in his arms, he'd awakened this morning with a demandingly hard cock.

But worse still was finding Charlotte blissfully asleep

beside him. During the night she'd managed to kick off the sheets and let her nightshift twist up around her waist. She was lying on her side with one knee curled up, displaying not only that splendid leg and wonderfully rounded bottom, but a good deal more besides, rosy and ready and enough to rouse a dead saint. If he hadn't been hard already, that luscious sight would have done it in an instant.

As much as he despised himself for enjoying the sight of her like that, he hated himself infinitely more for actually considering waking her to make delightful use of what she was unconsciously offering. Most men he knew would not think twice of doing that, but he'd only to remember how she'd wept last night after he'd tried his very best to be considerate and respectful. How shocked would she be if she'd known he was ogling her? And how horrified would she have been if he'd actually acted on his raging impulses and claimed his rights as a husband only hours after he'd already exercised them?

He wouldn't do that to Charlotte. He couldn't, not and live with himself, and once again the image of his profligate father, both with his mother and with the harlots he'd bought, rose unbidden like a fearsome, looming ghost. Over and over Charlotte spoke of how she trusted him, and to take advantage of her as she slept would have been the surest way to destroy that trust forever.

But as far as he was concerned, that must be an end to sleeping with her. He had enjoyed it, enjoyed it immensely, because he also liked her immensely as well. After only a handful of days as her husband, he'd already become so fond of her that he could no longer imagine his life without her in it. He wouldn't deny that. But while she might trust him, he didn't trust himself.

And he had to stop thinking about Charlotte asleep *now,* before they embarked together on another round of those infernal wedding calls. To sit across from her in the carriage and in drawing rooms and be able to think only of her with her nightshift rucked up and her bottom in the air . . .

He took the last flight of stairs two at a time, determined to wear himself out. He'd request that Giroux bring only the coldest of water for washing, too. Muttering darkly at his own lack of restraint, he was already untying his neck cloth when he entered his rooms.

"Good morning, March." Charlotte was sitting at his table, reading his newspaper spread out before her, and very likely drinking his coffee, too, albeit with so much cream that it was nearly white. She was wearing that dark pink dressing gown again, the one that made her look like a blossoming rose, and she'd added the pearls once again to her ears. She hadn't tied it as tightly today as she had before, and as she leaned over the open paper he'd a generous view of her pale breasts there by the window in the morning sun.

Whatever good the ride might have done him went right out that same window, too.

She stretched her arms out to her sides and yawned prettily. "I slept so well last night, March. I trust you did as well?"

"Absolutely," he lied. What else was he to say when she asked him like that? And he had slept well, up until the point when his cock had awakened him.

"You look very handsome this morning," she said, smiling warmly as she looked him up and down with open approval. "I like you dressed that way."

He wasn't accustomed to having a woman study him so thoroughly, even if it was his wife. He wasn't wearing anything extraordinary, just the usual white leather breeches, red waistcoat, and dark woolen coat that Giroux had chosen for him.

"It's what I wear to ride," he said, and immediately

felt like an idiot. What she could do to him simply by smiling! "I was riding in the park, you know."

"So Giroux has told me." She plucked a piece of toast from her plate, spread strawberry jam to the crust, and began to tear off tiny pieces daintily to feed herself. "I like to ride, too."

"I didn't know you rode." Another stunningly stupid comment. Of course she must ride, since she'd grown up in the country. He tossed his hat on another chair and sat beside her, taking the cup of coffee that the footman offered. He told himself it was only to be hospitable, and had nothing to do with Charlotte's dressing gown or her feet in those green mules with the high, curving heels. Though it was quite . . . engaging to watch how she crossed one pale, bare leg over another so the mule dangled from her toes and displayed the curve of her instep and ankle and calf and made him remember everything else above that. Quite engaging, and seductive as hell.

What malicious devil inspired him to desire his own wife like this?

"I do like to ride," she continued blithely, no notion of how she was depriving him of his wits each time she jogged her toe to keep from dropping her mule. "I'm good at it, too. My sisters and I used to race one another on the beach. We didn't ride on ladies' saddles, either, so we could go every bit as fast as any of the men. Once I overheard an old man at church call us the Wylder she-devils for riding like that, which was terribly shocking and rude, but very funny, too."

She paused long enough to lick a large drop of jam from her finger, running her tongue neatly along its length, then grinned at him.

He watched her licking that jam and understood perfectly why that old man in Dorset had called her a she-devil. The Wylder she-devil. Most appropriate.

"I should like to race you, too, March," she said, her eyes widening with anticipation. "I promise I'll ride properly, like a lady, so I'll be slower, but I'll wager I'll still beat you, so long as I have a good, fast horse."

The idea horrified him. "Good horse or not, Charlotte, I won't have you risk your neck racing through Green Park," he said. "I'll see that you've a proper horse and would be delighted to have you accompany me, but no racing."

"Very well, then, not in the park," she said. "But the next time we visit Greenwood, where I won't shock anyone, we'll see which of us is the faster. I'd venture you're a horseman, because it will be in your blood. I know next to nothing of your great-grandfather's politics, but most every picture in this house shows him on a horse. I know he was a racing king, and rode the courses himself."

"He did," March said, relieved to shift the subject to his royal ancestor on horseback. "He was faster and more daring than many of the hired jockeys."

"Well, yes, but who is going to dare to beat the king? A silver cup for your trouble, sirrah, and now off to the Tower you go." She used the jam knife for a vivid representation of the executioner's axe. "Besides, you have his royal thighs. I saw that from the pictures, too. A gentleman cannot be a good rider without possessing well-muscled thighs. *Royal* thighs."

That made him gulp his coffee and splutter it back into the saucer with some decidedly unroyal coughing. She jumped up with her napkin to blot his waistcoat, cooing and tut-tutting over the outrageous heat of the coffee, as if spilling it weren't his own damned fault.

And hers.

Stepping back, she lowered her chin to look up at him from beneath her lashes. "Did you mean what you said before? You will let me ride with you?"

"I will," he said as evenly as he could, "so long as you vow not to ride like a she-devil."

She grinned and ducked her head, something he'd learned meant she was pleased, which in turn pleased him. He did like the idea of riding with her. He'd have her company, but without any of the seductive hazards of a closed carriage.

"I've one more question, March," she began, and the way she was blushing before she'd even asked made him wary. "I know you wish me to be your proper wife and duchess and all, and I am trying to be so. But that picture behind you, March—I vow, that shepherdess is wearing my pearl earrings, and I do not think she looks entirely proper."

As if he, too, were seeing it for the first time, March turned in his seat to look at the painting in question. The shepherdess wasn't proper, nor had the painter intended her to be, and the incongruous pearl earrings were the least of her impropriety. With eyes half closed and the most wanton of smiles, she lounged provocatively on a mossy stone, her gauzy chiton looped high over her bare legs and so low on top that one plump, round breast was completely uncovered. To make certain no one over-looked this bare breast, she cupped her fingers beneath it, as if offering it to the viewer—which March had always believed was the entire point of the picture.

"That's my great-grandmother, Nan Lilly," he said. "She's painted as a shepherdess, yes, but she was really an actress. And, of course, my great-grandfather's mistress, and the first Duchess of Marchbourne. Because of all that, it's quite a famous picture, but it's also one of my favorites, which is why I have it hung here. That's the king on the other wall."

With fresh interest, Charlotte turned to study the portrait of his great-grandfather, and March did as well. Being a royal portrait, it wasn't nearly as informal or appealing as the shepherdess—how could it be, with a crown and all that ermine besides?—but March had always liked the sly, rakish twinkle to his dark eyes that the king hadn't quite been able to suppress, even while wearing a crown. That was the reason he'd hung the two portraits across from each other, so the pair could remain together, and he gave a little bow of respect to the king, as he always did.

But Charlotte had already turned back toward the other portrait.

"Nan Lilly." She tipped her head to one side, thoughtfully touching one of the tear-shaped pearls. "Did the king give her the earrings before he made her a duchess, or after?"

"Before," he said, looking up at Nan's face. "In the portraits of her after she's a duchess she's, ah, more completely dressed."

Charlotte rose and went to stand before the painting. "But of course she and the king never married."

"Of course not," March said. "Nan never married anyone. She was a duchess in her own right, without a duke."

"So while she was faithful to the king, he wasn't constant to her," she said. "I mean as constant as he could be to her, along with his true wife, the queen."

"No, he wasn't constant," he admitted. He generally avoided speaking of his family's scandalous history, but with Charlotte it wasn't difficult at all. "Breck's family descends from another mistress, and I've two more cousins, Hawkesworth and Sheffield, who can say the same. They were his favorites. I've heard there are at least a score of others whose bastards weren't legitimized or granted titles. It's what makes my family so different from those of other peers."

She looked back over her shoulder at him, the pearls swinging gently against her cheek.

"I suppose the rules are different for kings," she mused. "But do you know if he gave Nan the earrings as payment to her for being an accomplished strumpet, or as a gift because he loved her, enough to make her a duchess because she couldn't be his wife?"

"How can I answer that, Charlotte?" he said, mystified by why she'd ask such a curious question. He left his chair and came to stand behind her, resting his hands lightly on her shoulders as he, too, looked up at the portrait. "Everything happened a hundred years ago, and I doubt anyone knows the truth now, least of all me."

"I hope he loved her," she said with a fervor that startled him. "I hope he loved her passionately, and with all his heart."

"I hope she loved him as well," he said. He did, too, and he always had, though he doubted he'd ever said it aloud. "Nan was said to have been a merry, cheerful creature, able to make the king laugh no matter how grim his royal duties."

"If she hadn't, then we wouldn't be here today, together in this house, would we?"

"No, we wouldn't," March said. "It's a strange, disgraceful conundrum on which to base one's entire family and fortune."

"It is," she said softly. "How strange, too, to consider how very little difference there is between an actress and a duchess, or a bad woman and a good one."

Abruptly she turned to face him, resting her palms on his chest to smile up at him. "High time we dressed and began our day, yes?"

Their day did begin, another full day that included wedding calls, visits to her mantua-maker and his bookbinder, and a dinner in their honor given by some of his friends. Everywhere they went, Charlotte was her usual charming, beautiful self, dazzling all she met, and when he was congratulated again and again on his good fortune to have gained such a prize of a wife, he could only agree, and grin like the happy bridegroom that he was.

Yet throughout the long day, he couldn't help but feel as if their conversation before the painting somehow lingered with Charlotte. He hoped she didn't have second thoughts about joining a family with such a shameful history, not that anything could be done to change that now. He understood if she did; there'd been plenty of times at school when he'd fervently longed for a more ordinary pedigree. True, his children would carry Nan's lowly blood, but they'd also have a share of the king's stock as well, and there could hardly be any shame in that. At least he'd always believed the one compensated for the other, and he prayed that nothing as foolish as a century-old scandal would come between him and Charlotte.

There was no doubt, however, that something wasn't right between them, and he couldn't begin to fathom what it might be. He'd followed Breck's advice to the letter. Not even his royal ancestor could have treated her with more kindness or generosity.

Yet once again when he'd gone to her bed and performed his duty toward her in the most respectful way he could, she'd wept. Not with sobs or wails, but quietly, as if she'd known she'd no cause for complaint. She hadn't complained, either, even when he'd asked what was wrong.

Nothing, she'd said, *nothing,* even as the tears slid silently down her cheeks.

And afterward, as he'd walked the long hall back to his own bedchamber, he'd never felt more helpless, nor more alone.

CHAPTER
🎋 15 🎋

"Are you certain you're at ease in that saddle?" March asked, his brows drawn together with concern as once again he nudged his horse closer to hers. "An unfamiliar saddle can be the very devil, especially a sidesaddle."

"March, please," Charlotte said, no longer able to hide her exasperation. She'd been excited beyond measure to come out this morning with him. As he'd promised, he'd surprised her with a smart chestnut mare, and she'd surprised him with her new scarlet riding habit, tightly fitted and bristling with brass buttons like a soldier's uniform in the very newest fashion, and topped by a quite magnificent black plumed hat. The sun had just risen, the dew still sparkled on the grass, the park was nearly empty, and everything looked so new and fresh that anything seemed possible—or it would if only he'd stop acting as if this were the first time she'd ever climbed on a horse's back, and insisting they walk at this ridiculous snail's pace.

"I've told you before that I've been riding forever, March," she said as calmly as she could, which, under the circumstances, wasn't very calmly at all. "I am not an idiot on a horse. If the saddle weren't right, I would have said so in the yard. The saddle is right, the bridle is right, the horse is divine, and the weather and the morning are perfect."

"I'm glad you are pleased, and I thank you for it," he said. "Though I can take neither fault nor praise for the morning."

She sighed, wishing he wouldn't be quite so serious. "That is true," she said, "and if I topple from my horse, then it would not be your fault, either, but entirely mine."

"I don't wish it to be anyone's fault," he said. "What I wish is that it won't happen at all."

"Well, then, I'll grant you that wish." She shifted her reins to one hand and fluttered her fingers toward him like a country fair conjurer. "There, Your Grace. It will not happen."

Still he didn't smile. "I'm only trying to make you happy, Charlotte."

She sighed, and despite the glorious morning, her heart sank a little lower. If he truly wished to make her happy, then he would have stayed with her the night through, instead of leaving as if she were somehow distasteful to him. Yesterday things had gone so well between them. She'd loved how he'd trusted her enough to tell her about his great-grandmother and the king, and she'd loved, too, that he'd given her Nan Lilly's pearl earrings. He spoke so seldom about his family that she'd realized the significance of that confidence, and it had pleased her far more than the earrings themselves.

And if he saw no real shame to Nan's humble beginnings and her illicit love for the merry old king, then perhaps, too, he might be persuaded to be a bit more merry himself, especially in the bedchamber. For her part, she certainly wouldn't have objected to being a little less like a duchess and a little more like an actress. But he hadn't been merry, not at all. If anything, last night he'd seemed even more respectful and somber, as if she were made of twice-glazed porcelain instead of flesh and blood. She couldn't begin to think of it again from fear that she'd begin weeping with despair here in the park.

Instead she forced herself to smile. "I *am* happy, March. I only wish that we could—"

"Halt, Charlotte, please," he ordered, guiding his horse directly before hers so she'd have no choice. At once he dismounted, bending down to peer at her boots. "There's something not quite right about that stirrup."

But to Charlotte's mind, there was something not quite right about everything, and at last she could bear it no longer. She dug in her heels and cracked her reins, and before March could stop her, she was gone.

The mare was equally happy to rebel, as Charlotte had suspected she would be, and given rein, she flew across the dewy grass. Charlotte didn't know the park and she didn't know where she was headed, nor did she care. For the first time since she'd left Ransom she felt free and alive, and the exhilaration overcame everything else. She could forget propriety and being a duchess. With the wind in her face and the reins in her hand, she was once again simply Charlotte, and it was a glorious feeling.

She could faintly hear March calling to her. Of course he'd follow, and she'd a pang of remorse when she remembered how he hadn't wanted her to race in the park. Yet she didn't want to be caught, not yet, and besides, it was exciting to have him chasing after her.

Just ahead of her was a thick copse of trees and mulberry bushes, and she swiftly guided the mare away from the open grass, over a shallow gully, and into the shadows of the trees. She didn't exactly intend to hide from March, but she wouldn't mind if he had to do a bit of hunting to find her, either. What better way to prove that she was at ease on horseback?

Breathing hard, Charlotte reached forward to pat the mare fondly on her shoulder. She was delighted with the horse for both her speed and her spirit, and she had to admit that despite all his worry and concern, March had found her an excellent mount. She leaned forward across the horse, craning her neck to look for her husband. She'd expected him to be here by now; she hadn't had that much of a head start on him. Uneasily she hoped he hadn't fallen or suffered some other mishap because of her.

"Have you escaped the villain, sweetheart?"

Charlotte gasped and twisted around in her saddle. How had she not heard the man come up behind her? He was thickset and ruddy-faced with sandy hair, and from the way he effortlessly controlled his large black gelding, he was clearly as strong as he appeared. At least from his dress—a dark blue coat with silver buttons and fawn-colored leather breeches, much the same as March's—he must be a gentleman, though true gentlemen would not come creeping up behind ladies in the park.

"I beg your pardon?" she said in as frosty a voice as she could muster.

"Come now, don't play coy with me," he said, smiling warmly. "I saw how you came racing through the trees there. You'd only do that if the devil himself were after your soul. That, or your husband."

She flushed. "My reasons are none of your affair, sir."

He laughed. "So it was the husband. Pity. I'd rather it were the devil, with some interesting reason for desiring your soul. Though who could blame him, when there is so much of you worth desiring?"

She gasped again, this time with indignation. "You've no right to speak so boldly to me," she said. "You wouldn't dare if you knew who I was."

"You're a lady who likes to take risks," he said, sweeping his black cocked hat from his head, "and that's sufficient for me. John Tinderson, Marquess of Andover, your servant, and your savior, if you've need of one."

"I am the Duchess of Marchbourne," she said, borrowing Aunt Sophronia's haughtiness, "and I need nothing from you, Lord Andover."

"Marchbourne's bride?" For a moment he stared in astonishment before he quickly recalled himself, and he bowed as much as he could from his saddle. "Forgive me, Your Grace, I'd no idea. His Grace should take better care of such a prize."

"He does," she admitted, not wanting March to be faulted. "Or rather, he tried to. I'm the one who ran away."

"A runaway bride." His respectful smile became much friendlier. "If you're ever in need of a sanctuary, ma'am, please consider my home as yours. I wouldn't want to think of a lady like yourself wandering about London like a lost lamb."

"Charlotte!" March appeared around the bushes, and sharply wheeled his horse to a halt to come to her. "Damnation, I've been hunting all over for you!"

In the short time Charlotte had known March, she'd judged him to be a temperate man, even mild-mannered, but not now. She'd never seen him so angry, his face flushed and his dark eyes flashing, and at once she realized that absolute contrition was her best—no, her only—course.

"I'm sorry if I caused you trouble, March," she began, "very sorry, but I only wished—"

"Have you any idea of how I feared for you?" he thundered. "This isn't Dorset, Charlotte. This is London, and you can't begin to understand the perils that wait for a woman alone."

"But I wasn't alone," she protested. "At least, not for long. Lord Andover has been with me."

March stared at the marquess as if seeing him for the first time. "Andover. Good day."

"Good day, Your Grace," the marquess said, his expression cordial. "May I offer my congratulations upon your marriage to this beautiful lady?"

"No, Andover, you may not," March said curtly. "The last thing I wish is to have my wife dallying in the park with you."

"*Dallying!*" Charlotte exclaimed. She wasn't sure which was more shocking: his suspicion, or his rudeness toward Andover. "March, I was not dallying. I was waiting for you, and Lord Andover greeted me while I waited. That scarce constitutes *dallying.*"

"It does with Andover." March continued to glare at the other man, and it was almost as if he'd inexplicably redirected his initial anger at Charlotte toward the marquess. She could sense it like a wall between the two men, so thick that Charlotte wondered if some long-held rivalry existed between them, some ancient, bitter insult that had nothing to do with her.

"I assure you, sir, that there is absolutely no cause for concern on your part," Lord Andover said, and Charlotte was sure that the marquess's knowing little smile was not helping his case with March, or hers, either. "Even I can stand before you in perfect innocence, and your lady as well. But I will say that Her Grace rides most splendidly. Perhaps you both would honor my hunt this season."

"We must decline," Marchbourne said. "My wife does not hunt."

"But I've always wished to try it," Charlotte said, hoping that the notion of hunting might distract March into a better humor. "It sounds most exciting."

"I have declined, madam," he said, his words brisk and clipped. "Now let us return home, if you please. Good day, Andover."

Again Lord Andover raised his hat, his smile so winning that Charlotte couldn't help but smile in return. If there was in fact some bad blood between her husband

and the marquess, then it must be entirely on March's side, because Lord Andover didn't seem at all disturbed.

"Now that you reside here in London, ma'am," he said, "I'll look forward to the frequent pleasure of your company."

"That, Andover, will be a pleasure I reserve entirely for myself," March said, already turning away. "Come, madam."

The sun had risen high enough to dry the dew and lift the mist, and bright beams slanted through the trees. There were more riders in the park now, as well as babies with their nursemaids and older children tossing bread to the ducks in the canal and flying bright paper kites. From the parade ground in the distance came the martial sound of drums and shouted orders as the Horse Guards held their morning review, and closer by a man trundled his hurdy-gurdy to a prime place beneath a shady tree and began to crank his wheezing, rattling instrument, his hat on the grass for coins.

But despite so much gaiety around them, March rode beside Charlotte in stony silence, a silence Charlotte didn't dare break until they'd nearly reached Marchbourne House. Mama had always maintained that disagreements were much better dealt with at once, rather than being allowed to fester and grow worse. Although Charlotte was certain that applying the lancet to this particular disagreement was going to be painful, she was determined not to let it poison her marriage any more than it already had.

"I have told you I am sorry for riding off as I did," she began, "and I'm sorry to have worried you."

Still his steadfast silence remained, but Charlotte plunged onward.

"I've told you, too, that I was innocent of anything beyond a handful of words with Lord Andover. What more do you wish me to say, March?"

He didn't look at her, but continued to stare resolutely ahead. "Not now, madam. I will not have us observed and gossip spread that we are quarreling already."

"Why not, when it is true?" she said tartly. "And please do not call me 'madam,' as if I were Aunt Sophronia."

"What else would you have me call you?"

"You could begin with my name," she said. "Then you could progress to the kinds of things ordinary men call their wives, such as 'sweetheart,' or 'dearest,' or—"

He drew his horse up sharply, forcing her to do so as well. "Would you like to know what you'll be called if you insist on familiarity with men like Andover? A strumpet, and a harlot, and a whore, because that is how he treats married women, seducing them and destroying their names so thoroughly that their husbands and children disown them."

"Did he do that to you, March?" she demanded. "Did he steal away some other lady you fancied?"

He stared at her, appalled. "No, Charlotte, he did not. There has never been any other lady but you."

"Then why can you not believe that it's like that for me as well, March? That you are the only gentleman for me?" The curling plume on her hat fluttered forward over her face, and furiously she batted it aside. "If I speak a handful of words to Lord Andover or to your cousin's mistress, Mrs. Shaw, no harm will come to me. Riding my horse fast will only give me pleasure, not magically transform me into some dreadful, debauched woman."

"You're my duchess, Charlotte," he insisted doggedly. "I can only treat you one way."

"Why can't you treat me less like a duchess and more like a woman?" she pleaded. "Why can't you trust me enough to act for myself? Consider your great-grandmother Nan. She managed to be a woman, a mistress, a mother, an actress, *and* a duchess, and quite nicely, too."

He flushed. "She had no choice, Charlotte. She was a

base-born wench. You're a Wylder, from an ancient and honorable family, and your father was an earl."

"Which only means I have no choices, either." She couldn't keep the despair from creeping into her voice. "You want me to be your own precious, fragile version of a duchess, bound so tightly by—by *respectability* that I can scarce breathe."

"But I wish you to be happy, Charlotte," he insisted. "Without respectability and honor and regard, no lady can be truly happy."

She shook her head, wishing more than anything that she could make him understand. He could talk all the day long of being happy, but she was positive that he was no happier than she. Now that his anger had faded, his dark eyes were full of sorrow and confusion. She wished that they could return to that afternoon when they'd been together in the tree, when he'd been gallant and she hadn't had a care beyond rescuing Fig.

She thought again of her mother, and how, whenever Charlotte and her sisters had quarreled, Mama had always insisted that they pretend they were one another, and see the quarrel through the others' eyes.

Perhaps that was her difficulty with March. Perhaps she had become so wrapped in her own unhappiness that she hadn't bothered to see his.

She shifted the mare closer to his horse, both so her hat's plume would stop blowing and tickling her cheek and so she could reach across to lay her hand lightly on his arm.

"My own husband," she said softly, though there were no others within hearing. "I've never been a duchess, and neither, for that matter, have you. Yet between us lies this saintly, noble ideal of a lady that I doubt I'll ever match. Was your own mother like that, March? You've never spoken of her. Is that whom you wish me to be more like?"

She thought she couldn't have phrased her question with more gentleness. It was true, too. March had never spoken of his mother, and all Charlotte knew of the previous duchess was how she'd decorated the rooms that now belonged to her.

But while she'd hoped that her question might help her better to understand her husband, it was clear from the stricken look on his face that she'd asked too much.

"My mother was far from anyone's ideal, Charlotte," he said, each word clipped sharp by sorrow, "nor was she happy in her married life, not for a day, not for a minute. I would never wish you to be like her. I would never wish that lot on anyone."

Though surprised, Charlotte didn't back away, nor did she lift her hand from his arm.

"I'm sorry, March," she said. "For her, and for you, too."

He looked away, down at her hand on his sleeve. "I am sorry, too," he said. "For her. For her."

Awkwardly he placed his own hand over Charlotte's— only for a moment, but long enough. Then he turned his horse and began back toward the house.

It was not exactly the answer Charlotte had looked for, but at least it was a beginning, and a beginning was always better than an end.

Later that afternoon, March sat on a narrow, uncomfortable chair in the drawing room of Lady Barbara Finnister, barely listening as Lady Finnister offered an interminable telling of how her husband, Sir Henry, had won five hundred pounds on the turn of a single card at the faro table. The room was stuffy and close with the windows shut, and made stuffier still by the enormous amount of French scent that wafted from Lady Finnister's person.

The baronet was an old acquaintance and popular at court as well, but this was the first time March had met this particular Lady Finnister. She was the third wife of twice-widowed Sir Henry, who, to complete the mathematical equation, must be at least three times his young wife's age. But Lady Finnister was very close in age to Charlotte, which was likely why the two of them were chattering away so freely.

March couldn't think that they'd have much in common besides their youth, for where Charlotte was as fresh as country cream from Dorset, Lady Finnister was London bred, and so thickly painted and powdered that March couldn't begin to guess her true colors. He much preferred his Charlotte, and as if sensing his approval, she glanced at him and smiled.

After this morning, he should be thankful that she'd ever smile at him again. When she'd raced away from him in the park, he'd thought the worst he could imagine was finding her lifeless in the grass. Then he'd come across Andover grinning at her like some rakehell wolf with a lamb, and he'd realized that the worst was beyond imagining. To find her with another man, even innocently, had not only shocked him but also wounded him to the core.

No: if he was honest, it had wounded his heart. Because though he'd yet to admit it to Charlotte herself, he was slowly realizing he was falling in love with his wife. He could think of no place he'd rather be than in her company, and when they were apart, all he thought of was how swiftly he could be with her again. When she smiled, he smiled. When she was sad, he felt her unhappiness as keenly as if it were his own. In a few short days, she'd become the centerpiece of his world.

And then he had found her beside Andover. But instead of calmly listening to his wife's explanation, then gathering her and escorting her away, the way a proper husband should, he'd raged like a madman, first at Andover and then at Charlotte herself. Pure and simple, he'd been jealous. He hadn't recognized it for what it was at first, jealousy being a rare emotion for dukes who'd been given everything. He knew that concern and affection for her had made him behave so, but that was still no excuse. He'd made exactly the kind of public scene that he'd always wished to avoid. If that hadn't been bad enough, in the middle of his raging he'd been acutely aware of how desirable Charlotte had looked, her hair disheveled beneath her hat, her face flushed from riding, and that wickedly close-fitting red habit accentuating every curve of her figure.

And in return, she'd proved herself the better spouse and behaved exactly as a lady should. She'd apologized for worrying him. She hadn't thrown her hat or stamped her foot, the way some women would have. The few sharp words she'd said had made sense, while his had not, and she'd managed to ease his temper with understanding and kindness.

She'd said she'd never be the perfect duchess he wanted. After this morning, he wondered if it was the other way around, and that he might never be the duke or husband that she deserved.

It was a sobering thought, and he'd had plenty of time to think it again and again during today's round of visits. Inwardly he'd resolved—again—to do better by her. She might require his guidance in certain matters, yes, but he didn't need to order her every move. It once again came down to learning to trust her, and he'd have to admit he was having a devil of a time doing it. He'd still been in school when he'd come into his title, and from that day everything in his life had been done because he wished it so.

But Charlotte was his wife, not a servant or tradesman. He shouldn't expect her to oblige him in every tiny matter. She should be free to make her own decisions, as a duchess should, and it was up to him to trust her and give her that freedom.

Which was why he was still sitting in Lady Finnister's drawing room, long after the usual fifteen minutes that a wedding call was required to take. This was their last call of the afternoon, and if Charlotte was enjoying herself, then for her sake he would bear with it. She should have friends of her own in London, other ladies whom she could call upon for tea. Then she'd be happier and stop brooding over grim subjects such as his poor mother.

"Isn't that so, Your Grace?" Lady Finnister smiled brightly at him, her face somehow too small beneath her enormously frizzed and powdered hair. "Would you not agree?"

March smiled weakly, unwilling to agree to an unknown question, but also not wishing her to know he'd stopped listening at least five minutes before.

But Charlotte, bless her, jumped in to rescue him.

"You'll have to answer for me, March," she said, smiling charmingly at him over the top of her fan. "Having never so much as seen a roulette wheel, let alone wagered against one, I can't venture if such a game of chance is truly the most excitement one can have in London."

"Ah, games of chance." He smiled his thanks to her, and thought what a useful marvel a wife could be. "I must confess I do not often play myself, Lady Finnister."

"Oh, but you must!" she exclaimed, bouncing on the edge of her chair. "You and the duchess both. To watch the wheel spin, to see the ball bounce, to feel one's heart leap with excitement—ah, there is nothing more thrilling in London, no, no, in the entire world!"

"Lady Finnister and Sir Henry are having a small entertainment here tonight, March," Charlotte said, sounding like the voice of rational sanity compared to Lady Finnister's silliness. "There will be music and gaming and a supper, and she has kindly invited us to return later and join them."

"You must join us, Your Grace, you must!" Lady Finnister begged, her clasped hands raised in supplication. "Oh, please, you simply must!"

Instantly he decided he must do no such thing, not when this squealing woman demanded it of him. Gaming had never held much allure for him personally, nor did he enjoy the company of those in the grip of feverish play, squandering vast fortunes on the turn of a pasteboard card. Besides, he'd been counting on a quiet evening at home with Charlotte, culminating in a visit to her bedchamber. He prayed tonight she wouldn't cry, but would instead find some measure of pleasure in his attentions.

He watched her now, leaning forward to set her teacup down on the table before her, and offering him a splendid glimpse of her breasts, round and plump and framed by lacy white ruffles. What mere game of cards or dice could rival that?

With her chin still lowered, she smiled up at him from beneath her lashes, displaying her dimples to devastating effect.

"If it pleases you, March," she said, "I should like to attend."

That was all she asked, and it was enough. That visit to her bedchamber would not be denied, but simply be postponed until later this night. He'd give her anything, anything at all, when she looked at him like that.

"If it pleases you, Charlotte, then of course," he said. "Lady Finnister, we are honored."

CHAPTER

16

Eagerly Charlotte gazed from the carriage window as it crept toward the house of Sir Henry Finnister. When Lady Finnister had said she'd invited a few friends, she'd clearly been being modest. To Charlotte it seemed that there were more hackneys and private carriages clogging this street than had been in Drury Lane before the theater.

"I cannot believe this crush," she marveled. "Lady Finnister made it sound as if only her closest friends were coming tonight."

"That may well be true," March said. "Likely she only has a few thousand or so in that category."

"March, be serious," she said, dropping back onto the seat across from him with a little *whoosh* of silk. Her gown, a *robe à la française* of peach-colored French brocade with a swirling pattern of peacock feathers, had been delivered earlier that day, and Polly had assured her it was exactly what was required for such an evening. It was cut very low in the bodice, so low that even the lace kerchief Polly had tied over her shoulders seemed to veil her breasts more for provocation than for modesty. That, too, Polly assured her was in the best French taste. What had mattered more to Charlotte, however, was how March's eyes had lit when she'd joined him, and how now his gaze was wandering freely over the gown, and her in it.

"I'm perfectly serious," he said. "Finnister's a man with many fingers in many political pies, and most of those clamoring to attend his wife's gatherings have more interest in currying his favor than in her hospitality."

"Politics," Charlotte repeated with dismay. "Oh, March, I know nothing of politics, nothing at all. And here I'd thought we'd be playing games."

For the first time that evening he laughed, and Charlotte was glad to hear it. He'd been quiet all day, subdued, as if his earlier strong words in the park had exhausted him. But he had also clearly been striving to be especially agreeable, and he'd surprised her by agreeing to return to the Finnisters' house this evening. Perhaps it was his way of apologizing, or at least trying to make things better between them.

She did worry, however, that she'd have to fight to keep the other ladies away from him tonight. His quietness only made him more attractive, at least to her. Sitting across from her in the half-light, he was unfathomably handsome, dressed in dark wine-colored silk with cut-steel buttons that sparkled like stars. He wore her favorite jewel, too, an elegant small heart-shaped shirt buckle, studded with rubies, that nestled in the snowy linen ruffles on the breast of his shirt. She hoped that any other ladies who might see the ruby heart would know that the gentleman who wore it belonged to her alone.

"Some would say politics are no more than gaming," he was saying, fortunately unaware of her thoughts. "Anyone who has sat in either house would agree. But I doubt you'll be disappointed by Lady Finnister's offerings. I've heard she prides herself on having more games than a Venetian casino. But take care, Charlotte. Have your fun, but choose a game such as whist or backgammon, where there's more skill than chance. There'll be plenty playing for deep stakes, too, and I don't want you washed away."

"Or swept off in one of those Venetian canals," Charlotte said cheerfully, clapping her palms lightly together with anticipation. At Ransom, they'd played hands of whist for seashells from the beach, all that Mama had permitted, and in the stables they'd learned put from the grooms—which, of course, Mama had never known about. As exciting as that had been, she couldn't wait to try these new, fashionable games. "I'll do well enough, March. I'm as skilled as any gamester I'll find in a drawing room. I won't shame you."

"I am serious, Charlotte."

"So am I," she promised. She felt as if this were the ride in the park all over again, with him worrying too protectively over her, which of course only made her more determined to prove her ability, and to earn his trust, too.

But he looked so doleful that she laughed and leaned across to kiss him, a quick brush of her lips across his.

"Thank you," she said softly. "I know this isn't your choice of diversion, and that you agreed for my sake alone."

He smiled crookedly. "I only pray that we don't both expire from a surfeit of Lady Finnister's gaiety."

She laughed again, unable to imagine such a thing. Yet when at last they entered the Finnisters' house, Charlotte realized at once that a surfeit of gaiety was no exaggeration, but a very possible danger.

The same rooms that she and March had visited this afternoon were now packed with elegant folk, drinking and laughing and flirting and conversing as loudly as possible, each striving to outdo the other. Crowds clustered around the tables set for cards, with the spectators every bit as excited as the players themselves. In the next room, both gentlemen and ladies sat at a long green-covered faro table, leaning forward and anxiously waiting with open mouths for the dealer to announce each new card.

But the crowd around the roulette wheel in the last room was the loudest of all, craning their necks and pressing against one another to watch the little ball bounce and jostle around the spinning wheel until it finally settled into a numbered slot. Then they threw their hands in the air with either despair or delight, shrieking and swearing and hopping in place, for all the world like people who'd lost their wits entirely.

"I told you they raved like the lunatics in Bedlam Hospital," March said, leaning close to Charlotte's ear so his words could be heard over the din. "Rational, respectable people to meet by day on the street, but you see how gaming reduces them to this sorry state."

Charlotte glanced up at him, her hand holding tightly to his arm. He seemed bemused by the sights around him, nothing more, and it was strange to think that these raving folk could be fine lords and ladies. Despite March at her side and Nan Lilly's pearl-and-diamond earrings hanging from her lobes, she felt like an insignificant country mouse in this loud, brittle company, and in truth she was more than a little intimidated both by the crush and by the ferocity with which the ladies and gentlemen played.

"We can leave if you wish," she said. "We needn't stay."

"No reason for us to sound the retreat just yet," he said. "I'd like them to see my beautiful wife."

"And I for them to see my handsome husband," she answered promptly, relaxing a bit. She'd liked that "us" he'd used, showing they'd face this together. She liked it very much. Besides, he was right. She liked to think of herself as brave, even daring, and she would not retreat just yet. Resolutely she raised her chin and squared her shoulders, so obviously that March noticed.

"Preparing for battle, are we?" he asked.

"Yes," she said. "I am. I won't have it said that the Duchess of Marchbourne is a coward."

"No one who has ever seen you ride would say that of you," he said wryly. "Ah, here's our hostess, ready to make a prize of us."

"Oh, Your Grace, Your Grace!" Like an eager spaniel, Lady Finnister bounded and pushed her way through the crowd, her hoops bouncing around her. She was lavishly dressed with her hair piled high, dusted with lavender powder, and decorated with brilliants and nodding ostrich plumes in the French fashion. She came to a lurching stop to curtsey far too deeply than was correct, though it did serve to make all around them at the gaming tables take belated notice and bow or curtsey as well. "Oh, I am so, so honored!"

"Thank you for including us, Lady Finnister," March said. "Lady Marchbourne was particularly delighted by your invitation."

"Then you must play, Lady Marchbourne," Lady Finnister said, popping her eyes for emphasis. "You *will* play! But before we find you a place at the table, you must admire my new picture. It was brought and hung this very afternoon. Quite divine, I vow."

With a flourish of her brisé fan, she pointed to the large painting hanging on the wall behind them. She'd a right to be possessive, for the new painting was a full-length portrait of herself. Dressed in a filmy gown with gold slippers on her feet and a gold bow in her hand, the painted Lady Finnister gazed soulfully up at a new moon hanging over her shoulder.

To Charlotte, whose experience with painted portraits was limited to the grim, beruffed specimens at Ransom Manor and those at Marchbourne House, this picture was the finest she'd ever seen. The artist had discovered a luminous beauty and grace in Lady Finnister that wasn't ordinarily visible in the lady herself, at least not to Charlotte; clearly the painter must be a genius at his art.

"I'm portrayed as Artemis, goddess of the hunt, which is the reason for that silly bow," Lady Finnister said. "And goddess of maidenly virtue, too. Sir Henry wishes me always to say that, you know. But isn't it a perfectly lovely picture?"

"It is, Lady Finnister," March said, staring up at the painting. "Never was there a more beauteous Artemis."

He made his pronouncement solemnly, a solemnity that Charlotte now realized he employed whenever he wished to be polite in a challenging situation. It made her feel clever and wifely—and closer to him, too—that she'd noticed this about her husband.

"Ooh, thank you, sir," Lady Finnister said, preening in the glow of that same solemnity. "It is a Rowell, of course."

"A rowel?" asked Charlotte, mystified.

"Sir Lucas Rowell," March said. "He's the artist of this fine work. A painter of considerable accomplishment and perception. He's a favorite with the king for his portraits of the queen and the royal princesses."

"His Majesty rewarded him with a knighthood," Lady Finnister said, glancing side to side to make sure there were no royal ears to overhear. "When you are presented to Their Royal Highnesses, ma'am, you'll realize for yourself that Sir Lucas is a master of diplomacy as well as art. La, plain as curdled milk, the lot of them."

She tittered behind her fan. March did not laugh—doubtless the poor plain princesses were related to him in some way—and Charlotte didn't laugh, either. It was hardly the princesses' fault to have been born plain, and besides, Lady Finnister might do better to consider how her portrait outshone her own beauty before she made jests about others.

"I've always admired Sir Lucas's work, though I've never sat for him myself," March said, turning back to Charlotte. "Perhaps we should consider asking him to paint a pair of marriage portraits of us. Would you like that?"

"Oh, yes!" exclaimed Charlotte. While the idea of sitting for a great painter was exciting, she was overjoyed that March wished to commemorate their marriage like this.

"Sir Lucas comes very dear, you know, and Sir Henry had fits over his fee," Lady Finnister said. She puffed out her cheeks, screwed up her mouth, and lowered her voice to mimic her husband. " 'Fifty guineas for a few daubs of paint and varnish, and your feet shown bare as a pauper's! Why, I could buy the whole cursed moon from the sky for fifty guineas, damn my eyes if I couldn't!' "

"I should like to know where Sir Henry takes his custom," March said. "I've never seen the price of a cursed moon at less than a hundred."

Startled, Charlotte looked at March. He'd kept his solemn face, but his dark eyes were bright indeed, especially when he glanced at Charlotte. Her too-serious husband had made a jest. It was a small jest, to be sure, and likely would have gone unnoticed in clever company, but she'd heard it, and she'd understood the effort it must have taken for him to make such a comment at all—for her sake, she knew, for *her*. She grinned with delight.

"A hundred for a new moon, March," she said. "But for an entire moon, fully ripened, I'd venture the price would be nearer to five hundred."

He couldn't help but smile now, the jest shared between them. "Five hundred, yes. But only for the best-quality moon, with a fine polish and patina."

"Ah, Your Grace, I can see you're in a fine humor for wagering!" Lady Finnister said, determined to bring the attention back to her. "Which table shall it be, then? Faro, roulette, or loo?"

"I'll let Lady Marchbourne choose for herself," March said. "I need to speak a few words with Sir Henry, Lady Finnister, and so I'll entrust my bride to you while I do."

He raised Charlotte's hand to his lips and kissed it, his gaze still intent on hers, as if parting from her even for a few moments was nearly beyond bearing. Then he turned and made his way through the crowd.

Lady Finnister sighed dramatically. "His Grace is so handsome and gallant. How blessed you are, ma'am, to have such a husband."

Charlotte looked after him, his height and unpowdered dark hair making him stand out among the others.

"Yes," she said softly, more to March than to Lady Finnister. "He is gallant and handsome, and I am truly blessed."

"Well, yes, you are," Lady Finnister said. "But now, ma'am, we must introduce you into a game. What do you prefer? Quinze, loo, all-fours, piquet, or hazard? A place at the roulette wheel, or before the faro bank?"

Charlotte didn't recognize a single one of the games, let alone how to play them. "What of whist?"

"Bah, a tedious diversion for old hens," Lady Finnister said with a dismissive sweep of her fan. "We can, and will, do better than that for you, ma'am. Loo will be best, I think. 'Tis wicked fast, and easily learned."

She led Charlotte through the crowd to a large round table and unceremoniously asked another lady to give her seat to Charlotte. Introductions were made with a complement of bows and curtseys, and a footman helped Charlotte settle into her chair. There were six other ladies and gentlemen around the mahogany table, with many more gathered to watch. The table was specially designed for the game of loo, with shallow, scalloped recesses before each player. In each of these recesses were piles of small mother-of-pearl fish, some players with more, and some with very few.

"Now, these are quite cunning," Charlotte said, plucking up one of her fish and making it swim through the air before her, much to the indulgent amusement of the other players.

"Those are your counters," Lady Finnister explained quickly as she claimed the chair beside Charlotte's, "and this place before you holding the fish is your pond. The house bank has staked you to twenty-five counters. You must decide your wager and enter you stake in the pool, there in the center of the table, before you're dealt your hand. Then you can decide if you wish to play your hand, or pass and forfeit your stake."

Charlotte nodded. It sounded similar enough to put, the old rooking game she'd played with the stable grooms at home, and her confidence grew.

"There are three tricks to a play, ma'am," continued Lady Finnister, "and if you don't take at least one of those, then you're loo'd, and must forfeit the whole amount of the pool."

"All?" asked Charlotte with surprise.

"All, Your Grace," said a man standing close behind her. She turned and discovered Lord Andover, the gentleman from the park. "You're wise to be cautious, ma'am. It's Lady Finnister's pleasure that we play the unlimited game in her house. With a table of seven, as here, it means that four lose with every hand, and thus the pool quadruples with every hand as well."

Charlotte nodded and quickly turned back toward the table. It wasn't her fault that Andover was here, or that he stood behind her chair, but she could only imagine what March would say if he found the marquess there.

"His Lordship doesn't like my rules because he's unlucky, ma'am," Lady Finnister said tartly as she glared at Lord Andover.

"Pray forgive me, Lady Finnister," Lord Andover said easily, "but it isn't a question of my luck so much as your desire for a fast game."

Lady Finnister flushed, her cheeks so red that the color showed beneath her paint.

"The benefits of an unlimited game are clear, ma'am," she said to Charlotte, though she still looked at Lord Andover. "The play never lags or grows flaccid, and the rewards are much greater for those who dare reach for the sweetest prize."

Lord Andover only smiled and bowed toward Lady Finnister. But from the way others around the table smirked and raised their brows knowingly, there was clearly more to their acquaintance than luck and loo. A flaccid game? The sweetest prize? Who described a hand of cards in such a fashion? March had said that Lord Andover seduced married women. Could Lady Finnister have been one of his conquests, or had she been the one pursuing the marquess?

"We also play with a Pam card, ma'am, that black fellow the knave of clubs," Lady Finnister continued, her voice more brittle by the word. "His value is wild."

Lord Andover leaned over Charlotte's shoulder again, as if only to point to the cards on the table. "A wild knave is always useful in a lady's hand, ma'am, as he can obligingly masquerade in any way she requires to reach her goal. Especially for a flush. A flush will loo all the other players and clear the table. What greater pleasure can there be than to claim the pool and the ponds of all your rivals?"

Now Charlotte was the one who blushed. Or rather she flushed, her whole face burning as she began to comprehend the marquess's meaning.

"Thank you, Lord Andover," she said, and nothing

more. She didn't dare. Instead she pointedly stared down at the shining fish in her pond, trying to concentrate on the game instead of the scandal that was so obviously swirling around her. She felt like a tiny little fish herself, swimming in a pond where she did not belong. Clearly loo in London was a good deal more complicated than whist with her sisters at Ransom.

"Shall we begin, ma'am?" Lady Finnister said, stacking her fish into three precise little piles. "Your wager, if you please."

With a deep breath Charlotte counted out five of her fish and pushed them into the center. The other players followed, and the hands were dealt. Charlotte's cards weren't good, and in the next instant—or so it seemed—she'd lost, and her first fish were swept away. But worse still was realizing that she must now stake the next pool as well, and suddenly she found herself with twenty of her twenty-five counters gone and only five remaining, quite lonesome, in her pond.

"Tell me, please," she whispered to Lady Finnister. "How much does each marker represent?"

"Not much," Lady Finnister said. "Only ten guineas."

Ten guineas. Charlotte swallowed hard. She might be a duchess, but ten guineas still seemed like a prodigious amount of money. Only yesterday she'd generously increased Polly's salary to eight guineas, a sum befitting a lady's maid—more than any of the servants were paid at Ransom Manor—and that eight guineas was for the whole year. Entire families in the country could live well on twenty guineas. A full-length portrait by Sir Lucas Rowell was fifty. Here she'd already lost twenty markers, or two hundred guineas, and that was only after two hands of loo.

"Do you wish to continue to play, ma'am?" Lady Finnister asked delicately. "You must enter the pool again if you do. I will gladly have the bank raise your stake—"

"Yes, yes, please do," Charlotte said with fresh determination. She couldn't let March see how much she'd lost, not after he'd cautioned her against the hazards of gaming. She had to win back those guineas before he returned to her, and with a sigh of relief she watched as a footman scooped a fresh pile of fish to clatter into her pond.

But before long, those fish, too, were forfeited and claimed by others, and another scoop as well. Feverishly she tallied her losses in her head: oh, preserve her, she'd lost over *seven hundred guineas* in a quarter hour's play.

"Your play, ma'am," Lady Finnister said gently. "You've just enough for a fresh stake. If you wish, the bank will oblige—"

"Thank you, no," Charlotte said quickly. "I've no wish to borrow more."

Lady Finnister tipped her head to one side, considering.

"Those earrings are monstrous fine, ma'am," she said. "No one here at the table would object if you added those to your wager. Your luck's sure to change, you know. It always goes that way for beginners."

Charlotte's hands flew to the earring, her fingers touching the heavy, swinging pearls: Nan Lilly's pearls, the gift from the king, and now given to her by March.

"Matched pearls like that are rare, and worth a pretty sum," Lady Finnister continued, her words a covetous purr. "If you don't wish to place them on the table, I'll take them now for a hundred guineas."

Certain Charlotte would accept, she began to count out her markers.

But Charlotte placed her hand out to stop Lady Finnister's.

"Not the earrings," she said firmly. "I'll play with what I have."

She pushed the last remaining markers forward and with a deep breath took up her cards. At last she'd received a good hand, and for the first time that evening, she won. Her share of the pool came her way, filling her pond. But she'd much further to go to recover her losses, and resolutely she pushed all her winnings into the pool again.

And she won again, and again, and again after that.

Before long, Charlotte had a small mountain of fish before her, the heaped mother-of-pearl gleaming softly in the candlelight where her pond overflowed with markers. She'd gone far beyond winning back her losses and what she owed the house's bank, yet still she played on, unable to resist the heady delirium of winning.

The crowd around the table grew. They cheered her with each new hand and wager, and roared when she won. While the ladies watched her play with envy, the gentlemen watched with desire—both for her luck and for her beauty.

"What is that racketing?" asked March, two rooms away. "Sounds like a pack of heathens."

"It could well be heathens," Lord Willoughby grumbled with an extra snort of disapproval. He was an older gentleman, powerful in the House but grim company everywhere else. "Many of the women here are as wanton and free as any savage's wife. Maybe more, considering how many feathers they thrust into their hair."

March only smiled. Not even Willoughby's grumpiness could spoil his humor this night, and besides, he liked the black plume that Charlotte was wearing in her hair, curling to one side of her face like an apostrophe.

His smile widened unconsciously as he thought of her. Things were going well, very well, with Charlotte this night. He'd resolved to trust her as she'd asked, and to his surprise it had worked. She'd been so happy and beguiling in the coach that he'd nearly had the carriage turned round for home so he'd have her to himself for the evening. She was becoming more and more a part of his life—even, perhaps, the best part. Already it had become difficult for him to remember a time when she wasn't his wife, and after only a fortnight of marriage, too. The tiniest things about Charlotte enchanted him: the graceful way she turned her head, how she smiled up at him, the unruly curls at the nape of her neck, and the way her laughter bubbled up so full of merriment that he was helpless to resist it, and her with it.

"I came here tonight for the single purpose of speaking a word or two to Sir Henry about the plans for the Wey Navigations, but though this is his house, I've yet to see him," Lord Willoughby was complaining. "Nothing but these jabbering young fools that are his wife's friends. Her 'set,' they are called. Bah, I would call them something else entirely, were I not a gentleman."

He held his glass out for a servant to refill. "The problem is that young wife of his. Vain, silly chit. No good can possibly come from a young wife." He frowned at March, majestically swaying back and forth. "You, Marchbourne. You have a young wife as well, do you not?"

"I do." March did not see the need to point out that, being a young man himself, a young wife made perfect sense. "But while my duchess is young, she is neither silly, vain, nor a chit. She is the eldest daughter of the late Earl of Hervey, and I am honored that she is my wife."

"Hervey, eh?" Willoughby squinted, clearly striving to recall the name. "Died young, with only a gaggle of girls? John Wylder, the fourth earl. I recall him now. His daughter must have brought you a pretty penny."

March smiled. In truth, he never thought of Charlotte's fortune. He'd plenty of his own, and besides, that wasn't why he wed her. "My lady has much to recommend her."

The howling crowd at the gaming table sounded again, and Lord Willoughby visibly shuddered.

"Like savages," he said succinctly. "Pity the poor gentleman who must wake to such racketing in his bed each morn."

But March was instead thinking of his own wife, in her own bed, and how much he'd like to be there with her.

Lord Willoughby was still grumbling, more to his brandy than to March.

"Painted, spendthrift young hussies, all of them," he said. "They wouldn't recognize a decent woman if they stumbled over one."

"Then you shall meet my duchess," March said. "Come with me, Willoughby, and I'll present her to you, so that you might see that youth and decency, yes, and beauty, too, are not exclusive."

Lord Willoughby made a final disgruntled snort of skepticism. "Then amaze me, sir," he said. "I'll gladly bow before your paragon."

March bowed, and turned to lead the way back to the room where he'd left Charlotte. He was looking forward both to seeing her again and to making Willoughby eat his tiresome words. Eagerly he searched the tables, hunting for Charlotte's unpowdered dark hair and the curling black plume. He spotted Lady Finnister's lavender-dusted hair first, in the center of a noisy crowd of hard-bitten gamesters. Likely she'd know where Charlotte was, and March headed toward her.

But at that moment, the crowd at the table whooped and crowed again, celebrating another's good fortune. At first March thought it must be Lady Finnister herself, which seemed entirely in keeping with her personality. Then he realized it was the lady beside her, the lady with the black plume in her hair. As March watched, stunned, Charlotte took up two of the pearly little fish from the table, and made them first bow to the cheering onlookers, then turn and kiss their tiny fishy lips together, as if congratulating each other. The crowd loved it.

"Flagrant, wanton creature," Willoughby sputtered behind him. "Shameless, shameless!"

Reluctantly March could almost agree. At once he pushed his way past the others to reach Charlotte, laying his hand on her shoulder. Laughing, she turned about, and her eyes lit with obvious pleasure.

"March!" she exclaimed happily. "You're just in time to see me triumph. Verily, verily, I am the luckiest fisherwoman of the evening."

Her eyes bright and teasing, she made the two fish markers kiss once again. Surely she didn't mean for the markers to represent themselves, did she? Newlywed fish, kissing to the delight of every last raucous soul here in Finnister's parlor?

"Charlotte, please," he said, all he could think of to say in the circumstances. If she'd made a show of the lovesick fish when they were alone in her bedchamber, he would have laughed as loudly as anyone else—perhaps even more loudly. But he was a private man, and this should have been a private entertainment. He'd always prided himself on possessing a certain dignity in public company, a reserve that was part of his rank, and he'd expected the same from his duchess. Didn't Charlotte realize that there was not one iota of dignity about kissing fish?

Clearly she didn't, not the way she was grinning. "I won, March," she said proudly. "Quite monstrously, too. I told you I'd skill with gaming, didn't I?"

Belatedly March noticed the sizable mountain of glittering markers before Charlotte's place. When he'd told her to play and enjoy herself, he'd imagined a discreet little game for ladies, not the kind of perilously high stakes that led to duels and ruin.

And talk. Damnation, all London would be chortling over his bride's boldness and daring with a wager in mixed company as well as those infernal kissing fish in her fingers. Yet here she was, still smiling up at him over her shoulder, so blithely, so innocently, that he really was at a loss for the proper words.

So of course he said improper ones. "Shall we leave, ma'am?"

Her brows rose sharply with surprise. "Now?"

He took a deep breath, a breath that sounded as loud as a gust of wind in the suddenly silent room.

"Now," he said. "If you please."

"As you wish." She slid from the chair, shaking out her skirts. "Let me gather my winnings—"

"No, leave it," he said, glancing at the towering pile of markers she'd won. "You've no need of any of it."

Charlotte bowed her head and nodded, outwardly agreeing as she placed the two last little fish on top of the pile. But bright red patches had appeared on her cheeks, and her lips were furiously pinched as if to bite back words that should not be said. Lady Finnister patted her arm in consolation, and the others around the table remained silent, too, not from embarrassment or shame, but from the hope that the Duke of Marchbourne would say some delicious, scolding, scandalous thing to his wife that could be repeated.

March, however, would rather be damned than oblige them. He'd already spoken enough—more than enough, really. In silence he took Charlotte's hand, and in silence he led her from the table.

"I won fairly, March," she began again. "Truly. I didn't cheat, or cozen, or—"

"No, Charlotte," he said. "Not now. Not here."

And in silence, the Duke and Duchess of Marchbourne left the house.

CHAPTER

 17

In all her life, Charlotte had never encountered any-thing so deep and inscrutable as March's silence.

Other people might refuse to talk, but his silence now was something entirely different. It reminded her of a well: she could lean over the side and peer deep into the bottomless darkness, but no matter what she said or even shouted into it, only her own words answered.

This was the silence he kept as they left the Finnisters' house, and the same silence that was her chilly com-panion on their way back to Marchbourne House. It accompanied her past the waiting servants and up the marble staircase, and when she started toward her own rooms, March wordlessly made it clear that she was to continue with him to his rooms instead.

He sent the servants away and shut the door so that they were alone, and when he motioned for Charlotte to sit, she perched on the very edge of his settee with her hands clasped tightly together. There was a well tended fire in the grate before her, as there was in nearly every hearth in Marchbourne House, but she felt none of its warmth, not with his silence filling the room, and she kept her cloak pulled around her shoulders. She watched as he crossed the room, poured himself a glass of wine, and drank it down with his back to her, still without a word.

Finally she could bear it no more.

"Clearly I have erred in some fashion, March," she began, speaking to his back, "and I am sorry for distressing you. But until you tell me exactly where I have misstepped or given offense, I can neither explain nor apologize any further. Nor will I beg forgiveness for sins I have not committed, nor—"

"Stop, Charlotte," he said without turning. "You're not making sense."

"Hah," she said. "And here I thought that was your specialty this evening."

"Mine?" He wheeled around to face her. "You would tell me that I am the one lacking sense?"

"Yes," she said as evenly as she could. She did not wish to quarrel with him again, but she didn't wish to be trapped into being a meek little mouse of a wife for the rest of their lives together, either. "I will tell you so, because it is true. You encouraged me to divert myself by joining the play at the gaming tables while you spoke to your associates, and I did exactly that. You *told* me to do that, March."

"I didn't tell you to act like a professional gamester and win so extravagantly."

"But the entire point of playing *is* to win!" she exclaimed. "Fortune smiled on me tonight, true, but I also warned you that I was a good player. Yet you didn't believe me, did you?"

"I didn't say that," he protested. "Not at all."

"You expected me to lose," she said, unable to hide her disappointment. "It's just like the riding, isn't it? You do not believe me to be accomplished in any way. Or is that what a duchess is supposed to do? Not try to excel? Would you rather I were an unaccomplished dullard, unable to do anything for myself?"

"Not at all," he said quickly. "It's more that a peeress

shouldn't, ah, call attention to herself quite so boldly. You had every eye in the room watching you play."

"You would rather I'd lost?" she asked. "You'd rather I'd been one of those ladies who fuss and fluster at a gaming table, and cannot even keep the cards in their fingers?"

He didn't answer, which was answer enough.

"Very well, March," she said. "But why stop at that? If you do not wish me to be noticed, then I will cease to follow fashions, and dress instead in the plainest of Quaker gray. I will give up my stays, and cut my hair short. I'll wear an untrimmed cap that ties beneath my chin, and cover my bosom with a thick coarse kerchief."

He frowned. "There's no need to be so dramatic, Charlotte."

"It will be the last time, I promise you that." She pulled the black plume from her hair and tossed it aside, then unhooked the heavy pearls from her ears. "And you had better take these, too. They cause too much notice, you see."

He ignored her outstretched hand with the earrings. "It wasn't just how much you won, Charlotte," he said. "It was that business with the markers, pretending that the fish were, ah, kissing."

She flushed, and let her hand with the earrings slowly drop to her side. "I did that to make you laugh," she said. "I thought you'd be entertained. I realize now that I was woefully mistaken."

"I *was* entertained, Charlotte, or at least I would have been if you hadn't chosen to entertain everyone else in the room as well. They were laughing at us instead of the fish, Charlotte, picturing us as—as besotted newly-weds."

"Which I rather thought we were," she said, her voice brittle with disappointment. "How foolish of me!"

"We are the newlywed Duke and Duchess of Marchbourne," he said. "We are not some newlywed Darby and Joan, frolicking in the hay to amuse the rest of the village."

He set the empty glass back down, tapping it lightly on the table before he finally left it. Wearily he crossed the room, finally coming to stand before her. "What am I to do, Charlotte? Can you tell me that?"

With one hand she pulled the cloak more closely about her shoulders. "What should you do with me?"

"Of course with you," he said. "What other meaning could I have?"

She looked up at him. With the fire behind him, his face was in shadow, and she couldn't make out enough of it to tell his mood. His voice was resigned, which frightened her. What if, after tonight, he'd decided that he was done with her? A husband—especially one who was a duke—could do that with a wife who didn't please him. What if he sent her away to live alone in one of his distant houses, so she'd never trouble him again?

If he banished her, her heart would break.

She bowed her head, staring down at her wedding ring, the firelight dancing off the clustered diamonds.

"Are you that unhappy?" he asked.

Surprised, she looked up swiftly. "Unhappy? You believe that I'm unhappy?"

"It's the reason for your discontent, isn't it?" he said, his voice heavy with sadness of his own. "If you were happy being wed to me, then you wouldn't be so restless."

"But I am neither restless nor unhappy, March, not at all!"

"Then why do you cry when I come to you at night?"

She caught her breath. "I—I did not know you noticed."

"How the devil could I not notice?" he asked, his frustration clear. "I try to treat you with every respect and courtesy, every kindness, and yet still you weep."

"I—I can't help it," she confessed miserably. "I don't know why. You are gentle and courteous, as kind a husband as can be, and yet—"

"I love you."

She looked up sharply. She wasn't sure that she'd heard the words from him, or only imagined them.

"I love you, Charlotte," he said again, more strongly this time. "I love you, and I cannot imagine my life without you in it."

"Oh, March." She let her cloak slip from her shoulders to the settee and quickly came to stand close before him. Now she could see his face clearly, and his emotions as well, writ achingly plain across his handsome face.

He loved her.

She could see it in his eyes even more clearly than she'd heard the words, and for the first time since they'd been wed, he'd lowered his guard of ducal propriety and let her peek inside. It hadn't been easy for him, but that made it all the more special. Bravely he loved her; he cherished her, he wanted her above all other women. In that single, heart-stopping moment, it was all there for her to see and relish.

But there was more to see, too, in the tension in his mouth and the tightness of his jaw. To her shock, she realized from the sadness and resignation in his face that as glorious as his declaration was to her, he also feared, even expected, that she wouldn't return it.

She wasted no time in correcting him.

"I love you, too, March," she whispered, her voice breaking with the perfection of saying it aloud. She reached up and held his face in her hands, making sure he'd never doubt her again. His stubbled jaw was rough against her palms, and she could feel the beating of his heart beneath her fingers. "I love you, and I do believe I was always meant to love you."

He smiled, and she felt that, too, with her fingers, his mouth curling up at the corners against her thumbs.

"I believe it so for me as well," he said softly. "I love you, Charlotte. Do you know I've never said that to any other?"

She smiled, too, the joy so tight in her breast that she feared she'd weep from it.

"Nor I," she said. "Nor should you, ever, ever, except to me."

As if to prove it, he took one of her hands in his own and turned his face toward her palm, kissing her there on the softest part. She shivered with delight, and with remembering.

"You kissed my hand like that the first time we were alone together," she said. "In the back room at the mantua-maker's. I didn't want you to stop."

"I wouldn't have," he said, kissing the inside of her wrist. "Except that your Aunt Dragon was thumping on the door outside, determined to protect your virtue."

She chuckled. "I vow she would have broken it down if we hadn't opened it."

"She's not here now, is she?" Using her hand to reel her in closer, he kissed her mouth. From the way he kissed her, Charlotte knew that even if Aunt Sophronia had somehow appeared at that very moment in her dragon guise, he would have ignored her, even if she had broken down the door. But what was a mere dragon before her duke? If only he would always be like this!

No, there was more than that. They both must change. If only they could forget the others crowding round their marriage, offering advice and suggestions and criticisms. If only they could simply be March and Charlotte as lovers, and not the imposing duke and duchess.

"Oh, March," she pleaded softly. "Why can we not always be like this, without a thought for what others think or say? What does our rank or station matter if we love each other?"

He was listening closely, watching her with such intensity that it gave her courage to continue.

"My own husband," she said, reaching up to run her fingertips over his lips. "I only wish to please you, you know. I don't give a tinker's dam for what anyone else might think or say. You're all that matters to me, March. All."

"All?" he repeated, the single word full of wonder.

"All," she said. "And I—"

But what she said was lost between them as he swept her back into his arms to kiss her with astonishing purpose, deepening the kiss until she melted against him. What choice did she have, truly? She loved being kissed like this, until her head grew dizzy and her bones dissolved inside her, and she was happy to yield to him in any way that she could. He tasted of the wine he'd just drunk, but it was his own masculine taste that made her giddy and robbed her of her sense. Really, it was just as well he kept his arm around her waist. If he let go now, she'd likely sink to the floor at his feet.

He must have sensed how weak she'd become, because his hand slid lower, his fingers spreading to fondle and squeeze her bottom even as he pushed her belly more tightly against him. Countless layers of clothing separated them, but she could still feel how hard and hot his cock had become as it pressed against her. She sighed raggedly into his mouth as they kissed. Excitement was gathering within her, too, that irresistible, unladylike heat that she'd felt only on their wedding night, when they'd both had too much to drink.

Aunt Sophronia had told her it was unseemly to feel so, unseemly and slatternly and unbefitting a lady of her rank and station. But where was the sin in it if she and

March loved each other? How could any pleasure that felt as fine and right as this be wrong?

She tightened her arms around his broad back because she needed his support, but more because she wanted to. He was tugging at the back of her skirts, tangling in the cloth as he struggled to reach her within all that linen and silk and the cane of her hoops. Abruptly he stepped back, and she gasped in disappointment.

"Go to your maid, Charlotte," he said, breathing hard. He clenched his hands tightly at his sides as he willed himself not to touch her further. "Have her undress you and prepare you for bed, and in a quarter hour's time, I'll come to you."

On any other night she would have done as he'd asked, returning to Polly and her own bed to wait in misery for his bleak, empty visit. But tonight she knew he loved her, and that changed everything. She glanced up beyond March to the portrait of his great-grandmother behind him, and Charlotte could have sworn that Nan Lilly's smile was for her.

No one should ever call the Duchess of Marchbourne a coward.

"I believe, March," she said, her breathing rapid, "that I'd rather stay here with you."

She retrieved her pearls from the table where she'd tossed them, and slowly hooked them back into her ears, the only things she intended to put back on. Slowly, too, she untied the lace kerchief from her shoulders and let it drift behind her. At once his gaze left her face to stare at her mostly bare breasts, raised and presented to him by her tight-laced stays. In the French fashion, of course.

He was either scowling or simply concentrating very hard on her breasts.

She sighed deeply, making sure that his concentration was well rewarded.

"Forgive me, March, but I no longer care what is appropriate and what is not," she said, lifting her arms to begin pulling the pins from her hair. "I told you that before."

"You did," March said, but with a decided lack of conviction—or rather, his conviction was more completely focused on her breasts. "That is, ah, true."

"Of course it's true," she said. "You're March and I am Charlotte, and I love you, and you love me."

She drew the last pin from her hair and shook it free, combing her fingers through the heavy waves so that they rippled over her shoulders. March didn't say anything, but she was quite sure she hadn't lost his attention. This was an *interested* silence, nothing like the one he'd used before to keep her away. Lightly she rested her hands on his chest.

"I'll act as your servant tonight," she said, already unfastening the heart-shaped shirt buckle. The buckle pinned the opening of his shirt closed, and to free the prong she had to slip her fingers inside his shirt, brushing against his chest. "There will be no more need for you to summon Giroux than for me to call Polly. If you'll let me, that is."

"How could I stop you, Charlotte?" he asked, his voice strained.

Deliberately she tucked the little heart in the front of her stomacher, glittering between her breasts. "If you wished to, you could."

"I could," he agreed, leaving the rest unsaid. He could but he wouldn't. It was as if he'd given himself permission, and she fervently prayed he wouldn't change his mind.

With a little smile she slipped her hands inside his jacket and eased it away from his shoulders and arms. She was surprised by how heavy it was: her clothes were as insubstantial and light as air, but his were weighed down with embroidery and buttons.

Buttons, and more buttons. While his coat had been open, his waistcoat wasn't, and one by one by one she undid the long row of small cut-steel buttons, fifteen in all. She didn't rush. She pushed each glittering button through its silk-stitched hole with care as her fingers made the slow progress down his chest and lower. She bent before him, and finally knelt before him, her skirts settling around her. From the way March tensed and shifted, struggling with his self-control, she suspected it all made for a teasing torment for him, which made her go more slowly still. She took extra time with the last buttons at the bottom of the waistcoat, and if her fingers brushed over his very evident cock inside his breeches, it was no more than artful accident.

Finally she reached the last button and swept the waistcoat from his shoulders. Her gaze met his for a moment, his dark eyes so full of smolder that she flushed and swiftly looked away. She was very much playing with fire. There was no other nor better way to describe it, and wondering how long he'd let her continue only made her game more exciting.

She stepped around him, as much to escape his gaze as to continue undressing him. She reached up and brushed his queue over his shoulder, and was surprised to see that the square buckle on the back of his stock was covered with rubies, too. Such a pretty, costly trinket, to be hidden by his collar, his hair, and his coat, and yet as she unfastened it and slowly drew the neck cloth free, she marveled at how many other such things she did not yet know about her husband. Even now she took a long minute to study him greedily, smoothing the white linen of his shirt over his broad shoulders and admiring the elegant fit of his breeches. It was a shame that gentlemen's long coats hid their backsides so completely, for at least her husband's was a handsome sight indeed, rounded and muscular from riding.

Swiftly she returned to his shirt, unbuttoning the cuffs before she stepped back before him to undo the two last buttons at his neck. From habit he raised his throat to make it easier, and she couldn't help but kiss him there, beneath his chin.

He started, then grinned. "Giroux never does that."

"I should expect not," she said, smiling at the notion of the staid valet ever taking such an outrageous liberty with his master. "But I could not resist, March. Indeed, I could not."

As if to prove it, she again kissed his chin, and his jaw, and then, inevitably, his lips as well. Yet while they kissed, she continued undressing him, pulling his billowing shirt free of his breeches and sliding her hands along his torso beneath it. His skin was warm and sleek, the play of his muscles beneath her hands fascinating. After that first night, he'd always taken care to come to her with his nightshirt, and whether it was unladylike or not, she'd missed . . . *this*.

But now as they kissed, he was beginning to undress her, too, though with more urgency than finesse. Before long he'd managed to remove her gown, petticoat, and hoops, and he'd even unpinned her stomacher from her stays, only once stabbing himself on a pin.

"Ouch," he said, breaking away from kissing her to stick his finger in his mouth. "Damnation, but there's a lot of sharp points to you."

She chuckled again. "Even roses have thorns."

"I'd rather think of a bramble bush," he said, turning her around. "At least once you pass the thorns, there's a sweet berry inside. What kind of devil's knot does your maid tie in your stays?"

"I don't know what Polly does, because I never see it." She turned her head to look back at him over her shoulder. "So you would rather think of me as a berry than a rose?"

"Of course," he said, fighting with the knotted lace. "A rose is good for admiring and nothing more, but a berry is not only beautiful, but sweet and juicy."

"'Sweet and juicy'?" she repeated, for it seemed a nonsensical compliment. "How can I be as juicy as a berry?"

"You'll see," he said, his voice so low and full of dark promise that she shivered. "There goes the knot."

There the knot went, and there went her stays, too, falling forward from her chest. She'd barely shrugged them free before he reached beneath her arms and into her shift to cup her breasts. She gasped with surprise and then with pleasure as he caressed her, tugging and teasing her nipples into stiff little peaks. Her breath quickened into little sighs of joy, and she closed her eyes and sagged back against him, covering his hands lightly with her own.

"You're beautiful, Charlotte," he murmured, kissing the side of her throat. "So beautiful."

If all he did with her tonight was this, then she'd be happy, it felt that fine. But she was greedy and wanted more, and besides, she longed for their play to last the night. She slipped free of his embrace and darted out of his reach.

"You've far too many clothes compared to me," she said breathlessly. He'd left her with only her shift, the fine Holland so sheer that she might as well be naked, and her shoes, stockings, and garters. She bent to pull his ruby-covered heart from her discarded stays, and tucked it instead in the neck of her shift. The weight pulled it down perilously low across her breasts, exactly as she'd hoped. "It's your turn now."

"Easily remedied," he said, quickly pulling off his buckled shoes and reaching for the buttons on the fall of his breeches.

"Let me," she said, stopping his hand. She knelt, but

instead of unbuttoning his fall, she began with the fastenings on the leg of his breeches, four small buttons and a buckle as well. When that was done, she untied his garter and pushed his stocking down along his well-muscled calf, then scurried over to the other leg to repeat the process.

"Charlotte," he said, his voice faintly strangled. "This is torture."

"I know," she said, brushing her lips over the back of his now-bared knee. "But if I'm to be a proper valet—"

"A proper valet would have been sacked by now," he said, and abruptly hauled her back to her feet.

"Then I'm glad I'm an improper one," she said, grinning wickedly as she reached down at last to the buttons on his fall.

"Improper, indeed," he growled. "If that is what you wish, I'll show you improper, and to the devil with what anyone else may think."

There was no refusing him, not the way he was kissing her now, and if he'd put an end to her charade as his valet, she couldn't imagine a better way. She'd never seen his bedchamber, and she'd no time to admire it now. She'd only a fleeting impression of a great deal of marble and painted goddesses floating across the ceiling and an enormous bed with woodwork and hangings that were all black and gold. Then she found herself in the middle of that bed, sinking deep into the featherbed and staring up at a canopy of gold brocade. March was with her, too, his expression so dark and determined that she smiled with anticipation. This was what she wanted, what she'd had with him that one time and what she'd ached for ever since.

"March," she said, her voice trembling with love and eagerness, holding her arms out to embrace him. But he didn't join her, not as she'd expected. Instead he knelt between her legs, gently easing them apart and feather ing the lightest of kisses along the inside of her knees and her thighs. She liked having him tease her like this, his jaw rough and his mouth hot on her skin. She giggled, partly because it tickled, and partly from not knowing what he meant to do next. But she learned soon enough, when to her shock he began kissing her most private place.

"*March!*" Scandalized, she tried to pull away. He'd promised her impropriety, and she couldn't imagine anything more improper than what he was doing to her now. "March, please!"

"We will forget everything and everyone, Charlotte, exactly as you wished," he said, his hands gripping her thighs to keep them open. "No one matters here but us."

Relentlessly he kissed her and licked her and teased her with his tongue, and after her first surprise had faded, she realized how delicious this—this *devouring* could be.

She felt herself grow impossibly wet, swelling and filling with pleasure, and the more she writhed against him, the stronger and more delicious the feelings became, coiling and tightening her entire body. Shamelessly she arched against him, and clutched knots of the sheets at her sides. He'd complained of her torturing him, but nothing she'd done could compare to this. Still holding her legs apart with his arms, he gently used his thumbs to part her further and uncover the center of her pleasure. He licked her there, *there,* and the tension broke and joy rushed over her, waves and waves of it so bright and sweet that she cried out with it.

She was still limp and gasping when he came up beside her. She wasn't surprised that he'd taken off his breeches or that his desire for her was blatant; she wasn't surprised by anything now.

"I want this gone," he said, shoving her shift up over her body. "I want to love you as you are, with nothing between us."

She pulled it over her head, and when it tangled on her arm, he pulled harder, tearing the fragile fabric and tossing it aside with an impatience that excited her all the more. His much-prized control was in the same tatters as her shift, and knowing she was the reason was a heady feeling. When he kissed her, urgently, she could taste herself on his lips, the musky sweetness of her own arousal. Quickly he settled over her, between her legs. She hadn't time to recover from her first pleasure, or to steel herself for the rough intrusion that she'd learned to associate with him.

But this time was different, so different she could scarcely believe it. When he entered her, there was no discomfort at all, but only a blissful friction that made her sigh with delight. With each powerful stroke, he filled her completely, wonderfully. She loved the feel of his skin against hers, the roughness of the hair of his chest against her breasts, loved the working of the muscles of his back as she held him and the deep, rasping groans as he plunged into her. Instinctively she curled her legs around his hips and moved with him, reveling in the tension that was building within her once again.

Abruptly he rolled onto his back, bringing her with him so that she was sitting astride him.

"There," he said, his eyes hooded and his breathing ragged. "Ride me, my own brave lass."

With her hands braced against his chest, she moved tentatively, sliding up and then down with a shuddering sigh. He seemed to fill her more completely this way, and the sensations were more intense.

"Take the lead," he said, placing his hands around the narrowest part of her waist to guide her. "Race with it. Ride me hard, and find what pleases you best."

She nodded, and began moving in earnest. Naked though she was, she still wore her earrings, and the pearls swung back and forth against her neck. Quickly she found the rhythm that pleased her and him as well, or so she guessed by the way he bucked beneath her. Faster and faster she rode him, her heart thumping and her blood pounding and every scrap of her body intent on finishing the wild, glorious race with him. She was close, so close, and when he reached up to stroke her where she was most open to him, she climaxed again and brought him with her, his final cry of release a deeper match for her own.

Afterward he pulled the coverlet up and held her close, her body curled against his and his arm protectively across her. She'd never felt closer to him, nor more in love, either. She listened to his breathing, slow and calm, and when she twisted around to face him, she saw that his eyes were closed and his lips parted. With his dark hair tangled around his face and his features relaxed and at peace, he had never looked more content, nor more handsome. She was almost afraid to break the spell, yet she couldn't resist brushing her lips over his in the gentlest of kisses.

"I love you, March," she whispered, barely breathing the words as she drifted off to sleep. "Oh, how I love you!"

Later he kissed her awake and made love to her again, their passion as fiery as before. He'd bid her to face away from him and hold on to one of the thick carved bedposts for support. She'd laughed at the foolish posture, until he entered her from behind and she discovered that the deliciousness of it far outweighed any mere foolishness. Exhausted, she laid atop him, their sweaty limbs tangled intimately together.

"Why didn't we do this before?" she asked drowsily. "Why, I wonder?"

"That's easy enough to answer," he said, and for the first time that night she saw the old darkness flicker across his face, ready to close her out. "There's reasons enough, aren't there?"

No, no, please, no, she thought desperately, now sharply awake. *Don't retreat from me again!*

"Forget them," she said urgently. "Whatever reasons you might dream aren't worth remembering. This is what matters, March, here between us. Please, oh, please recall what I said! Here we're only lovers, March, and the only ones we need please are ourselves."

"We did do that, didn't we?" he said. "I've never loved anyone as I love you, Charlotte. More than the world, and the moon in the heavens, too."

But there was weariness in his smile and melancholy in his kiss, and though he slept again, she lay awake long after that, her hand linked tightly into his as if that would be enough to keep him close and safe.

At last she slept, and woke with the sun streaming in fine lines between the still-closed curtains. She blinked, not recognizing March's bed, then rolled over to find him gone and only his impression on the pillows remaining.

Of course. Of course. Though her heart plummeted, she knew she'd expected it to be so.

"Good morning, Your Grace," Polly said cautiously, holding her usual morning tray as if they were in Charlotte's bedchamber instead of March's. Behind her stood an uneasy footman, his eyes carefully averted.

At once Charlotte jerked the sheets over her bare breasts and shoulders, clear to her chin. "Good morning, Polly. Good morning, Giroux. Is His Grace in the next room?"

"No, Your Grace," the footman said, as intensely uncomfortable as a man could be. Still concentrating on the carpet, he stepped forward to hand Charlotte a letter. "His Grace was unavoidably called away to Greenwood. He did not wish you to be disturbed, ma'am. He left this for you, ma'am."

To Greenwood. He'd run far this time, clear to the country, and her heart sank even lower. She might chase him from one room to the next in their house, but she wouldn't follow as far as the country. She couldn't, not with the distinct possibility that he might only run farther if she did.

No. Yet she didn't doubt that he loved her. Even her ever-sinking heart knew that, and the glorious lovemaking of last night had proved it. Nor did she doubt that he'd come back to her, for the Duke of Marchbourne would never risk the public scandal of abandoning his duchess entirely.

But though the duke would return, it was the man she feared for. What demons drove him from her? What could make him feel such guilt over loving her, and being loved in return?

She forced herself to smile. "How kind of His Grace to let me sleep," she said, taking the letter to read later in private. "Of course I recall now that he was to leave for the country so early. La, sometimes I believe I'd forget my own name."

Polly smiled with relief. "Would you like me to fetch your dressing gown, ma'am?"

"Thank you, yes," Charlotte said. "Giroux, would you please locate the address of the painter Sir Lucas Rowell, and have a carriage for me at eleven to take me there?"

As she moved her head, the pearls that March had given her swung against her neck, a silent reminder of her absent husband. She couldn't begin to understand what devils possessed him, not yet, but she would. She *would,* and she would fight them, and she would win: for his sake, for hers, for theirs.

And she'd already a plan to start.

CHAPTER

❧ 18 ❧

Charlotte sat on the same seat in the carriage, in the same place, as she did when traveling with March: facing forward, slightly to the right of center so he wouldn't step on her skirts. Of course there was no danger of that while he was somewhere in Surrey instead of here with her in London, but sitting in the same place somehow made the carriage feel less empty and Charlotte less alone.

She looked down at her muff, a beautiful concoction of silk satin, loops of French ribbon, and white swansdown, large enough to hide March's letter tucked deep inside. The heavy paper lay against her hand, the raised wax seal so thick she could read it with her fingertips.

She wasn't sure why she'd brought it with her now, except perhaps as a talisman. It wasn't really even a letter, but more of a note, and she already knew the hastily written words by heart:

> *My dearest Charlotte,*
> *Forgive me if you can for what I have done & know*
> *that I love you above all others.*
>
> > *Yr. husband forever,*
> > *M.*

There'd been no mention of what he'd done that needed forgiving, why he'd left, or when he would return. Not that Charlotte had expected any. To her regret, it seemed that she and March had spent almost all of their married life together apologizing and forgiving, and she prayed that they'd soon learn simply to love and accept as ordinary people did.

She felt very young and very alone in this, and wished desperately for her mother's wise counsel, the only person in whom she might confide without feeling she was somehow betraying March. But was this only part of learning to trust each other, one more part of learning to love? Perhaps every new husband was unsure like this, a devoted and consummate lover one moment, only to withdraw and flee the next? At least March's note had ended with a pledge for the future, and those few comforting words of love—*know that I love you above all others*—were the ones she kept repeating over and over to herself.

Those same words had also given her the courage to be in this carriage now, on her way to the studio of Sir Lucas Rowell. She'd never met a true artist, let alone sat for one, especially not one with the daunting reputation and talent of Sir Lucas. She hoped to persuade him to paint her portrait as quickly as possible, so that she might send it to March at Greenwood. March held portraits in the highest regard; they were his favorite form of painting. She'd only to remember how much he liked and respected the portrait of the first duchess in his parlor, and how other members of his family stared down from nearly every wall in his house. To him portraits represented family and permanence, which was why he'd suggested that they have their portraits painted in honor of their marriage.

But Charlotte was determined not to wait for that. A portrait of her now would prove to March that she already considered herself his wife and his duchess, and always would. It would be a part of her there with him, and she hoped her painted image would inspire him to return more quickly to the flesh-and-blood reality.

The carriage stopped, the door opened, and with her head high in her plumed hat, Charlotte waited while her footman knocked on Sir Lucas's door. She still wasn't accustomed to the response that her new title drew. Sir Lucas's poor housekeeper nearly tripped over herself welcoming her into the artist's house, while his dogs barked at her footman and other servants raced about like headless hens.

Sir Lucas himself hurried into the hall to greet her. He was a middle-aged gentleman with a bulbous nose, and he wore a fur-trimmed velvet cap on his head and a canvas coat brilliant with daubs of every color of paint.

He ushered her through the house and back to his work-room, a room the size of a small ballroom with extra tall, curtainless windows along one wall, thrown open to the garden beyond. It wasn't a tidy room. New canvases and completed pictures leaned haphazardly against walls and chairs, and costumes, drapery, and painterly props were strewn here and there. Plaster casts of ancient statues served both as inspiration and as makeshift tables, with a blank-eyed Venus balancing an empty teacup on her head. A long table for mixing paint and cleaning brushes stood to one side. The room's centerpiece was Sir Lucas's easel, with a half-finished portrait of an as-yet-faceless general. Standing in for the general was his gold-braided coat and hat, arranged on a wooden mannequin on a low modeling stage before the easel. A red and blue par-rot in a brass cage chattered and squawked, and despite the open windows, the oily scent of paint and turpentine mingled with the aroma from a pot of fresh coffee on a nearby table.

Quickly Sir Lucas cleared a chair for Charlotte.

"I cannot begin to tell you what an honor it is to have

you here, Your Grace," he began. "A great lady of your beauty and rank in my humble studio!"

"I am the one who is honored, Sir Lucas, to be in the presence of such genius," Charlotte said, her eyes wide as she looked about the exotic clutter. "I saw Lady Finnister's portrait last night, and judged it the loveliest and most like I'd ever seen."

Sir Lucas beamed and dramatically swept his cap from his head as he bowed.

"You are too, too kind, ma'am," he said. "But as handsome as Lady Finnister's picture might be, ma'am, I am sure the one I'd make of you would surpass it in every degree, if you'd but honor me with your patronage."

Charlotte smiled, imagining Lady Finnister's indignation if she'd heard that. "I wish not one painting from you, Sir Lucas, but three. My husband the duke and I wish you to paint us as a pair to mark our wedding."

"A splendid notion, ma'am," Sir Lucas said, his eyes brightening at the prospect of the sizable commission. "I would venture you'd want the portraits full-length, to mark so momentous an occasion properly."

"That will be for my husband to determine," Charlotte said, "though I would expect he'll have no wish to scrimp on paintings destined for Marchbourne House."

"No, no indeed." Sir Lucas rubbed his paint-stained hands together with anticipation. "And the third portrait, ma'am? Who is the subject to be, ma'am?"

Charlotte took a deep breath, hoping she'd be able to explain her wishes. "I wish a portrait of myself, Sir Lucas, as a special gift for the duke. Are you familiar with an old painting from the last century of the first Duchess of Marchbourne?"

"The shepherdess, ma'am?" He hurried to rummage through a nearby portfolio and returned with an engraving of the painting, the kind of cheap print of famous folk often pinned to the walls of taverns and common houses. "Is it this one?"

"It is," Charlotte said, unable to keep from blushing at the sight of the bare-breasted Nan Lilly in the artist's presence. "I wish to have myself painted in a similar pose, thought not quite so—so—"

"So antique," Sir Lucas suggested delicately. "It was a different time, with far less refinement than our present day."

"Yes," Charlotte said with relief. "Then you understand. I would like to be painted sitting the same way, with the same sort of setting, so that the duke will at once see the connection between us."

"A cunning conceit, ma'am," Sir Lucas said thoughtfully, nodding. "You are to be congratulated for your invention. Dare I ask if the earrings you wear now are—"

"The same ones?" Charlotte touched the pearls, wistfully thinking again of March. "They are, Sir Lucas, and I would especially wish that they be included. This, too."

She pulled a bundled handkerchief from her muff and unwrapped March's ruby heart pin. She'd retrieved it this morning, still pinned to the tattered remains of her shift. "It belongs to His Grace, you see, and has special meaning to me."

"A wondrously pretty bauble, ma'am," he said. "I could show it pinned to your bodice, but it would be much more sentimental if you were to hold it in your open hand, as if offering your own heart to His Grace."

"Oh, yes, I'd like that." Swiftly she looked down at the little heart, hoping Sir Lucas wouldn't notice the tears that had suddenly filled her eyes. "Then we are agreed, sir. How quickly can the painting be produced? I should like it sent to the duke this evening, if possible."

"This evening, ma'am?" The painter's mouth fell open with astonishment. "Forgive me, ma'am, but as much as I regret disappointing a lady like yourself, that is impossible. A painting such as this takes weeks, even months, to complete. There must be sittings, and sketches, and preparation of the canvas, and painting, and curing, and framing."

"I did not realize," Charlotte said, disappointment sweeping over her. "I've no knowledge of painting, you see."

"But all is not lost, ma'am, all is not lost." Sir Lucas tapped his fingers against his cheek, thinking. "If you wish to send His Grace a token, a memento, then we could oblige him with a drawing of you in chalks. To be sure, it would only be a preliminary drawing, with none of the subtleties of a painting in oils, but I am certain I could produce an agreeable and pleasing likeness within an hour or two, if Your Grace would be so kind as to sit for me."

Within a quarter hour—and with the assistance of Sir Lucas's housekeeper as a lady's maid—Charlotte had changed into a fanciful costume of gauzy linen and silver ribbons that bared her arms and feet but nothing more. Holding the old print for comparison, Sir Lucas had taken great care to arrange her pose and her drapery to match Nan Lilly's as closely as possible. He pinned a fresh sheet of paper to a board at his easel and began, with much furious scowling and muttering and sweeping, scraping strokes of the chalk over the page.

Sitting perfectly still was much more difficult than Charlotte had ever dreamed, yet though her nose itched and her right foot fell asleep, the very idea of the picture was wildly exciting, and she could scarce wait to see it done. She'd no idea of how long she posed, which was likely the reason there was no clock in Sir Lucas's studio.

"We are close, ma'am," Sir Lucas said absently, as if sensing her impatience. "We are close."

"Might I see it, please?" Charlotte begged, taking care

to move only her eyes toward him and not to shift her head from how he'd placed it. "Please, Sir Lucas?"

The artist stepped back and with a flourish tossed the chalk aside. "You may indeed, ma'am."

Charlotte hopped from the stand and ran to the easel, and gasped with delight. The drawing was extraordinarily beautiful, larger than she'd expected, in black chalk with white as a highlight, and done with remarkable detail for such haste.

"That's me!" she exclaimed. "That's me exactly, Sir Lucas!"

"You as a fanciful shepherdess at any rate, ma'am," he said, clearly pleased by her reaction. "I doubt you'll ever be seen like this ambling through the park, but His Grace will know you at once, and that's what matters, isn't it?"

Charlotte nodded. The longer she looked at the drawing, the more she realized how Sir Lucas had captured much more of her mood than she'd realized. Though the pose was as mannered as the original, he'd sensitively discovered a longing in her face and in the way she held the ruby heart in her outstretched hand, a poignancy that she hadn't expected. She truly was offering her heart to him. How could March resist such a picture, or mistake the love that would come with it?

"Thank you, Sir Lucas," she said softly. "It is *perfect*."

The housekeeper came bustling in, her hands in her apron. "More company, Sir Lucas, more guests," she announced. "Lady Finnister and Lord Andover."

"Not company, but the very dearest of friends!" exclaimed Lady Finnister, racing toward Charlotte. "Good day, Your Grace, good day! What a charming, charming surprise to find you here, when my only paltry business was to ask after copies. I know you said you wished Sir Lucas to paint your portrait, but I'd no notion you meant today!"

She held her arms outstretched as if expecting Charlotte to forget propriety and welcome her embrace.

But Charlotte hadn't forgotten last night's disasters, or how they'd come about, or how she didn't at all think of Lady Finnister as being her very dearest friend, or really any manner of friend at all. Instead of returning Lady Finnister's exuberant greeting, Charlotte pointedly kept her hands clasped before her, and waited for Lady Finnister to curtsey, as was proper before a duchess, even a duchess in the makeshift garb of an ancient shepherdess.

Belatedly Lady Finnister realized her error and turned her unwanted embrace into a fluttering curtsey. Lord Andover bowed without prompting, but there was nothing respectful about the way his gaze remained on Charlotte, wolfishly taking note of everything that her wispy costume revealed. Beneath his scrutiny, Charlotte blushed, heartily wishing she hadn't. She wrapped one of Sir Lucas's extra lengths of drapery over her bare shoulders and arms, against both the chill and Lord Andover's gaze.

"Come, my lord, let us play the critic," Lady Finnister said, familiarly tucking her hand into Lord Andover's arm. Whatever friction might have existed between them last night was gone today, and they lolled against each other with such ease that Charlotte wondered if the brittle words she'd heard last night at the gaming table had been meant only as some kind of provocative flirtation.

Sir Lucas turned the easel to better display the drawing. "It was Her Grace's idea to pose in the manner of the first duchess, a pretty conceit to amuse His Grace."

"How perfectly charming!" exclaimed Lady Finnister. "Sir Lucas, you must draw me exactly the same way for Sir Henry."

"He could, my dear, but the effect would not be the same," Lord Andover drawled, leaning closer to the picture. "Only a duchess can pretend she's a shepherdess. It goes with the strawberry leaves."

"Oh, Andover." Lady Finnister rolled her eyes and tapped his arm with her furled fan. "I should like to see you as shepherd, or perhaps just a sheep."

Lord Andover ignored her, instead studying the drawing against the old print that Sir Lucas had pinned to the top of the easel for reference.

"It's a fine likeness, Sir Lucas," he said, "but I do find some fault with the costume. The original shows the lady in becoming dishabille. For the sake of capturing true beauty, shouldn't the copy be equally revealing?"

"No, Lord Andover, it should not," Charlotte said tartly. "It is a gift meant for my husband, not the wall of a bawdy house."

Lord Andover laughed, his gaze wandering to her breasts. "All the more reason for you not to be so coy. Being male, His Grace must surely enjoy the sight of your charms."

"But being my husband, Lord Andover," Charlotte said, her indignation growing as she pulled the improvised shawl more closely around her, "he'd rather not share any part of me with other males."

"Pray be easy, ma'am, be easy," said Lady Finnister, her voice placating. "Lord Andover is only trying to provoke you. It's his way, you know, and signifies nothing. But where is His Grace? If my husband were half so handsome as yours, I'd never let him stray from my sight."

Charlotte wouldn't have, either, if it had been up to her. "The duke was called to the country on a sudden emergency," she said. "I expect him back as soon as the affair is resolved."

"To the country?" Lord Andover asked with surprise. "What manner of emergency could possibly draw a bridegroom away from his bride's bed so soon after the wedding?"

"Hush, Andover." Lady Finnister raised a single painted brow. "I hope we were not the cause of that emergency, ma'am. La, I've never seen a husband grow so angry over his wife's winning as yours did last night."

"It was a private, petty misunderstanding between us, Lady Finnister, now resolved," Charlotte said as severely as she could. It was too late to undo what had been done, but she still could try to keep their private life private, exactly as March had so wisely counseled. "It was of no lasting consequence."

"Of course not, ma'am," Lady Finnister said. "Our merry mob will be playing again this evening at my house. If His Grace returns in time from the country—or even if he doesn't—we should be thoroughly honored to have you return to us."

"Especially if His Grace doesn't return, ma'am," Lord Andover said, leaning closer to Charlotte. "There's nothing to be gained by being lonely in London, nor any virtue to it, either. And as your friend, I—"

"But you are not my friend, Lord Andover," Charlotte said, as sharply as she could. "Nor do I ever believe you shall become one."

"Oh, ma'am, pray do not be so severe to poor Andover," Lady Finnister said, patting the marquess on the arm as if to console him. "He means no ill toward you."

"You need only try me, ma'am." Lord Andover smiled, and dared to wink as well. "Unlike husbands, I bring only pleasure and amusement."

"There, ma'am, you see how it is," Lady Finnister said. "You must join us this evening. The company will be quite bereft without you."

"Thank you, Lady Finnister, but I must decline," Charlotte said quickly. "I wish to be at home when His Grace returns."

With that in mind, she left the studio as soon as she could, and returned to Marchbourne House. She'd canceled the day's wedding calls, not wishing to make them without March at her side, but without his company, the afternoon stretched interminably. She began letters to her mother and sisters, but tossed them unfinished into the fire. She picked up a half-dozen novels, only to put each aside after a page or two. When Polly brought her dinner to her room, she realized she'd no appetite, and pushed the tray away untouched.

She sat by the window, sighing. Sir Lucas had arranged for her portrait to be sent that very afternoon, and she imagined it strapped to the back of some fleet courier's saddle. She hoped March liked the picture; most of all, she hoped it would make him return to London, and to her.

But as the sun set and the empty evening stretched before her, she was forced to realize that he likely would not come back that day or even that night. Greenwood Park was many hours from London, and it would be nearly impossible for him to have journeyed there this morning, done whatever it was he was determined to do during the day, and come back to town.

Whatever March was doing, he was clearly doing it without her. The more she considered this, the more lonely and despondent she became. They hadn't even been wed a fortnight, and already her husband had left her. He'd told her it wasn't her fault, but how could it not be? Somehow she'd driven him away, and not knowing the reason only made it worse. She'd felt better when she'd been at Sir Lucas's studio, because then she'd been taking action, however empty it might prove to be, and not merely waiting. Now the vast house seemed so empty that even the silence echoed, and she'd never felt more alone, nor more unhappy.

She was so lost in her misery and in missing March

that she started when Polly came to the door again. With her was a footman from the front hall and, more surprising, a footman who wasn't hers.

"Forgive me for interrupting you, Your Grace," Polly said with a hasty curtsey. "But this man says he has a most urgent message for you from His Grace."

"From His Grace?" Eagerly Charlotte rose to address the man. "What news have you of the duke? Have you brought me a letter, a note?"

"Your Grace." The footman bowed low, his expression blankly inscrutable in the manner of the best-trained servants. "I regret that I have not, ma'am. His Grace did not wish to take the time to write, but sent me to deliver his message in person."

That was so unlike March that immediately Charlotte feared the worst. "He isn't injured, is he? Not harmed, or ill?"

"Not at all, ma'am," the footman said quickly. "He is attending my mistress, Lady Finnister, at her home, and wishes you to come join him there."

"The duke is with Lady Finnister?" Charlotte frowned, both perplexed and doubtful, too. Given March's feelings regarding Lady Finnister—and he'd made no secret of them—she couldn't imagine why, if he had in fact returned to town, he'd gone there, rather than here. Yet she'd no real reason to doubt the servant, especially now that she recognized his livery as belonging to the Finnisters. "He is there now?"

"Yes, ma'am," the footman said. "His Grace arrived in the company and coach of His Grace the Duke of Breconridge, who brought him direct from the company."

That did make sense. It was entirely like Brecon to have fetched March back from the country, and likely, too, that Brecon would then have thrust March into the raucous company of the Finnisters as a way of improving his spirits—and hers.

She frowned, still considering. "Parker, how long would it take to ready a carriage for me?"

"Forgive me, ma'am," said the other footman. "Lady Finnister sent her own carriage for your use. It waits at the door."

"How kind of her," Charlotte murmured. It truly did seem as if everything had been arranged. The three servants stood in respectful silence before her, waiting for her to make up her mind. She could stay here alone, or she could join March. What kind of decision was that?

"The blue silk with the pink ribbons, Polly," she said. "And quickly, too. I do not wish to keep His Grace waiting."

March dropped heavily into the old armchair before the fire, stretching his stockinged feet before him toward the warmth. He'd two of his favorite dogs asleep before him, and another snoring lightly with her chin on his knee. Since he'd arrived at Greenwood this afternoon, he'd purposely not stopped working. With Carter at his side to take notes, he'd been everything a conscientious lord and landowner should be. He'd gone from surveying a freshly sprouted field to smiling at the foals in the stable enclosure, from viewing the new bricks relining the icehouse near the lake to inspecting the old drain near the dairy. He listened to the head gardener's report and agreed that there should be fewer cabbages planted and more asparagus, and he'd knelt in the empty dolphin fountain to peer into the pipes with the engineer to make sure for himself that it truly did need fresh lead plumbing before it was filled for the season.

When the sun had set, he'd moved his labors to his library, going over every ledger book and record with Carter as if they hadn't done it only two weeks before. Only when Carter had been literally falling asleep in his chair had March released him, the tall clock in the great hall chiming two in the morning.

Yet March himself remained restless, his thoughts still far too uneasy to give way to the peace of sleep. He'd been able to push away his memories of last night as long as he'd been occupied and around others. Now, with only the dogs and the fire before him for company, those memories came rushing back to torment him: Father and Rome, ruined temples and lewd paintings, and Father's endless drinking and belligerence. And women: jeweled courtesans, brash actresses, or low, filthy creatures from the river, they were all the same to Father, and all used the same way, too. No matter how March had tried to bury his head in his pillow, he heard the same every night, Father's drunken laughter and the women's, too, and then the terrifying roars and grunts and exclamations and cries that had sounded more like animals than humans. He'd had no choice, not with Father. What he'd been forced to witness had stayed with him ever after.

Yet why should he believe that he was any better? The old saying was that blood will tell, and it had told last night. What he'd done to Charlotte, how he'd treated her—he'd never forget that, either. No matter how he tried, he couldn't escape.

He was the Duke of Marchbourne, and he was his father's son.

CHAPTER

19

Charlotte paused in the doorway to Lady Finnister's parlor, eagerly scanning the room for her first glimpse of March. Seemingly nothing had changed from the night before, with the same elegantly dressed company engaged in much the same pursuits around the same tables.

But everything that had seemed brilliant and exciting last night had now lost both its brilliance and excitement without March to share it, and she made her way into the crowded room, determined to find him as soon as she could. "Oh, Your Grace, how happy I am to see you!" exclaimed Lady Finnister, rushing to greet her. "I never dreamed you would come, I never thought—that is, it's *such* a pleasure to have you back among us."

"Thank you," Charlotte said, "and thank you for the kind use of your carriage as well. Now, if you could please tell me where I could find the duke—"

"Oh, the carriage was nothing, nothing at all!" Lady Finnister's laugh was shrill, and to Charlotte there seemed to be a false, nervous note to it as well. "I am most honored to have assisted you, ma'am."

Charlotte smiled and tried to ease past her, but Lady Finnister abruptly seized her by the arm. It was a bold, improper familiarity, but what startled Charlotte more was the anxiety she saw in the other woman's eyes.

"I could not help it, ma'am," Lady Finnister confided

in a swift, urgent whisper. "How could I? I pray you might understand, one lady to another. His rank is so much greater than mine, and when he asked, I could not refuse."

Charlotte drew back with surprise. She couldn't imagine March imperiously demanding the use of the Finnister carriage, not the way Lady Finnister was making it sound.

"Please don't distress yourself," she said as kindly as she could. "I'm sure he never intended to impose in any way."

But Lady Finnister only shook her head, her painted eyes watery with unshed tears. "He waits for you down that passage, in Sir Henry's library."

"Then I must go." Charlotte's heart raced with anticipation as she made her way through the crowded rooms, past the gaming tables, and down a short hall to the library. Clearly this was Sir Henry's male domain in a house dominated by his wife, with manly leather armchairs and bronzes of fighting gladiators, and the overbearing reek of tobacco, even with the two windows open over the garden.

But to her sorrowful disappointment, there was no sign of the one male she wished most to see.

"March?" she called uncertainly as she walked deeper into the room, hoping against hope that he'd suddenly pop out from behind a tall-backed armchair, or perhaps that Chinese screen. She glanced from the open window, wondering if he'd gone to the garden. "March? Are you here?"

"Alas, dear lady, I fear he is not," Lord Andover said, the latch on the door closing shut with an ominous click. "That is, alas for you, but most fortunate for me."

Charlotte turned to face him, so swiftly that her silk skirts swung whispering around her ankles. "Lord Andover!"

"Your servant, Your Grace," he said, bowing deeply, though still somehow managing to leer at her. "I cannot tell you how pleased and honored I am to have your company to myself."

"And I cannot tell you how displeased I am by it," she sputtered indignantly. "Now please open that door at once, so that I may pass. I came here to meet my husband, not you, and when he learns of your—your presumption, he will surely have strong words for you."

"Oh, I've no doubt of that, ma'am," he said, sauntering slowly toward her instead of opening the door. "But you needn't fear me. I have only the highest regard both for your honor and for your husband's temper."

"I am glad of that, Lord Andover," Charlotte said, backing away. Where *was* March, anyway? "Because you do not wish to discover which is the more fierce."

He showed too many of his teeth when he laughed. "Your honor is fierce, ma'am?"

"If necessary, my honor can be as fierce as any tigress's," she said, striving to sound as fierce as she claimed, and not as uneasy as she felt. "Now let me pass, else when the duke joins us—"

"Alas again, ma'am, but His Grace will not be joining us," he said, relentlessly closing the distance between them, "not unless he has sprouted angel's wings to carry him here from Greenwood."

"But he sent for me himself," Charlotte protested, and even as she spoke, she realized the appalling truth. The Finnister carriage, the footman with his verbal message instead of a written one, Lady Finnister's halting apology—it all made dreadful sense to her now. The marquess had learned March had left town from her at Sir Lucas's studio, and her trust and eagerness had made her gullible. March wasn't here and never had been, and she was the greater fool for believing the lies.

"You—you *lured* me here," she said, not hiding her

disgust. "You say you respect me and my honor, and then you act in this vile, deceitful fashion!"

Lord Andover's smile was more of a smirk. "There is no deceit in the game of love, Duchess. Now that we are alone, I hope you will put aside these tedious scruples so we might explore more . . . more enjoyable pleasures together, yes?"

He reached to touch her cheek, and she swatted his hand away. He wasn't as tall as March, not much taller than she herself, but he was as broad-chested as a bull, and she'd no wish to test her strength against his.

"Might I remind you that you promised to respect me, Lord Andover?" she said, trying to sound haughty and aloof. "And my husband, the duke, as well?"

He wasn't impressed. Instead he pushed closer, his arms arching out on either side to corner her. His ruddy face had grown even more red, his expression so determined that the first flutterings of real fear rose in her chest.

"Your husband, you say," he said, his eyes gleaming with desire. "If Marchbourne's not man enough for you, Duchess, then I'm happy to serve you in his stead."

"*You!*" she exclaimed, holding her hands out to keep him back. It wasn't much use; she'd backed away so far that she'd almost reached the wall, and now she was cornered with no further retreat. "You're not a tenth of my gentleman-husband—nay, not a hundredth. Away with you, sir, before I make a row and disgrace you!"

"No, you won't," he countered, breathing hard. "You'd be the one disgraced, ma'am, not I. Anyone you summon will see that you are here with me of your own will."

He was almost right. To be discovered in an unseemly tussle with Lord Andover would shame both her and March. What she did in the next few moments could bring more scandal crashing into his exemplary life than he'd ever experienced, and she loved him too much to do that to him. She *couldn't*.

"Come now, Duchess, let's amuse ourselves," Lord Andover coaxed, inching ever closer. "Show me this tigress in you. Yes, yes, show your Wylder blood! Show your claws, ma'am, and by God, I'll tame you."

"You will not, sir, not at all." She jerked to one side and remembered the open window, there like a gift from Providence. Without a second's hesitation she sat on the sill and swung her legs over, the same as she'd done thousands of times at Ransom Manor. She reached for the thick branch of the oak tree that stood obligingly nearby and pulled herself onto the branch, her hooped skirts fluttering and tangling around her legs. Desperately she tried to find her footing, the leather soles and high heels of her mules slipping on the smooth bark, until she kicked them off and they fell to the garden path below. Her feet in silk stockings were better, much better, and with a small sigh of concentration she sidled down the branch to the trunk and away from Lord Andover, her skirts rustling along with the oak leaves.

"What in blazes are you doing, Duchess?" the marquess demanded furiously from the window. "Are you mad? Come back here at once, before you fall and break your empty skull!"

"I'd sooner fall than return to you, Lord Andover," she shouted back. "I'd sooner remain here all the night long."

"You're a teasing, taunting bitch, that's what you are," he roared back, his anger and frustration spilling over. "Come back here at once, I say. Come back here now!"

But Charlotte had no intention of leaving her branch, and tucking her skirts around her legs, she crouched on her new perch. She looked down and saw the astonished, upturned faces of guests who'd been strolling in the garden, with more people streaming from the house to gawk at the rare sight of a duchess in a tree.

"Good friends, you see my plight," she called down to them. "To preserve my virtue and my husband's honor from this rogue who pretends to be a gentleman, I was forced to flee here. Nor shall I come down until I know I'll be safe."

"Shame on you, Lord Andover," scolded a lady from the gathering crowd. "To chase a poor lady like that!"

"You'll be next, Andover," called a gentleman. "March will dangle you over a branch when he hears you've dragged his lady into your scandal, see if he won't."

The bystanders laughed, and Charlotte cringed, horrified. The last thing she wished was for March to feel he must defend her honor. But if she was being regarded as the victim, then there wasn't truly a scandal, was there?

"There is nothing scandalous about me," she called down. "It's all Lord Andover's fault, not mine, nor my husband's."

But to Charlotte's mortification, there was laughter and applause in reply, not the understanding or sympathy she'd hoped for. Oh, why wasn't March here to rescue her again from this tree, the way he had the first time they'd met?

"Charlotte?"

She leaned around the branch to see who'd called her by her given name.

"Charlotte," the gentleman said again. "Good evening, my dear."

It wasn't March, but it was his favorite cousin, the Duke of Breconridge. Nothing shocked or scandalized Brecon, and even now he was smiling at her as genially as if he were addressing her in her carriage, instead of speaking to her as she swayed barefoot in a tree.

"Can you return to the window?" he asked. "Or must I send a footman to bring you down?"

He met her in the library, holding her shoes—retrieved from the bushes by a servant—in one hand. Lord Andover was gone, nor was there any sign of Lady Finnister, either. Brecon didn't shout or rail or do anything else to cause a scene, leastwise a greater scene than Charlotte had already managed on her own. With a pleasant half smile on his face, he escorted her from the house and to his own coach waiting at the door.

"I trust you won't object to riding with me," Brecon said. "I thought this way we could talk, just the two of us."

He handed her into the coach, and the footman shut the door. He placed his hat on the seat next to him, settled back against the squabs, and sighed deeply.

"My dear Charlotte," he said. "I've heard a great peck of nonsense regarding my cousin this evening, but I'd rather hear the truth from you. Where is March?"

Charlotte sighed, too. "He was called to the country on—"

"No," Brecon said. "We both know that's an excuse, not the truth. Why isn't he with you?"

It was the one question she could not answer: not to Brecon, not to herself. Without a word, she burst into tears.

"I thought as much," Brecon said, handing her his handkerchief. "Weep as long as you please, if it makes you feel better. I'll wait."

"No, no, crying accomplishes nothing," she sobbed, struggling to control herself. "I—I know I shouldn't have climbed into that tree—"

"Do you truly think I give a fig about that?" he asked. "Andover is a boor, but you served him exactly as he merited. There's no lasting harm, and besides, you've entertained a good many folk this evening. Pray recall that I'm not your husband. You may dance among the treetops at the palace for all I care. But if you've made March suffer—ah, that is altogether different."

"He suffers, yes," she said, "but so do I, and I can't begin to know what is wrong."

Now that she'd started crying, she couldn't stop. Already Breck's handkerchief was sodden, and still the hot tears streamed down her face, fueled by her frustration and misery.

"I love March and I would swear by all that's holy that he loves me, too," she said, her voice choked with emotion. "Yet each time that I feel we've become closer, closer still, he draws back and away. He always blames himself, but he never explains why, so I am sure it must be my fault instead, and oh, Brecon, I am so, so unhappy without him!"

Brecon drew another handkerchief from his coat pocket. "You can tell I spend much time in the company of ladies," he said as he handed it to her. "Is this the first time March has actually left you?"

She took the fresh handkerchief and blew her nose. "If you mean leave London, then yes. But he—we have never spent the entire night together. He—he finishes, and leaves me for his own rooms. Oh, I am being most wretchedly disloyal to him by telling you that, but it saddens me terribly."

"You're not being disloyal, Charlotte, not at all," he said, sadness of his own in his voice. "I wish you both to be happy, and to be happy together."

"Most times we are," she said wistfully. "Last night we were most wonderfully happy, or so I believed. I tried my best to please him, and he pleased me very much."

"Then he has pleased you," he said with great delicacy, "as a husband should please a wife?"

Charlotte blushed and looked down at the tight, teary ball she'd made of the handkerchiefs. She doubted she could speak to her own mother of such a private, personal matter, and here she was discussing it with Brecon.

"When he forgets he is a duke," she said with care, "then he pleases me, oh, above everything in this world. But when he—and I, too, for I wished to be a lady for him—when we think more of our duty than of making love, then there is no joy for either of us. Last night I believed we had finally found our way, but then he was gone when I woke, with—with only apologies."

"Apologies," Brecon repeated, shaking his head. "I feared that was so. He has done that since he was a child, you see, apologizing for things that did not require an apology, at least not from him. If he cannot make it right, by will or by order, then he must apologize."

"Yes, yes," Charlotte said, marveling at how precisely this described March. "That's him exactly, though I wish it weren't."

"He's reason enough for it, I suppose," Brecon said. "You Wylders were always a cheerful family. I know you lost your father at an early age, my dear, but surely you recall the love your parents shared?"

"Oh, yes," she said, smiling as she remembered that long-ago happiness. "They loved each other and us, too, very much. Mama misses Father still, and it's been years and years. That is what I wish to have with March: that happiness, that trust, and that passion."

"But you see, you have the memory of your parents to guide you, that knowledge of how a marriage should be," Brecon said with an understanding that surprised her. "March does not."

"But his parents—"

"His parents were not like yours," he said firmly. "That is all I'll say of them. March must tell you the rest himself, Charlotte, when he is ready. As his wife, you must know his past before you can make your shared future. I can see no other way."

Charlotte listened thoughtfully. When she wondered what haunted March, she'd never once thought of his parents. Why would she, when her own parents had only shown her love and the fondest indulgence?

Brecon leaned across the aisle toward her. "Go to him, Charlotte," he said. "You need to be together, not apart. Go to him at Greenwood."

"To Greenwood?" She gave her head an anxious little shake. "I can't, Brecon. I can't. What if I go to him and he leaves me again?"

"He won't," Brecon said firmly. "I know him well enough to give you my word on that. If you go to him, he'll stay with you."

She tried to smile, but failed. "I do not know if I'm that certain. Or that brave."

"If you're brave enough to climb that tree as nimbly as a cat, then you've the courage to go to Greenwood after your husband." He smiled and reached out to cover her hand with his own. "Go to March, Charlotte. Talk, and listen, and hear whatever he tells you. Above all, love him. Love him, and the rest will mend itself."

CHAPTER

 20

Washed, shaved, and dressed to meet the new day, March sat at his breakfast table with the London papers spread before him and tried very hard to pretend that he'd slept in his bed instead of slumped awkwardly to one side in an armchair, and only an hour or so at that. His humor was foul and his neck was stiff, and his eyes felt as if sand had been rubbed beneath his lids.

Yet in that short, restless sleep, he had dreamed of Charlotte, and she had been the first thing he'd thought of when he'd awakened as well. Charlotte, safe in London and safe from him. How fine to dream and think of what he could not have, he thought as he irritably sawed his knife across his toast, damning the very crust that would confound him this day.

"The midsummer rents will fall due at the end of the week, sir," Carter was saying, cradling in his arms yet another gloomy account book with all the fondness of a mother for her firstborn. "When you have returned from your survey of the north fields later this morning, sir, I might suggest that we review the accountings together, as is your usual practice."

But for once, March wasn't listening. Instead he was leaning back in his armchair, the better to see the hired cart that was drawing before the front door. No one called at Greenwood at this hour of the morning, especially not in a cart with London markings on the side. Curiosity overcame propriety, and he left his napkin beside his plate and went striding into the front hall to see for himself. Two men were carrying in a large, flat package, wrapped and tied in brown paper, while his butler hovered beside the open door.

"What the devil is this?" March demanded. "I've ordered nothing from London, and if it's meant for below stairs, then it should be brought to the back, not to the front hall."

"It appears to be a gift for you, sir," his butler said apologetically. "These men are from the workshop of the painter Sir Lucas Rowell."

"Aye, Y'Grace." The first man balanced his share of the parcel's weight against his hip and carefully drew a letter for March from inside his waistcoat. "This be for you, Y'Grace. From Her Grace the Duchess o' Marchbourne."

Swiftly March glanced from the sealed letter to the parcel, regarding it now with considerably more interest. He felt a fool for how fast his heart had begun to beat, simply because his wife had sent him some manner of gift.

From Charlotte, from Charlotte, beat his heart. *From Charlotte.*

"Bring it to the back parlor," he said gruffly. "You may set it against the bench in there."

He followed the men and the package, Charlotte's unread letter clutched in his hand. With care the man unwrapped the parcel, setting it gently on the bench to lean against the wall, and then stepped away.

March stared, speechless. How in blazes had Charlotte persuaded Sir Lucas to make such a beautiful portrait of her in so little time? There was an immediacy to the drawing that March had never seen in more finished paintings. To see Charlotte smiling at him, her face so full of eager longing and hope, tore at his heart, and when he began to realize other things about the picture—his ruby-studded shirt buckle in her open hand, how the pose mimicked his favorite portrait of the first duchess—he was overwhelmed. People did things for him because he ordered them or paid for them, or because he was a duke.

But only Charlotte acted from love.

Without looking away from the picture, he sent Sir Lucas's men to the kitchen to fortify themselves for the journey back to London, and he dismissed Carter, too. Finally he was alone, and at last he opened Charlotte's letter.

My own dearest darling March,

Please might this TOKEN *remind you of me & demonstrate the regard I have for my place in your heart & as the* FOURTH *duchess, tho' not so far removed from the* FIRST. *O my dearest husband, pray return! There can be nothing in that infernal country to compare to the* LOVE *I have waiting for you if only you would come back to*

Yr. most loving wife in ALL WAYS,
Charlotte

He read it again, and again after that, hearing each breathless word in her voice. It was as if she were here with him, tormenting and comforting him at the same time, and he wondered if she'd any notion of what a blessed torture that would be. No matter that it was morning, he poured himself a glass of brandy and squared his chair before the picture. The rest of his day could wait. He must sit here now, before Charlotte. Her love for him—and his for her—had so much power that he'd no choice.

From his first glimpse of her, high in the tree above

him, he'd known she was a brave woman. But for her to let Sir Lucas capture her like this, with every emotion plain on her lovely face, took a rare kind of courage. She'd offered her love as completely as a woman could, and she didn't care who knew it.

And what had he done for her? He'd taken her innocence and her trust and her love, and then he'd left her. Once again he'd behaved exactly like Father. No matter how he tried to be a better man, he couldn't escape the past.

He stared at her portrait now, struggling to think only of her, yet still the old nightmares of his loveless, bitter childhood returned. The longer he sat there, the hours slipping by, the darker and more oppressive his thoughts became. He ignored the polite knocks at the door, doubtless from Carter and from servants. He didn't hear the carriage in the drive, or the exclamations in the front hall that marked an arrival. All that existed for him was Charlotte's portrait and the mire of his own thoughts.

"Do you like the picture, then?"

He turned quickly in his chair, certain he'd imagined her voice behind him.

"Do you like it, March?" She was standing near the door, unhooking her traveling cloak in the most ordinary way imaginable. She was like sunshine itself, so beautiful that it hurt him to look at her.

"Damnation," he muttered. "Are you real?"

"Am I *real*?" she repeated, perplexed. "La, what manner of welcome is that?"

She tossed her cloak on a chair and came to him. Swiftly she bent and kissed him, her lips brushing sweetly across his. He was too shocked to kiss her back, and she frowned, her gaze searching his face.

"You look dreadful, March," she said with concern. "Are you ill? Should I send for a doctor? What is wrong?"

"Nothing," he said. "Everything."

"Goodness," she said. "How am I to answer that?"

He shook his head, rubbing his hand across his forehead. He was making no sense and he knew it, which meant that he wasn't as mad as he feared. Not quite.

He looked from her back to the picture. "Tell me, Charlotte," he said. "How did your father die?"

"My father?" She pulled a chair close to his and sank into it. "It was long ago, and because I was so young, I only knew what they told me."

"Tell me now," he said. "Tell me what they said."

"Very well." She smiled sadly. "It was a butterfly that killed him, they said. A white butterfly. It flew out from the mulberry bushes near the stable gate and startled his horse, and Father fell and landed on his neck. The friends who were with him told Mama that he was laughing and jesting one moment, and the next he was silent and dead, it happened that fast."

"A white butterfly," he said, stunned by the ordinariness of it, and the purity of it, too.

She nodded. "I was terrified of butterflies for years afterward," she confessed. "I still don't like them, not at all. Strange how things like that linger, isn't it?"

He rose quickly, seizing her hand to raise her to her feet as well. It was time for this, past time, and he couldn't put it off any longer.

"Come with me," he said, pulling her after him. "I'll show you."

"Show me what, March?" she asked breathlessly as he led her from the room and up the stairs. "What will I see?"

But he didn't answer, not until they were in the distant parlor to which he'd banished his father. The portrait of the third Duke of Marchbourne was very grand, almost regal, with him in his ducal robes and the old-fashioned long wig of a generation before. But not even all that red velvet could mask his father's nature, the innate cruelt in his heavy-lidded eyes and the dismissive sneer that passed for a smile.

"There," he said, staring up at the portrait. He hadn't been in this room for years, yet the impact of Father's painted face struck him like a blow, so hard that he had to force himself to stand before it. "That's my father, Charlotte."

"Goodness," she said. "He's very . . . very regal, isn't he?"

March laughed bitterly. "He'd be proud to hear you say that. Father never forgot his royal blood, or how it made him superior to everyone else. Can you tell how he died?"

She shook her head. "How could I tell that?"

"It's there, Charlotte, it's there," he assured her. "This was painted only months before he died. You can see the pox that killed him, eating away at his flesh and his mind until he went mad from it. No pretty butterflies here, are there?"

The artist had been kind and flattering. There were no signs of the sores his father had tried vainly to cover with black plasters and patches, none of the pallor that hinted of the grave. The artist hadn't showed how most of Father's teeth were gone, how ghastly his smile had become, or how his eyes had grown cloudy as blindness stole his sight.

But March couldn't look at his father's once hand-some face, so much like his own, and not see how the pox had destroyed his soul as surely as it had destroyed his flesh.

"I'm sorry, March," Charlotte said softly. "I'm sorry."

"Save your grief," he said curtly, still confronting his father's painted self. "His death was his own doing, as surely as if he'd taken a knife to his own throat."

"But he couldn't always have been a monster," she said slowly. "Before he was sick, he must have been a better man, else my father never would have agreed to a match between us."

"I have heard it said that my father was more of a gentleman as a young man," March said, though he didn't believe it himself, and never had. "I can only judge what I know of him from my own memory."

"But my father—"

"Charlotte, I know your father was a paragon, but he was also only an earl," he said wearily. "Of course he would have agreed to a match if my father proposed it. To wed one's daughter to a duke: what father would refuse that?"

Charlotte didn't answer, clearly not believing her perfect father could be so mercenary. Well, so be it, thought March, and though he tried to be cynical, he couldn't help but envy her a bit, too.

"Was the picture painted in Italy?" she asked tentatively. "The setting looks the same as the picture of you as a boy that's in my rooms."

"Rome," he said. "That's where we were. I hadn't wanted to go with Father, but he insisted, taking me from school in the middle of the term. A last grand tour, he'd called it, a voyage with his only son and heir."

Gently her fingers moved against his. "That must have been quite an adventure. You weren't very old."

"Eleven," he said. "But because I was tall for my age, the whores all judged me older."

"The whores?" she asked.

"With Father there were always whores," he said, bitterness filling his mouth like bile. "Our lodgings stank of their perfume and their bodies. He didn't care. No matter how cruelly he used them, there were always more to be bought."

"But you were a child, March," she said. "What could you have known of your father's sins?"

He closed his eyes, unable to meet Father's gaze any longer.

"I knew because I saw them," he said. "Father made me watch. To be a man, he said. He wanted me to be a man. He made me watch him with the women, and he bid them touch me and—and handle me, and though I knew it was wrong and sinful, I would let them because it pleased Father to share his debauchery. But I hated it, and I hated the women, but mostly I hated Father for making me part of his wickedness."

He remembered their touch, the coaxing cleverness in their fingers, and how little it had taken to destroy his innocence. He'd been ashamed of himself, especially when they'd used their mouths as well, and Father had laughed and called it the best sport a man could know. But it hadn't felt like sport to him, not at all, and he'd lived in a sick dread that others would discover his secret. There was no one he could turn to, no one who could help him, not when it was his father's idea and his father was a duke.

"It wasn't your fault, March," Charlotte said, her voice soft. "You were still a child, no matter what your father said."

"Mother knew it, too," he insisted. "She saw it in my eyes as soon as we returned to England. She said I was no better than Father. She said that my soul was poisoned by sin and that my blood was black with it, just like Father's. She wanted nothing to do with me after that. She said that Father had broken her heart, but that I had trod upon the pieces."

Still in his traveling clothes, he had stood between his parents in the drawing room as they raged at each other over his head, using words and accusations that no child should hear parents say. By then he'd understood that he was only a tiny part of the anger and loathing they bore toward each other, yet even his insignificance had wounded him. He hadn't taken either side, but stood with his shoulders straight and his gaze focused on his mother's chinoiserie cabinet. Only later, when at last he was alone, had he seen how he'd bloodied his own palms, neat rows of semicircles where he'd clenched his hands so tightly his nails had cut the skin.

"But your mother must have loved you, March," Charlotte insisted. "There's the portrait of you in the bedchamber, where she could see it first thing in the morning and last thing at night, the way I do now."

Slowly he opened his eyes and once again met the scornful painted gaze of his father, looking down at him as he always had.

"That picture of me was painted when we first reached Rome," he said, turning away from him and back toward her. "Before everything else. Before I changed. She wouldn't have kept it otherwise."

"I don't believe that," Charlotte said, appalled. "How could any mother feel like that about her only child?"

"Because she was my mother, not yours," he said evenly, a truth not even she could deny. "She was right about me, too. I *am* my father's son. No matter how I've tried to be the gentlemanly husband you deserve, I always sink back to his wickedness."

"Whatever are you saying, March?" Charlotte asked. "You're the most gentlemanly gentleman I have ever met. There's not one scrap of wickedness in you anywhere."

He groaned and shook his head, glancing back over his shoulder at Father's portrait.

"Consider how I've treated you, Charlotte," he said. "I have, and to my endless shame, too. Think of that last night in my bed, of all the reprehensible things I did to you—"

"But you didn't, March, not for a moment!" She reached up and cradled his face in her palms, forcing him to look directly at her. "What we did was make love,

March. We did what we're meant to do, which is to give each other pleasure as husband and wife. Without love, I suppose our actions might be the same as those of your father and those—those vile women, but the joy would not be there. It's love that makes it special, my dearest, dearest husband, love and love alone."

How desperately he wanted to believe her! "What you ask of me, Charlotte, what you ask," he said, still bowed beneath the weight of his parents' history. "I can't deny the past."

"Nor am I asking you to," she said, the pearl earrings swinging against her cheeks. "I won't ever tell you to ignore your past or to forget your parents. For better or for worse, they're part of you."

He did not need her to remind him of that. "Charlotte, please—"

"Hear me, March, I beg you," she pleaded, her eyes wide and blue as the sky. "Your parents are part of you, yes, but I'm part of you now, too, as our children will be. I know you cannot change the past, but you can make your future as bright as ever you could. *Our* future, March."

Yet still he hesitated, torn and tempted at once. She was like an angel standing before him, offering redemption. His first tastes of her love had been impossibly, unforgettably sweet. Could he truly deserve the joy she promised? Could he ever be worthy of her and this glorious shared future?

He hesitated, and she saw it, disappointment flickering through her eyes.

"Love me," she whispered. "That is all I ask, March. Just—just love me."

She rose on the toes of her slippers to kiss him gently, a kiss that was meant to seal that pledge, that promise, and at last it was enough. He pulled her into his arms and kissed her as if all the world depended on it, and for their world, perhaps it did. He bent to slip his arms beneath her knees, and she yelped as he swept her into his arms.

"Goodness, March," she said breathlessly. "What is this?"

"It's what I should have done in the beginning," he said, carrying her from the room. He stopped beside the door's frame and did not look back. He wouldn't let his father rule him any longer. He knew better than to believe his past would never trouble him again, but he prayed that with Charlotte at his side, he would be able to keep it in its place.

"Shut the door for me, Charlotte," he said. "Shut it as hard as you can."

She grinned, and with one hand she shoved the door with such force that it slammed behind them, the sound echoing down the hall.

"There," she said proudly. "Done."

"Entirely," he said, and for the first time he smiled. "There are no portraits in my bedchamber."

"None?" she said, circling her arms around his shoulders. "Then I suppose we must make pictures of our own."

He laughed, and she laughed, too, though she clung to him more closely.

"I vow, March," she warned, "if you drop me because you were weak from laughing, I shall be hard-pressed ever to forgive you."

"I won't drop you," he said, carrying her down the long hallway. "I may not ever put you down again."

But he did, of course, onto the center of his bed. He left the windows open, with the sun free to stream around them, and the sweet scent of the newly mown field grasses drifted in on the breeze. Before this day, he'd never have taken her to bed in the middle of the afternoon, thoroughly unseemly for a proper married couple. Now he could think of nothing better. This was how he wanted it always to be between them, without any artifice or shadows or haunting ghosts, and as she pulled off her clothes and smiled at him, he knew she'd make it so.

This time he'd no doubt that they made love. He took care to woo her with a hundred little endearments and as many kisses peppered all over her creamy pale body, and he caressed her in every way he could imagine and a few more besides. When at last she begged him to enter her, he was more than ready, too, feverish with desire and the need to join with her. He'd never felt anything more right than her body beneath his, moving with him in mindless, perfect unison, and together they explored every inch of his oversized featherbed.

But even they couldn't make it last forever, and they found their release together, letting their cries sound through the open windows and fade over the fields beyond. Afterward they lay curled together, letting the breezes cool their sweat-sheened bodies. He pulled her closer, relishing how neatly they fit together.

Gently he swept her damp hair to one side and kissed the nape of her neck. No matter how wrongly his father had treated him, he had arranged the marriage that brought him Charlotte. Strange to think how much love could come from so much hatred, and stranger still to think that for that single, glorious, fortuitous decision, he would forever be in his father's debt—perhaps even enough, in time, to be able to forgive him.

"I love you," he said quietly. "My Charlotte, my wife."

She chuckled happily. "I love you, too, March."

"As it should be," he said. "As it should be."

She twisted to face him, her soft breasts pressing against him as she braced her arms on his chest. He was surprised to see the uncertainty in her eyes, in how she nibbled on her lower lip.

"What is it, sweet?" he asked, lightly touching his forefinger to that plump lower lip. "Tell me."

She smiled crookedly. "You will not leave, will you? If I fall asleep, you will be here when I wake?"

"Yes," he said, his voice reverberating with confidence. "Nothing will make me leave you."

Her whole face seemed part of her smile, her happiness so complete that he couldn't keep from kissing her again, and again after that.

"Now," he said. "There's nothing more to tell me, is there?"

She frowned as if thinking deep thoughts, then sighed mightily.

"There is one small adventure that you might wish to know of, Your Grace," she began. "It involves an open window and a tree."

He sighed, too, but with amusement, not concern. "Could it be that you made the acquaintance of that tree, Your Grace?"

"I fear I did," she admitted. "It was a tree in Lady Finnister's garden."

He hadn't expected that. "Lady Finnister's? Why the devil were you there again?"

"It's a long story," she said quickly. "She lured me by claiming you were there, and because I wanted so badly to see you, I went, and then that odious Lord Andover was there, too, and he would have seduced me if I'd let him. But I didn't. I climbed from the window instead."

"Into the tree?"

"Into the tree," she said. "Then I used that lofty bower as a pulpit to denounce the dishonorable behavior of the Marquess of Andover."

She was smiling still, but she was also holding her breath, waiting for his reaction. Last week, even this morning, he might have been angry, even furious, but no longer. Now he felt lazy and content and thoroughly entertained to think of Charlotte denouncing Andover from the branches of a tree. If she said he hadn't seduced her, then he hadn't. Andover was lucky she hadn't tried to box his ears in the bargain.

"You are not angry?" she asked warily. "There were rather a great many people below me, and Lord Andover was monstrously angry. He was *inflamed*."

"I'll wager he was," he said, idly twisting one of her curls around his finger. "I wish I'd been there to see it for myself."

"You do?" she asked with such charming astonishment that he laughed.

"I do," he said, pulling her down to kiss. "Now tell me more, sweet. Tell me everything."

CHAPTER

21

It was, decided Charlotte, the most perfect month of her life.

As much as she'd enjoyed London, she was at heart a country lady, and now at last she'd a country gentleman as her match. It pleased her that March was such a conscientious lord and landowner, and to her delight he welcomed her to join him each morning on whatever his day's business at Greenwood might be. Because she was so comfortable in the saddle, she kept pace with him with ease, and together they rode the lands and made plans for years to come. Slowly, too, she began to meet Greenwood's tenants and other workers, and in many instances she found their company a good deal more agreeable than that of the grand folk she'd called upon in London.

There were, of course, several dutiful calls to make here in Surrey, too, from the flustered wives of country squires nearly overwhelmed by receiving His Grace's bride to tea to solemn introductions to the mayor and bishop of nearby Guilford. But Charlotte survived even those visits with graceful aplomb; it was easy to be charming when one was happy, and she was so openly happy now that the whole world wished to be happy with her.

The whole world, and March most of all. She was blissfully, hopelessly, endlessly—she couldn't invent enough ways to describe it—in love with him, and knowing he felt the same for her only made her joy even more indescribable. In these sunny weeks, he'd become not only her husband but her best friend as well, and whether day or night, they seldom parted, and never wearied of each other's company.

Greenwood became their honeymoon and wedding trip, and the servants soon learned to announce themselves loudly, for there was no telling where or when the duke and duchess would next be seized with sudden desire. They made love in the drawing room and the garden, beneath the bright June sun and the night stars, on the roof by moonlight, and in the water of the lake—though the last became more a splashing, laughter-filled experiment due to the chilliness of the water.

But one morning in July, their blissful summer changed abruptly.

The first trays for the morning had just been brought up, with March's coffee and Charlotte's chocolate, plus sweet buns and bacon. This had become their customary beginning of the day, sustenance enough before a quick ride, followed by a larger breakfast later in the morning. March had already left their bed, while Charlotte remained curled against the pillows. Although she was usually up with the larks, she was having a difficult time mustering herself from bed this morning. She still felt drowsy and tired, and perfectly content to lie here and watch her handsome husband. He *was* handsome, too, his dark hair falling over his shoulders, his jaw still unshaven, and his silk banyan falling open over his bare chest.

"You're looking exceptionally piratical this morning, March," she said languidly. "I rather like it."

He looked over his shoulder at her, his brows raised in surprise. " 'Piratical'?" he repeated. "That's a fine thing to call me. Likening me to the lawless, villainous brigands who plunder the ships and goods of respectable folk. And you know as well as I that Giroux would rather perish than let me go about with a stubbled jaw."

"What would Giroux know of rogues and pirates?" She chuckled, bunching a pillow beneath her cheek. At heart he was still so eminently honorable, and that was one of the things she loved about him. "What if I were part of your plunder? Would that make being a pirate more agreeable?"

"Plunder, you say?" he said. "Perhaps then I could be persuaded."

He took up a silver butter knife from the tray and brandished it like a miniature cudgel, attempting to look villainous. He didn't, not at all, and she laughed again.

"Do not provoke me, fair maiden," he warned, pointing the butter knife at her. "Else ye shall be forced to pay the consequences."

He lifted the silver cover on the tray and plucked a large piece of bacon from the plate beneath. He bit into the bacon as savagely as he could, clenching it in his teeth.

The scent of the plate of bacon wafted toward her, greasy, grilled, and heavy. Most mornings Charlotte found it quite delectable. But now, to her surprise, it affected her in the most sudden and horrifying way: her stomach clutched and roiled, and she'd barely time to bolt from the bed to her dressing room before she retched over the chamber pot. When she was done, she sat cross-legged on the floor, feeling clammy and weak and still too unsure of her stomach to return to the bed.

"My poor girl," March said, sitting on the nearby bench to commiserate. Gently he reached out to rub her back. "Perhaps that second custard last night was one two many."

"Do not mention custard," she ordered, holding her arms around her stomach. "Ever."

"I cannot fathom what else it would be," he said. "Unless you've acquired some sort of general plaguish illness from one of the tenants' children."

"Oh, March," she said dolefully. She knew the reason, and if she was honest, she'd known it for a while now. "For such a clever gentleman, you can be remarkably thick-witted. We've been wed seven weeks now."

"Fifty-one days," he said. "I've kept track."

As disarming as that was, she refused to be distracted. "Fifty-one days, then. In all those days, I've never refused you, have I?"

Still he shook his head, mystified. Could he truly be so dense about women?

"March, please," she said. "Fifty-one days, and I haven't had my courses. I'm with child. *Your* child."

The mystification turned instantly to amazement. "A child?" he said. "Are you sure?"

"As sure as I can be," she said, drawing her knees up and hugging them close. "Considering how often we've applied ourselves to the task, I should be more surprised if I weren't."

"A child," he said, marveling as he stared down at her. "A baby."

"This is when you should be rejoicing," she said. "I've done exactly what you required me to do. I've proved myself as fertile breeding stock, capable of producing an heir to your dukedom."

"Don't say that, Charlotte."

"Why not, when it's true?" she said, unable to keep back the bitterness. Tears stung her eyes, and she didn't try to keep them back, either. "Peers need heirs, and dukes need them most of all. You wouldn't have married me otherwise."

"Charlotte, please." He came to sit on the floor beside her and slipped his arms around her shoulders. "I agree, yes, that's why we married. I can't deny it. But since then I've come to love you for yourself."

She tipped her head back to nestle against his shoulder and sighed. "You won't love me when I'm huge and fat."

"Of course I will love you," he said gallantly. "I'll love you more."

"I only wish we'd had more time to be us together," she said forlornly. "I love you so much, March, and a baby will change things."

"*Our* baby," he said firmly. "Doubtless things will change, Charlotte, but only for the better. You have my word that I'll make sure of it."

He did, too. She'd thought herself pampered as his bride, but that was nothing compared to the attention he lavished on her now. No wish was too small to be obliged, no whim too peculiar. She blossomed, both with love and with the growing child. March insisted on bringing a trio of long-faced physicians from London to pronounce her in perfect health and sagely assure the duke that the child would be the much-desired male.

"That's nonsense," Charlotte said indignantly. "They can't tell that. No one can. They're only saying that because they know dukes want sons, and they can double their fees if you're pleased."

"Having neither son nor daughter, I don't care which comes first," March said. "A son is more useful to the estate, of course, but I will love a daughter every bit as much."

"You're sure to have one or the other, my love," Charlotte said philosophically. "Those are the only choices, you know."

But the doctors also advised that they remain at Green

wood, where the country air was more felicitous, which pleased Charlotte, even if they then forbade riding, which displeased her very much. March offered a pretty compromise in the form of a smart two-wheeled cart that Charlotte could drive herself, so long as she promised not to race. Reluctantly she agreed, and he had their arms painted on the door and the spokes of the wheels picked out in gold.

And so, for Charlotte, the happiest month of her life stretched into the happiest summer. But happiness is a fragile thing, and just as a butterfly had destroyed her family's happiness when she'd been a child, it now took only a single sheet of paper to bring havoc to the joy she shared with March.

The letters from London were always presented to March in the same fashion at Greenwood: in his study after dinner, on the same square silver tray engraved with twin dolphins that he remembered from boyhood. There were seldom any surprises resting on those two dolphins: letters from friends and acquaintances, bills from tradespeople, and appeals from politicians and charities were the usual fare.

One oversized letter stuck out from the others. The address had been printed in purposely clumsy letters rather than written in a decent hand, as if the writer wished to keep his regular penmanship secret. There were no clues with the closure, either, the page having been sealed with a blot of common candle wax. Curious, he cracked it open with his thumb and opened the sheet.

It wasn't a letter or a tradesman's bill, but a print, the kind common in shops and pinned to the walls of taverns and public houses, an engraving made after a famous portrait by a better artist. This one was a crude pastiche, two paintings of varying styles combined into one awkward picture.

To his shock, he recognized them both. The lower half was the portrait of his great-grandmother Nan Lilly, her breast provocatively bared as it had been for the last century. But in place of her face was another, a face that was even more familiar: Charlotte's face as drawn by Sir Lucas Rowell. The same drawing that even now hung on the wall before him had been clumsily altered to fit atop Nan's body, the sweetness of her expression at jarring odds with the wanton pose beneath it. Worse still was the doggerel verse engraved beneath it:

A noble house of bastard blood,
Tho' royal at the core,
Their ladies do what e'er they could,
To always play the whore.

There was nothing more written on the print. Whoever had sent it to March had clearly felt the print and verse were message enough. Most likely the sender wasn't the author, anyway, but some "friend" who wanted to be sure March didn't miss seeing the print.

But who would have created such a hateful scrap of slander? Charlotte was too new to society to have enemies or rivals, and as far as he knew, he didn't have any, either. To be sure, in school he had been taunted by boys from older, more noble families about the source of his own nobility, and he'd bloodied his share of nose over it. Now that he was grown, no one dared say such things to his face, though he knew plenty did behind his back. He *was* the Duke of Marchbourne, after all, and while he'd Nan's common blood in his veins, he also had the king's.

But for some anonymous coward to attack Charlotte publicly like this infuriated him beyond reason, beyond sense. It wasn't just a grievous, mocking insult to h wife and duchess, but an act of pure cruelty directed at a lady who would never harm another.

"What word from town, my love?" Charlotte came through the doorway, a basket full of just-picked flowers from the garden on her arm and his dogs trailing devotedly around her skirts. "Anything of interest?"

"Not at all," he said, attempting to slide the print to the bottom of the pile so she wouldn't see it.

He wasn't fast enough, not for Charlotte's sharp eyes.

"What is this you're trying to hide?" she asked mildly. She set the basket of flowers on the floor and darted around his chair to pull the folded print free. "Have you run up an exceptionally high reckoning with your tailor that you don't wish me to see?"

"Please, Charlotte, that's nothing you should see," he said sternly, trying to wrest it away from her. "Give it to me."

"Why should I, when you order me as rudely as that?" Laughing, she stepped backward with her prize, and opened it before he could take it back. Her laughter vanished at once, her smile faded, and her cheeks flushed as if feeling shame for her printed, pieced-together self.

"I told you that you'd not wish to see it," March said. "I'm sorry that you did."

She gave a jerky small shake to her head, enough to make the fine ruffles on her linen cap flutter about her face. "No, it's better that I do. But who would concoct such a dreadful thing? You don't think Sir Lucas—"

"No," March said. "Sir Lucas would not debase his art that way. He might be selling prints of his drawing of you—that's to be expected, considering who you are—but he would never make a version like this, or risk ruining his career."

"But it must be someone who has seen the drawing, to copy it so," she said. "Perhaps it was copied by one of the apprentices in his studio?"

He felt the anger growing inside him, fueled by the sight of her standing there, with one hand holding the vile print and the other resting on the slight swell of her belly. He doubted she even realized she'd placed that protective hand there over her unborn child; she did it instinctively now, a natural gesture for a mother. Now, too, it was his turn as a husband and father to defend them.

"Here, Charlotte, please," he said, stepping forward to reclaim the print. "I don't want you distressed any further by some stranger's malicious jest. Give it no more thought. I'll make sure the villains who did this are discovered and punished."

But she heard the anger in his voice, or perhaps because she knew him so well, she simply sensed it.

"If you truly don't wish to distress me, March, then you won't go chasing off after 'villains,' " she said, resting a cautionary hand on his arm. "I don't require an avenging fury on my behalf. The worst that's been done is that I've been called a foul name that we both know isn't true, and shown with an ample chest that we both know isn't mine, either."

"Don't diminish this, Charlotte," he said sharply. "This is an egregious slander against you, me, and our child as well. By insulting your virtue in this fashion, they're also implying that I'm not the father of your babe, and I won't have our child dogged with that all his life."

"Or hers," she said. "You must remember that possibility, March."

"Charlotte, don't wander," he said. "There could be scores of these things about London by now. I want the printer and the artist found and punished for libeling you, and all the copies burned and the plate destroyed."

"An avenging fury indeed," she said wryly. "If you make a fuss like that, then you'll only make more people speak of it, and wish to find a copy that's escaped your wrath. Better simply to let the whole affair drift away as a seven-day wonder, and then be forgotten."

"But it won't be forgotten," he insisted. "Scandal never is."

"Oh, yes," she said, "especially if the scandalmongers are treated to the delicious tattle of the mighty Duke of Marchbourne with his scourge in hand, raging after some low printer of penny broadsides."

He looked down into her bottomless blue eyes and wished desperately for a way to make her understand. He knew he didn't sound rational to her. If he thought more about it, he likely wouldn't sound rational to himself, either. Trying to track down who knew how many prints scattered over the countryside would be next to impossible, and finding the man responsible for creating the scurrilous print would be even harder. But for her sake, he'd do it. For her, he'd do anything.

"Charlotte," he began again. "I must do this for the sake of your honor and good name."

"I know you feel that way, my love, but I wish you wouldn't." She slipped her arms around his neck and gazed up at him, the kind of imploring no sane man could resist. "Please, March. For my sake, ignore it."

He frowned and grumbled. "It's not as if I'll be chasing the rascals through the streets myself, Charlotte. I'll have my lawyers look after it. A few inquiries should be sufficient."

Her arms tightened around his shoulders. "A few inquiries would be excessive. Put it from your thoughts, my love, as I already have done."

He grumbled again and kissed her, letting her think he'd agreed. Which he hadn't, not exactly. But while he was busily kissing her, she pulled the folded print from his fingers and swiftly tossed it into the grate.

"There," she said. "Now it's truly done, and that's an end to it."

But as March watched the paper curl and blacken in the flames, he wasn't nearly as sure.

"I wish we didn't have to come to London," Charlotte said, curled in the corner of the coach. "I wish we could always stay at Greenwood. And I most heartily wish I did not have to be presented at court. Why couldn't His Majesty wait until I was done breeding?"

"Because His Majesty is extraordinarily old," March said, sitting across from her, "and he might not be able to wait another five months for you. Besides, how can I refuse his wish to meet my beautiful wife?"

"Your portly wife," Charlotte said gloomily. Although she seemed finally over the worst of being ill in the mornings, her waist was thickening and her breasts were blossoming at an astonishing rate. Already Polly had had to change her stay laces three times to longer lengths, and the gap in the back was yawning so large that she'd soon outgrow them altogether, and require new ones in a properly gargantuan size. "Clearly this child takes after you, and is determined to be the most prodigious baby ever born."

"All the more reason for you to be presented to His Majesty, so that he might marvel," March said. "But you are not portly, Charlotte. Far from it. You *are* beautiful. You're even more beautiful now than when we wed."

His gaze wandered lower. "I especially like that gown on you. Every gentleman there tonight will be ogling you and envying me."

She grinned—not at the possibility of other gentlemen ogling her, but at the idea of her own husband doing exactly that. He wasn't offering idle flattery, either. In these last weeks he'd frequently demonstrated that he found her more luxurious figure irresistible.

Not only was she happy to reap the benefits of his attentions—and often, too—but it also meant he hadn't time to be fussing over that ridiculous lewd print and whoever had circulated it three weeks before. She understood why he'd been upset, for no one prized honor and respectability as much as March did. But he hadn't said a word about it since, and she was relieved beyond measure. A lustful March was much, much better than an angry, vengeful one.

She leaned forward, offering him a better (and quite spectacular) view of her décolletage, draped in diamonds.

"Perhaps we should send our regrets to Lady Tewksbury," she suggested in a low, breathy voice, running her hand along the inside of March's thigh. "I find I'm feeling weak, and I must return home to my bed."

March groaned. "Don't I wish we could," he said. "But this supper's in our honor, and even if you were lingering at death's door, Lady Tewksbury herself would come and haul you back to grace her table."

A quarter hour later, they were in Lady Tewksbury's drawing room. March had been right: as soon as they stepped through the door, the countess had swept down upon them like some bright-feathered bird of prey, and hadn't relinquished possession yet. One after another, Lady Tewksbury introduced Charlotte to a seemingly endless line of eager, aristocratic faces that were all new to her.

And then, finally, came one that was all too familiar.

"The Marquess of Andover, ma'am," Lady Tewksbury said as he bowed before Charlotte. He'd been drinking already, enough that she could smell it on him, and his broad face was even redder than usual. Yet still she blushed furiously, remembering that the last time they'd seen each other, he'd been roaring out a window while he'd been berating him from a tree.

"Your Grace," he murmured as he rose. The expression beneath his powdered wig was blank and impassive, without a hint that he, too, recalled how they'd last parted. "I am honored, ma'am."

She nodded, and that was all. Then he moved on to repeat much the same exchange with March, and Charlotte gave a quick sigh of relief as another Lord and Lady Someone were introduced to her. The couple smiled and bowed and curtseyed, as pleasant as could be, but Charlotte instantly forgot the names that went with their pleasant faces because what happened next blotted out everything else.

"What was that you said, sir?" March demanded, his voice so loud and furious that every other conversation in the room ceased.

He addressed Lord Andover; it could be no other gentleman. But Lord Andover had already moved away from March into a crowd of other guests, all of whom now melted away from him. He turned slowly, a half smile on his face, as if March had only called to him in greeting from across a park.

"Sir?" he said blithely, the exact kind of feigned innocence calculated to anger March further. "You address me, sir?"

"Damnation, Andover, you know that I do," March thundered. "I heard what you said, and I mark your meaning."

"Forgive me, sir," Lord Andover said, his disingenuous smile twitching into a smirk, "but I was merely amusing these gentlemen here with a scrap of verse, though I disremember where I heard it first."

Charlotte grabbed March's arm before he could speak again. She knew her husband better than anyone else did, and she understood all the reasons why this print was such an irritant to him and so dangerous to them both.

"Stop, please, my love, don't do this," she begged. "It doesn't matter, not at all."

He put his hand over hers protectively, but to her sorrow he didn't turn away from the marquess. "If it was so amusing, Andover, then pray repeat it for the entertainment of the rest of the company."

The marquess seemed to sway gently on his feet, his pale-lashed eyes glassy. Clearly he was more drunk than Charlotte had realized, drunk enough to behave like this, and her dread for what could happen only grew.

Too late the random pieces fell together to make an unsavory whole: how Lord Andover had seen both her portrait and Nan Lilly's side by side in Sir Lucas's studio, how she'd rebuffed his attentions twice and humiliated him publicly. What better way to humiliate her in return than to order that dreadful print engraved, printed, and shared among his friends? He might even be the author of the accompanying verse that he'd obviously just repeated in her husband's hearing.

"Don't press, March," Charlotte pleaded. "Can't you see that he's too far in his cups to care what he says?"

But March ignored her. "Repeat what you said, Andover," he ordered curtly. "Repeat it now so all may hear."

"I cannot, sir," Lord Andover said, still smirking, and pointedly bowed toward Lady Tewksbury. "The verse will offend the true ladies in the room, since it contains reference to . . . whores."

She felt March tense, the muscles in his arm beneath her hand stiffening. She wouldn't be able to stop him if the madness of his anger made him lunge at Andover, and the scandal that would result would be far, far worse than any name-calling.

"Don't," she whispered, all she'd left to say. "Don't."

She felt him warring with his temper, struggling to contain it. Then, as gently as he could, he slipped free of her hand and went to stand directly before Andover. When he spoke, his voice was low and unexpectedly measured, and Charlotte realized that his anger had risen to an entirely new and more dangerous level.

"You owe my wife an apology for that, Andover," he said. "I expect to hear it now."

But Lord Andover shook his head. "She's the one who should apologize to me," he snarled. "The sneaking little whore."

Instantly March's fist flew forward to find the fleshy underside of Andover's jaw, and with a single efficient punch he knocked the marquess to the floor. Women screamed, men swore, and everyone gasped and chattered, but they still heard March as he spoke to Andover, stunned and sprawled on the floor.

"You will offer your apology to my wife by noon tomorrow, Andover," he said, "else my friends will call on you by one."

He took Charlotte's hand and kissed it. He bowed to their shocked hostess, and then with his head high he led Charlotte from the room and the house, and into the greatest scandal in anyone's memory.

CHAPTER

22

It wasn't supposed to come to this.

With his hands clasped behind his back, March stood by the window in the long drawing room, staring out at the park without seeing any of it. Behind him sat Charlotte, her eyes red with weeping and her hands clenched in her lap. Brecon, tight-lipped and tense, sat across from her. Tea, coffee, wine, and biscuits were set on the table between them, as if any of them could muster an appetite. There wasn't any conversation, either, and the only sound in the room was the ticking of the ormolu clock on the mantelpiece, relentlessly counting the minutes until noon.

It was all his own fault, of course. March knew that. If he hadn't let himself be ruled by anger, if he hadn't jumped at Andover's taunt, if he hadn't spoken so rashly before so many witnesses, if he hadn't challenged that smirking scoundrel and demanded an apology for Charlotte . . .

If, if, if.

Now it was too late, and growing later still with every tick of the clock. Andover wouldn't present himself here at Marchbourne House, and he wouldn't apologize, either. Andover never apologized to anyone; it wasn't his way. He'd nothing to risk in this. No wife, no children, no reputation, and he'd long since gambled away his income and his estates. For Andover all that was left was the ex-

citement he could wring from dangerous situations. A
duel was only another part of the game of seducing other
men's wives. For Andover to be able to stake his own
wretched, empty life against that of a duke with rank,
wealth, and power second only to royalty's: what greater
thrill could there be than that?

It would be the easiest thing in the world for March
to withdraw his challenge. He was a duke. He could as
much as do what he pleased. In some quarters, he'd be
praised for obeying the empty laws against dueling, laws
that no other gentlemen ever paid much heed. He might
even win the approval of the king, who'd been voca
about how much he hated the practice. Most of all, he'c
please Charlotte and spare her from the anguish that
one way or another, she was sure to endure on accoun
of him.

But then it was precisely for her sake that he couldn'
walk away now. She'd been slandered and dishon
ored by a man with no right to be called a gentleman
March had to defend her. He wanted her to be proud c
being his duchess and the mother of his children, an
he wanted those children to be proud of him, too. H
didn't want anyone telling Charlotte she'd married int
a family bred from bastards, or that she was no bette
than Nan Lilly simply because she shared his bed.

There was his own honor and name to protect as we
Charlotte was the bravest woman he'd ever known, ar
he didn't want it said that her husband was a spinele
coward who issued challenges only to back away. If pe
ple whispered behind his back now about his family
background, then they'd do it a hundred times more b
cause he'd only confirmed their worst suspicions. He
be a gentleman without honor and a disgrace to t
peerage. He would, in short, become an outcast.

And Charlotte deserved far better than that. Her lo

had been his salvation. The least he could do for her in return was to defend the honor of that love.

He started when the clock began to chime, solemn and slow, twelve times. He waited until it was done before he took a deep breath and turned to face Charlotte and Brecon.

"Very well, then," he said, forcing himself to smile. "It's decided. Brecon, you'll call on Andover on my behalf. Make whatever terms are customary."

"Andover will choose pistols," Brecon said, his face grim. "He always does."

"All the better," March said. When it came to the duel itself, he felt strangely confident, trusting both to fate and to his own abilities as a marksman. He had fought two other duels before, again over Nan Lilly's legacy to his family. The first time had been with swords. He'd been nineteen and terrified, yet he'd escaped with only a scar on his arm so insubstantial that Charlotte had never noticed it. The second was by pistols, and again he'd been the victor, with his opponent likely carrying the ball in his thigh to this day. Now, with so much more at stake, he could only pray that his luck held.

"We'll be using my pistols," he said, "the French pair, and they'll be like old friends in my hands."

Clearly worried, Brecon shook his head. "I'd always rather trust my fate to a blade and skill, especially now that you've settled on accepting first blood. Gunpowder's as likely to misfire as not, and then you'll—"

"No more!" Charlotte rose abruptly. "Enough of this— this *foolishness,* March. Guns versus swords! What manner of question is that, when both can only lead to bloodshed? You must stop this *now.*"

Brecon nodded, though his expression didn't change. "You have heard all my arguments and those of your good lady as well. You will not be persuaded?"

March sighed. He *had* heard all the arguments, from

Brecon and Charlotte both. There couldn't possibly be anything left to say.

"I thank you for your concern, Brecon," he said gravely, "but you know my decision."

Brecon bowed. "Very well. I'll go to Andover and present your compliments, and make the other arrangements as well."

He reached out and patted March's shoulder, an old and familiar show of affection between them. "Take care, cousin, and spend this time with your lady well. Good-bye, Charlotte, and be easy. This is a serious affair, yes, but I believe we can trust in your husband's aim and God in his mercy that matters will go well."

Charlotte didn't answer, which was never a fortuitous sign with her. Brecon realized it, too, and the look he shot March as he left the room was so brimming with male commiseration that, under other circumstances, March would have laughed aloud.

But there was nothing to laugh at now with Charlotte. March wrapped his arms around her and drew her close. At first she was stiff against him, her anger with him and his decision like a palpable barrier between them. Gently he threaded his fingers into her hair at the back of her neck, below the bristle of her hairpins and above her nape, and rubbed his fingers in small circles, the best way he'd discovered for calming her.

"I know you're unhappy with me, sweet," he said softly. "I know you're angry about this duel. And I know you believe me the greatest ass in Christendom for sending Brecon off to act as my second."

"Because you *are* the greatest ass in Christendom," she cried miserably, pushing back far enough in his embrace to stare up into his face. "There is no believing about it, but only the same sorrowful knowledge that women have always, always learned of the stubborn, wasteful stupidity of men!"

She'd been so distraught this day that she'd given up blotting her tears hours ago and had instead let them run unchecked down her face. Her eyes were puffy and red with them and her lashes spiky and wet, and the salt and likely the bitterness as well had blotched her cheeks and nose. By most standards, she wasn't very pretty like this, but because each one of those salty tears represented her love for him, he'd never seen her look more beautiful.

"Charlotte, please," he said gently. "Please. I wish you would trust me that this is for the best for both of us, to preserve our family's good name."

"How can anything as dangerous as a duel be for the best?" she demanded. "What do I care about your good name at the cost of your life?"

He sighed again, and not for the first time with her, he longed for some magical words to explain that she'd accept. "I won't deny that there is danger, Charlotte."

"Don't treat me like a child, March," she said, cutting him off. "I know what will happen. I've sat here while you and Brecon discussed this whole foolish affair, haven't I? I know that at dawn tomorrow you will meet Lord Andover beneath the two oak trees that mark the beginning of Hounslow Heath. I know that Brecon and Andover's second will pretend to stop you one last time, and then explain the rules of your idiocy. And I know that you will then both shoot guns at each other with the intention of making the other bleed."

"It's called drawing first blood, Charlotte," he said patiently, "and it means that whoever bleeds first has lost. We'll only fire a single shot apiece, too. It's not as we'll be hacking away at each other with swords. But this will be as good as having him apologize to you, and will end the scandal forever. In that way, perhaps it's even better than an apology."

"Oh, yes, better, better, better," she said, drumming her fists against his chest. "He will be aiming at you, too. What if you are the one who does this 'first bleeding' instead? What if you are maimed, or crippled, or blinded, or any other of a score of misfortunes that can occur when a lead ball meets a mortal's flesh and bone? Pray, how can that be better?"

Why had this made so much more sense when he and Brecon had discussed it in a calm and manly fashion?

"Because it simply is," he said softly. "For the sake of honor, it is."

She closed her eyes and didn't answer, her mouth twisting with silent emotion. He wished there'd been time to bring her mother to town to support her through this. Of course, he'd dutifully written to Lady Hervey, explaining what had happened and assuring her that Charlotte would be provided for, but having her here now would have helped immeasurably.

"I want you to go to bed and rest now," he said, kissing her forehead. "You're exhausted, and you'll make yourself ill. I must go out for a short while, but I'll be back soon."

"You're going to your solicitor's," she said forlornly, eyes still shut. "You're going to make certain your affairs are in order in case you die."

That was exactly where he was going, among other places, and her prescience was unsettling. He was confident, yes, but he wasn't so confident as to believe he was immortal.

"It's my duty to make certain preparations for the, ah, for the future," he said awkwardly. "Because I love you and our child."

"If you truly loved me, March," she countered quickly, "you wouldn't want to leave me a widow and our child without a father or so much as a memory of one, and—and—"

She couldn't finish. She gulped, fighting a great, racking, shuddering sob, and sank against his shoulder.

"Oh, my love, my love," she said through a fresh wave of tears, her fingers feverishly twisting and clutching at the lapels of his coat. "Didn't you promise you'd never leave me again?"

"I told you, I won't be gone long," he said. "I'll be back so we can dine together."

"That's not what I meant," she said sorrowfully. "I meant leave me forever, which is what you will do if Andover kills you."

"Oh, Charlotte," he said. "Please don't."

"No," she said, her voice at once soft and fierce. "No. I won't have it, March. You say you're acting from love, to protect me, and I mean to do the same. I love you too much to let you go. You'll see. I'm going to fight for you, March, and honorably or not, I don't intend to lose."

"What the devil is that supposed to mean, Charlotte?" he asked, frowning down at her. But she only shook her head and slipped free, and before he could catch her, she'd run from the room and toward the stairs.

"Charlotte!" he called. He began to follow her, then stopped. He'd be wise to let her go, off to Polly's solicitous care and her own bedchamber to rest. There wasn't anything that, as a woman, she could do to stop the duel now. Her words were brave and blustering, but empty of any real threat, the kind of thing that someday they would laugh over together.

At least he hoped they would, and with that lonely thought and the front of his coat soaked with her tears, he left the house for his carriage, and the offices of his solicitor.

Charlotte paced back and forth across the soft carpet in Aunt Sophronia's parlor, too agitated to sit. Dusk was beginning to settle on the square outside, and the candles had already been lit. It had taken Charlotte longer than she'd thought to develop her plan and collect the pieces she'd need, and she was so weary now that she wondered that she could walk at all. Her pregnancy did that to her; she'd no stamina. She'd need her aunt to help her tonight, need her very much, but the sorry truth was that she wasn't sure her aunt would agree.

The footman opened the parlor door and Aunt Sophronia bustled in, her small white dogs bounding before her.

"Oh, my poor, dear Duchess!" she exclaimed. She paused to curtsey, then seized both of Charlotte's hands in her own. "I have heard the terrible news. Whatever possessed His Grace to make such an impulsive challenge and to such a man as Lord Andover?"

Charlotte took a deep breath to steady herself. She had resolved not to cry before her aunt, nor to show any other sign of weakness. If she did, then her aunt would surely refuse her. If she was to be of any help to March at all, she must be strong and she must be confident.

"He believes he is defending my honor," she said carefully as they sat. "He believes he has no choice but to fight Andover like this, to preserve my good name and our family's with it."

"That's a very noble endeavor, to be sure," Aunt Sophronia said, patting her lap for the dogs to join her, "and I've no doubt that the duke intends only to win. Gentlemen always believe they're invincible, don't they? Brave oaths and pistols at dawn, then pop, pop, one man is dead in the grass and the other's off to France to avoid being charged with murder. *Very* noble indeed, I am sure."

Charlotte's fingers spread over her belly, as if she could cover the ears of her unborn child to keep it from hearing that.

"Forgive me, Aunt, but I would rather be more optimistic," Charlotte said as firmly as she could. "For the sake of my child."

"Of course, of course," her aunt said, glancing down

at Charlotte's waist. "I've not seen you since you became *enceinte*. I congratulate you on your efficiency, Duchess."

"Thank you, Aunt," Charlotte murmured. "We were blessed."

"The duke has proved to be quite the virile gentleman, hasn't he?" Aunt Sophronia laughed and winked, bawdy enough to make Charlotte blush. "Now that he's filled your belly properly, we can only hope that you carry a boy to secure the dukedom no matter tomorrow's outcome. I'll never forget the dreadful trial for your poor mother, those long uncomfortable months in mourning, only to give birth to another daughter and lose your father's estates entirely."

Why must her aunt say such dreadful things, thought Charlotte unhappily, as if her father's early death and her mother's grief-stricken last pregnancy weren't already mixed in with her fears for March?

But she must not cry. For March's sake, she must be strong.

"I don't intend for the duel to have that sad outcome, Aunt," Charlotte said. "I mean to have it end before it's begun, with no one grievously hurt, let alone killed."

Her aunt made a puffing sound with her lips puckered together. "How would you accomplish such a thing? Surely you must know by now that when gentlemen have determined their course, no mere woman can deter them, no matter how she wishes it."

"But *I* will, Aunt Sophronia," Charlotte said, her voice resonating with resolve. "That is why I have come here."

Her aunt frowned suspiciously. "What manner of mischief is this, niece? Need I remind you of your rank, or that your husband is willing to risk his life to defend your honor?"

"You needn't, because that is exactly why I must do this," Charlotte said, and quickly she shared her plan.

Her aunt listened, her head tipped skeptically to one side as she slowly combed her ring-laden fingers through the curling fur of one of her small dogs.

"None of that will be easy, child," Aunt Sophronia said when Charlotte was done. "You are counting on a great many things falling exactly your way to make such a plan succeed, and there is still much room for disaster."

"I know all of that, Aunt," said Charlotte, and again she felt her eyes well perilously with tears. "But I cannot sit back and be idle, not when March's life is at risk."

"Fah, at risk from his own male foolishness, you mean to say." Aunt Sophronia raised her head and thrust out her chin, her nostrils flaring, and all Charlotte could think of was how March called her the dowager dragon. "Truly, it is not to be borne. But then, you are a Wylder, and it's not in your constitution to be idle in such a circumstance."

"Will you help me, Aunt?" Charlotte asked. She came as close to pleading as she dared; she'd no other recourse if her aunt refused. "Please?"

"Of course I shall help you," Aunt Sophronia declared. "We have all gone through a great deal of trouble to secure His Grace as your husband, and I will not see him wriggle free to the hereafter without a fight."

"How can you tell me Her Grace is gone?" March glared at the line of servants before him: coach driver, housekeeper, butler, footmen, grooms, parlor maids, Giroux, and Charlotte's maid, Polly. "She is the Duchess of Marchbourne. She cannot simply vanish into nothingness."

"Forgive me, sir, but it's as we said before," the driver said, beads of sweat thick in his eyebrows. "We carried Her Grace to Lady Sanborn's house in St. James's, and she told us t' leave her there, that she'd stay the night an' return tomorrow in her ladyship's coach. I saw her go inside myself, sir, wit' my own eyes."

"Then why the devil did Lady Sanborn tell me that she hadn't seen Her Grace at all?" March demanded. "Where could she have gone?"

Not one of them answered, their eyes staring straight before them.

A mystery like this was the last thing he needed tonight. His various errands had taken much longer than he'd expected, and when he'd returned home he'd found that Charlotte had vanished, with no message or clues. He had gone to her aunt's house but learned nothing from the dragon. He had then tried every house where Charlotte had an acquaintance, and received only pitying denials. Then he'd come back to Marchbourne House in the hope that she'd returned, but there was still no sign of her.

He was worried beyond measure, and desperate beyond reason. It wasn't that he feared she'd met with foul play, though he couldn't entirely put that grim thought from his head.

No, what he feared most was Charlotte herself. He remembered how distraught and angry she'd been before he'd left, and how she'd told him she meant to fight for him. He'd discounted those last words, blaming them on her distress and her pregnancy. Now he knew he shouldn't have.

This wasn't an ordinary woman. This was Charlotte.

He was certain she was off busily hatching some sort of plot to stop the duel. He had appalling visions of her appealing to the king himself to beg for his interference, or worse, to Andover to change his mind. He could even imagine her appearing through the morning mists brandishing pistols of her own like a pirate maid. The only thing he knew for sure was that if Charlotte did not wish to be found this night, she wouldn't be, and nothing he could do would change that.

He retreated to the drawing room, determined to wait there until she returned. *If* she returned. Instead of the fine supper (he refused to call it his last) he'd planned to share with her, he ate in his armchair, alone before the fire. To keep himself busy, he cleaned the matched pair of dueling pistols, then cleaned them again, refusing to trust this task to a servant. Then he carefully replaced them in their fitted case, ready for the morning. As the hours passed on that same ormolu clock, he remained where he was, unable to bear the thought of his bed without Charlotte in it beside him.

At last he must have fallen asleep, because Giroux was gently touching his shoulder to wake him.

"Good morning, sir," he said. "It's time to rise."

It didn't seem like morning. The drawing room was dark except for the candlestick in Giroux's hand, the windows darker still. With a start he remembered his appointment at dawn beneath the oak trees, and he was instantly awake.

"Did Her Grace return?" he asked. "Is she home?"

Giroux shook his head. "No, sir," he said sadly. "Her Grace is not at home."

He missed her more than he'd dreamed possible. He loved her more than any man should love a woman.

But most of all, he could not bear to consider that he might die this morning without kissing her again.

CHAPTER

23

"Are you certain this is the place, ma'am?" Aunt Sophronia's footman spoke cautiously through the carriage window, not unlatching the door until Charlotte spoke. "This place, ma'am?"

"Of course she is certain, Pratt," Aunt Sophronia said, leaning toward the window. "She is a duchess, while you are a cowardly ninny."

"Aye, my lady," Pratt said patiently. "It's just that it's a terribly dark and lonesome place to put a lady like Her Grace down."

"But that's exactly why we're here, Pratt," Charlotte said. "Duels aren't held on the Horse Guards Parade, for all the world to see. They're supposed to be secret. Now will you please open the door so I can climb down?"

Contritely Pratt did, and Charlotte clambered down into the grass. It *was* dark, with the sky still full of stars. The quarter moon was setting, low in the sky, and the slightest gray of the coming dawn showed on the horizon. Against this she could make out the darker silhouettes of her landmarks, the old twin oak trees with their branches widespread and sprawling, and nothing else around them except open fields and scrub.

"It's just as well that it's dark, Charlotte," Aunt Sophronia said. "No one would ever mistake you for a duchess dressed like that."

"That's my purpose, Aunt," Charlotte said, "as you know perfectly well. I don't want anyone knowing who I am."

She settled her hat more securely on her head. She'd needed to dress for practicality, not elegance, and she was thankful she hadn't tossed away her old boy's clothes from Ransom, as she'd been ordered to do. She wore her fisherman's jersey, which still smelled faintly of the sea, and her most comfortable, broken-in boots. To her despair, she'd been unable to fit into her old breeches and had had to borrow a pair in a larger size from the servants' laundry. She'd braided her hair tightly and tucked it up into a dark knit cap, and for the first time in months, she wore no jewelry beyond her wedding ring, and that only because it was hidden by her gloves. Everything was calculated to blend in with the dark.

"Should I take down one of the lanterns, ma'am?" asked Pratt. "You'll need to light your way."

"Thank you, no," she said briskly. She pulled the cloth haversack from the coach and slung the strap over her shoulder. "I'll see well enough."

"You are certain about this, Charlotte?" asked Aunt Sophronia, a quaver of worry in her voice. "It's all quite mad, you know."

"It *is* quite mad." Charlotte smiled up at her aunt. Now that she was actually on her way, she was more excited than fearful. "But so are duels."

"Take care, Charlotte," Aunt Sophronia said. "And may God be both with you and with His Grace."

"Thank you, Aunt," Charlotte said. Excited or not, she knew she needed all the heavenly protection she could muster. "Hurry now, Pratt, I don't have time to lose."

With the footman trudging respectfully behind her,

she led the way across the grass to the larger of the trees and looked up into the branches. The tree was old, the branches weaving and thick, with plenty of leaves. She couldn't imagine a better tree to climb.

"Give me a hand up, Pratt, if you please," she said to the footman.

"Ma'am?" he asked uncertainly.

"I need to reach the first branch," she explained, "and then I'll do well enough. Pretend you're helping me mount a horse."

"Very well, ma'am." He linked his hands together to make an impromptu step, and helped her up.

She was glad of his help. She was heavier than her old self, and she doubted she could have climbed up to the first branch without him. Now she'd be fine.

"Thank you, Pratt," she said, breathless more from excitement than from exertion. "You may go now, and tell the driver to leave."

"Ma'am?" asked the footman, his upturned face pale beneath her. "You'd have us leave you here alone, ma'am?"

"Yes, yes," Charlotte said. "I won't be surprising anyone if they see my aunt's coach, will I?"

"But ma'am, Lady Sanborn's orders—"

"My orders are that you leave me here, and at once," she said, striving to sound again like a duchess and not a thick-waisted boy in a tree. "I'll be well enough. I'll be returning home later with His Grace."

"Very well, ma'am," Pratt said, his reluctance obvious. "Take care, ma'am, and good fortune to you."

"Thank you," she said, and resolutely began climbing deeper into the tree. It was easy to see where the duel would take place. The branches of the two trees arched together like a natural roof, with a wide flat place beneath that was bare of grass. The branches were so wide that the climbing was easy, and she soon found a comfortable place where she'd be in perfect position, yet well hidden by the leaves. She braced herself against a crook, then took the haversack from her back and settled it in her lap. All she must do now was wait.

When she'd made her plans this afternoon, it had seemed wonderfully clever and daring, sure to succeed. Now reality was stealing away much of the cleverness, and the danger and uncertainty of what lay ahead took the excitement from the daring. As she watched her aunt's carriage lumbering off into the darkness, she shivered, and not from the early morning chill, either. If she couldn't make this work, then all she'd have accomplished was securing a splendid view of March being shot.

She tucked her hands beneath her arms, trying to stay as calm as she could. She hoped March wasn't too terribly angry with her for avoiding him last night, but just as he'd said he was fighting this foolish duel for her sake, what she'd done was for him. She hoped he'd slept well and was feeling keen and refreshed this morning. She hoped his pistols were ready, and that Giroux had made sure he'd had an excellent breakfast.

She hoped he was thinking of her with some kindness and not simply irritation, and most of all with love.

She felt tears sting her eyes and quickly dashed them away. She *had* to succeed. She couldn't lose March, her husband, her duke, her lover, and her best friend. She wished he were here beside her, laughing and teasing her and kissing her, to make her feel more cheerful and less lonely.

No. Sternly she reminded herself that she wasn't alone, and she put her hand over her belly.

"Isn't this an adventure, lamb?" she whispered softly.

"What a tale you'll have to tell one day, ah? How you and Mama climbed up a tree and surprised Father by saving his life against his will!"

That made her chuckle, and as she did she saw the two carriages coming her way. Almost time, almost time, and quickly she opened the haversack to draw out her weapons.

She'd made them herself, and was proud of her ingenuity: a dozen (better to be overprepared) apples, each armed with shards of broken glass poked into the skin. She arranged them gingerly before her, wary of the sharp glass. As hazardous as glass-studded apples might be, she prayed they'd be a much safer way of drawing that dreadful first blood than any lead ball could be. She'd also brought a bag of smaller missiles—acorns, in honor of the oak tree.

Her heart racing, she watched the carriages draw up beside the road. Andover had come in a hired hackney (for secrecy or economy?), while March arrived in his usual ducal splendor. It took all her willpower not to call out to March as he stepped down. Though she couldn't make out his face, she could tell by how straight he stood and the way he squared his shoulders that he was ready, confident, and a bit nervous as well. He was dressed entirely in dark clothes, without so much as a hint of white linen. Of course, she realized with shock: no white on the chest to serve as a clear target.

She prayed to God that her little trick would work.

She watched the men walk quickly toward the tree. There were six: March, Brecon, Andover and his second, a gentleman with a lantern, and another carrying a case. This last must be the surgeon, and again Charlotte felt fear ripple through her. The men didn't waste any time on small talk or chatter, with March and Andover standing apart with their seconds. The duelists removed their hats and cloaks and stood before the starter, who again asked them to consider reconciliation. When they refused, Brecon presented the pistol case, and Andover went first, testing and balancing each gun in his hand before choosing one. Quickly the rules were announced—twenty paces, a single shot, the winner to be determined by first blood.

To Charlotte, it all seemed like a foolish play, a play with the most serious consequences imaginable. By the light of the single lantern, their faces were taut and serious, and she had to swallow her own anxiety. March and Andover counted out their steps and took their places.

To Charlotte's luck, Andover was almost directly beneath her. He looked down at his gun, fiddling with the lock. His ginger-colored hair looked pale and oddly vulnerable in the moonlight. A fine target, she decided, and before he moved away, she threw one of the acorns directly at it.

"My God, what was that?" he exclaimed, clutching at his head. His second hurried over, ready to assist.

"Here's the culprit, my lord," the second pronounced, pouncing on the acorn. "A nut."

Andover swore again, and composed himself as best he could. As he did, Charlotte threw an acorn toward the surgeon, just to make sure the falling nuts appeared random. The surgeon exclaimed and flailed about.

"Who the devil picked this infernal place, anyway?" snapped Andover.

"The choice of location was previously agreed upon by both parties, my lord," said the starter solemnly. "You cannot change it now without forfeiting."

Charlotte prayed he would. Alas, he did not.

"Begin again," he barked, and once more the paces were counted.

An apple ready in her hand and her heart beating painfully in her breast, Charlotte looked to March, and breathed a silent little prayer toward him.

Be safe, my love, be safe, be safe . . .

She listened for the starter's final count to begin. She'd have to time this exactly: too soon and they'd stop the count; too late, and—well, she would be too late.

"One," intoned the starter. "Two."

She hurled a glass-studded apple at Andover's hand precisely on the three.

Everything else happened in a single roaring instant. A shockingly loud crack, a flash, and a cloud of acrid smoke as March's gun fired. A howl of pain from Andover as he staggered to one side, clutching his wrist as he dropped his unfired pistol. At once his second and the surgeon hurried toward him. The surgeon took his wrist, holding it up for inspection.

"Blood, Your Grace," he announced gravely. "A profusion."

"Congratulations, Your Grace," the starter called to March. "You have your satisfaction."

Waves of relief washed over Charlotte, and she had to cover her mouth with her hand to keep from laughing with joy. She'd done it. She'd saved March, and her honor with it.

"Blast him, he doesn't!" Andover shouted, pulling his hand away from the surgeon. There *was* a profusion of blood, covering his hand and wrist. Furiously Andover shook it as if he could shake away the pain. "Damn him, he fired first! I was struck before the last count, before I could fire, before—"

"What is this, my lord?" Andover's second bent over, and to Charlotte's horror he picked up the apple, the shards of bloody glass glinting red in the lantern light. "What manner of foul cheat is this?"

He looked up into the tree, and the other men looked up, too. But Andover grabbed his pistol from where he'd let it drop and cocked it again. His face livid with fury and pain, he pointed the pistol upward, directly into the branches at Charlotte.

"No!" she wailed, scrambling along the branch with one hand over her belly and her child. "No, no, no!"

She heard the gunshot and shrieked, expecting the pain that surely must follow. Beside her a branch cracked and shattered, dropping to the ground, but no pain followed. Weeping, not understanding her deliverance, she dared to look down again, and saw March wrestling with Andover to hold him down to the ground. There was blood everywhere, on the dirt and on the two men.

"March!" she cried, praying that the blood wasn't his. "March!"

The other men caught Andover's arms and dragged him back, and at once March was on his feet, staring up into the tree.

"Charlotte, are you there?" he shouted. "Charlotte, are you hurt? Damnation, are you there?"

His voice so full of desperate love, love for her, that Charlotte's throat tightened with love of her own, and she was so overwhelmed that she almost couldn't answer.

"Here, March," she managed to croak. "Here. I'm fine, and—and I love you, March!"

At once he rushed to the trunk of the tree. "Stay where you are, Charlotte," he ordered. "Be easy, and I'll come and rescue you."

He'd used almost exactly the same words when he'd tried to rescue her once before, when they'd first met in that tree long ago. It was so perfect, so gallant, that she wept, thinking of how ridiculously much she loved him.

Then she also remembered how very bad he was at climbing trees and what had happened the last time he'd attempted it to rescue her. As quickly as she could, she made her way down the length of the branch, down the trunk, and into his arms.

"You saved me, March," she said, laughing and crying at once. "Exactly as you said you would."

"You saved me, Charlotte," he said, holding her as tightly as he could. "Exactly as you weren't supposed to do."

"Well, no," she admitted. "But at least you have your satisfaction."

"Satisfaction." He smiled and kissed her, then kissed her again. "Satisfaction, indeed."

As was to be expected, the duel was the talk of London for the rest of the year. There were so many delicious aspects to discuss and dissect, from the bravery of the duchess to the devotion of the duke. It was declared by both the surgeon, who inspected the injury, and the seconds, who served as witnesses, that Lord Andover had been wounded by March's shot before Charlotte's apple had added its own insult, and therefore the duel was in fact honorable and complete. The fact that the marquess not only had lost but then had attempted to fire at the duchess instead was regarded by all as the lowest infamy, so low that some of the papers called for him to be taken and tried for attempted murder, or horsewhipped at the very least. The calls became sufficiently loud that Lord Andover decided a sojourn on the Continent was in order, and quickly departed.

But the duke and duchess soon found their own celebrity wearying as well. With the impending birth of their child as an excuse, they retreated to Greenwood, where the only conflict between them rose from predicting whether the babe would be a boy and heir, or a girl for both of them to indulge. But to everyone's delight and amazement, it was discovered in the spring that both parents were correct, when the duchess was brought to bed with twins, a boy and a girl. It was just as well that there were two babies. When the duchess's mother and aunt and sisters descended as promised, there was so much female spoiling and coddling and cosseting and baby talk that the duke was said to be overwhelmed by it. Overwhelmed, and never happier.

But what made London talk most was the gift that the duke presented to his duchess on the birth of their twins. Most gentlemen in such a circumstance would have offered a piece of costly jewelry, or perhaps a priceless painting. The duke, however, was more original. He chose the largest tree at Greenwood and had an elaborate, elegant tree house built within its branches for his duchess—where, it was rumored, the duke and duchess spent much of their time in seclusion together.

"This truly is heaven," Charlotte said, lying close beside March in the oversized hammock that hung between the branches. The hammock swayed slightly in the breeze, and Charlotte smiled, staring up through the leaves to the stars strewn across the summer night sky. "And you, my own love, are quite heavenly for having thought of it."

"You deserve it," he said, kissing the side of her neck. "Besides, it was the only way I could think of to keep you from climbing any more trees."

"Ha," she scoffed, lazily running her fingers through his hair. "That's only because I'm much better at tree climbing than you shall ever be."

"Perhaps," he said. "But there are a great many other

areas in which I excel. Areas, I'm told, that are much more interesting than tree climbing."

"Truly?" she said, laughing softly. "Then perhaps you should demonstrate, Your Grace."

"With pleasure, my love," he said, pulling her close. "Only with pleasure."

Read on for an exciting preview
of Isabella Bradford's next novel

When the Duchess Said Yes

❦ ❦

London
April 1762

It was duty that had drawn the Duke of Hawkesworth
back to England. More specifically, duty, and lawyers,
and a woman he'd never met but was bound to marry.

Bored already, Hawke sprawled in his chair in the
playhouse box, pretending to watch the abysmal opera
before him. He'd been away nearly ten years, long
enough that he suspected those in the other first-tier
boxes were desperately trying to decide who he must be.
It wouldn't be easy. He knew he'd changed, grown from
a schoolboy to a man, and he'd grown into both his
broad frame and his title with it. Thanks to a long-ago
Mediterranean grandmother, he'd dark hair and dark
eyes, and his face was so unfashionably tan after the
long voyage that those in the other boxes had likely all
decided he was swarthy, even foreign.

The thought made him smile. Well, let them peer at
him with their opera glasses and whisper behind their
fans. They'd all come to recognize him soon enough.

"Those two dancers with the scarlet stockings," whispered the Marquis of Petershaw, an old friend and the
first to welcome him back to London. "The ones with
the golden hair. A delectable pair, eh? Sisters, I'd wager.

Should I send our compliments for a late supper, the way we did in the old days?"

"We were randy schoolboys in those 'old days,' Pertershaw, ready to mount anything female that didn't kick us away," Hawke said, bemused. "We weren't exactly discerning."

Pertershaw's round face fell. "I judged them a fine pair of doxies."

"They are, they are," Hawke assured him, not wanting to belittle his friend's tastes. But the truth was that Hawke's own tastes had changed with the rest of him, and in comparison to the vibrant, voluptuous women he'd left behind in Naples, English females seemed pale, bland, and thoroughly insipid, just as English food now tasted underseasoned and overcooked. "I'm not in the humor for such entertainment, that is all."

"You, Hawke?" His friend's brows rose with disbelief. "I've never known you to refuse feminine company."

"You forget my reason for returning," Hawke said, as evenly as he could. "I am to be wed, and my days with that manner of strumpet are done."

"Perhaps on your wedding night," Petershaw said, "but not forever. Not you."

Hawke only smiled, letting his friend think what he pleased. Petershaw would anyway, regardless of what Hawke told him.

"No, not you," Petershaw declared with a suggestive chuckle that also managed to be admiring. "Not at all! I'm going to send a note down to the tiring room for those little dancers, and I'll wager you'll change your mind before the evening's done."

He went off in search of a messenger before Hawke could answer. Hawke sighed, sadly wondering if he'd lost his taste for English friends, too. But then Petershaw could afford to be impulsive with dancers, milliner's assistants, and whatever other pretty faces caught his fancy. He was a third son with no need to wed or sire heirs, and he was completely free to scatter his seed wherever he pleased.

But the truth was that Hawke's smile masked a great many misgivings about his own upcoming marriage. He was, of course, obliged to follow through with the betrothal that Father had long ago arranged for him. It wasn't only a matter of honor, of not abandoning some poor lady of rank at the altar. No, Father had mistrusted his only son so thoroughly that he'd bound this marriage and his estate together into a tangled knot of legal complexities and obligation that could never be undone. Father couldn't prohibit him from inheriting the dukedom, but he could—and had—restricted the estate necessary to support the title. In other words, unless Hawke married the lady of Father's choosing before her nineteenth birthday, he would become a duke without a farthing.

Restlessly Hawke tapped his fingers on the polished rail before him. Accepting his fate didn't mean he found it agreeable. Far from it. Ten years had passed since Father died, yet Hawke still resented both him and that infernal will. Still, though his father expected him to marry, at least he didn't expect him to be faithful. Their family had been founded on the legitimized by-blows of a king and his mistress a century before, and every Duke of Hawkesworth since had followed suit and kept at least one mistress. It was a tradition Hawke fully intended to continue. He'd marry this lady, remain honorably faithful to her long enough to produce children, and then, with the title secure, his duty complete, and his family well provided for, he'd depart for Bella Collina, his beloved villa in Naples, never to return.

In theory it was a most excellent plan, one that had given Hawke much comfort on the long voyage to England. But as he idly glanced around at the well-bred faces in the other boxes, his heart sank. He'd forgotten how unappealing his fellow aristocrats could be, and one lady after another struck him as smugly complacent as they preened in their jewels and costly gowns, their painted faces and towering white wigs no more attractive to him than the two dancers that Petershaw had spotted.

Glumly he wondered what his bride would be like. Wynn, his agent, had written that she was a beauty. But then every bride was considered beautiful, and what, truly, could Wynn have written instead? There was no portrait enclosed, never a favorable sign. Wynn had mentioned that the lady had been raised in the country and wasn't accustomed to society, let alone to sitting for portrait painters, but Hawke had immediately imagined some bland, stolid, milk-fed creature, more like a farmer's daughter than an earl's, with a round face and wispy pale hair.

By unfortunate coincidence, his wandering gaze had settled on exactly that sort of young lady, not two boxes away, who set off her pasty pallor and snub nose with black velvet patches scattered over her cheeks. To Hawke's dismay, she'd noticed him, too. She smiled, flashing teeth marred by too much sugar and tea, and coyly winked at him over the blades of her fan.

He nodded curtly in return, only enough to be polite, then swiftly turned away, back toward the portly singer.

But before his gaze reached the stage, it stopped, stopped as completely and abruptly as a gaze could be stopped. He couldn't look away if his life depended upon it, and in a way, perhaps it did.

She was standing alone at the front of an empty box, leaning forward with her hands on the railing. From her pale pink gown and the strand of pearls around her throat, she appeared to be a lady, but she bore no resemblance to any of the other ladies in the entire house. If she was alone like this, unattended, then she was likely a courtesan, some wealthy gentleman's costly plaything despite her youth.

Not that Hawke cared, and in a way that made her even more fascinating. He'd stolen women away from other gentlemen, and he was quite willing to do it again. She was undeniably pretty, even beautiful, and fresh in a way that wasn't fashionable for London, let alone for whores. Her face was bare of paint and artifice, rosy and glowing by the light from the stage, and her hair was unpowdered as well, so dark that it blended into the shadows around her. She was tall, too, with a slender grace that didn't depend on tight lacing, and the way she bent forward, offering a generous view of her breasts framed by the pink silk, was unconsciously elegant.

That was it, then, the intangible that compelled him to look at her. She was a beauty who didn't seem to care about being one, unashamed of being unaware. It charmed him, he who'd been sure he'd seen and admired every kind of female beauty; no, it captivated him. And the longer he watched her, the more intrigued he became.

In his eagerness, Hawke leaned forward, too, almost as if mirroring her pose. Suddenly she looked from the stage directly toward him, as if she'd felt the power of his interest clear across the playhouse. She looked at him openly, studying him without any coyness or coquettishness, and slowly raised one hand to smooth a loose curl behind her ear. Automatically he smiled, more with pleasure than with any seductive motive, and to his delight, she smiled in return.

He had to learn who she was, no matter the inconvenience this would cause to his wedding plans. His unwanted bride had already waited a good long time for him, and surely she could wait just a little longer. He had to meet this beauty now, as soon as possible. At once he rose, intending to leave his box and find her, and crashed directly into Petershaw.

"Here, Hawke, no hurry," he said, his broad face beaming as he put his hands on Hawke's shoulders to steady himself. "I've made certain that those two little hussies will be waiting for us after the performance, and then—"

"Damnation, Petershaw, not now." Hawke untangled himself from his friend. "That beauty in pink, there, in the box directly across the way. Do you know who she might be?"

He turned back to point her out to Petershaw.

The box was empty. The girl was gone.

Hawke swore again, and raced through the door of his box into the corridor. She couldn't have gone far. Her box was on the same ring, and if he hurried, he was sure to find her.

But the opera's second act had just concluded, and while applause rippled through the house behind him, the doors to all the other boxes opened and their occupants streamed into the corridor in search of refreshments or one another. At once the narrow passage was filled with people, with the ladies in their wide hooped skirts claiming three times the space. Though Hawke did his best to press through, by the time he'd finally made his way to the other side, the young woman in pink was nowhere to be found, and doubtless long, long gone.

"Whose box is this?" Hawke demanded of the attendant standing beside the door.

"The Earl of Farnham, my lord," the man said.

"Your Grace," Hawke corrected impatiently. He didn't know Lord Farnham, but then he didn't know much of anyone in London now. "I'm the Duke of Hawkesworth."

"Forgive me, Your Grace," the man said, mortified, and bowed hastily. "I did not know."

"There was a young woman here this night, dressed all in pink," Hawke said. "Was she a guest of Lord Farnham's? Do you know her name?"

The attendant's brows rose with surprise. "Lord Farnham's not in attendance tonight, Your Grace. Forgive me for speaking plain, but his lordship must be eighty if he's a day, Your Grace, with scant interest in young ladies."

"You saw no young woman in pink?"

"No, Your Grace," the man declared soundly. "None at all."

"What is this all about, Hawke?" Petershaw asked beside him. "Who the devil is this chit in pink that has you in such a steam?"

Hawke sighed with frustration, and a certain amount of confusion as well. He didn't know why finding this girl had become so important to him; he could not put her smile from his thoughts, nor, truly, did he want to.

"I do not know who she is, Petershaw," he said, "beyond her being the most beguiling creature imaginable. It would seem she has vanished clear away."

"Now that's the Hawke I recall, always with his nose to the trail of a vixen." Petershaw grinned slyly. "Where's that dutiful, dull bridegroom now, eh?"

Petershaw had intended it only as a jest, a sly and slightly envious jab at Hawke's reputation with women. But instead it struck Hawke as a sobering reminder, as determined to douse his desire as a bucket of water from an icy river. It should have been, too, especially for a man such as Hawke, who seldom denied himself anything. As delectable as the smiling girl in pink might be, she was not for him. For the foreseeable future, he was doomed to keep to only the most respectable of paths, and grant to his bride exclusive rights to his honor, his title, his fortune, and most of all his cock.

A sobering reminder, indeed. A grim, depressing, damnably sobering reminder.